JENNY LEE

Anna K

A LOVE STORY

FLATIRON
BOOKS
NEW YORK

ANNA K. Copyright © 2020 by Jenny Lee. All rights reserved. Printed in the United States of America. For information, address Flatiron Books, 120 Broadway, New York, NY 10271.

Excerpt of *Anna K Away* copyright © 2021 by Jenny Lee

www.flatironbooks.com

Designed by Anna Gorovoy

The Library of Congress has cataloged the hardcover edition as follows:

Names: Lee, Jenny, 1971– author.
Title: Anna K : a love story / Jenny Lee.
Description: First edition. | New York : Flatiron Books, 2020.
Identifiers: LCCN 2019045206 | ISBN 9781250236432 (hardcover) | ISBN 9781250759856 (international, sold outside the U.S., subject to rights availability) | ISBN 9781250236425 (ebook)
Subjects: CYAC: Dating (Social customs)—Fiction. | Love—Fiction. | Korean Americans—Fiction. | Wealth—Fiction. | Family life—New York (State)—New York—Fiction. | New York (N.Y.)—Fiction.
Classification: LCC PZ7.L512533 Ann 2020 | DDC [Fic]—dc23
LC record available at https://lccn.loc.gov/2019045206

ISBN 978-1-250-23644-9 (trade paperback)

Our books may be purchased in bulk for promotional, educational, or business use. Please contact your local bookseller or the Macmillan Corporate and Premium Sales Department at 1-800-221-7945, extension 5442, or by email at MacmillanSpecialMarkets@macmillan.com.

First Flatiron Books Paperback Edition: 2021

10 9 8 7 6 5 4 3 2 1

For my husband, John—my love, my favorite,
and my happily ever after.
This book would not exist without you.

Who's Who in *Anna K*
(in order of appearance)

LOLLY S.
Seventeen, junior at the Spence School. Girlfriend of Steven K., older sister of Kimmie.

STEVEN K.
Eighteen, senior at Collegiate School. Older brother of Anna, boyfriend of Lolly.

DUSTIN L.
Eighteen, senior at Stuyvesant High School. Homework tutor to Steven, younger brother of Nicholas.

KIMMIE S.
Fifteen, sophomore at Spence. Younger sister of Lolly.

ALEXIA VRONSKY
(ALSO KNOWN AS VRONSKY OR COUNT VRONSKY)
Sixteen, sophomore at Collegiate. Cousin of Beatrice.

ANNA K.

Seventeen, junior at Greenwich Academy. Younger sister of Steven, girlfriend of Alexander.

ALEXANDER W.
(ALSO KNOWN AS THE GREENWICH OG)

Nineteen, freshman at Harvard University. Boyfriend of Anna K., older half-brother of Eleanor.

ELEANOR W.

Fifteen, sophomore at Greenwich Academy. Younger half-sister of Alexander.

BEATRICE D.
(ALSO KNOWN AS BEA)

Seventeen, junior at Greenwich Academy. Cousin of Alexia.

NICHOLAS L.

Twenty-one. Older brother of Dustin, boyfriend of Natalia.

MURF G.

Sixteen, sophomore at Greenwich High School. Childhood friend of Vronsky, stable hand at Staugas Farms.

NATALIA T.

Eighteen, lives in Arizona. Girlfriend of Nicholas.

Part One

I

Every happy teenage girl is the same,
while every unhappy teenage girl is miserable
in her own special way.

The whole thing was a fucking disaster. Lolly found out her boyfriend Steven was cheating on her while she was getting his Apple Watch outfitted with a new wristband at the Hermès store on Madison Avenue. Steven didn't even know she had his Apple Watch. Twenty minutes ago, he decided to do back-to-back SoulCycle classes, while Lolly begged off staying for the second class with him. (Her new gluten-free diet lacked the necessary carbs for her to handle doing a double sesh without passing out.)

She was telling him the truth while also needing the time and access to his Apple Watch to take it to the store for a new wristband, his present for their eighteen-month "screw-a-versary," which happened to be the very next day. (Lolly didn't love commemorating their first official date with this crude moniker, but Steven called it that. Lolly went along because she loved him.) So while Steven was climbing an imaginary hill to the steady beat of Dua Lipa's "IDGAF" at the East 83rd Street studio, Lolly was fifteen blocks south standing at the counter of Hermès.

She was deciding between the traditional double-wrap band in iconic orange leather and the more hetero choice in matte black. She was admiring the orange band on her own delicate wrist, when Steven's Apple

Watch vibrated and a tiny tit pic flashed on the screen, followed by the gray text bubble containing the letters: DTF? *eggplant emoji*

Lolly tapped the touch-screen to see the photo again. Confirming the worst, she froze until her fight-or-flight impulse kicked in. Lolly chose flight, forgetting to take off the new band as she ran out, and was stopped by the burly security guard who blocked the door. Lolly, never good at holding back tears, started to sob pitifully, staring down at her beloved Gucci sneakers (the ones with the glittering snakes) that Steven had bought for her this past Christmas. Unsure of what to do, the security guard placed his arms around the crying girl. She pressed her face into his poly-blend jacket and whispered, "It's a mistake. It must be a mistake. Please let it be a goddamn mistake."

Eventually the beautiful Japanese saleswoman decked out in head-to-toe Hermès, who had been helping Lolly before, took charge of the situation and brought her into the back room. She sat her down on a small couch and gave her a Perrier, which gave Lolly hiccups and made her start crying even harder. The whole scene was quite embarrassing for all parties involved. Kimiko, who had worked at Hermès for ten years, was no stranger to the rampant cheating of the city's wealthiest citizens, many of whom were her clients, but there was something about witnessing this seventeen-year-old girl's loss of innocence IRL that unexpectedly moved her.

Once they had gotten rid of her hiccups, Lolly asked if she should scroll through the rest of her boyfriend's messages or not. Kimiko said in a quiet voice, "Better to find out how bad it is now when you're not alone." Soon both women were mesmerized by the appallingly graphic nature of Lolly's boyfriend's relationship with the mysterious "Brad." Steven had used a fake name in his contacts, but there was no chance "Brad" was a guy judging from the plethora of female body parts being photographed and sent to Steven over the last several weeks. There was even one blurry up-the-skirt video that made both women wince and groan in unison.

Lolly purchased an Hermès Iris belt buckle and reversible strap in bleu saphir and bleu Brighton to thank Kimiko for her kindness and left the store fifteen minutes later, Uber-ing straight to Steven's parents' massive four-bedroom penthouse apartment at 15 Central Park West (his parents were currently in Aspen skiing) to wait for his cheating ass. She tipped Gustavo the doorman a Benjamin not to tell Steven she was upstairs, citing a surprise gift and waving the orange Hermès shopping bag as proof. The doorman took her money, but clearly warned Steven anyway because ten minutes later her bf showed up carrying red deli roses in his still sweaty hands.

He had managed only the words "Lolly baby, what's wrong?" before his mother's favorite Lalique Tourbillons amber vase whizzed past him and smashed into the marble foyer floor. He stared at his normally demure girlfriend in shock when she said, "Just tell me one thing Steven . . . !" her voice now building in ferocity, "When's your screw-a-versary with Brad?!" She was now holding up his Apple Watch as digital proof. Steven stared at it and knew he was irrefutably busted.

Steven's momentary confusion quickly turned to sheepish shame and he activated full grovel mode. He tried to approach her, but she backed away from him. "Don't come near me, you . . . you . . . disgusting pig! That's right, I saw all the vile thirst trap pics that slut Brad sent you!" she screamed. At the mention of the pictures, the latest naked pic that Steven had seen on his phone after class popped into his brain and the tiniest lascivious smile flickered across his face. He was an eighteen-year-old boy, after all.

Unfortunately, Lolly caught Steven's smirk.

The noise she emitted was more animal than human and she ran past him, almost knocking him over in the process. Having nowhere to run except the end of the hall, Lolly opened the door to the master bedroom and slammed the heavy door behind her. She locked the door and ran straight into Steven's mother's walk-in closet. She threw herself face-down on the bloodred crushed-velvet chaise at its center and began to cry harder than she had ever cried before.

Steven tried talking to Lolly through the door, but he was met only with the occasional sound of things being thrown at the door. An hour later he was in the living room watching SportsCenter highlights and eating his third pepperoni Hot Pockets when he received the following text from his buddy Kaedon: Dude, did U buy ur gf a fur coat?!!!

Steven paused the TV and quickly discovered he was already unfriended and blocked across all Lolly's social media accounts. (So much for their 453-day Snap streak!) He texted Kaedon back: screenshot?

Seconds later he received a selfie of a possibly naked Lolly wearing one of his mother's fur coats. Lolly, being much tinier than his mother, looked ridiculous in the chevron-quilted Russian sable, her eyes wild and ringed with mascara. She looked like a rabid raccoon . . . one who just found out that her boyfriend was cheating on her and was royally pissed. He shook his head and knew the situation was now far beyond his skills to rectify. Steven fired off a string of texts to his sister Anna in Greenwich, Connecticut, telling her he was in dire need of her immediate in-person assistance. His sister was younger than he was, but much wiser, especially when it came to relationships and all the tricky emotions that came with them.

Ten minutes later he received a text from Anna announcing her arrival into Grand Central at 8:55 P.M. Before he could text back telling her to take a car, two more texts arrived explaining the latest snowfall was backing up traffic, with Google Maps showing how a train would be the fastest way into Manhattan for her. Anna's last text stated she expected him to pick her up at Grand Central in person so she could hear his side of the 911 gf emergency!! Steven replied with only the single character k, as there was no emoji to depict the grand scale of how fucked he truly was.

II

After playing Shadow of War to clear his head and sipping some of his dad's Glenmorangie Pride 1974 scotch to calm his nerves, Steven tried once again to talk to Lolly through the door. A moment later he finally received some indication of his girlfriend's state of mind, but it wasn't good. Lolly pushed the black-and-white photo strip of the two of them, which they had made together in the photo-booth at her little sister Kimmie's bat mitzvah a year and a half ago, underneath the door. This picture was at one time (like four hours ago!) Lolly's most cherished possession, which she carried around in her LV wallet.

Steven often found his girlfriend staring at the photo strip, but it had been in a different condition than the one he was looking at presently. His eyes had been poked out in each of the four pictures and she had also drawn tiny dicks on his forehead.

"Lolly, baby, it didn't mean anything. It's you I love. I swear." Saying this out loud he knew it was true. When Steven was fourteen years old, his father discovered him getting a BJ from Jenna H. while her parents were over for dinner. His father sent the humiliated girl out of the room and sat Steven down and told him two things. First, he needed to get better at hiding if he didn't want to get caught. And second, the more important lesson, Steven needed to learn the difference between loving sex with girls and loving the girl he was having sex with.

At a loss for what to say and knowing Lolly adored Anna, as every girl adored his younger sister as soon as they met her, Steven announced Anna was on her way into the city, hoping Lolly would take this as a sign he wasn't giving up easily. But again, he was met with only silence. He did however get a text from the doorman alerting him to the fact that Dustin L. was on his way up. Steven sighed, pissed at himself for forgetting to cancel his thrice-weekly homework tutoring session. He stood up in the hallway and headed toward the front door.

He considered talking to Dustin about his current dilemma, as Dustin was one of the smartest guys he knew, but Steven decided there was no way Dustin would take his side. Dustin was technically one of Steven's oldest friends, as their mothers had happened to attend the same mommy-and-me music classes, so they played together as babies every Tuesday and Thursday and were "best buds" until the age of five. But then Dustin's parents divorced, and he went to public school while Steven went to private, which meant they hadn't run in the same social circles for years and had only recently gotten back in touch when Dustin became Steven's homework tutor.

Currently Dustin was a senior graduating with honors from Stuyvesant in June, while Steven was a second-time senior at Collegiate. Steven had attended Collegiate for elementary school but was kicked out in fifth grade when he got busted pantsing a classmate during PE. Next, he was kicked out of Xavier in seventh grade for pot, then Riverdale in ninth grade for fighting. He then attended Horace Mann for a few semesters and was now back at Collegiate on a very short leash.

Steven had his mother to thank for his reinstatement. She'd had to call in a few favors to make it happen. And since one of the conditions of his academic probation was maintaining a high GPA, his mother had hired a string of overpriced homework tutors that all quit after a week or two, citing Steven's poor attitude (i.e., filthy mouth) and even worse work ethic. At her wit's end, his mother finally had the brilliant idea to call Dustin's mother to see if Dustin, whose impressive academic accomplishments were always touted on fb, would agree to work with Steven as his new homework tutor. His mother knew that while her son had little respect for the authority of adults, he coveted the approval of his peers.

Dustin had been adamantly opposed to tutoring Steven when his mother brought it up to him last October. He pointed out that he and Steven were only "friends" because of the happenstance of their two mothers meeting, and by all accounts, the two boys could not have had more different childhoods. "We have nothing in common!" Dustin moaned. "What will we talk about?"

"What you're being paid to talk about . . . homework," was her calm reply.

Dustin let out a deep sigh and rolled his eyes. Where Steven was a good-looking, rich party boy from Manhattan's highest social circle, Dustin was none of those things. Dustin was adopted and knew nothing about his biological parents. Well, he did know that his teenage mother had left a note saying he should be given to Tamar L., "the nice social worker lady who was smart and kind, when she was just a kid from a fucked-up home living with her messed-up mom." She wanted a better life for her own kid, which is why she knew she should give him up.

And so, one Friday night on her way to temple for her first Shabbat service in quite some time, Tamar received a call from a social worker at a hospital and was given one hour to decide if she wanted to become the mother of a two-day-old newborn. Taking it as a test of her lapsed piety, she leaned forward and gave her cab driver the address to St. Luke's on 112th Street. When she told her husband about her intentions and explained her taxicab epiphany, Dustin's soon-to-be adoptive father didn't give it a moment's hesitation (even though they already had a three-year-old) before saying, "I'm in!" And Tamar was consumed with a feeling of security that she had married the right man. Eighteen years later, Dustin's mom still told this story, but with the caveat that while she was right about adopting Dustin, she had spoken too soon about her now ex-husband.

Dustin had grown up to be a quiet, serious boy whose adoptive parents continually made jokes to their friends that their own genes could have never produced such a smart kid, and Dustin, knowing the routine, would respond that he was pretty sure his biological parents could never have raised him to be such a good Jewish boy. (Only recently with the rise of Drake's popularity was Dustin's blackness combined with his Jewish upbringing thought of by his peers as "cool" rather than "weird.") What people didn't know was that Dustin was also prone to panic attacks and had been in therapy for his anxiety since the age of ten, which was why the thought of tutoring a "crazy rich kid" like Steven tied his stomach in knots. "No way. I can't do it, Mom," Dustin said. "Steven's the epitome of the one percent, and me helping him is like going over to the dark side. I'm no Kylo Ren."

Dustin's mother, being a very practical woman, calmly explained to her son that he was making far too much of a big deal over the matter. "You're being too emotional, Dusty," she said. "This is not *Star Wars*. This is real life, and it's not fair of you to write Steven off just because he was born into great wealth. No one's saying you have to be best friends with him. This is a job where you're providing a needed service and getting paid well for doing it. You'll make more money in the next eight months than I make in an entire year." The going rate for homework tutors in Manhattan was easily two hundred bucks an hour, and Steven's mom was of course offering more, which meant Dustin would be clearing over two thousand dollars a week along with a bonus of ten grand if Steven ended the year with a GPA above a 3.2.

"Don't you see how insane that is?" Dustin replied. "You're a licensed professional who spends her days helping the underprivileged, people who actually need help. You're the one who's always saying social workers and public-school teachers are the two noblest professions that are grossly undervalued in today's world. How can you in good conscience suggest I do this?"

"Stop being so melodramatic! You're going to college next year and this will spare you working at some crappy part-time job for spending money. That's the way I'm looking at it, and so should you." Dustin found his mother's viewpoint to be simplistic and shortsighted but when he tried to tell her as much, she refused to debate the matter with him further and instead insisted he talk the matter over with someone else before turning it down.

Dustin decided to end the matter quickly by going to the highest authority first, the rabbi at their temple. Much to Dustin's surprise, Rabbi Kennison agreed with his mother, citing the example that she herself had worked at McDonald's in high school. "I asked every customer if they wanted to supersize their meal; does that mean I'm responsible for the obesity problem in America?" she asked. Before Dustin could answer, she added that Dustin would be performing a mitzvah by using his God-given intellectual gifts to help another. "What if Steven grows up and becomes a senator because you helped him with his studies?"

Dustin would have scoffed at the idea that the kid who once ate a June bug on a dare when they were four years old could ever become a senator, but the fact that the current president was once a reality star who cheated on his pregnant wife with a porn star gave him pause. Instead Dustin thanked her for her counsel and immediately called Dr. N. and requested an emergency therapy session. After fifty minutes of therapy, Dustin was no closer to a decision. He eventually reasoned that all teenagers, rich and poor alike, probably had the same capacity for good or evil, and the best way to combat evil was through education—that is, if no lightsaber was available. (Dr. N. casually mentioned at the end of the session that if Dustin turned down the job, perhaps he might recommend his nephew for the position, as he was a poor law school student at Fordham. Dustin found this suggestion ethically questionable.) After a week of intense hand-wringing, Dustin accepted the tutoring job, warning his mother that if he felt even a twinge of inner turmoil, he'd quit.

What Dustin found after his first month was that the nine hours a week he spent tutoring Steven was not in fact an Aristotelean battle between good and evil like he had feared (nor a biblical, Shakespearean, philosophical, or even George Lucasian one), but was instead fun. His childhood friend wasn't as entitled and insufferable as Dustin had assumed he would be. Steven had grown up to be very much the same as he was when he was a toddler, a charismatic boy with a good sense of humor who enjoyed expensive toys and was happy to share them with his friends (and who would probably still eat a bug if he was dared to do so).

By the second month, Dustin had begun to find his time spent with Steven amusing, even though he would never admit it to his mother. On more than one weekend, Dustin found himself looking forward to their Monday study session, when Steven would no doubt regale him with some outlandish story from his "lit AF" weekend. The two boys had polar opposite high school student experiences: Steven's were all drugs, nightclubs, and hot girls while Dustin's were mostly coffee shops, study groups, and smart girls who always, always "friend-zoned" him.

By the end of the fall semester Dustin had whipped Steven into fighting academic shape, witnessed Steven ace his finals (without cheating), and found himself prouder of Steven's 3.3 GPA than his own 4.0 (though with APs his GPA was actually higher). The two boys celebrated their shared victory over a massive steak dinner at Peter Luger in Brooklyn, and when Steven toasted Dustin for achieving the impossible—Steven's father told him he was proud of him for the first time ever—it dawned on Dustin that he was going to miss Steven during the monthlong winter break. The fact that he had been proven so wrong about his old friend didn't annoy Dustin, but instead filled him with joy. Feeling superior to his peers often made him lonely, and that night over a feast fit for a king, he felt a profound sense of connection to someone his own age, and he liked it very much.

This was when Steven invited him to his annual New Year's Eve party, which, though he didn't know it at the time, would forever change the course of Dustin's life. It was never Dustin's soul that was at stake upon reuniting with Steven, it was his heart. The reason for this was that Steven's girlfriend, Lolly, had a little sister, Kimmie, who was to become Dustin's newest infatuation and perhaps his greatest love.

III

Unlike Steven, Dustin had always been an intense, bookish kid, which meant he didn't have many friends, but this never bothered him because he had no time to be social. He put all his time and effort into his schoolwork, the debate team, and worrying about global warming and the rising sea levels. However, he did have one source of real joy: movies. Sitting in a dark theater, he could momentarily stop worrying about his extensive AP course load and just breathe. Because of this escapism, he had seen an impressive number of films, with his favorite guilty pleasures being the high school comedies of the eighties and nineties. It was these very movies that ignited the flame of his one super-secret, shameful fantasy that he had never admitted to anyone in his entire life, not even his therapist.

This fantasy was that Dustin wanted to end his high school career by going to his senior prom not with a pack of guy friends, or even a smart Ivy League–bound girl whose GPA he admired, but with a gorgeous, completely out-of-his-league hot girl (he didn't even care if she was smart). And he didn't want just any pretty high school girl, he wanted a girl who was on the not-so-secret "secret" Manhattan private school Hot List that came out every year during the Christmas holidays, ranking the top ten private school girls in every grade. (He knew, of course, that the very existence of such a list was shallow, misogynistic, and demeaning to girls, but it's not like he actively participated in the making of the list; he just viewed it. And then promptly hated himself for doing so.)

Dustin was wise enough to know this reverie of his was fueled by the fantasy-filled teen movies he loved, where the "nice guy" always ended up with the "hot girl," but he didn't care. He wanted what he wanted, and even though he felt guilty for having such a frivolous hankering, especially when the entire political landscape was a shit show these days, he let himself off the hook by viewing the matter scientifically. What he was experiencing was a biological imperative, or to put it more crudely, it was because he had just as much testosterone as every other teenage boy in America.

This prom fantasy of Dustin's had morphed into an entirely different beast six weeks ago, on the night of Steven's annual New Year's Eve party. This infamous party came into existence four years prior when Steven had no choice but to attend Baruch, a New York City public school, for the first semester of his freshman year after he managed to get kicked out on his first day of Riverdale Country School. Steven, worried he was going to lose his social standing while he waited for his mother to get him into a new private school, asked his father to let him throw a New Year's Eve party, while his parents spent the holiday as always at their beach house in Maui.

His Korean father, who was constantly worrying about his half-Korean son fitting in with the best of New York society, agreed and gave his son the sage advice that for a party to be memorable, it needed not only to be lavish but exclusive as well. It was his father's idea that Steven should restrict his party to only upperclassmen (private school juniors and seniors) even though he was himself only a freshman. And to attract these cool upperclassmen his father paid handsomely for A$AP Rocky to perform. It was his mother's idea to "paper the party" with twenty young Wilhelmina models paid to be pretend guests, something she had heard about from a friend who made his fortune investing in nightclubs. The original party was an enormous success, and Steven's reputation as the host-with-the-most (models and booze) was now legendary.

This very party five weeks ago was Dustin's first time being invited, though he had heard stories about the infamous gathering over the years. When Dustin showed up that night, he had convinced himself that the party, like most things in this town, was more than likely 50 percent hype, but as soon as he entered, he knew he was wrong. This party was unlike anything he had ever seen before.

It was as if Santa Claus had quit the toy-making business and opened a strip club. Sexy models dressed like holiday elves circulated the professionally decorated party, handing out truffle mac-n-cheese balls and poached purple potatoes with caviar. There were two top-shelf liquor bars manned by scantily clad bartenders. (This being her second year as gf of the host, Lolly had made sure there were hot male bartenders as well.) There was a stream of professional DJs who were in charge of the music. And right when you entered the foyer, the first thing you saw was a seven-foot-tall ice sculpture fountain of Rick and Morty, in which champagne poured into Morty's hand, then would travel through Morty (sitting on Rick's shoulders), and come out Rick's "Pickle Rick" dick perfectly chilled.

The fountain was the most Instagrammed photo of the party.

Steven's parents' only new rule this year was that there would be no smoking cigarettes inside because of the fifteen-million-dollar Matisse-cigarette-burn incident of last year's soiree. Solving this problem was easy. They simply opened their roof access, the stairs in the hallway outside of Steven's front door. (Steven's parents shared the floor with only one other family and the C.s were gifted the K.s' Parisian pied-à-terre keys for their holidays to ensure they wouldn't be home to deal with three-hundred-plus teenagers rampaging on the rooftop.)

After wandering from room to room in the main party, Dustin decided to go check out the roof before he dumped his coat in Steven's sister's bedroom. Upstairs he found throngs of people smoking spliffs and cigarettes under heat lamps, a Ping-Pong table and an ice hockey table in full action, and a pop-up shop from Serendipity 3 manned by someone dressed in a penguin suit. Overwhelmed by the sheer insanity, Dustin got himself a hot chocolate and walked over to check out the view. Central Park was breathtakingly beautiful, still blanketed in white from the first early snowfall of winter. As Dustin stared out across the park, he couldn't help but wonder if Steven's dad had paid for it to snow.

Turning to scan the crowd of faces, Dustin didn't see one person that he knew, and he realized the only people who had spoken to him since arriving were paid waitstaff. He made the decision, after finishing his hot chocolate, to leave before Steven even knew he had shown up. This party was obviously not his scene and these were not his people, and admitting this allowed him to finally relax. When Dustin checked the time on his iPhone, he saw an alert reminding him that OSIRIS-REx was going into orbit around the asteroid Bennu, and even though this was happening 70 million miles away he looked up anyway and found the night sky to be quite calming. He was gazing upward when he heard a sweet voice ask him what he was looking at with such fierce concentration.

When he looked down to see who had spoken, his first thought was that he had gotten a contact high from mistakenly walking into the kitchen pantry earlier, which was being hotboxed by three Dalton seniors, because the girl standing before him looked like a blond angel, otherworldly and ethereal, sparkling in a silver dress with a pale pink pashmina wrapped around her shoulders to cover her wings.

As a man of reason Dustin did not believe in the phenomenon known as "love at first sight," but in that moment it absolutely happened to him. He spoke to this gorgeous girl about how he had the *New York Times* Astronomy and Space calendar alerts on his phone and how he had just received a notification, and she told him that she never really "got the whole stargazing thing" until she spent a year living out West where there were no tall buildings and the sky was bigger than she ever believed possible, chock-full of a zillion stars. Dustin adored her use of "chock-full" and how she guilessly admitted she hadn't understood that bright city lights were the reason why she never saw the stars in Manhattan.

Dustin gently corrected her, explaining that on a clear night it was possible to see a few constellations if you knew where to look. He then explained why the spacecraft OSIRIS-REx's first orbit around the asteroid Bennu was significant and how exciting it was that such a thing was happening in space while they were standing there. "Can you even imagine the years of preplanning that went into this one event? It's such a huge accomplishment for all involved."

"Sure sounds that way," the angel, whose name he didn't even know, replied and then shivered in the wind. Pulling her wrap tight around her shoulders she told him she needed to go find her sister, but she hoped they could talk more later. And then she was gone. If she hadn't touched his arm telling him it was nice to talk stars with him, he would have wondered if she had ever really been there at all.

He ended up staying at the party until a little after midnight, which he owed to the good fortune of running into two girls he knew from SAT prep class who let him tag along with them for the evening. Stephanie and Tasha were friends of Steven's girlfriend from Camp Laurel in Maine, and they both admitted to being first-time party attenders as well. Dustin was relieved to hear they were as overwhelmed as he was by the spectacle, but they said they were sticking it out to the bitter end, unsure if they'd ever score an invite again.

Luckily the two girls were chatterboxes, so Dustin stayed his usual quiet self and just listened while secretly scanning the crowd for the girl from the rooftop. It was only minutes after the New Year was welcomed, via screams and confetti cannons, that he saw her again. He was in the library sitting on a couch with Tasha and Stephanie, when his mystery blonde hurried by the doorway. He pointed her out to Stephanie, and she matter-of-factly informed him the angelic beauty was Kimmie, the little sister of their friend Lolly.

"I didn't know Lolly had a sister," was all he had to say before Stephanie and Tasha unpacked Kimmie's entire life story. Kimmie had just started Spence as a sophomore, because her freshman year had been spent living in Nevada and training to be an Olympic ice dancing hopeful. Six months ago, she moved back home after a terrible spill during a competition when Gabe, her skating partner and gay BFF, mistimed a deep outside edge lift, lost his balance, and fell backward, causing her to fall forward and shatter her kneecap. She spent the whole summer recovering from surgery and was told her career as an ice dancer was over.

Tasha then added, "Well, if I had to choose between the Olympics or being on the Hot List, I'd pick the Hot List for sure."

At the mere mention of the list, Dustin choked on his now-warm champagne, which escalated into an embarrassing coughing fit. After getting pounded on the back by both girls, he finally managed to get out in a raspy voice, "She's on the list?" Dustin tried to sound as casual as possible, because truth be told, he hadn't known the list was even out yet.

Stephanie nodded. "She came in at number three, which is incredible since she didn't even campaign for it."

Tasha added, "And she doesn't dress slutty like all the other girls."

"Well, not at school," Stephanie said. "But there's plenty of videos of Kimmie in some skimpy-ass ice dancing outfits on YouTube."

"Do you thinks it sucks for Lolls to have such a gorg little sister?"

"Nah. I'd rather have a bf like Steven than be on the list."

"Same."

Newly awash in so much information, Dustin, not wanting to give either girl reason to be suspicious, artfully changed the subject and then left the party twenty minutes later. He chose to walk home across the snowy park so he could replay the night in his head, marveling at how every choice he'd made in his entire life led him to that serendipitous encounter on the roof. As much as he tried to stop himself from going there, near the end of the walk he couldn't help but imagine what it would be like to walk into his prom with Kimmie S., the third hottest sophomore in all of Manhattan.

IV

School had been back in session for almost two weeks, and Dustin had seen Steven six times and had been unable to find the courage to talk to him about Kimmie directly. When he thought about why this was, all he could come up with was that he didn't know if he wanted to hear the truth. Because if he were to learn he had only a miniscule chance in hell with her, where would that leave him? But as Dustin crossed the park in the late afternoon for tutoring, he thought about what he'd just discussed in therapy. Today was lucky number seven and he was finally going to grow a pair and confess to Steven his love for Kimmie.

Dustin knew something was wrong as soon as he stepped into the apartment, and Steven embraced him in an awkwardly long bro-hug. He then said, "Dude, you can't even believe my day. Come in. Come in. Good you're here."

Dustin's first thought was Steven was on drugs. While getting himself some water in the kitchen, he checked his friend's eyes. Steven's pupils looked normal given the amount of light in the room. Dustin's older brother was currently in rehab, so he had some experience with people on drugs, and though he knew Steven used, he was certain Steven wasn't currently high.

To Dustin's surprise, Steven settled down in the formal dining room at a table that could comfortably seat twenty-four people. He made a big show of opening his physics textbook, telling Dustin they could start working on his problem set right after they had a shot. Ordinarily, Dustin would have refused, but he needed to steel his nerves. The booze was surprisingly smooth and when Dustin said as much, Steven replied, "It fucking well should be, this shit is ninety-five hundred bucks a bottle!"

When Dustin heard this, he shook his head, grabbed the bottle, and did some quick calculations. "We just imbibed seven hundred and sixty dollars' worth of booze!"

"And we're doin' it again!" Steven said, pouring two more shots.

Dustin, unable to deal with his growing anxiety, blurted out, "Is it absolutely impossible to believe Lolly's little sister would ever go out with me?" and then downed his second shot.

Steven sat back in his chair, let out a slow wolf whistle, and said, "Dustin, you dirty dirty direwolf, you." (A love of *Game of Thrones* was one of the few things the two boys had in common.)

Dustin ignored the whistle and kept going. "Ever since I met Kimmie on New Year's Eve she's all I can think about. My father caught me watching her ice dancing videos on my iPad and now is probably wondering if I'm gay. Thank god I met her after I got into MIT, because that girl is a GPA-wrecker."

"Is that nerd-speak for crazy hot? Me likey." Steven laughed at his friend's outburst, set the front legs back down on the floor, and then said quite seriously, "Real deal, I think Kimmie would be into a smart guy like you. Plus, girls high-key freak out over the status that comes with dating seniors." Steven paused, which Dustin instinctively knew meant trouble.

"But . . . ?" Dustin prompted.

Steven nodded and continued, "But . . . she's currently caught the attention of Count Vronsky and may be a little under his spell right now. But hang tight, 'cause no girl lasts long with him." Steven was sorry to give his friend the bad news, but he felt he owed it to Dustin to clue him in on who he was up against.

Dustin furrowed his brow, digesting the news. "Please tell me 'Count' is a nickname and not his actual official title." Steven told his pal that it was indeed a nickname, but one born from a rumor that Vronsky's father's lineage could be traced back to a legit Russian royalty. The second theory on why he was known as "the Count" was because it took five minutes for him to count all the girls who had dropped their panties for him, but Steven kept this part to himself, instead adding, "But, seriously, Lolls thinks the Count's a passing fancy and you could be the slow and steady tortoise that wins Kimmie for a prize."

"Race," Dustin corrected. "The slow and steady tortoise wins the race, not a prize."

"Same thing!" Steven countered back in all seriousness. "You gotta assume if you win a race you'd also win a prize, yes? Dustin, my friend, I've got another expression for you . . . 'Lighten the fuck up, dude!' This is some real-ass life shit we're talkin' about, not English lit!"

It was Dustin's turn to laugh at Steven's comment and at himself. It was in Dustin's nature to be inordinately precise about details, which served him well in school, but made him seem uptight socially. Dustin asked, "Hey, why would Lolly know I have a tortoise in the race at all?"

Steven admitted he had been aware of Dustin's interest in Kimmie for a while now. Lolly was the one who put it together after joining the two boys during their study session last week. She told Steven that Dustin had awkwardly managed to bring up Kimmie's name three times while they worked on Steven's calc homework, which could only mean one thing. Hearing this caused Dustin to drop his head to the table and thump his forehead a few times. Steven put a hand on Dustin's shoulder and promised his friend he was willing to help him with his Kimmie quest in any possible way. Dustin thanked him profusely and said he'd repay the favor any way he could.

Steven, emboldened by their bonding session, decided it was now his turn to confess his own girl troubles. Dustin listened to everything Steven said without interruption, only raising an eyebrow when Steven admitted that Lolly happened to be in the very same apartment with them at this very same moment.

Dustin chose his words prudently before giving his opinion on Steven's tale of woe, but no matter how hard he tried to find a way to side with his friend, he couldn't do it. He strongly disapproved of Steven's cheating on Lolly. It made no sense to Dustin that any man could make a case where it was okay to cheat on his girlfriend. The way Dustin saw it, why bother to make a commitment to someone if you had no intention of honoring it? Sure, he knew that plenty of boys cheated on their girlfriends with the reasoning that their girlfriends were holy terrors, but Lolly was no such terror. Steven tried to explain to Dustin that staying faithful was harder than it looked, but even as he said it out loud he knew his words were lost on him. He also knew that staying faithful for Dustin wouldn't be difficult, as he was made of sturdier moral stock than himself, for sure. And Dustin, who was somewhat of a rookie when it came to kicking game, probably had fewer temptations to deal with in general.

"Dude, it's not like I don't have banger's remorse, 'cause I do," Steven admitted.

"But do you have remorse because you did it, or because you got caught?" Dustin asked.

"I'd say fifty/fifty."

"And I'd say, thank you for your honesty," Dustin said, and he meant it, too.

After an hour passed, Steven told Dustin he had to cut their time short so he could pick up his sister at Grand Central. Anna was coming in for damage control. Dustin, now understanding the extenuating circumstances at hand, found himself offering to edit and proof Steven's paper on the flaws of the American prison system for him. Truth be told,

Dustin welcomed the idea of a little busywork because he had nothing better to do that night except obsess over Kimmie, which was the last thing he wanted. The thought of doing yet another deep dive through her Instagram feed, where he would stare at heavily filtered "artistic" photos of nature, made him want to scream. (Kimmie's most annoying trait so far was that she, unlike most other teen girls, rarely posted selfies.)

As Dustin gathered up his things to go, it occurred to Steven how he might help Dustin and himself with one simple idea. "You should go to Wollman Rink right now because Kimmie's there skating. She was recently cleared by her surgeon to skate again and Lolly said 'skating puts Kimmie in her happy place.' And if you show up when she's in her happy place, then maybe some of her happy place could rub off on your happy place, nome sayin'?"

Dustin shook his head vehemently at the suggestion. "No way, I can't. Do I look like a guy who can fake his way through a staged run-in? Nope, nope, nope!"

Steven waited for Dustin to quiet down before he continued. "C'mon, you'd be doing me a solid by going to talk to her." His rationale for this request was that he needed Kimmie to cover for Lolly's absence to their father and stepmother. "Lolly's going to be in no shape to see the 'rents tonight and Anna's gonna need some time to talk her down off the crazy ledge!"

The last thing Dustin wanted was to get in the middle of Steven's messy love life, reminding his friend that the messenger was the one who always got killed. "Text her yourself."

Steven, now exasperated, raised his voice slightly. "C'mon dude, think about it. What am I supposed to text? 'Yo, Kimmie, I straight-up cheated on your sis and now she's gone all Sylvia Plath and locked herself in my mother's walk-in'? Dustin, do it for me. I'll pay for your Uber, hell, seize the moment and take her to Serendipity 3 for frozen hot chocolate, which I'll also pay for. Buy her the thousand-dollar sundae with the gold leaf, for all I care. Trust me, that's a total panty-dropping move!" Steven pulled out his phone. "What's your Venmo again? Seriously, let me *assuage* my guilty conscience by helping you with Kimmie. Vocab word! I win."

Dustin laughed and then closed his eyes for a moment and tried to picture himself sitting across from Kimmie in a cozy leather booth, watching her perfect mouth blowing on her hot chocolate. He shook the picture out of his head and waved off any more talk of money, heading out the door without agreeing one way or the other. Steven called after him, telling him he should trust him because the only subject he was smarter than Dustin in was girls.

Dustin almost reminded Steven that his current girl problem disproved his last statement but didn't. He was positive his friend wasn't in the right mind-set to handle the hard truth.

V

Steven was staring up at the arrivals and departures board in Grand Central when he found himself standing shoulder to shoulder next to Alexia V. (known around town by his nickname the Count, or just Vronsky), who was also scanning the board above them. "Hey man, what brings you here?"

Vronsky gave him a big grin. "Would you believe I'm here to pick up my mother? She's recovering from a broken ankle and is still using a cane. She attended a dinner party at my uncle's in Greenwich, gave her driver the night off, and is now taking the train back by herself. She didn't ask me to pick her up, but why else would she have sent me her arrival time?"

Steven returned his smile and decided that on close inspection Count Vronsky was every bit as handsome as everyone said he was. As they were both newish to Collegiate and Steven was a senior, everything he knew about Vronsky was strictly based on reputation. "If I was a betting man, I'd wager there's another reason. Gotta bank some 'good-boy points' for the future, perhaps? That's what I do whenever I can. What choice do we have when blessed with formidable women for mothers?"

Vronsky roared with laughter in response, slapped Steven on the back, and then proceeded to neither confirm nor deny anything. Instead he answered a question with his own. "And you? What brings you out on a snowy evening without a proper overcoat?" Steven looked down and realized Vronsky spoke the truth. He had been so distracted trying to get Dustin out the door and not be late himself that he had left the house in only a Loro Piana cashmere cardigan and his black Burberry cashmere beanie.

"A beautiful girl," Steven answered, but quickly realizing this was not the right time for him to be so cavalier, added, "My sister, Anna. She's coming in from Greenwich, too."

Vronsky frowned. "Did I know you had a sister?"

"Anna's a junior at Greenwich Academy. She's the equestrian of the family and can't bear to be too far away from her precious horses, so she mostly lives at the Greenwich house. Plus, she has two giant dogs she's obsessed with. She's always saying it's her duty as a mom to give her fur babies a proper backyard to romp in."

"Gotta love the girls who love riding," Vronsky said with a sly grin, then quickly added, "Horses."

Ordinarily Steven would be all over Vronsky's statement, piling on his own vulgar jokes, but since they were talking about his sister, he kept himself in check. "Maybe you know her boyfriend, Alexander W.?"

Now it was Vronsky's turn to straighten up, even adding the flourish of tightening an imaginary tie. "No shit? Your sister is the gf of the Greenwich OG. Interesting."

"Not really." Honestly, if Steven never heard another word about Anna's umchina boyfriend it'd be fine with him. "Umchina" was one of the few Korean words Steven had learned from his Korean grandmother. There's no English translation, but it basically means the perfect son of your mother's friend, the one you're constantly compared to. For Steven, the Greenwich OG was his umchina because his mother couldn't help but list off every single one of Alexander's many accomplishments in Steven's presence. She once even went so far as to say, "Greenwich is so fortunate to have someone like Alexander representing it."

Alexander W. had been his sister's boyfriend for the last three years, earning his nickname, the Greenwich OG, for being the only privileged white male in the country to have gotten into all eight Ivy League schools his senior year. He was old-money Connecticut from a good family, had published his first op-ed piece in *The New York Times* at age sixteen, was valedictorian at Brunswick, and spent two weeks of every summer teaching disadvantaged youths how to sail (which Steven found moronic, as if poor kids sat around wishing they could sail). He for sure would be the Democratic presidential nominee in another twenty years if the current president didn't decimate the American democratic system for all eternity. Alexander was presently a freshman at Harvard University but traveled back to Greenwich often to be a devoted boyfriend to Anna. Only the formidable Greenwich OG could get away with being a college guy who still had a high school girlfriend.

Anna was seventeen and two years younger than Alexander, but she had always been quite poised for her age. The perfect couple's "meet cute" happened at the White House Easter Egg Hunt when she was thirteen. Alexander was there because his dad was a big supporter of Obama, and she was there because at thirteen she played the violin in an award-winning string quartet, otherwise comprised of high school girls. If you believed the stories, it was said that when Alexander watched Anna play, he felt an overwhelming sense of déjà vu, even though he was certain he had never seen her before in his life. What he did know was that he no longer cared about helping little kids find Easter eggs. His only goal was to meet the beautiful girl who played the violin like she was sent down from the heavens to do so.

Alexander introduced himself to Anna at the dessert buffet and was so taken with her delicate beauty up close he dropped a piece of cherry pie on her white dress. Horrified over the mishap, he quickly arranged to have Anna borrow a dress from Sasha, President Obama's younger daughter. (To this day, Anna is still friends with Sasha.) What they later figured out was that Alexander had seen Anna play the violin for his aunt's second wedding at the Saugatuck Harbor Yacht Club in Westport the previous summer. Utterly smitten, Alexander begged his dad and stepmother to invite Anna to fly home with them on their private plane instead of letting her take the train. His stepmother had never seen Alexander behave in such a way before, and in an effort to win favor with her husband's only son, she called Anna's mom and arranged the whole thing.

By the time Anna arrived home, she had the "promise" of her first boyfriend, since she wasn't allowed to "officially" have a boyfriend until she turned fourteen. Alexander had no problem waiting and the two had been the perfect couple ever since. The long-term plan was marriage, of course, but the post–high school plan was that Anna would attend Harvard or Yale and Alexander would go to law school wherever she ended up.

Steven once asked Anna whether it was scary to have her entire life planned out at such a young age. "We live in America now, so it's not like you gotta do the whole Korean arranged marriage for the good of the family status thing, you know?"

She just smiled at her brother's sarcasm and told him, "Alexander is a good person. He needs me and I'm happy to be there for him." Steven was quick to remind her that Alexander was not a dog and to ask her about her own needs, to which she simply replied that Alexander adored her, and she liked how easy their relationship was from the very start. She was relieved to not have to deal with the drama of dating, which she had little time or patience for. Alexander was everything a girl could want, plus it helped that her parents approved of their relationship. There were very few boys that their father would ever trust his precious daughter with; in fact, Alexander may be the only boy that fit the bill. In Korea, societal status was paramount, and Alexander's father was the top of the Greenwich elite. It was this importance their parents placed on social standing that Steven disagreed with the most.

"Track twenty-seven," Vronsky said, breaking Steven out of his thoughts.

"What did you say?" Steven asked.

"Their train, it's arriving now."

Steven nodded and hurried after Vronsky, for whom the crowd seemed to part, as he walked toward the escalators in his Brioni camel overcoat, his extra-long Tom Ford cashmere scarf dragging on the ground behind him.

VI

Anna K. told Mrs. Geneviève R. she'd be back to say a proper good-bye, but she needed to look and see if she could spot her brother, Steven. "Please know if your son isn't here we'd be more than happy to give you a ride home. And, if neither one shows up for us, I'm pretty capable my-self."

It was rare for Geneviève to be impressed, but this delightful young creature was a firecracker. "Absolutely, my dear. I truly believe men need us women to show them their purpose in the world. For instance, meet-ing a woman's train on time."

Anna smiled at the socialite's words while standing in the doorway of the train car. She looked around and finally spotted her brother. She called out to him, but he didn't hear, so she stepped onto the platform, waving to get his attention.

What Count Vronsky first noticed about the exquisite girl were her eyes, dark deep pools that sparkled beneath incredibly long lashes. She looked like a perfect porcelain doll standing so straight and tall in her pale gray Max Mara cashmere coat. He also admired that she didn't wear much makeup like most teenage girls. As he stood watching, Steven bear-hugged her. Ah, so this was his younger sister?

A sharp rapping noise broke his gaze, and he turned to find his mother waving at him, as she banged her cane against the window once more for good measure. Having no other choice, he hurried into the train car. "Mother, dear," he called out, which was exactly how Geneviève preferred to be addressed by her favorite son.

"Alexia, your scarf. It's dragging on the ground like you're some kind of animal." His Parisian mother, a grand dame of New York society, never had a hair out of place, let alone a rebellious scarf. He quickly flung the unruly end over his shoulder and held out his hands to help her to her feet. She no longer had to wear a boot on her injured foot, but she still had it tightly taped and wrapped for security.

"Mother, you shouldn't be wearing heels."

"Darling, two-inch heels for me is the same as wearing flats," she murmured, kissing her handsome son on both cheeks.

"Oh good, you found him." At the sound of her voice every hair on the back of his neck stood at attention. He forced himself to turn around slowly to meet her.

"Did my mother doubt I'd show up?" he asked, his eyes twinkling.

Anna found herself blushing, not out of embarrassment but because she was so startled by Vronsky's good looks, his dirty-blond locks falling over a face that was movie-star handsome. But it was more than his appearance: he exuded a confidence that could only be described as a king-of-the-jungle magnetism. She was sure her face registered wonderment that she would be susceptible to such a thing. "Not for one moment. I was probably projecting my own doubts about my brother showing up for me."

"Anna, please meet my son Alexia, or Alex as he prefers to be called. Alexia, this remarkable young lady was kind enough to keep an old dame like me entertained for the entire trip. She's quite special, this one," Mrs. R. said.

Anna held out her hand to shake the one he was already extending. "A pleasure to meet you, Alexia, your mother has told me so much about you I feel like I know you already."

Vronsky groaned. "Believe only the bad stuff. My mother often crowns me with a halo I don't deserve."

Before Anna could reply, Vronsky's mother snapped, "Nonsense, you're the most eligible bachelor in the city. Such a shame Anna's already taken by the OG, or I'd insist you ask for her hand immediately."

Anna and Alexia traded secret smiles at his mother's use of the nickname, both certain she had no idea that OG stood for "original gangster" as opposed to "Old Greenwich" like she probably assumed. Vronsky's mother barreled on, as was her way. "We traded stories of our children, my human ones and her four-legged ones. Anna is an accomplished rider and has two show dogs competing in Westminster next week."

Anna, embarrassed by the praise, quickly corrected her. "I'm not showing them myself, my handlers Lee Ann and Ali will be doing the honors.

But it's true, I'm a girl who prefers the company of animals to people." Vronsky studied her face while she spoke, barely registering her words. She was truly the most stunning girl he had ever seen, a perfect blend of Eurasian beauty: almond eyes and sleek shiny dark hair combined with high cheekbones and a perfect WASPy ski-slope nose.

The conversation ended abruptly as a commotion erupted outside of the train. There was suddenly lots of shouting and people running by their window.

"Wait here, let me see what's going on," Vronsky said. Anna nodded, stepping toward Vronsky's mother and helping her sit back down.

He returned a few minutes later followed by Steven, reporting it was safe for them to leave now. Anna asked what was going on, but both boys exchanged looks and remained silent. Anna demanded, "Tell me; I want to know."

Vronsky gravely explained that a homeless man was the source of the uproar. The man had two dogs and was insisting that one of them had jumped out of his arms onto the tracks and was hit by the train. Anna gasped at the news. "Our train? Oh god, is it true?"

Her eyes were already welling up when Vronsky, compelled to be honest with Anna despite her reaction, confirmed the ugly truth. "I'm afraid so."

"That's so awful!" Anna cried, not bothering to wipe away her tears. She felt a roiling in her stomach. *This is a bad omen*, she thought. The four of them were on the platform heading to the escalator when Anna turned to see two police officers on the scene, one of them placing the still howling homeless man in handcuffs. Anna stopped walking. "Why are they arresting him?"

Steven explained that the homeless man had shoved the train conductor during the commotion. He then put his arm around his sister trying to usher her onto the escalator, but she refused to move.

"But what about his other dog? Didn't you say he had two? What's to become of that dog?" Anna pulled away from Steven and took two steps forward, but Vronsky put his hand on her arm and gently stopped her.

"No, don't. I'll go make sure his other dog is taken care of. Can you make sure my mother gets home for me?"

Anna met Vronsky's eyes and immense relief flooded through her. "You will? That's so sweet of you. Of course, we'll take your mom home."

Geneviève remained silent during the exchange, proud of her son for stepping up to do the right thing, but aware that he was far more concerned with doing the right thing for the beautiful girl's sake than the dog's.

Vronsky's mother had boasted a great deal about her son's accomplishments (romantic and otherwise) on the train, so Anna was already impressed, but this move was above and beyond. What kind of sixteen-year-old boy possessed the type of heroic goodwill she'd just witnessed? It was like her pain had become his as well. In that moment she felt as though his crystal blue eyes had seen her secret self, which was ridiculous because how could such a thing be possible when they had only just met?

VII

Dustin had no problem picking out Kimmie from the swirling mass of skaters at Wollman Rink. She was wearing a deep purple faux fur jacket with matching earmuffs, and even though her knee was not 100 percent, she was still the best skater on the ice. She moved with such grace and ease, Dustin couldn't take his eyes off her and was embarrassed to discover he had been holding his breath while he watched. He walked to the railing, unsure of how to get her attention, finally deciding he'd call out the next time she skated by. But three times she whooshed past, and three times he was unable to speak as he stared at her beautiful face. Eventually two middle school boys in hockey skates playing tag crashed into a few novices and a little boy belly-flopped onto the ice, landing so hard that he spun a full 720 degrees in his navy Patagonia snowsuit directly into Kimmie's path.

"Kimmie, watch out!" Dustin's voice was so urgent that several people, Kimmie included, looked his way. In one bunny hop movement, Kimmie made a full stop an inch from the fallen boy. She bent over and helped the little guy to his feet and delivered him back to his parents. As Dustin watched this small kindness, he felt a pressure in his chest that made him wonder if there were any known cases of teenagers dropping dead of heart attacks.

Kimmie skated straight to him with an expression he couldn't read, so he quickly pulled off his own hat, reasoning that perhaps she didn't recognize him. He gave her a friendly wave. Kimmie smiled and waved back, stopping in front of him with a dramatic flourish, the shavings of her braking blades hitting the low guardrail.

"Hey, Dustin. Are you here to skate?" she asked.

"I suck at skating. Shitty ankles," he replied. "I'm here for you." His words jumbled out faster than he wanted, and he winced. "Not here for you in a creepy stalker way, or anything."

"I didn't think so. You seem too serious to be a stalker and too nice to be a creeper."

"I would think stalker sorts are actually very serious," he replied, still unable to control his words around her. "But I'm not one . . . yet."

She laughed at this, cocking her head in surprise at his dryly delivered wit. "So now that you have my attention, whatever will you do with it?" she asked, flushing with embarrassment because what she'd meant as a joke came out sounding far flirtier than she'd intended.

"Sorry, I don't mean to be cryptic. Steven sent me. Steven, your sister's—"

She frowned, interrupting him. "I know what Steven you're talking about."

"Yes, of course you do." This was going quickly from bad to worse.

"And what news do you bring from the scoundrel that is Steven from the House of K.?" she asked, straight-faced.

"Uhhh . . ." Dustin hesitated.

Kimmie laughed at his confusion. "Don't tell me you're the one guy who hasn't watched *Game of Thrones?*"

Dustin smiled with relief. "Oh no, I'm a fanboy. I've read all the books."

"Me, too," she admitted, even though her mother once advised her that boys don't always like girls who read books. "Seriously, what does the dickhead have to say?"

Of course, Kimmie had already heard the news from her sister, which meant Steven had sent him on a ridiculous mission with the sole purpose of getting him some face time with Kimmie.

"You know?" he asked, wanting to verify what he suspected to be true.

"I do. Lolly texted me all about 'Brad.' She's okay, isn't she? I told her I'd come and get her, but she said no."

"I didn't see her myself. But I'm sure she's fine, or rather as good as can be expected. Honestly, I didn't want to get involved, but Steven asked me to come, as a favor. The rink's on my way home." Even though he knew he'd said enough, Dustin kept going anyway. "I'm Steven's homework tutor. We were friends when we were little because of our moms," he added, helping her connect the dots on why a guy like him would be friends with Steven.

"I know," she said simply, which made Dustin wonder whether she knew because she had specifically inquired about him after they had met, or whether this was news she had learned from Lolly in everyday conversation. If Tasha and Stephanie, the two chatty girls from the party, had taught him anything, it was that teenage girls seemed to talk about anything and everything with one another. Chatting was like breathing for them.

"You're shivering," he said.

"Only because I stopped to talk to you. Don't worry, I'm used to the cold. I like it."

"Can I buy you a hot chocolate at Serendipity?" He had no idea where his boldness was coming from.

Kimmie looked confused. "Steven sent you to take me to get hot chocolate?"

"No. He sent me to ask you if you would cover for your sister with your parents tonight. She's going to be home late." He felt immediate relief now that his mission was over and done with. "I'm the one asking if you want to have hot chocolate with me. Or a frozen hot chocolate, since you like the cold."

Kimmie studied Dustin's face for a few seconds, then checked her phone pretending to look at the time. When she saw she had no new texts, she looked up and smiled. "Sure, why not? But you should know I'm a feminist so I'm going to have to pay for myself."

"Cool. I'm a feminist, too, so I'll let you pay for mine."

Kimmie surprised herself by laughing out loud again. But no one was more surprised at Dustin's wit and charm than he was.

VIII

After they dropped off Vronsky's mother at 834 Fifth Avenue, Steven joined his sister in the backseat of the Uber Select. Anna had been very quiet during the entire journey so far and he knew she was still thinking of the poor dog who had been hit by the train. And while this was true, Anna's thoughts were also on the handsome boy who was at this moment rescuing another helpless dog. *Is he a dog lover, like me?*

Steven grabbed his sister's hand and squeezed it, and as if he knew what she was thinking, he said, "Hey, thanks for coming to this dog's rescue, too."

They were crossing Central Park and the snow was still falling, faster and thicker than before. "Perhaps we'll have a snow day?" she said, pretending she had been thinking of the weather.

"Dude, I'd fucking kill for one," he responded, checking his phone to see if there was any news yet. "Sorry, I know you don't like it when I call you 'dude.'"

Anna heard something in her brother's voice that made her realize it was time to deal with his massive screw-up. She pushed all thoughts of dead dogs and blue-eyed heroes from her mind and turned toward her brother in the dark of the backseat. This was not the first time she had come to his rescue, and she knew it was far from the last. She had been covering for him since they were little kids. "Okay, I'm ready," Anna said. "Tell me everything."

And Steven did. He told her how he met "Brad," whose real name was Marcella, a seventeen-year-old public-school girl from the South Bronx who had approached him at the Union Square Starbucks a few days before Christmas on a dare from her friends. "She walked right up to me, smacked me in the chest with the back of her hand, and said, 'Gimme twenty bucks.' When I asked her why me, she said I looked rich and bored. Then she . . ." He trailed off.

"I need to know everything Steven, just tell me. I'm not a baby."

Steven continued, "She told me I looked like I had BDE." He paused and then finished. "You know, Big Dick Energy."

"I knew that," Anna lied, but then let out a small laugh. "Okay, I didn't. But she really just walked up and said that when she didn't even know you?" Anna tried to picture herself ever doing such a thing, but it seemed impossible.

"Marcella gives zero fucks. She'll say anything to anyone."

Anna's eyes widened at her brother's admiring tone, but she didn't say anything. Steven went on to say he gave Marcella a twenty to buy coffee for her friends but found himself asking her if she wanted to grab dinner. She accepted on the spot, abandoning her friends, and the two of them ended up at Joe's Pizza where he watched in awe as she ate half an order of garlic knots and two slices of pizza, finished the end of his calzone, and washed it all down with a large pink lemonade. "And she did it without once talking about carbs, calories, the evils of refined sugar, or apologizing for her large appetite. It was baller AF!" Steven explained he was further entranced with Marcella because she seemed so much freer than any girl he had ever met before. She wasn't polite or perfectly dressed. She laughed at all his jokes and kept telling him he was funny for a rich dickhead.

"Lolly thinks you're funny, too," Anna reminded him.

Steven agreed, but he couldn't help but point out that Lolly often refrained from laughing at his dirtier and meaner jokes, always calling him out when he said something in poor taste. "I keep telling her since I'm half a minority I'm allowed to say off-color things." Anna swatted her brother even though she had heard him say this type of thing plenty of times as well.

"See, you do it, too. You can't help but correct me, but here's the thing. I'm just talkin' shit. I'm not racist, so what's the big deal? Comedians do it all the time. I know I said Marcella seemed so free, but maybe it's me. Maybe what I liked about her was she allowed *me* to feel free. Don't you just want to be yourself sometimes, Anna? Flaws and all?"

Though Anna did understand her brother's feelings, she also didn't want to encourage his way of thinking at this moment. She knew this was a reaction to how hard their father was on him, all this talk of wanting to be free. Their father kept her on a short leash, too, but with her it seemed overprotective and endearing, almost. With Steven, it was different somehow. Steven never talked about it with her, though she often wished he would. So now she stayed silent and motioned for him to continue, because it was clear he had more on his mind.

"I'm so fucking tired of everyone having to be so PC all the time," Steven said. "Why does everyone get offended over every little thing these days? I'm eighteen, why can't I just have a little fun when I want to? I didn't ask to be born into privilege."

It was here that Anna spoke up, reminding her brother that having fun had never once been his problem, though she conceded it was certainly difficult to deal with the high expectations placed upon them by their parents. And since Steven was the only son, which in Korean culture meant that the responsibility to step up and take care of the family would fall on his shoulders when he was older, Anna knew he had the tougher road. "I know you're upset, and I know it sucks for you, how Dad can be so tough. . . . But we're getting off track, Steven. Can you finish telling me about the girl?"

Steven told her that after pizza, they had gone to Ace Bar in Alphabet City and played arcade games. Marcella's cousin was the bartender there and let them drink. At the end of the night, Marcella dragged him into the girls' restroom, took him into a stall, and . . .

Anna nodded. "I'm pretty sure I can guess what happened next."

Her brother was totally hooked after that, and he'd been seeing her in secret now for the last two months or so.

"But do you have feelings for Marcella?" she pressed. "Not sexual ones, I mean, but real ones. You know, like heartfelt feelings."

"Anna, I barely know the girl. She's sexy and DTF. I love Lolly. But sometimes . . . well, you know how boring it can get when you've been in a relationship for a while."

"Actually I don't know," she replied, looking out the window. "Don't look for sympathy from me. I've been with Alexander double the time you've been with Lolly."

"Exactly my point! You two must know what I mean, or at least he must."

There were so many things that annoyed her about her brother's statement, she barely knew where to begin. "Are you implying Alexander cheats on me?" Anna asked, going straight for it.

"No, in fact, I'm sure he doesn't. Your bf is much too good of a person, whereas I'm a tremendous shitbag."

Anna was aware their mother often tortured her brother with comparisons to her seemingly perfect boyfriend. "I know this sucks. But stop deflecting. If you say you love Lolly, then why cheat?" she asked, knowing her brother didn't have an answer. She was willing to wager her brother rarely knew why it was he did most of the things he did.

"I don't know," he replied as if on cue.

Anna knew this was the best she was going to get from him now and moved on. She asked Steven whether this was the first time he had cheated on Lolly, and after a long silence he said it wasn't. She fired him a look of sisterly disapproval. "Are you sure you want to stay with Lolly? Because plenty of guys in this town stay single and hook up with a new girl every weekend. Maybe that would suit you more. Honestly, you don't seem ready to be a boyfriend. Like, at all."

"I know that's what it seems like. But that's how I know I love Lolly, because I *want* to be her boyfriend. She's good like you. And no one's sweeter. She also keeps me reined in, which you know I need. She makes me want to try harder to be better myself. Marcella means nothing to me. Though she had this dope tongue ring . . ."

"Ew. Enough about her. Steven, you've got to end it." Anna loved her brother, but she didn't like him as a person in this moment. She knew that boys were very different from girls, but hearing her brother talk made her feel the gap between the sexes was much wider than she'd ever imagined.

"I know. I will. And the tongue ring wasn't a reference to anything lewd, it was something I saw because she laughed a lot. You know, because she thought—"

"Steven, you're funny! Everyone thinks so; why do you always hyperfocus on this fact?" Anna said in an exasperated tone.

"Because it's my thing, Anna! I'm not perfect like you, and I'm certainly not better than perfect like your fucking boyfriend, okay?" Steven rarely raised his voice to his sister and he felt immediately ashamed at doing so. But Anna just didn't get it. Steven's dad had impossibly high standards when it came to him, and it wasn't fair. He'd never told Anna, but on more than one occasion their father had commanded he come to his study, where he lectured him about how hard he had worked to get their family where they were. As an immigrant, Edward said he worked four times as hard to be seen as equal to a Caucasian. It was true that he had been born into wealth the same way Steven had, but Edward's Korean father sent him to America to be educated. He was shipped off to an East Coast boarding school when he was only ten years old. Children of any race and upbringing can be cruel, but entitled white children were often especially cruel. His classmates were not welcoming in the slightest. So he had to fight hard to earn their respect, working with a speech tutor to lose his accent until he spoke perfect English, exceling at sports, and making sure he ranked at the top of his class when it came to academics. The only way he was able to garner the attention of girls in his school was by careful calculations on his part.

Marrying Steven's mother, Greer, was not only about love, but also about Edward's desire that his future children would travel an easier road than he did. Edward had the money and the intelligence, but it was Greer's old-family name that opened the right doors in society. Edward warned his son that as a half-Korean, half-white man, Steven would face racism, not as overtly as he had, but in subtler ways. Steven needed to understand it would always be present. Steven's father told him how he would never truly fit in with Koreans or with Caucasians; however, if Steven played his cards right, his own future children would have it easier. He could not afford to fuck up, and as far as Edward was concerned,

Steven was a disappointment from the moment he got kicked out of Collegiate in the fifth grade.

Steven hated the pressure, always feeling torn between being the person his father expected him to be and figuring out who he wanted to be for himself. Steven wished he could tell Anna the truth, but he could never bring himself to do it. "God, I'm sorry. I don't mean to yell. I'm just . . . I know you're trying to help. I'm just an insecure asshole."

Anna ignored her brother's outburst. "I'm happy to help, Steven, but you can't see this Marcella ever again. And you must break it off over the phone or text. You're too weak to do it in person." Anna knew she was being harsh, but it was time for a little tough love.

"Do you think Lolly will take me back?" he asked.

"Are you one hundred percent sure you want to stay together?" Anna asked. "I mean, really think about it, Steven, you can't do this to her again. Seriously. And if there's a next time, don't even think about calling me—"

"I do want her back! And I won't cheat." Steven sighed. "But do you think she'll take me back?"

Anna looked out the window into the snowy night. "I don't know. She probably will . . . but you do know she's much too good for you, right?"

"I know," Steven said, feeling his sister's disappointment, wanting to be a better person not only for Lolly and Anna, but for his father as well. It just didn't seem right that it was so fucking hard to be good.

IX

The car pulled up to their building and the doorman rushed over to open Anna's door. She turned to her brother. "Give me an hour alone with her. Go and get Lolly's favorite dessert." She stared him down. "You do know what your girlfriend's favorite dessert is, don't you?"

"Joe Allen's banana cream pie. But Anna, c'mon, the shows are getting out now. Times Square will be insane . . ." He stopped talking immediately, her gaze burning a hole in his forehead. "I'll be back in an hour."

Anna smiled at the doorman, who was holding an umbrella and waiting for her to exit the car. She took his hand and stepped to the curb with purpose.

Upstairs in the apartment she made two cups of Dulsão do Brasil and grabbed a couple of coconut waters before walking down the hallway toward her parents' room. Anna had only lived full time in this apartment when she was in elementary school, even though she still had a bedroom here. She loved so much about the city, but lately she preferred it in smaller doses. She felt most like her true self when she was on one of her Dutch Warmbloods, Mark Antony (named for the cartoon bulldog and not the Roman politician) or Cleo (named for the tiny cat who liked to snuggle in Mark Antony's fur), or when she was romping around in the backyard with her Newfoundlands, Gemma and Jon Snow.

She knocked and told Lolly she wanted to talk to her alone, adding that she thought they should do so while trying on her mom's clothes. She never doubted Lolly would refuse her, and she was right, Lolly opened the door right away. Anna entered, offering Lolly her choice of Nespresso or a coconut water. Lolly reached out for the coconut water, twisted off the top, and chugged it down. Crying for hours over an undeserving boyfriend certainly made a girl thirsty. After Lolly calmed down, the girls dressed in never-before-worn Japanese silk robes they had excavated from deep within Anna's mom's closet. Anna told Lolly she could keep the kimono she was wearing (pale pink with cherry blossom trees in a repeating pattern) because she was positive her mom didn't even remember she had it. Anna explained that her mother once told her that although her parents were fine with her dating Anna's father during Yale Law, they were shocked when she announced that they were engaged. Though her parents were much too WASPy and polite to say so, she knew they weren't thrilled she was marrying a Korean man. To make matters worse, her parents threw her an over-the-top lavish engagement party with an Asian theme to it. As if they were announcing to the world: "See, everyone! Our daughter Greer loves all things Asian. Even the men! Not our fault."

Anna's mother had been horrified by the party, of course, but she never told her parents how she felt. Anna's father, meanwhile, who certainly had the most right to be upset about the party, took the whole thing in stride. He was used to racism in all its forms, but Anna's mom was shocked by it. For the first few years of their married life, Anna's mom kept receiving Asian-themed gifts, sushi plates, fancy chopsticks, and very expensive Japanese kimonos. Anna's mom said it pissed her off at first, because she felt they were given as a slight, but eventually she got over it and realized that most people were stupid and had no idea that Asia was divided into many different countries, each with their own distinct histories and cultures. Now twenty-one years later, she and Anna's father were still married, while most everyone else in their social circle was on their second or third divorce. Greer said she couldn't believe it used to upset her so much when she was younger, meaning that their marriage had withstood the scrutiny and skepticism of others for years now, and thus was stronger for it. But that still didn't mean she ever wore the kimonos.

"Well, I heart this robe and I'm going to wear it forevs, and it's nuts your dead grandparents weren't into your dad. I mean, he's why your brother is like crazy fucking hot. I mean everyone knows if you mix in a little Asian, you'll get beautiful kids. Look at you! I'd kill for your skin. Tell me the truth, when was the last time you shaved your legs, even?" Lolly ran her hand across Anna's smooth and hairless shin. Which is when Anna realized that Lolly had entirely missed the main point of her story, which was that time heals all wounds. Lolly was sweet, but she wasn't the brightest flame in the candelabra.

Anna lay down on her back and looked at the ceiling. Above her parents' bed was a new Baccarat crystal chandelier that was dazzling when on but seemed foreboding when off. It was currently off. "Oh my god, I'm so full of pie I could burst," Anna groaned, closing her eyes to it. The banana cream pie that Steven had left outside the door an hour ago was now half gone.

Lolly rolled on her back, too, and then let out a very long and deep sigh. "I don't know how I can stay with him, Anna. I'm just so humiliated." Anna didn't have to look over at her brother's girlfriend to know she was crying again. This was how the entire night had gone: one moment they were laughing and telling each other stories, the next moment Lolly was crying and lamenting that her life was ruined. Anna had no problem with girls who cried, because she herself had cried over a dog she had never met earlier that evening. So, she was in no way cry-shaming Lolly, but Anna did find herself surprised by the sheer number of tears she produced. Anna wondered how her friend could have any tears left. The waterworks strengthened Anna's resolution that something could be done about this terrible predicament. Though what the perfect solution was to be, Anna still had no idea.

Lolly now rolled onto her stomach. "I mean, he pretty much ruined Hermès for me. Like forevs. How can I ever see their 'H' again without remembering what happened to me there?"

Anna had always been told she had a gift when it came to animals, having soothed many a stubborn horse in her day. She assumed the key was that she was a very patient person by nature, so her grand plan in dealing with Lolly was to keep the night going for as long as it took. Eventually Lolly would grow tired and decide what she was going to do one way or another.

Going along with this supposition, Anna tried some of the techniques that had worked on horses. She was careful to keep her voice low and steady when she spoke. Next, she brushed out Lolly's long golden hair (remembering what one of her riding instructors had told her about brushing a horse: long strokes to keep them calm). After the brushing, the two girls looked up fun hairstyles, and, following a video from the Braid Queen of YouTube, Anna gave Lolly the Princess Leia double side bun look. The entire time Anna played with Lolly's hair she reassured her that although she was understandably upset now, she was through the worst of it and things could only get better. Anna didn't know if this was true, but right now she knew she had to believe it if they were to make it through this night together.

Clearly, a lot of what was driving Lolly's misery was fear. Fear of having to make a definitive decision about her romantic life. Fear of making the wrong decision about it. Fear of loss if she broke up with Steven. Fear of hating herself if she didn't break up with him. Fear of having no boyfriend and being single again in the wilds of Manhattan. Fear of looking for a new bf and not finding anyone better. And the big one, fear of dying unloved and all alone.

"What about the fear of loving the wrong guy?" Anna asked.

"You mean the wrong guy 'cause your brother sucks a bag of dicks?" Lolly asked in all seriousness.

"No," Anna said. "I mean what if you spend your whole life loving the wrong guy?"

"Elaborate, please," Lolly said, reaching for the pie box again.

"I mean, I know I love Alexander, but what if he's the wrong guy? Like what if there was some other guy who I'm supposed to love that was . . . better? For me." As soon as she said the words out loud, she regretted it. She needed to stop thinking about that moment when Alexia Vronsky turned to face her on the train. It was impossible that he could be as gorgeous as she remembered him.

"Impossible!" Lolly cried, echoing Anna's secret thoughts. "Alexander is the best guy on the planet. He would never in a million billion years do to you what Steven did to me. Oh god, are you and Alexander having problems, too? Because if that's the case, then I should give up now." Lolly let out a melodramatic sigh. "I mean, if the world's most perfect couple can't make it work, then what hope is there for the rest of us?"

Anna sat up suddenly. "No, no, Alexander and I are fine. He's perfect. We're happy. Sorry, I didn't mean to freak you out. I don't even know what made me ask that. I'm just tired, I guess. And since we were listing fears, I thought I'd throw one of my own in the ring." Anna rarely opened up to her friends about her relationship with Alexander, and when she did broach the subject, everyone always had the same reaction as Lolly: that her boyfriend was perfect and she was lucky to have him. When other girls complained about their boyfriends, Anna found she rarely shared their problems. The only complaint she had about her relationship was that sometimes she found it a little dull, but she assumed this was because they had been together for so long already.

Anna stood and walked around the room to regain her focus. She needed to come up with a new approach. Now was definitely not the time to begin questioning her own heart.

X

Kimmie was having a much better time at Serendipity 3 with Dustin than she thought she would. Their initial meeting at Steven's New Year's Eve party had left her with a completely different impression of him. They had only spoken for a few minutes on Steven's rooftop, and she barely remembered what they had talked about. Normally she had a flawless memory for conversations, but her poor recollection could be blamed on the Veuve Clicquot that had her more than a little tipsy.

On the elevator up to the party, Lolly had specifically told Kimmie, "Make sure you eat something before you start throwing back champagne." Kimmie hadn't experimented with alcohol like most kids her age due to the fact she was always in training, so she basically had no tolerance. She had had every intention of heeding her sister's advice so she "wouldn't end up the puke-and-rally girl or passed out in a pile of coats" as Lolly had warned, but that entire evening had gone in a direction she never could have imagined.

It wasn't fair to blame her sister for what happened, but Kimmie did feel Lolly could have at least walked her around the party, maybe introduced her a bit before abandoning her to go find Steven as soon as they walked in the door. The party was already in full swing because they had arrived much later than planned. (Kimmie had watched her sister taking selfies in different dresses to see which one looked the best in different lighting for what seemed like hours.) Kimmie tried to push her way into the living room but instead found herself jammed into the corner right next to a hideous ice sculpture fountain, when a cute guy sporting a man-bun offered her a glass of champagne, which she accepted immediately, eager to make a friend.

Why oh why did she have to ask him who the pair depicted in ice was? Though Man-Bun didn't have to be such an asshole and laugh in her face. She can still close her eyes and see the guy's sneer and hear his stupid voice, "How the fuck do you not know who Rick and Morty are?"

She couldn't believe a stranger would be so awful to her. She should have thrown her glass of champagne in his face, but instead drank the entire thing down and escaped to the roof.

Hoping that eating marshmallows from the hot chocolate bar would counteract the effects of the champagne, Kimmie stuffed her cheeks like a chipmunk with a sweet tooth. This was when she noticed Dustin standing by himself looking up at the night sky. She liked his face immediately, and that he didn't have a man-bun. He looked so serious and out of place in this anything-goes crowd, which also made her feel better, because he looked exactly how she felt, herself: overwhelmed and wanting to be anywhere else.

Suddenly, Kimmie remembered what she and Dustin had talked about on the roof: space exploration involving a meteor, or was it an asteroid? Dustin had a vast knowledge of astronomy, which he babbled on about for a while, but she liked that he talked too much when he was nervous. She assumed that was why he was babbling, and that she was the cause of his nervousness, which she also enjoyed.

She was the opposite of Dustin. When she felt nervous, she clammed up. She hated this aspect of herself, mainly because when she was quiet, people accused her of being stuck up. She had heard a few of the other skaters talk about her that way. "Kimmie's such a snob. She thinks she's better than everyone else because she's a rich bitch from New York City." She should have had tougher skin by now, but she really didn't.

When she went downstairs to look for her sister, Kimmie'd had every intention of finding Dustin again later to continue their conversation. But on her way downstairs she ran into Steven heading up and he turned and followed her back down into the crowded hallway. It was so loud when he asked if she wanted Molly, she honestly thought he said, "Do you want to meet Molly?" Thinking he was referring to a person instead of a drug, she said, "Sure, I'd love to." Steven pulled out a little bag of crystals and told her to open wide. Kimmie had never tried drugs before, as all competitive athletes were regularly drug tested. But that chapter of her life was over, so nothing was stopping her from experimenting now.

Also, she didn't want to look like a baby in front of Steven, especially since her sister told her she had him to thank for letting her attend at all. Lolly was the one who didn't want her there because she didn't want to be responsible for her, but Steven had argued back, "Kimmie's had a shit year. She deserves a little fun." Lolly gave in, more because she always let Steven have his way, as opposed to being a cool older sister. Honestly, she was terrified and didn't want to do it, but was too much of a wimp to tell Steven she'd misunderstood him. So she did as she was told, tilting her head back and opening wide.

Most of her first drug experience took place when she was alone, sitting in Steven's mom's massive soaking tub. (The master bedroom was the only room off-limits for the party, but Kimmie had ignored the sign and gone in anyway, assuming she had special dispensation as sister to the gf of the host.) For the next two hours, she was blissed out on MDMA happily playing with the most exquisite and wonderfully scented bath bombs she had ever seen. Steven's mom kept a tall glass jar of them by the tub. They were so sparkly Kimmie was convinced that Steven's family was so rich they bought bath products with real crushed-up jewels in them. Her father was a named partner in a big corporate law firm so they were rich, too, but Lolly told her they weren't rich in the way Steven's family was rich. Steven's family had "fuck-you money," like Beyoncé and Jay-Z money, which was a different league entirely.

When Lolly found her two hours later, Kimmie was happy as a clam sitting in the empty tub, her dress covered in shimmery colorful bath bomb dust. Lolly took in her little sister's dilated pupils and knew immediately what had happened. Soon both Steven and Lolly, who were rolling themselves, stared down at her like she was a tiny guppy in a large fishbowl. Kimmie closed her eyes and listened to Steven tell her sister that he had given Kimmie a kiddie-menu portion and reminding her it was a party and that she needed to lighten the fuck up. Lolly got pouty at Steven for swearing at her but she didn't stay mad, because she never could. It was like Steven had some sort of magical spell over her sister, one snap of his fingers and she fell in line when he commanded.

The room was quiet and Kimmie wondered whether they had left her, so she opened her eyes to find her sister and Steven making out pressed up against the bathroom wall. Steven was rubbing his hands all over her sister's body and her sister was making these gross moaning noises. Steven eventually picked up Lolly, tossed her over his shoulder, and carried her giggling out of the bathroom. On his way out Steven told Kimmie that she'd soon feel "right as rain."

Thirty minutes later Kimmie felt well enough to go ring in the New Year and rejoin the party. As she was pushing through the crowd trying to get to the kitchen for some Fiji water (she had a serious case of dry mouth going), someone standing behind her reached around and handed Kimmie a glass of champagne. For a split second she thought it must be Dustin and was happy, but when she turned around she found herself staring not at Dustin, but at the most beautiful teenage boy she had ever seen. Blond hair and blue eyes had never been her type, but this guy was too gorgeous for her to care about types anymore. She remembered thinking he was like a beautiful piece of sea glass in a pile of boring old seashells.

"Do you have someone to kiss at midnight?" He spoke up, trying to be heard over the pulsing dance beat of Migos' "Bad and Boujee" remix.

"No!" she yelled back, surprised at her boldness.

"Shall we then? It's bad luck to ring in a New Year without a kiss from a beautiful girl."

The next thing she knew, everyone around her began counting down from ten. Kimmie was soon screaming along with the other three hundred partygoers, and when they reached number one, she closed her eyes and lifted her chin to this handsome, nameless, shimmering sea glass of a boy. He kissed her, giving her the most magical kiss of her life. (There had only been three others, but still!) Fireworks were going off in her head just like in the movies, though she realized later what she had heard was the TV. It was the first time Kimmie felt truly happy since her "accident," the accident that she was trying so hard to bury and walk away from. That was the advice her dad gave after her surgery: "You're young, kiddo, sometimes dreams don't work out. Find a new one and move on. A pretty girl like you has plenty of options." So that's what she had been trying to do lately, to be more like her sister, Lolly, and find happiness in friends, clothes, Instagram, or even a boyfriend. Though it was nauseating to listen to Lolly gush over Steven, Kimmie sometimes found herself envious of her sister's relationship. Maybe a boy could give her that same feeling she had had out on the ice, a this-is-exactly-where-I'm-supposed-to-be-in-this-big-wide-world kind of feeling. And now here was this boy who thought she was beautiful and picked her to kiss when he could have had any girl at the party, so she decided to give in and enjoy it.

After midnight the boy thanked her for the kiss, asked for her iPhone and said he'd put his number in it, instructing her to text him so he could take her for high tea. After he handed her phone back, he winked and wished her a Happy New Year. He then turned and disappeared into the drunken writhing crowd now dancing to the Bieber version of "Despacito."

She didn't want to look at his name until she was alone, so she pushed her way through the drunken crowd again, heading to her secret bathroom. Passing the library, she glimpsed Dustin sitting on a couch between two girls. She wasn't sure if he saw her, and knew it was rude not to wish the one friend she met at the party a Happy New Year, but at that moment she didn't care. She was on a mission to learn the name of the beautiful blond boy who had slipped his tongue into her mouth at midnight.

"V is for Vronsky" was what he wrote for his first name in her contacts, and he put "Count" under the heading of title. Ten minutes later, Steven and Lolly had found Kimmie twirling around in the spacious bathroom with her arms outstretched singing "V is for Vronsky, V is for Vronsky, V is for Vronsky!" Over and over she twirled, oblivious to Steven and her sister standing there in the doorway, watching her. The last thing she remembered from the night was hearing her older sister yell at her boyfriend. "OMFG, Steven! Kimmie's still all fucked up! Kimmie! Snap out of it!"

"Kimmie?" Dustin said, his voice snapping her back to reality.

"Yes?" she answered, feeling guilty for thinking about another guy when she was with a perfectly nice one now.

"I'm going to the restroom," he said.

Kimmie smiled and nodded, but as soon as Dustin left the table she pulled her phone out to check for texts. She had one new one, which filled her with hope, but she frowned when she saw it was from her friend Victoria. Kimmie ignored her friend's text and instead composed one of her own, hitting "V is for Vronsky," which was saved in her favorites. She typed: Missed you at the rink tonight. Hope you had a good day. *pair of ice skates emoji* *snowman emoji* She hesitated for a moment, debating whether the ice skates emoji would be seen as redundant or as cute like she intended. She deleted the pair of ice skates, left the snowman, and hit send.

Bubbles appeared immediately and her pulse quickened in anticipation, but they soon disappeared and left her feeling annoyed and stupid. She wished she hadn't sent any emoji at all now. She put her phone back in her mini Prada backpack and looked up to see that Dustin hadn't even made it to the restroom yet. He was talking to four teenage boys she didn't recognize and the whole table erupted in laughter from something Dustin said.

So weird, Kimmie thought to herself. *Who knew nerds could be so funny?*

XI

Dustin didn't even have to go to the bathroom, but he needed a break from Kimmie's dazzling beauty. He had to admit the evening was going far better than he'd imagined possible, and he hoped to finish strong, which was exactly why he was in the men's room doing some of the breathing exercises his therapist recommended he try whenever he felt anxious enough to bring on one of his panic attacks.

The secondary reason he had to come to the bathroom was he had to answer his mom's texts before she had a panic attack of her own, did a "find my phone" search, and called his father to track him down and bring him home. Dustin not calling to let his mom know he wasn't coming home for dinner was completely out of character for him. Then again, being out with a gorgeous blonde on a Thursday night wasn't just out of character for him, more like he'd been taken over by a much cooler alien life-form that was living its best life in his body. He needed to call his mother, but first he needed to calm down. When he was around Kimmie he could barely breathe, let alone think straight, which reminded him that he had his inhaler in his pocket. He hadn't needed it in months, but he still carried it around for peace of mind. He took it out and was about to take a hit, when he stopped and looked at himself in the mirror. "Don't be a herb. You can do this," he said, realizing that the only characters in movies who gave themselves pep talks in the mirror were losers. Except for maybe John Travolta in *Pulp Fiction* right before Uma Thurman OD'd on heroin and had to get a shot of adrenaline straight to her heart. Which reminded him, he should probably get back to Kimmie. He texted his mom a quick apology and explained where he was and who he was with, deciding it was better for her to spin about a girl than worry he was on drugs.

He had been surprised Kimmie was allowed out so late on a school night. When he asked her about it, she said she and her sister were at their father's town house for the week, and her father was working late on a huge case. Kimmie then mentioned in the next breath that whenever her dad worked late, her "Stepmonster" would use this as an excuse to go out on the town with her friends and drink too much. Her real mother was much stricter about school nights, but she was in Saint Lucia with her new celebrity chef boyfriend who was opening a restaurant at some fancy resort, which meant no one was keeping track of her or Lolly's whereabouts.

When Dustin heard this, he told Kimmie they could go grab dinner first if she preferred, but she said, "Frozen hot chocolate is a perfectly nutritious dinner in my book." He was happy she had a sweet tooth, because he had a big one himself.

While they waited for their order he had asked her whether she was heartbroken over her career-ending injury, hoping it wasn't too soon for so personal of a question. She'd seemed fine to talk about it, quickly saying her dad told her it was pointless to wonder what would have happened if she hadn't busted her knee up, because she did. And her mom still got angry and looked for blame even though it was no one's fault.

Kimmie said Dustin was sweet to ask, though, and then commented that since she had been home not one of her so-called friends here had bothered to ask her that question. She was disappointed but wouldn't go so far as to say she was heartbroken over the whole thing.

Now Kimmie turned the tables and asked Dustin whether he had ever had his heart broken. "Not really," he said. His longest relationship to date lasted exactly one session at Harvard Summer School last year. He told Kimmie the truth and said he'd had his version of a "camp romance" with a girl named Susie S. from Philly but it never got serious. "We both were into classic films, but let's just say it takes more than understanding *Last Year at Marienbad* to make my heart sing." Kimmie didn't respond for a long time, and he was getting worried. "Talking about another girl is rude," he added, hoping this would prompt her to say something. "And coupling it with a pretentious French cinema reference probably made it unbearable. I'm sorry."

"Don't apologize. I totally get it. And, besides, I asked," she said in a half-hearted way that made him question whether she was being honest. What Dustin didn't know was that Kimmie was only quiet because she was silently praying he wouldn't ask her if she had ever been with someone who made her heart sing. She was no idiot. She knew Dustin liked her, and she liked him, too. She just didn't like him enough, or maybe she just liked that he liked her. She had felt her heart sing only once in her life and it was on the same night she had met Dustin, but it wasn't him—it was Count Vronsky who had played her heartstrings.

It was this whole awkward exchange that drove Dustin to excuse himself to the bathroom in the first place. On his way there, he stopped to talk to a few guys he knew from school. Since it was a table of four teenage boys, they had noticed who Dustin was with and demanded details. Nerds like them didn't have hot chocolate with gorgeous girls on the Hot List, unless she was a blood relative or needed to copy homework. Dustin knew he could have told these guys any story he wanted, but that was not his way. He told them the truth, which was that he had no fucking clue what was going on. His brutal honesty was lauded with laughter all around.

As Dustin approached the table after the bathroom, he saw that

Kimmie had a smile on her face and looked lost in thought. *God, she's so beautiful*, he thought. *I wonder if she's thinking about me?* "What are you thinking about?" he asked, taking his seat across from her.

"Nothing much," Kimmie lied, looking down at her hands. "I guess I was wondering what was happening across the park with Lolly and Steven." Upon hearing herself, she realized there was truth to her statement as well. Lolly was her sister, so of course she was wondering if she was okay.

"Do you think they'll work it out?" Dustin asked. The whole situation was causing him much consternation. Whether he liked it or not, he was personally invested, especially now that he was benefitting from it. Even though he believed that Lolly should break up with Steven for what he did to her, it was obvious how much Lolly adored Steven. And there was a small part of him that hoped they would make it because he'd be lying if he hadn't thought about the four of them hanging out together. Perhaps Anna could help smooth things over.

"I don't know," Kimmie said. "But if I were her, I'd dump his ass."

"Just so you know, even though I'm friends with Steven, I think he's one hundred percent in the wrong," Dustin said. "And if you could, please tell Lolly I'm sorry she's had to deal with all of this."

Kimmie studied Dustin's serious face and could tell he meant everything he'd just said. His honesty shone through, which was why she felt so safe and secure in his presence.

After the check arrived, Dustin convinced Kimmie to let him pay by reminding her that one of the cornerstone tenets of feminism was a woman's right to choose, and if she chose to let him pay for her dessert, then she was still a feminist in good standing. She laughed, agreeing to his logic, which pleased him because it made their outing if not a real date, then at least date-like, which gave him the confidence to ask if he could walk her home, to which she said yes.

"I believe you say what you mean, Dustin. And I like it," she told him as they strolled across Park Avenue.

"I say what I mean, I do what I say."

"What's that from?" Kimmie asked.

"It's a quote from one of my favorite movies. *Heat* with Al Pacino."

"Al Pacino wasn't in *Heat*. That was Sandra Bullock and Melissa McCarthy."

"They were in *The Heat*. I'm talking about the movie from the nineties with Pacino and De Niro. Written and directed by Michael Mann. One of my dad's ex-girlfriends who lived with us when I was younger loved it and was always telling me about it. Eventually my dad let me watch it with her. It was only my second R-rated movie. It's a cat-and-mouse bank heist movie with one of the most famous shoot-'em-up scenes of all time."

They were now only a block and a half from her father's brownstone off Madison Avenue, standing at the corner, waiting for the walk signal to change. Their time together was almost done.

"That's a weird movie for a woman to like," Kimmie said, unaware she was being sexist.

"I thought so, too, but she was much cooler than my dad. And even though it was this high-octane action movie it was also a love story. All the men in it loved the women in their lives, which she found romantic." Speaking of romantic, the two of them were now standing in front of her house in the middle of a snowstorm. If Dustin had the ability to freeze time right then he would've rushed to the nearest electronic store, bought a drone with a 4K camera and night vision, and recorded this moment in time. If he could get a fish-eye lens on the camera, he was sure he could create a snow globe effect, with the twirl and dazzle of snowflakes in the night air and this beautiful girl he was with, cinematic proof that this night actually happened.

"Did you find it romantic when you saw it?" Kimmie asked.

"Not when I was twelve. But I watched it again last year and I understood what she meant. Though to me, *Heat* is more a movie about honor. Honoring your friends, honoring your job even if you're a thief, honoring your commitment to justice if you're a cop. Most of all it's about honoring the code you choose to live by, whatever that code may be. But even though the men in the movie loved their women, they couldn't do right by them. Sometimes people can't help but make poor choices and hurt the ones they love, I guess." Dustin suddenly felt foolish going on and on about a movie she had never seen. "Sorry, I'm a hopeless film nerd."

Kimmie grabbed his arm and looked him squarely in the eyes. "Stop. You don't sound like a nerd at all. You sound passionate, which is a wonderful thing. If anything, you're making me want to watch the movie right this second, but more for the romance aspect. Call me a cynic, but with all the shit going on with Lolly and Steven I'm not feeling so big on the honor of men . . ." She paused, knowing that Dustin may be perhaps the first man of honor she'd met in New York so far. Last year, she would have put Gabe, her ice dancing partner, into this category, but he'd proved to be a disappointment as of late, barely calling her anymore now that he had just paired up with some Swedish skater named Maja.

"Don't. I mean, you can, of course. I'm not trying to tell you what you can and can't do," Dustin fumbled. "But maybe we could watch it sometime . . . together? The two of us or with others." *God, I'm a babbling fool around her.*

"Perhaps. But not tonight. It's late and I should go." Kimmie smiled and ran up the steps to her front door. Once at the top of her stoop, she turned around to face him. "Thank you for the frozen hot chocolate and the walk home," she said, followed by a little curtsy.

Dustin answered her curtsy with a deep bow. "The honor, my fair Kimmie, was all mine."

Kimmie entered the front door and hurried to the living room window to watch Dustin walk off into the snowy dark night. Did she detect a little spring in his step? Yes, she most certainly did.

XII

Anna and Lolly had grown tired of talking and took a mental break to watch Beyoncé's *Lemonade* videos. This was Lolly's idea, her rationale being that Queen Bey had been cheated on by her man, and this album was how she worked her way through the experience. Anna wasn't sure if this was a good idea or not, but she was getting desperate to reach some sort of resolution and was willing to try anything. They watched the whole thing in total silence, and afterward Anna turned off the TV and faced her friend. "Okay, it's your turn to face the music. Lolly, are you ready? Do. You. Love. Steven?"

The first time Anna asked Lolly this same question hours ago, Lolly's reply was that she didn't love him and in fact wanted him dead. Then it was, "Maybe I love him, but I know I shouldn't because he's a lying cheat monster." Then it was, "Okay, I love him, but I still want him dead. I'm fine with wearing black for a year." Then it was, "I love him, but I hate him, too." Then it was, "I love him, I guess, but clearly he doesn't love me." (Anna never let this statement go as she reassured Lolly a hundred times that she knew Steven absolutely loved her, and that his cheating on her didn't mean he didn't love her, it just meant he was a pathetic, idiotic teenage boy.)

Finally, they were at, "I love him, but how can I possibly stay with him after he humiliated me like this?" which seemed like progress to Anna. Though in response Anna said that she herself wasn't a girl who cared what people thought, since it was none of their damn business. Lolly agreed with Anna, but she knew Steven didn't. The example she used to prove her point was admitting to Anna that their whole screw-a-versary was a sham.

"I'm still a virgin," Lolly said in small voice. "I just let Steven tell people we're having sex."

Anna's curiosity was piqued. "What the hell are you talking about?"

Lolly sniffled and said she knew it was confusing, but the only reason she agreed to call it that was because of Steven's dumb male pride. A year ago, when it was time to celebrate the six-month anniversary of the day they first decided to be boyfriend and girlfriend and changed their status across all social media, Lolly found out that Steven didn't want to celebrate it. This caused their first big fight. Steven said anniversaries were for married people and he refused to do something so girly.

Normally she gamely went along with whatever Steven wanted, but this time she refused. She told him it was important to her to celebrate, and he should do it to make her happy. But Steven kept saying no and eventually after going around and around and not getting anywhere, she wondered if there was something else that was going on. Maybe he was upset over something completely unrelated but it was getting all mixed up in his head.

Anna, impressed by Lolly's astute thinking on the matter, gestured for her to continue.

"Well, turns out I was right. There was something else going on, which was that Steven finally admitted he was fine with me wanting to wait to have sex until I was ready, but he was embarrassed to let his friends find out we hadn't done it yet."

"Why would his friends find out?" Anna asked.

"That's what I said!" Lolly exclaimed. "So then he said if his friends found out he bought me jewelry for our anniversary when he wasn't even getting laid he'd get tons of shit for it."

"That's the stupidest thing I have ever heard," Anna said, and she meant it.

"That's what I said! But then he said, 'Now if we were celebrating our six-month screw-a-versary, that's something I could get behind.' He was joking, of course, you know in that way your brother jokes about everything. So without thinking, I asked him if I agreed to let him tell his friends we had sex on the night he asked me to be his girlfriend then could we celebrate it? And he said yes, and the rest is history."

Anna was a little shocked over how utterly ridiculous the whole story was. "And it worked? I mean, was everything fine after that?"

"Yep. Steven had his friends thinking he was a stud. And I got taken to Per Se for our six-month screw-a-versary and the diamond studs from Tiffany's that you picked out."

Anna smiled at this because she had forgotten about going with Steven to pick out the earrings Lolly was pointing to in her ears. "Wow, and you really don't care that people don't think you're a virgin?"

"Please, these days I'd be made fun of for wanting to wait. I mean, I know the truth, and who am I keeping my virginity for but me? I consider it one of the most mature relationship moments of my life. I found a compromise that Steven and I are happy with." Lolly told Anna her mother always said the number-one reason she divorced Lolly's father was because he wouldn't compromise. So Lolly had it ingrained in her that she should steer clear of any man who couldn't, because if that was the case, then the expectation would be that the woman always had to make all the sacrifices.

"What really makes me insane about finding out about his cheating ass today, of all days, was that my present to him, besides the stupid watch band, was I was going to give it up. For real."

This time when Lolly started crying again, Anna totally understood.

"Oh god, Anna, I'm such a disaster."

Anna shook her head and put her arm around Lolly's shoulders. "You're not a disaster. You just fell in love with one."

Lolly nodded sadly. "It's true. I love him. I love him so much."

Anna nodded and told Lolly that was why she was in so much pain. So now the only question to answer was: did Lolly love Steven enough to forgive him? Because if she did love him enough, then it was time to talk to him to see if they could work past this.

"Was it my fault? For withholding sex? Is this why he cheated on me?"

"No!" Anna spoke sharply this time. It was the only time she'd raised her voice the whole evening. "Never put the blame on yourself, Lolls. You loved him and wanted to wait and that's your choice. In fact, I admire you for it. Sometimes I think I should have waited longer myself. Alexander didn't pressure me, but when I knew he was going away to college I felt like I needed to do it. Before he left, you know?"

"I get that. I probably would have done the same thing. But it's all good, right? You've been together for so long and you love each other, so after a while it makes sense to just go for it, right? Is it as awesome as they say? My friend Miley says it's better than a shoe sale at Bergdorf's."

Anna gave a short laugh and started turning off all the lamps in the bedroom. She wouldn't have minded confiding in Lolly, but Anna never really talked to her friends about her sex life. Alexander thought that sex was something to be kept private, and she tried to respect that, even if she didn't totally agree with him.

"Right now the only thing you need to think about is whether or not you can forgive him. Because if you can, then you two can work it out, and who knows, maybe your relationship will be better for it. Sleep on it. Right here and now. I just got the alert that we have a snow day tomorrow, so you and Steven have all day to talk . . . if you decide that's what you want."

Lolly nodded and admitted she was sleepy; she was exhausted from all the drama and could no longer think clearly.

"Plus, Steven deserves to twist in the wind for a little while longer," Anna said with a smile.

"Hells yeah he does," Lolly said, already slipping into the high thread count Frette Lux sheets on Anna's parents' California king.

Anna stayed with Lolly until she fell asleep. She didn't have to wait long.

XIII

Leaving Lolly asleep in her parents' bedroom, Anna walked barefoot down the dark hallway to the kitchen where she put the rest of the pie in the fridge. She heard voices coming from the living room, which she assumed was the TV, but then after listening more closely she realized Steven was talking to some guy. Anna rolled her eyes, annoyed that while she had spent the last several hours mopping up her brother's mess, he had been hanging out and probably having a grand old time as usual.

Her phone vibrated and she looked down to see yet another text from Alexander, who had been trying to reach her for hours. *If it's not one boy, it's another.* She grimaced to herself. She walked back to her bedroom knowing she needed to call her boyfriend back before she was embroiled in her own boy trouble.

Alexander answered on the first ring, and it was obvious from his tone he was upset that it had taken so long for her to get back to him. Alexander didn't get the nickname the Greenwich OG by being the most patient person. But he quickly softened when she recounted her evening to him, murmuring how she was too good to her feckless and reckless older brother.

"He doesn't deserve a sister like you," he said, and it wasn't the first time he had spoken out against her brother. Alexander was not a fan of Steven's, but he knew better than to bash him too harshly, as Anna was quick to defend her brother despite his many shortcomings.

"You're missing the point entirely, Alexander. It's not me Steven doesn't deserve. It's Lolly. Can you believe they haven't even had sex yet? I thought for sure they had, but now that I know they haven't I feel that Steven's actions were not excusable exactly, but a little more understandable? God, I hate myself for saying that out loud, but maybe it's true? Didn't you once tell me that if men don't, you know . . . on a regular basis then . . ."

"Yes, but it doesn't give them permission to cheat. They made a commitment to each other and part of that agreement is to be only with each other. Steven could have jacked off in the shower like every other guy I know."

It was rare that Alexander ever talked about sex with her so candidly, and Anna couldn't help but be a little intrigued. "Is that what you do? You know, when I'm not around?"

"Anna, stop. I'm not discussing that with you. That girl would be an idiot not to dump him. How can she ever trust him again?"

"I don't think she will, dump him, I mean," Anna responded. "Lolly loves him. Like, not just in the regular way, but she like loves him—loves him. If she didn't there's no way she'd be this upset. She was an absolute wreck. I'm almost positive she's going to forgive him in the morning."

Alexander, now bored of this subject, asked Anna if she knew that her school was canceled for the next day. She had known, but for some reason pretended she didn't. "Really? Oh good, because I've been dreading taking the 7:02 A.M. back to Greenwich to make it to Latin by nine. Do you have a snow day, too?"

Alexander chuckled at this. "No, my sweet, college doesn't get snow days." Anna felt foolish for a moment, but this passed because how should she know how college operated in a snowstorm? Without pausing for her response, Alexander launched into a very boring story about his Globalization and Private Governance class, so she let her mind wander back to earlier in the evening when she first met Count Vronsky.

She had heard of him before but was positive they had never met until today. She knew plenty about his mother, though, a famous socialite known for her beauty, impeccable style, and many marriages. Mrs. Geneviève R. was her married name now because she had recently wedded her fourth husband, the CEO of the third largest pharmaceutical company in the world. Normally when a woman had multiple divorces she was looked down on by society, but Geneviève was in the rare position of still being held in high regard. (This was most likely due to the fact that each time she married, it was to someone richer and more powerful than her previous husband.) Her picture frequently appeared in *Vogue* or in the Style section of *The New York Times*, and Anna had recognized her immediately when she boarded the train.

As far as Anna knew, Mrs. R. had only two sons, both from her first marriage to Mr. Vronsky. Like Anna, Mrs. R. also had show dogs, but hers were Russian wolfhounds. She fell in love with the breed after meeting Vronsky's Russian father. The two women bonded on the train over their love of giant-breed dogs with tragically short life spans. Anna's first Newfoundland only lived to the age of nine.

She put Alexander on speaker while he droned on about losing his morning tennis match due to his elbow, and she told him he needed to see an orthopedist to get it checked out, all the while texting Magda, the Greenwich housekeeper, of her plans to stay in the city and asking to have her dogs driven down sometime tomorrow. Anna treated her two giant beasts like they were lapdogs and rarely traveled anywhere without them. This luxury was only available to her because her family had drivers and a private plane. And because her father doted on his only daughter. Anna's love of all animals was something they had always shared.

It was her father who had given her her first Newfoundland puppy when she was only five years old. She had seen one in a painting at a museum in London and couldn't believe it when her father said the giant creature she was pointing to was a dog. "He looks like the biggest stuffed animal in the store!" she cried with glee, which was a private joke between her and her father. He had told her whenever they went into a toy store she always managed to pick out the biggest and most expensive stuffed animal she could find saying, "I want that one." And because her father indulged her every want, her bedroom in Greenwich now contained a dozen or more massive stuffed animals lined up along a side wall to guard her when she slept.

The Newfie pup was a very special belated birthday present that was given to her when her father missed her fifth birthday party because he was traveling in Asia on business. On his way back home, he had pit-stopped in Vermont at a Newfoundland breeder and picked out a ten-week-old puppy with a champion bloodline named Doozy. The giant black dog became her constant companion, even accompanying her to the stables, content to sleep in the hay during Anna's daily riding lessons after school.

Doozy died two years ago, which was Anna's first experience with heartbreak. And even though she now had two other Newfies, she still wasn't over the pain of losing her first dog, which was probably why she had such a strong reaction to the dog's death earlier this evening.

"Anna? Anna, are you still there?" Her boyfriend's impatient voice snapped her back to reality.

"Yes, I'm here," she dutifully replied. "Are you on Adderall? You know it makes you cranky when you take too much."

Alexander ignored her question, which meant that it was true. But she was too tired to get into a discussion about whether he over-relied on it for his studies. His defense was always that he had a prescription for it and never bought it illegally like every other college student. "It's late, and you must be exhausted. You should get some sleep." He then asked, "Do you plan on staying in the city because of the snow?"

"Well, since there's no school tomorrow, I may just stay in the city for the long weekend," she answered, ready to get off the phone. The couple said their perfunctory I-love-yous and good-nights, and soon Anna was all alone in the quiet of her room. The room that was hers and yet didn't feel like it, since she was there so infrequently. Her parents were surprised when she told them at age fourteen that she had come to the decision that she wanted to go to high school in Greenwich instead of attending her choice of private schools in Manhattan. Her mother refused, mostly because it seemed like a monumental headache when it came to scheduling. But Anna's father heard his daughter out and was touched by her emotional plea to be closer to her horses and dogs and in the end said they'd find a way to work it out. When Anna had left the room, she stood and listened by the door for a bit, but her mother's first words were, "You know this is your fault, Edward. If you didn't acquiesce to her every wish, she'd understand that she's the child and we're the parents who decide what's best for her." But her father told her mother their daughter was capable of making her own choices and they had to respect that about her. They didn't want to raise a daughter who couldn't think for herself, did they?

Anna put on her Prada lipstick-print silk pajamas, threw on a pair of pink bunny slippers that Steven had given her for her birthday last year, and decided to go see what company her brother was keeping at this late hour.

She walked down the dark hallway and found Steven was standing in the foyer with his back to her. Suddenly none other than Vronsky himself strutted out of the kitchen with a bottle of Fiji. She took two steps backward, bumped into a wall, and knocked a painting crooked. Not only that, but she let out an embarrassing little yelp that made both boys turn their heads and stare at her. In her bunny slippers.

"Oh my god, Anna, are you okay?" Vronsky asked, taking a step toward her.

"Me? Yes! So great. I mean, I'm fine. Hello." She whipped around and busied herself by straightening the painting.

"Steven, thank you for your hospitality but I've stayed much longer than I meant to," Vronsky said, not taking his eyes off of her as Anna turned and stepped toward him. He cleared his throat and continued. "I just stopped by to thank you guys for making sure my mother got home safely tonight."

He had such a soft and wonderful voice to complement his beautiful eyes, which was pretty much the exact same thought he was having about her. Anna wanted to respond but found herself struck speechless by the intensity of his gaze. He continued, "I also wanted to let you know I found the man's other dog." He held up his hand, which had a large Snoopy Band-Aid on it as proof.

"Oh no, you're hurt. Did he bite you?" Anna padded toward him.

"No, no, I'm fine. It's just a scratch. My mother's dog walker insisted on the Band-Aid." Vronsky ripped it off, balled it up, and stuffed it in his overcoat pocket. "The dog's with her now. She fosters strays so it's a much better option than a shelter."

Anna was overcome by Vronsky's thoughtfulness, and it took all her resolve not to throw her arms around him and hug him. "Oh my god, you're my hero. That's so nice of you. I know it was silly for me to worry, but—"

"Not at all," he cut her off. "It just shows what a sweet girl, I mean, good person you are." The two of them locked eyes again, and now Anna felt light-headed. She forced herself to look away and put her hand on the wall to steady herself.

"I'm sorry, I've barely eaten today, except for that pie."

"Hey, is there any left?" Steven asked, looking up from his iPhone, oblivious to the situation unfolding before him.

"That's Lolly's pie and it's up to her if you can have a piece," Anna said, a smidgen more sharply than she should have. This whole unnerving situation was his fault after all.

The three of them stood in silence for another awkward beat. Anna needed Vronsky to leave immediately, but there was another part of her that desperately wished she could ask him to stay for pie, though she couldn't very well offer it up when she'd just told her brother he couldn't have any. Oh, what to do! "Thank you so much for stopping by . . . Alexia. Or should I call you Vronsky? Or is it the Count?" she asked playfully.

"You can call me Alexia. I like it when you say it," he said to her in a much more serious tone than he intended. It was as if he was no longer in control of his faculties when he was around her. And truth be told, he did like hearing his proper name when she said it. "I should really be going . . ." Vronsky finally made his way toward the front door.

"Aight, later dude! Maybe we'll check you at Jaylen's party on Saturday?" Steven opened the door and Vronsky slowly backed up until he was standing in the hallway waving good-bye. He couldn't take his eyes off Anna until the door closed in front of him and she was gone.

XIV

Vronsky felt restless when he walked out into the snowy night after leaving Steven and Anna's building. He waved off the doorman's offer to find him a cab and buttoned up his coat, wound his long scarf around his neck a few times, and started walking. The streets were practically empty because of the storm, but he barely noticed. His mind was singularly focused on one thing, and one thing only.

Anna K.

Never in Vronsky's life had he been so taken with a member of the opposite sex. And though he was only sixteen years old, he already had plenty of experience with girls.

Alexia's father had passed away three years ago, but even when he was alive they never had much of a relationship. Alexia's mother had primary custody of him and his older brother, Kiril, after they divorced. Entire years would go by without seeing his father, who moved to Thailand when Alexia was only seven. (Rumor had it his father had no choice but to leave the States because of legal trouble, but Alexia never cared enough to find out the real story.) It was Kiril who continually demanded they be allowed to see their father and eventually their mother gave in. She agreed to let the boys go to Thailand for three weeks over the summer with a well-paid nanny, who reported back to their controlling mother.

Vronsky had few memories of his early visits. He remembered discovering Bangkok arcades and spending nearly all his time and money there. But soon his brother introduced him to something that drove video games out of his mind. The first time he witnessed Kiril's sexual exploits, Vronsky had run terrified from the doorway. The second time he stood watching until his brother noticed him and yelled at him to leave. The third time he refused to leave until his brother got out of bed and forcibly removed him. And the last time he stayed and watched for a long time, his brother unaware of his presence. Alexia had been in

Kiril's closet, rifling through his brother's pockets looking for cash for tickets to the latest *Fast and Furious* movie. His own weekly allowance had been spent and his father was nowhere to be found. Alexia had hit the jackpot finding ten dollars in American money and was about to leave when he heard his brother's footsteps.

Panicking, Alexia crouched in the closet and pulled the door partially closed. Kiril entered the room with a girl close behind him. Alexia watched his brother pick up the girl as if she weighed practically nothing, place her on the bed, and immediately begin taking off her clothes. His brother then started stripping down, but the girl put her hand on his chest to stop him. She set a new pace by slowly unbuttoning his brother's Oxford shirt one button at a time.

Eventually, the girl spotted Alexia watching from the closet, but instead of telling his brother, she just smiled and put a finger to her lips to let him know his secret was safe with her. Alexia put his own finger to his lips to show her he understood. It was in that moment that he recognized the naked girl before him wasn't one of the young servants in the household but was one of his father's girlfriends. This incestuous infidelity blew the young boy's mind.

Alexia was of course mesmerized by everything he saw and spent the next hour watching his brother and this older woman engage in all sorts of sexual acts. It was this experience that caused Alexia to lose interest in playing video games, as he realized girls were far more interesting. He, too, wanted to feel what he saw in his brother's face that day: total ecstasy and rapture.

He lost his own virginity at thirteen, but not in Thailand. He was in New York and came home to find his brother back from college, throwing a party while their mother was at Canyon Ranch. Their mother always spent two months at a spa after she got divorced. Kiril told him their mother was like a snake and needed to shed her old married skin to reveal pretty, new scales that she'd use to trap her next husband. Kiril and their mother fought often, always posturing and trying to prove who was toughest. This type of aggression was never Alexia's way, mainly because their mother always babied him, which he much preferred over her yelling at him.

His brother wouldn't let him hang out with his friends, so Alexia went to go to bed. When he arrived in his bedroom he found a pile of coats covering the bed. In a rage, he started throwing all the coats of his brother's guests on the floor, but soon realized someone was asleep underneath the pile. She was a beautiful redhead with a smattering of freckles on her nose and cheeks, who more than likely was too tipsy to figure out which of the teddy bear coats belonged to her and gave up. Alexia grabbed a blanket and a pillow and fell asleep on the floor. Sometime before dawn, he woke up and the girl was on top of him kissing his neck and telling him he was the most beautiful thing she'd ever seen, as she slid off her thong and dropped it playfully on the carpet.

After that night his fate was sealed. He decided he was a guy who would never settle down. He loved the way beautiful girls made him feel, and he loved making them feel incredible, too. He loved the flirting, the dancing, the kissing, the cuddling, and was even happy to sleep over after sex, which he knew most other guys detested. To him, women were so much better than men. They smelled better, they dressed better, and they were so soft to the touch.

It was for this very reason that he was so desperately unhappy to be sent off to an all-boys boarding school in Maryland for high school (his father and brother had both graduated from the esteemed school). He missed the company of women. He missed fancy rich girls, the ones who shopped and gossiped. The ones who loved tea parties and Broadway shows. The ones who had little dogs they dressed up in sparkling crystal collars. The ones who spent hours and hours—and hundreds of dollars—in salons debating their hair and nail colors.

He barely made it to the Christmas holiday his first year at Georgetown Preparatory. When he arrived home for vacation and saw his mother, he wept in her arms and begged her not to send him back to that horrible, wretched place, and she didn't. Instead she allowed him to go abroad and become a ski bum for the rest of the year. It was because of this and his late birthday that he was now a repeat sophomore at Collegiate. He knew some people called him a mama's boy, but he didn't care. Being back in Manhattan and living with a full-time nanny was worth it.

This was why Vronsky was feeling so out of sorts when it came to Anna.

Yes, she was gorgeous and beautifully dressed, but there were hundreds of such girls in the city—he had a constant rotation of at least three such girls at any given moment. There was something special about Anna. Why else was he so taken with her after only meeting her once?

After he dropped the homeless man's dog at the dog walker's apartment, he'd headed over to Steven's house, hoping he could see Anna for just a moment more. It was Steven who answered the door and told him Anna was otherwise engaged with saving his ass from the wrath of his angry girlfriend. Having no other choice, Vronsky small-talked with Steven and waited. It figured that she finally appeared right as he was leaving, but Anna was worth the wait. By God, he would wait ten thousand hours to spend ten seconds with her.

Suddenly he remembered that Beatrice, his favorite cousin, was a classmate of Anna's in Greenwich. He stopped in his tracks, not caring that the wind was picking up and the icy snow was pelting him in the face, and texted Bea, who was a big party girl and often spent her nights in the city crashing at the SoHo apartment of her older stepbrother. Bubbles appeared, followed by a text telling him to come to her favorite hangout in the Village. She was with two hot models who were just his type. Giddy with anticipation, he wasted no time hailing a cab. His cousin would surely be able to give him what he ravenously desired: inside info on the winsome creature known as Anna K.

XV

Vronsky entered the Beatrice Inn to find his cousin sitting on the bar, her Jimmy Choo thigh-high boots dangling, and her head thrown back in abandon. Behind her an extremely tall hipster bartender poured their most expensive tequila into her mouth straight from the bottle. His cousin Bea had always been one of the most popular girls in Greenwich and by the end of freshman year she had secured her queen bee status and quickly set her sights on Manhattan.

Vronsky knew the key to her success wasn't that she came from one of Greenwich's oldest families, her surprisingly natural good looks, or her piles of family money—that was half the kids in Greenwich. What Beatrice had was information. No teenager can keep a secret and Bea was happy to be the one others confessed to. Beatrice never judged and how could she? For Bea had seen it all, heard more, and probably done worse herself. Her senior yearbook quote would surely read, "If you don't have something nice to say about someone . . . then come find me at lunch."

As promised, she was currently hanging out with two teen models, Daler and Rowney. They weren't old enough to drive but were both six feet tall and weighed a combined 202 pounds. Both girls walked runways in fashion shows all over the globe and were in the city for Fashion Week. If Vronsky had had the pleasure of their introduction two days ago things would have gone differently. But tonight he barely gave either one a second glance.

"Bea, I need to talk to you." Vronsky dutifully drank the shot of rye the bartender handed him. "Outside," he said in a low voice, "alone."

Beatrice peered out at her cousin through her mink eyelash extensions and nodded. Even though Bea was clearly wasted, she perked up like a shark at the promise of a bloody good story.

Minutes later the two of them were outside, their backs pressed to the wall, blowing cigarette smoke into the swirling snow. Bea listened to Vronsky's tale of first seeing Anna at Grand Central, Steven's infidelity, which had brought his sister into the city, and finally Vronsky's current state of mind.

Beatrice flicked her butt into the street, pulled out her vape pen, and took a long drag. She turned to face her handsome young cousin, reaching out to brush some snow from his blond locks in an almost motherly way. "Weird, not at all what I was expecting," she said with a wicked grin. "I can't believe you never met Anna K. before tonight."

"That's all you have to say?" he said with impatience. "What do I need to know?"

"That all depends. Do you just want to fuck her? Or is this a more serious malady?" Beatrice was nothing if not direct.

Normally he would have laughed at his cousin's crudeness, but he found himself unable to smile. "I'm afraid the malady could be serious."

She pulled the lapels of her fur jacket up and shivered. "Let's go back in, get drunk, and figure it out."

Vronsky exhaled and watched his breath waft up into the snowy night.

Inside, Beatrice dismissed her two model sidekicks for the night. They went all sulky, pointy elbows and pouty lips, until Bea handed over a baggie of party favors. While the waitstaff cleaned up around them, Bea and Vronsky sat down in a leather booth and talked.

Bea told her cousin that she and Anna were friendly from years of attending the same school and social functions, but they weren't close. "Such a waste," his cousin mumbled. "She's probably the most beautiful girl in Greenwich, but she never capitalized on what she could do with it." She paused here and stared at Vronsky.

"Present company excluded," he added, paying the flattery toll so Bea would continue.

Beatrice laughed brightly at his compliment. Vronsky was such a tasty-looking morsel, and more than once in a drunken horny stupor, she had thought about reaching over to check out his goods, but kept herself in check because as much as she lived for shock value, even she knew that getting busted for fooling around with family would be hard to recover from. Though she had heard from many sources that he was quite skilled in the boudoir, which is why she proudly started the rumor that his nickname "the Count" referred to the number of girls he had slept with.

"The problem is her snorendous and ridicu-perfect boyfriend." She explained that before Alexander left for college, he made sure Anna still ran with his friends, who were in a different crowd than the one Bea ran with. She made Anna sound like the adorable mascot of a few up-tight seniors at Greenwich Academy. "Those uppity Episcopalians aren't as evil as the Midwest mega-church psychos, but are almost as clique-y. Her boyfriend's half-sister Eleanor ran with a prudish rat pack of so called 'good girls' with iron chastity belts and matching headbands. My theory is Eleanor is secretly in love with the Greenwich OG and wishes she had the guts to go all Cersei Lannister with him."

Vronsky wrinkled his brow but stayed silent. Nobody understood the intricate politics of Greenwich and Manhattan teen society better than his cousin, but like any teenager she was prone to hyperbole at times. Beatrice fed on the shock of others.

"You know, Anna does the whole horse thing and equestrian girls are always so serious. I blame the boots . . . though the crop I could get down with."

Vronsky listened to Beatrice's convoluted theory about how girls needed a love of high heels to become comfortable with their sexual place in the world, and young girls who wore riding boots daily were sexually repressed late bloomers. His cousin's theory made no sense, but after a few more drinks he slowly started to understand what she was getting at.

There were only three social circles that had power in Greenwich: fun society girls who partied, which Beatrice herself led; a group she called the Three Cs for their obsession with church, charities, and college admissions, which was Anna's boyfriend's cohort. "And lastly . . ." Bea hiccupped, frowning. "I can't remember the third, but there are three."

"The third group are the rich boarding school kids who come back for holidays and the summer," Vronsky added helpfully. He already knew about the three circles, having heard Bea pontificate about this before. Social politics was her favorite thing to discuss when stoned, and Vronsky had spent many such evenings with his hard-partying cousin.

"Yes, yes, very good," Bea said, finding Vronsky's impatience funnier as the minutes passed. "Anna is a fascinating case because she's always floated freely between all three circles, never pledging allegiance to any one group. I've always found her to be a mysterious bird. She's well liked but kind of a loner who spends all her time with horses and giant dogs. At school she usually reads through lunch. Books! Not her phone, even." Bea hiccupped again.

Vronsky pushed a glass of ice water toward Beatrice, a not-so-subtle hint.

"You stinkstar!" she snapped. "If I didn't adore you, I'd tell you to fuck off. Of all the girls for you to fall for, does it have to be Anna? Her boyfriend is no small obstacle. Even though he's away, he still holds a lot of influence and the entire town thinks he walks on water. My dad once called him 'the pride of Greenwich.' This isn't an Asian fetish thing, is it, dear cousin?"

Normally, Vronsky would have laughed off his cousin's ridiculous comment, but tonight he wasn't in the mood for her crass sense of humor. She saw his lips tighten and she placed her hand on his arm. "Sorry, that was gauche. I only said it because you *do* have a pattern. Your first sexual experience was watching Kiril and that Thai girl. And you have had more than your fair share of hotties from the Far East. . . ."

"Dammit, Bea, I'm not here to discuss the psychology behind my sex life! I'm here because I, I . . ." He stammered, realizing he hadn't eaten very much and was now drunk himself. He gulped down his glass of water and wiped his mouth. "I'm here because I think I'm in love with her and I don't know what to do about it," he said, hanging his head, not in shame, but in relief. Honesty was difficult, but it was also exhilarating to say what had been on his mind for the entire taxi ride downtown. Vronsky knew without a doubt he had never been in love until he saw Anna K. step off the train a few hours earlier.

Beatrice reached across the table and grabbed her cousin's hands. "It's gonna be okay, V. I've got your back. I'll help you, I promise." She downed the rest of her scotch and looked Vronsky straight in the eyes. "Now, do you have a little snow-white for me? I need a bump so we can keep drinking."

XVI

Anna woke up the next morning momentarily confused by her surroundings. She sat up in bed, grabbed her phone off her nightstand, and gaped at the time. As a dog owner, sleeping past ten was never an option. She couldn't remember the last time she had slept this late.

She walked into the kitchen and found Marta, the housekeeper, baking cinnamon rolls. They exchanged pleasantries, and Anna made herself a double shot of Nespresso and went to see if her brother was awake.

Steven's door was closed and she should have knocked, but it hadn't occurred to her. She entered the room and stopped immediately when she realized her brother wasn't alone in bed. Lolly, half naked, was straddling Steven, her blond hair falling down her back, the two of them making out like the world was ending.

She averted her eyes and backed out of the bedroom in shock, quickly closing the door. She stood in the hallway, dumbfounded, and tried to blink away the visual of Lolly riding her brother. She wasn't sure how she felt about the spectacle she'd just witnessed but had no time to decide because Marta was waving at her down the hall. The doorman had just called. Lolly's little sister, Kimmie, was on her way up. Anna headed to the door breathlessly, thankful for the distraction.

Kimmie stepped off the elevator looking down at her phone and ran straight into Anna, who was standing in the outside hall waiting. "Oh my god, I'm so sorry!" she exclaimed, instantly annoyed at herself for being like the people she despised, the ones who roamed the city's sidewalks, staring at their phones like iZombies.

"Were you waiting for me, or the elevator?" Kimmie asked, truly confused.

Anna smiled warmly at the adorable blond sophomore. "You must be Kimmie. I'm Anna, Steven's sister." Anna gave Kimmie a quick hug and ushered her into the apartment.

Of course, Kimmie knew who Anna was, though they had only met in passing once or twice before. "It's so good to finally meet you," Kimmie said, trying to take off her Moncler snow boots and feeling unbearably self-conscious about the SoulCycle sweats she had lazily thrown on. Kimmie wished she had chosen her outfit more wisely, knowing there was a possibility she would run into Steven's sister, who Dustin had said was coming into town the night before. Kimmie knew she was beautiful in her own right, but in the presence of Anna she felt totally basic.

Soon the two girls were seated in the dining room, Anna drinking a second Nespresso while Kimmie picked at a chocolate croissant, waiting for the housekeeper to bring her a hot chocolate. As soon as Kimmie sat down, Anna had leaned forward and told her in a hushed tone what she had seen only seconds before Kimmie arrived. Not knowing how close the two sisters were, she chose her words carefully. "They were so busy kissing I don't think they saw me," she said. "Thank god!" she added with a small chuckle.

"So they made up?" Kimmie asked.

"Seems that way," Anna replied.

"Because of you." Kimmie had intended her words to be a compliment, but upon hearing them, she worried her tone sounded more like an accusation.

"Not really," Anna demurred. "She loves him, like, really loves him. She told me so last night. And I told Lolly only she had the power to decide Steven's fate."

"How so?" Kimmie asked, surprised at being taken into this older girl's confidence in such an intimate way. "I mean, you think she should stay with him? I know he's your brother but . . ." She trailed off, remembering all that her sister had texted her. She shuddered with revulsion.

"I think Steven's behavior was repulsive and reprehensible. I don't want to be so cavalier as to say 'boys will be boys,' but I told your sister the only way they could stay together is if she could truly forgive him. Otherwise it would never work."

"I'm not sure I could do it," Kimmie said. "In fact, I know I couldn't. It seems impossible to forgive my boyfriend for cheating on me like that. Not that I've ever had one."

"So you've never had a boyfriend?" Anna inquired very gently.

"Does that matter?" Kimmie's voice rose defensively.

"Of course not. I was just curious because I've had a boyfriend for so long that it's hard to remember what my opinions were when I didn't. Though I'm pretty sure I would have said the same thing as you."

"So having a boyfriend gives you different opinions?" Kimmie asked, now intrigued.

"Not exactly. I know it sounds like I'm making excuses for their thoughtless stupidity, but I'm not. I'm just saying boys and girls couldn't be more different in their wants and behaviors. And when you throw in raging hormones and mix it up with emotions, it's a wonder we don't all go mad." As Anna heard her own words out loud, she wondered if she was expressing her thoughts for Kimmie's benefit or for her own. From the first moment she had opened her eyes that morning, Anna had been thinking about Vronsky. This wouldn't have concerned her, if it weren't for the fact that he had been the last thing she had thought about before falling asleep as well.

"So the takeaway is that boys are stupid?" Kimmie asked, only half joking.

"Yes," Anna said, laughing. "My work here is done!"

Kimmie looked up to see Marta carrying a silver tray. She placed a teacup and saucer filled with steaming hot chocolate in front of Kimmie, along with a heart-shaped crystal candy dish with several large marshmallows. She placed half a pink grapefruit in front of Anna along with a grapefruit spoon, the kind Kimmie had first seen at the Mandarin Oriental hotel when she traveled with her mother to London. She remembered being so fascinated with the beautiful tiny jagged-edged spoon she slipped it into her purse at the end of the meal.

"If you were in Lolly's situation, would you forgive him?" Kimmie asked. "You know, if he wasn't your brother and all."

"You mean, if my boyfriend cheated on me could I forgive him?" Anna asked. She had wondered the same thing herself last night when she was counseling Lolly.

"I'm sorry, was that rude? I didn't mean to make you feel weird."

"It wasn't rude at all," Anna said, thoughtfully. "I have to be honest and say I don't know. Luckily, I've never been in that situation. I suppose it depends."

"But is there ever a situation when cheating is okay?" Kimmie asked.

"Probably not. But I'm hardly an expert on the matter. I've only ever had one boyfriend myself. But relationships are complicated, Steven is my brother, and I'll support whatever Lolly decides to do."

"Me, too," Kimmie said. She desperately wished for Anna to like her and had no problem changing her tune. "I know my sister loves Steven. She says it all the time. Maybe—" She paused. "—maybe this will make their relationship better? Stronger, I mean?" All this talk of love brought Dustin to Kimmie's mind, but she dismissed the thought of him quickly, assuming he'd popped into her head because of the hot chocolate. Her thoughts then jumped to Vronsky. Since meeting him at New Year's, she had seen him at least once a week, first for tea at the Plaza, then a walk through the park, and twice more in the evening for coffee.

Anna noticed Kimmie's smile and asked her who was on her mind.

"How did you know it was a who I was thinking about?" Kimmie asked, blushing with embarrassment, but happy for the opening to discuss what she really wanted to talk about. She assumed Anna knew Vronsky and was eager to get her opinion. Kimmie knew Anna was the girlfriend of the Greenwich OG, which basically made her royalty, like America's own version of William and Kate. *Perhaps Vronsky and I could be Harry and Meghan.*

"Just a feeling," Anna said, happy to have Kimmie here to gossip with. Anna was still wrestling with thoughts of Vronsky and she wasn't happy about it. She wasn't single like Kimmie, so she knew it was trouble to start daydreaming of boys that weren't her boyfriend.

Kimmie sipped her hot chocolate. "I met him at your brother's New Year's Eve party, and I've only seen him a few times since then."

"Oh, is this Dustin? Steven's old friend?" Anna asked innocently. "Your sister mentioned something about him last night. I hear MIT practically begged him to go there."

Kimmie frowned at the mention of Dustin's name and shook her head. "Not him. I mean, Dustin's sweet and may have a crush on me. But I like someone else, though I'm not sure he likes me back."

Anna found Kimmie's sudden shyness quite darling. "Of course he likes you back! Any guy would. Tell me! Who's this mystery man?"

"His name is Alex. Alex Vronsky, though you may have heard of him by his silly nickname Count Vronsky."

Anna's eyes went wide, but she quickly checked herself. "How odd, I met him for the first time last night. I rode the train in with his mother and he was there to pick her up at Grand Central."

Kimmie was thrilled. Vronsky didn't come visit her at the rink last night because he was with his mother, not because he was losing interest like she feared. She was so happy to hear the news she didn't notice that Anna's mood had changed slightly. "What was his mother like? Alex hasn't told me much, but I can tell they're close." Kimmie was thrilled to finally have a girl she could talk to about Vronsky. Lolly was always so judgy when it came to boys and kept warning her Vronsky was famous for being a huge flirt and a total playboy.

"She's incredible, so beautiful and elegant. She mainly spoke of her two sons. Alexia is clearly her favorite." Anna hoped Kimmie didn't catch her slip of the tongue calling Alexia by his mother's pet name, and continued, "She seems very involved in his life."

Kimmie was interested in Vronsky's mom of course, but she most wanted to hear Anna's opinion of Alex himself. "Don't you find him crazy hot? He's, like, movie star good-looking."

"He is handsome." Anna nodded, knowing it'd be strange for her to deny such an obvious truth. "You two would make such a good-looking couple." She knew Kimmie would love to hear about Vronsky's heroic actions with the homeless man's dog, but she purposefully withheld it. Vronsky rushing off to find the second dog was somehow tied to her, though she hadn't spent any time yet contemplating why.

Kimmie's phone dinged and she couldn't help glancing at it. It was a notification reminding her she needed to pick up her new dress from Bergdorf's that was being tailored.

"Anna, are you still going to be in the city tomorrow night? It's Jaylen S.'s sweet sixteen party. Her father rented out the entire 1 OAK club. You should come! I'd be happy to have someone else there I like."

Anna frowned slightly. "I'm not big on the club scene, but maybe. Steven mentioned it last night."

"I see you in lavender. Do you own a lavender dress?" Kimmie asked.

Anna laughed in response. "Who doesn't? But I don't have it here. I'm sure I can scrounge up something to wear. If I go."

Kimmie stood up quickly. "Well, obvi Lolly doesn't need a shoulder to cry on anymore, so I'm gonna go. Hey, I have to go pick up my dress at Bergdorf's. I don't suppose you'd have any interest in coming with me?"

Normally Anna would have jumped at the chance to go to her favorite store, but she knew this would only lead to more boy talk, which she was no longer in the mood for.

"Ooooh, I'd love to, but I can't."

It was then that Kimmie's sister walked into the dining room, humming. She was wearing an oversized men's terry cloth robe and her hair was wet from showering.

"Kimmie, what are you doing here?" Lolly asked.

"I stopped by to check on you, but I hear you're doing more than fine," Kimmie answered, quickly adding, "I mean, after your talk with Anna last night."

"That's exactly right," Anna said casually.

Lolly was on another planet, barely listening to either of them. All she knew was that she was starving and had planned to ransack the fridge for something to eat with Steven in bed.

"Anna, is there any pie left?" Lolly asked in a dreamy voice. "Steven wants some."

Anna nodded with a smile. This confirmed her suspicions. Lolly must have decided to forgive her brother for his transgressions, and in the process, also decided to give up her V-card. Anna thought it was probably a good thing, because now the date of their "screw-a-versary" was legit.

"Lolly, are you stoned?" Kimmie asked her sister. "You look totally high."

Lolly smiled. "In a way . . . In a way . . ."

XVII

Jaylen S. was the youngest daughter of retired NBA basketball legend Maceo S., who was now a popular sports commentator for ESPN. Rumor had it her sweet sixteen was going to be one of the biggest bashes of the year, even though it was only February. Her father had rented out 1 OAK in the Meatpacking District. The adults would be in the VIP area while every socialite teen who was anybody danced the night away. Jaylen S.'s godfather had been one of her father's teammates and was now a part owner of the Miami Heat. He was apparently showing up with his own kids and a private plane full of their hard-partying friends from South Beach.

The thing about new money versus old money? New money was way more fun. Old money came with lots of baggage—outdated and uptight societal rules of behavior that frowned on being showy with your inherited cash. New money had no such restrictions. If anything, it was expected for the nouveau riche to throw it and show it as much as possible.

The theme of Jaylen's party was '90s Hip-Hop. And the invitation was the coolest one Kimmie had ever received . . . once it was explained to her. She had been delivered a small box containing a little black plastic square object with a tiny screen and two AAA batteries. When she popped the batteries in, the screen lit up green but remained blank. Thinking it was broken, she showed it to Devon M., the law student who stayed with her and Lolly whenever their mom was out late or traveled.

"Where did you get this?" Devon asked, turning the object over in her hands.

"It's supposed to be a party invite, I think," Kimmie said. "What is it?"

Devon explained that it was a pager, a popular form of communication in the '90s before everyone had cell phones. "Haven't you ever heard of a beeper?"

Kimmie shook her head. "What does it do?"

"People used to use it to send phone numbers. You would call the number back when you got to a pay phone. Doctors used them mostly, so they could be reached outside of the hospital. Drug dealers used them, too, but eventually the cool kids adopted the look as well. Some beepers could receive text messages."

On cue, the pager vibrated and emitted a series of high-pitched beeps, startling them both. Just as Devon had explained, a message appeared. `Jaylen's illin' 90s hip-hop par-tay deets arrivin' soon . . . ish!`

Devon couldn't shut up about the invite for the next ten minutes. She even took a picture to show her boyfriend. She calculated the cost of such an elaborate invite, and said it had to be at least five Gs if not more. Kimmie had been surprised by Devon's interest. Devon rarely got personal with her, mostly because her mother had specifically ordered Devon not to become friends with her daughter. "Kimmie needs a French tutor and positive role model for the nights when I'm out late, not a BFF, got it?"

Kimmie couldn't help but brag a little, telling Devon about Jaylen's famous father and his many celebrity friends. Though if she was being honest, she had no idea exactly what an old-school '90s hip-hop party would be like. She'd never listened to much rap; Kimmie's musical tastes were more along the lines of Lorde, Billie Eilish, and Lana Del Rey. Later that night, Lolly tried to explain the significance of '90s hip-hop to her, which made Kimmie roll her eyes. She knew her sister worshipped at the altar of Taylor Swift, and she only knew about "old-school rap" because Steven loved it. Kimmie once caught Lolly making a "hip-hop terminology" cheatsheet and she told her she'd get better grades if she applied even half as much effort to her homework. Lolly deadpanned: "Bih please, the right bf is way more important than school."

Lolly later told her that a lot of girls were planning on dressing like Fly Girls, which was yet another '90s term Kimmie needed explained to her. Lolly was of course horrified at the idea of girls showing up to a party wearing jeans and high tops and informed Kimmie that she was going to wear a dress, and she should do the same.

"Make sure it's short. This may be the only chance to dress like a total ho-bag until Halloween."

Kimmie thought of this moment now as she stared at herself in the mirror at Bergdorf's. She wondered if Vronsky would approve of her new Zimmermann dress. She stared at her reflection, annoyed she hadn't made it another inch shorter when she had the chance three days ago. The saleslady recognized Kimmie's look of doubt and quickly suggested that perhaps what the dress needed were some sexy new heels to go with it. Relief flooded through Kimmie. That was exactly what she needed.

In the second-floor shoe salon, Kimmie tried on eighteen different pairs of heels and finally landed on a pair of Azzedine Alaïa signature cut-out white leather booties with a four-inch heel. They cost over twelve hundred dollars and she charged them to her mother's store credit card knowing that she'd have a few weeks before her mother spotted them on her statement. Her rationale was simple: her mother would surely be so pleased about her daughter landing Vronsky as her new boyfriend, all she'd have to do was explain how these shoes helped her get him. She'd still get in trouble, but Lolly had already paved the way for such behavior as she had been obsessed with fashion since middle school, throwing tantrums if she didn't have the latest designers to wear. Kimmie had never cared much about everyday clothes, though her competition dresses were always Vera Wang.

Since Kimmie had started at Spence, she cared more and more about what she wore to school. Mainly because Lolly pressured her. Apparently if Kimmie dressed poorly it reflected on her. For the last six weeks Kimmie had really elevated her fashion game. Even though she was loath to admit it, she knew it was because of her newfound interest in boys, or rather, the attention she now garnered from boys since appearing on the Hot List. Kimmie denied that she cared about the dumb list, partly because Lolly had never made it on, and it felt tacky to rub it in her sister's less critically-acclaimed face, and partly because she only really cared about one particular boy's attention.

Kimmie wanted to believe she was dressing up for Jaylen's party for herself, but she knew that was a lie. Perhaps if every detail was perfect, Vronsky would be so taken with her they'd spend the whole night dancing together and he'd ask her to be his girlfriend. Clearly things were getting serious between them, and the other night when she told him she liked him, he had looked into her eyes and said he really liked her, too.

Now that she was already going to get busted by her mom for the new shoes, Kimmie figured she might as well go completely rogue, deciding that she needed a little bit of flash to show her fun side. She walked out of the Chanel department with a new cross-body evening bag, a limited edition in neon-pink patent leather. If tomorrow night was to be her night, she wanted to look her best.

XVIII

Anna spent her snow day afternoon hanging out with Steven and Lolly. After Kimmie left for Bergdorf's, Lolly asked Anna if she could use her bathroom to blow out her hair and Anna agreed. While Lolly was busy, Anna used the time to check on her brother. He was in his bedroom with an iPad on his chest, playing Fortnite. Anna flopped onto the bed next to him, careful to pull up his duvet first, and asked him whether she should bring her dogs in or not.

"Are you staying through the weekend?" he asked, keeping his eyes on the screen.

"Maybe. Tell me more about the party tomorrow night. Can you get me on the guest list?" she asked in a teasing way, knowing full well her brother had a lot of power because of his own reputation in the party circuit.

Steven paused his game and turned toward his sister. "Anna, you could ask me for anything right now and I'd do it for you. Seriously, you saved my ass. I don't know what the hell you said to Lolly but she really came around. And around and around." He didn't wink at her, but he might as well have.

"Don't gloat, Steven. It's unbecoming," she answered with pretend sternness. She felt delighted over her good deed, proud of the part she'd played in her brother's happiness. And now that her brother and Lolly were doing it, perhaps they could avoid the same problem happening in the future. All the magazines she read stated men usually cheated for sexual satisfaction, while women tended to cheat for emotional connection. She kept this in mind for her own relationship, which of course explained why Alexander insisted they never go more than three weeks without seeing each other.

Anna lost her virginity to Alexander when she had traveled with his family to Bora Bora the summer before he left for college. Alexander's father and stepmother rented them their own two-bedroom bungalow (with a private plunge pool), which they shared with Alexander's half-sister, Eleanor. Eleanor was a freshman at Anna's school and they were friends more out of convenience than anything else. Obviously, Anna would never dare to be catty about Eleanor in front of Alexander, but the truth of the matter was Eleanor was tedious.

On the second day of their ten-day vacation, Anna came back to their bungalow after getting a massage to find that Alexander had decorated the entire living room with candles and flowers. He had arranged for them to dine in their room catered by a private chef. Alexander was an incredibly thoughtful boyfriend, but this sort of grand gesture was not really his style. Anna was taken aback. "What about Eleanor?" she asked. Probably not the best response, but it was the first thing that popped into her head.

"She's not feeling well and has decided to move into my dad and Whitney's bungalow. You know, to be close to her mom," he responded simply.

To this day, she had no idea what Alexander said to Eleanor to get her to go along with his plan to seduce her, because when she saw Eleanor the next day, she didn't seem sick at all.

"But what if she comes into the room?" Anna asked. Eleanor never even watched rated-R movies because she found gratuitous violence and sex abhorrent.

"They don't call me the Greenwich OG for nothing," he said, shaking his head and laughing. Alexander held up Eleanor's key card to show he already had it covered. "Can we please stop talking about my sister?"

Anna smiled. It was rare for her boyfriend to display a sense of humor about himself. She knew he found his given nickname to be ridiculous and had never once heard him refer to himself by it. But she found hearing him say it now surprisingly sexy.

She had never asked Alexander whether he was a virgin as well, mainly because she didn't know if it was something she could ask him, and also because she wasn't sure if she wanted to hear about the girls who came before her. By the time Anna learned that a lot of girlfriends grilled their boyfriends about their past exploits, it was too late to broach the subject with him. Then, that night in Bora Bora over their candlelit dinner, he told her it was going to be his first time, too. She knew she should be touched by this, happy that they would have a shared experience as a couple. But, in fact, she was disappointed to hear the news. While they shared a chocolate soufflé for dessert all she could think of was that if they were both virgins, how the hell were they going to know what to do?

They figured it out, of course, after much fumbling and awkwardness. It wasn't rocket science, after all. The sex hurt more than she thought it would, but by the second day, she finally relaxed enough to enjoy it a little. Yet Anna always wondered whether there was more to sex than what she was experiencing. Even for that split second when she saw Lolly on top of her brother, she felt more electricity in the room than any time she had been with Alexander. She wondered whether this was because her brother had a lot more experience and was better able to show Lolly the way.

"Done!" Her brother's voice brought her back to reality.

"What's done?" she asked, having forgotten what was last said between them.

"You're on the list for the par-tay. I'm psyched you're going. It's gonna be high-key lit. Set list should be dope AF. Hey, should I get a white stretch limo so we can roll up straight pimpin'?"

This was why Anna loved her brother; he knew how to have a good time and always had. "Fo-shizzle you should!" she replied and Steven shot her a smirk. "Isn't that an old hip-hop expression? Did I use it correctly?"

"I know you're not a dumb white girl, but you've never sounded more like one."

"Hey, take that back! You're not allowed to be mean to me yet. You owe me, remember?" Anna was holding a throw pillow and ready to smack him in the face.

He put his arms up in the air in surrender. "I take it back! You're right. On my honor, I'll be nice to you for . . ." He paused dramatically. "At least for another few days. Like maybe three."

"Oh please, like you have any honor." Anna smacked her brother in the face with the pillow and got up from the bed laughing. "Get the limo.

Why not?" She had always told herself she needed to try to be more like her brother, less careful and down for whatever. She decided right then to text Magda not to send her dogs in from Greenwich after all. She was going to a party tomorrow night and was going to stay out late, which meant the dogs would be left alone in the apartment.

Feeling good about her decisiveness, she now turned her attention to the next important matter. What was she going to wear? Her closet in the city had plenty of dresses in it, but she knew she wanted something extra special since clubbing wasn't something she normally did.

Perhaps she deserved a fun new outfit as a treat for being such a good sister. It wasn't like she didn't have the afternoon to go shopping. She smiled brightly, opened the Uber app, tapped "Where to?" and typed "Bergdorf Goodman."

XIX

Dustin was spending his snow day catching up on his movie watching. He split his time between his parents' apartments: his father was a doctor at NYU Langone and lived in the West Village with his second wife, while his mother lived modestly on the Upper East Side in a two-bedroom apartment. His parents had divorced when he was four years old and it had always been a pain to travel back and forth. But when he hit high school, he traded off weeks, which was easier.

During the school week he never had time to veg out because of homework, and on weekends his mom always wanted to spend "quality time" together. He knew it was because she was stressed about him going off to college, and he was trying to be empathetic and just do what she wanted. But luckily his dad was less sentimental and let him do as he wished. He would never tell his mom, but he preferred his dad's downtown neighborhood. He had just seen two foreign films, a Jean-Luc Godard double feature—*Pierrot le Fou* and *Alphaville*—in the Village. He then walked to Corner Bistro and ate a hamburger. He was now trying to decide what commercial blockbuster he should see next. Dustin felt that to be a true film lover, one needed to see both highbrow and lowbrow movies.

A few minutes later, he got a text from Steven about a party at a club in the Meatpacking District this Saturday night. Dustin assumed it was an errant text as he and Steven were not weekend friends. But then he received a follow-up text that said: Renting limo STOP Kimmie will b there STOP ur presence mandatory! STOP. Dustin smiled at the text, knowing the "STOPs" were in his honor. He once said to Steven, during an American history homework session about the use of telegrams in the early 1900s, that it was one of his personal regrets, being born into the age of smartphones as opposed to telegrams. He found telegrams to be much more dramatic. Steven's response had been, "You're a weird fucking dude, but I like it. You almost make nerds cool. Almost." Dustin had liked the compliment and thought about it from time to time.

A picture of a super cheesy white stretch limo straight out of a John Hughes movie appeared. The superrich were just different. They could do things on a whim like rent vintage limos for the night. Out of curiosity, Dustin googled the limo service and saw that a twenty-four-hour rental with a driver was running Steven two thousand bucks.

Dustin shook his head and sighed. People were starving, wars were being fought all over the world, so many people were suffering, and yet here was an eighteen-year-old dropping two Gs on some bullshit like it was nothing. It didn't seem right that some people had so much when others had so little. He knew he shouldn't go on principle, but when it came to Kimmie, Dustin's convictions were like a bunny getting batted around by a bear. He sighed and then texted back two words: I'm in.

My spot 8 for grub, leave @9 to cruise in limo, cuz we straight ballin' 2nite. Dress code 90s hip hop

Reading Steven's upbeat text, Dustin knew he and Lolly had made up. He guessed Steven's sister had swept in and saved the day. He was happy for his friend, but he couldn't help thinking Lolly should have dumped him for what he did.

He wondered what he should wear to such a party. He wondered who he should ask. He thought about texting those two girls he'd met at Steven's on New Year's, but worried if he asked them, they'd ask what party he was going to and what if they weren't invited and asked him if they could come along? Also, what did two white girls in 2019 know about '90s hip-hop anyway? Probably more than he did, a fact of which he was not proud. Dustin's palms were now sweaty. This was exactly why he hated parties. So many machinations and preparations!

He texted the one person he knew he could ask without feeling stupid. His older brother, Nicholas, was a huge rap fan, which was the only reason Dustin knew anything about it at all. His brother also happened to be the least reliable person on the planet, which meant he probably wouldn't even get a response.

He was wrong. His brother texted him right back and asked why Dustin needed to know about '90s hip-hop clothes. Dustin hesitated to admit the real reason and briefly considered lying and telling his brother he needed to know for a school project or a short story he was writing. Dustin hadn't seen his brother in months and hadn't texted with him since a three-line exchange during the holidays. He had wished his brother Happy Chanukah but got a one-line response telling him he had renounced all religion and no longer celebrated any holiday. He had texted back Happy New Year, but his brother had never answered.

Dustin decided to tell the truth:

Dustin

I need to know because I'm going to a
90s hip-hop party with a girl

Nicholas

Send pic of girl

Dustin

No

Nicholas

Give me 1 reason Y I should help

Dustin grimaced when he read this, hating his older brother for being such an asshole, and then immediately feeling guilty for it. His brother was a recovering heroin addict, the black sheep of the family, but still Dustin always tried to cut him a break.

> **Dustin**
> I'm your brother.

Nicholas
Try again.

> **Dustin**
> Never mind, forget I asked.

Nicholas
ur so fuckin' sensitive. I'll tell you for $$$

> **Dustin**
> How much?

Nicholas
$100.

Dustin knew this was a bad idea, because he was on strict orders from his parents to never give Nicholas money. He felt guilty about it, but he felt like he had no choice due to the Kimmie of it all.

> **Dustin**
> Fine.

Nicholas
Venmo me.

Dustin Venmo'd his brother fifty dollars and waited for the response he knew he'd get.

Nicholas
only got $50.

> **Dustin**
> You'll get rest when you give me info

Nicholas
dickwad! Wu Wear baggy jeans, FUBU hoodie, Air Jordans or the pump.

What's "the pump"?

Nicholas

Shaq sneakers, go 2 vintage shop.

Dustin

What shirt?

Nicholas

brand new fresh white tee, maybe a chain.

Dustin Venmo'd his brother another hundred dollars.

Dustin

I added an extra 50$. Go get a fancy
dinner in MN. Outback Steakhouse?

Nicholas

Go fuck y'self

Dustin

Thank you. Take care not to slip on
the ice.

Nicholas

I'm not in MN. In the Bronx

This was news to Dustin. Last he heard, Nicholas was on month three at the Hazelden rehab facility. His fourth stint in as many years.

Dustin

Do Mom and Dad know?

Nicholas

Dad, not Mom. I'm clean. @halfway house
workin at taco shop.

Dustin was shocked, and honestly didn't know what to write back. Mercifully he didn't have to because his brother texted again. Gotta bounce lil bro. Later.

Dustin googled vintage shops that carried FUBU, found a store nearby, and headed out. He couldn't believe his brother was back in town and hadn't let him know. Though on further reflection, he could absolutely believe it.

XX

When they arrived at the party, Kimmie knew she looked on point and was happy to see a red carpet at the entrance. Photographers lined up, waiting for arrivals. She was used to being photographed from ice dancing competitions and knew exactly how to stand: angle the head, twist the body, cross the ankles if possible, and a relaxed face. As she moved along the step and repeat, posing for the photogs with her frozen half smile, she had only one thing on her mind: how long she'd have to wait until she saw him.

She had not heard from Vronsky all day yesterday. She tried her best not to care about one whole day passing with no word, even though it seemed to her that an unexpected snow day would have been a perfect time to hang out. But she couldn't take the silence and caved, texting him this morning because she needed to make sure he was going to be there. She knew she was breaking the unwritten rule about girls waiting for boys to text first, but she was going crazy waiting. He had replied immediately, and they exchanged exactly seven texts back and forth. She made sure she didn't respond to the last of his texts. She told him about Steven's impromptu limo rental and said she'd be arriving with him, along with Lolly and Anna. She tried to word it so he'd know they had plenty of room in case he wanted to join them. But Vronsky didn't take the bait. He said he had things to do but he'd be there by midnight and that she should save a dance for him.

Only after they texted had she found out from her sister that Steven had invited Dustin to join them in the limo, and she was relieved Vronsky hadn't asked to come along. That would have been terribly awkward. She knew some boys would get jealous to find out she had caught the attention of a senior, but Vronsky was not one of those boys. Why would he ever need to be jealous of anyone when he was sure to be the hottest guy at the party?

The limo ride was more fun than she'd thought it would be. She was initially very disappointed when she climbed into the large cavernous car to find Anna absent from the group. Kimmie was developing a full-blown girl-crush on Anna, and it was a toss-up whether she was more excited to see what Anna chose to wear to the party or have Anna see what she wore. When she asked why Anna wasn't in the car, her brother said Anna had instructed them to go without her because she got stuck on the phone with her boyfriend, Alexander.

Apparently, some issue arose about Anna's decision to stay in the city for the weekend because she'd be missing Alexander's younger half-sister's monthly tea party. Anna had texted her regrets to Eleanor, and even though Eleanor texted back k she clearly meant no such thing. As soon as she had sent the text, Eleanor immediately called Alexander in Cambridge and pitched a fit about Anna's last-minute cancellation. Alexander was left with no choice but to call Anna to see if she'd reconsider. "Why not just head back to Greenwich after the party instead of staying in the city?" he asked her on the phone. Anna had told Alexander she would have maybe changed her mind if Eleanor had asked her directly, but this behind-the-back tattletale shit pissed her off.

When Steven relayed the story in the back of the limo, he acted the entire thing out using funny voices and soon the four of them were laughing so hard they could barely stay upright. They were clutching their stomachs in pain and screaming for Steven to stop. After Lolly got the hiccups she told Steven if he didn't stop, she'd throw up and then she'd have to change again. Still on his best behavior and knowing she was totally serious about the outfit change, he obeyed.

When the limo pulled up to 1 OAK, the photographers started taking pictures immediately, which was exactly the effect Steven had intended. After a quick discussion it was decided that Steven would exit first so he could help Lolly out of the car. Dustin would get out next, followed by Kimmie. Obviously, she couldn't object when she had no alternative, but Kimmie wondered if it would look like she and Dustin were a couple since there were only four of them, as opposed to five. She decided that when they got out of the car, she'd make sure to put a little distance between herself and Dustin so the paparazzi wouldn't take them for a couple. And if they asked to get a picture of the two of them, she'd insist her sister and Steven join them. She felt bad for thinking these things, but she knew Dustin had a crush on her and it felt wrong to give him any false hope. To make matters even more annoying, her sister was Team Dustin, and as they stood side by side in their shared bathroom putting on their makeup, Lolly went on and on that Dustin was a genius and sure to be very successful in the future. This line of reasoning did nothing for Kimmie. She was only a sophomore in high school and just didn't care about such things.

Exasperated, she finally snapped that she didn't care about Dustin's perfect SAT scores, she only liked him as a friend and that was it. Lolly, knowing the real reason Kimmie wasn't interested, countered, "FYI, Count Vronsky has screwed half the senior girls at Spence."

Unwilling to let her sister have the last word, Kimmie said, "Well, won't they all be jealous when I'm his new girlfriend?" Kimmie regretted sharing her secret desire with her sister, but at least her sister went back to styling her hair and didn't say another word.

The driver opened the back door and Kimmie listened to the shouts of the photographers. She was ready for the best night of her life to begin.

XXI

While they went through security and waited to check in, Dustin told Kimmie again how gorgeous she looked. This made her happy and she repaid the compliment, saying she loved his outfit, too. She had googled

"'90s hip-hop style" earlier and Dustin was dressed exactly like many of the guys in the pictures. "You look very authentic. Like you just arrived here from the nineties *Terminator*-style." She felt the urge to be extra nice to Dustin now since it was sure to be difficult for him to watch her spend the night dancing with Vronsky.

"Well actually, in the original movies, Schwarzenegger arrived from the future buck naked." As soon as he spoke, Dustin regretted it. Why was he bringing up nudity? He tried to recover by quickly adding, "The whole naked thing was a comedic device, something the director used to add levity to the serious tone of the movie." Now he regretted sounding like a film geek. "Hey, will you dance with me? When or if we ever get in?"

"I'm surprised you like to dance," Kimmie blurted. "Sorry, that came out weird. I guess when I think of geniuses, dancing isn't what comes to mind."

"Well, clearly I'm no genius because I really want to dance with you." Dustin now understood what made cocaine so addictive, because it was allowing him to just say anything he thought without worrying about it. He had been reluctant to partake earlier but Steven convinced him a line or two might be just what he needed to get out of his own head. He felt foolish succumbing to peer pressure, but he had been wildly anxious all day over seeing Kimmie and by the time he got to Steven's he was desperate to feel something else. Now he felt surprisingly optimistic about his prospects with Kimmie for the night, though he had a suspicion the drugs were the reason for that, too.

Kimmie agreed to dance with him, and she meant it. She loved to dance and didn't want to be one of those girls who only danced with other girls in a circle. She always felt sorry for them. She also felt it'd be a good thing for Vronsky to show up and see her having fun already, so he didn't think she had been standing around waiting for him.

The dance floor was already packed and a speaker-thumping remix of Craig Mack's "Flava in Ya Ear" blared as they walked in. The teenage bar was serving nonalcoholic cocktails sponsored by Red Bull, but it seemed like every kid in the place was packing a flask or a vape pen. The lines for the bathroom were also long, giving away those who were into the harder stuff. Steven asked Dustin if he wanted to accompany him to the men's room, but Dustin shook his head. His mission of dancing with Kimmie was already in motion, so he felt like he didn't need any more chemical help. He watched as Steven grabbed Lolly's hand and led her away and turned to see Kimmie holding out two Jell-O shots for him.

"Red or green?" Kimmie shouted at him over the music.

He was about to answer he'd take whichever one she didn't want, but he reminded himself that girls liked assertive men. "Green, definitely green." He took the tiny plastic cup she was offering and sucked it down. "What's in these?"

Kimmie laughed and shrugged. "No clue! Some club kid just offered me some," she said and quickly slurped down the red one. She was slightly nervous, because god only knows what they could contain, but since she'd arrived at the party her anxiety had risen and she needed something to level her out. There were so many people she wondered how Vronsky would be able to find her.

Kimmie grabbed Dustin's hand and led him out onto the dance floor. They were soon at the center movin' and groovin' to Q-Tip's "Vivrant Thing." Halfway through the song Dustin noticed Vronsky twenty feet away standing beside the dance floor, drinking out of a silver flask. Dustin recognized him from the Google search he had done as soon as Steven mentioned his name. Dustin had known he'd be good-looking, but he wasn't prepared for the extent of it. The only thing that made him feel better were the sheer number of pictures of Vronsky with so many different beautiful girls. It obviously made sense he was interested in Kimmie because Dustin found her more beautiful than any girl he had seen on Vronsky's arm, but he hoped that perhaps the Count was a guy who never settled for one girl.

When he saw Vronsky, he thought about trying to block Kimmie from view, but it was too late. Vronsky had spotted them already and even raised his flask in cheers upon catching Dustin's eye. Dustin held his breath, hoping his rival wouldn't approach them, and was relieved to see that it appeared he had no intention of doing so. Vronsky seemed to be too busy scanning the crowd for someone else.

After dancing to Jay-Z's "Who You Wit" and Lords of the Underground's "Chief Rocka," Kimmie wanted to see if Anna had shown up and motioned for Dustin to follow her. To make sure he didn't lose her in the crowd, he reached for her hand, happy when she let him hold it, as they snaked through the throng of partygoers toward the main bar. "You're a great dancer, Kimmie," he murmured into her hair when their progress was stopped by a group of people watching a shirtless guy pop and lockin' on the dance floor in front of them.

She smiled and nodded but didn't respond as she watched the guy now doing the robot. Not wanting to lose this opportunity alone with Kimmie, Dustin continued, "Now that you know I secretly love to dance, you'll understand I've been thinking a lot about my senior prom. It's still a few months away, but I was wondering if you'd think about going with me . . . as friends even, or whatever . . ." Honestly, he was smitten with Kimmie and he'd like nothing more than to start dating her seriously, but what he really wanted was for her to go to prom with him. If she agreed to go as friends now, that was fine by him. He'd spend the next few months getting closer to her with the plan that by prom she'd be in love with him, too.

She turned around to face him, her cheeks slightly flushed from dancing. "Dustin, I like you, really I do. But there's something you need to know. I'm . . . I'm in love with someone else. And I swear I'd go to prom with you as a friend, and you're so sweet to ask me, but I just can't. I don't think the guy I like would be into me going to prom with another guy, you know?"

Dustin was shocked by her honesty, which in a way only made him love her more despite what she was telling him. What else could he do but nod and try to play it cool? Despite being devastated, he managed to say, "Totally get it. All good, just thought, you know, I had to ask." Thankfully they were moving again, and continued onward through the hip-hop-hooraying crowd, no longer holding hands.

By the time Kimmie made it to the bar she turned around to find Dustin no longer behind her. His absence made her sad for a moment, but she knew she'd done the right thing just telling him straight what was going on with her and Vronsky. Kimmie climbed up onto an open bar stool so she could survey the crowd, which was when she finally spotted Anna talking to Steven and Lolly on the far side of the club. From what she could tell Anna was dressed in a sexy short black number, which slayed so hard Kimmie wondered why she had ever thought Anna should wear lavender.

Kimmie flagged down a bartender because she now needed a Red Bull before she could deal with making her way across the dance floor again.

XXII

Anna felt better after she took a healthy swig from her brother's flask. The vodka burned going down, but she needed to get over her frustration and relax a little so she could enjoy the night. She could count the number of fights she and Alexander had had in their three years as a couple on one hand. That was before tonight. She certainly wasn't looking to throw down with him, but she really found the whole convo to be infuriating. It had turned from a calm discussion to a fight when he demanded to know why she was being so selfish. "You hate the city. Why are you insisting on this?"

"I don't hate the city, number one. And secondly, it's a stupid tea party. Why don't you sit and drink tea with Eleanor and her god-fearing, grating friends for three hours on Sunday and see if you like it?" She was as stunned as he was by her outburst and fought the urge to apologize immediately. She was sorry for yelling but she wasn't sorry for what she'd said. It was something she had been feeling for a while but had never had the guts to say: Eleanor was perfectly nice but could be unbearably whiny and entitled if she didn't get her way.

Alexander didn't yell back, because it wasn't his way. He just said they would discuss it further when she came home from the party.

"Alexander, the party won't even get going until after midnight," she said, perhaps unwisely. "I'm staying out late; don't wait up for me. I'll call you in the morning."

He started to respond, but she cut him off saying she had to go and hanging up the phone. The whole thing made her feel a bit queasy, and invigorated. She was annoyed she missed the limo ride, but found her solitary Uber to be exactly what she needed, a little time to herself.

When she arrived at the party, Anna ran into a few people she knew from the summer she spent six weeks at Juilliard, one of whom was the cellist in a string quartet she used to play with. Anna had played violin since she was five years old and was, after almost ten years of lessons and daily practice, an accomplished musician. She had garnered lots of attention from her teachers who praised her proficiency but fretted over her lack of emotion when it came to her performances. These comments always irritated her because she was never quite sure what exactly was meant when she was instructed to "feel the music." She enjoyed playing when she was younger because she liked the praise, and it made her father happy, but as she got older it was hard for her to figure out if she liked it because she was good at it, or if she liked it because she actually liked it.

This all came to a head the summer after her sophomore year when she was asked to participate in a small European tour with her quartet. Everyone assumed she would be thrilled to go, but she wasn't. It was actually Alexander who pushed her to talk to her father about her feelings and even though she insisted "feelings" were never discussed in Korean or WASP households, she did finally get her nerve up. Her father's response was as pragmatic as always, which was that she needed to double down on her practicing so she could make an informed decision. At the beginning of the summer, Anna spent six weeks of intense private study with a world-famous teacher from Kiev, and by the end she played with more emotion. Unfortunately that emotion was a deep empathy for all the other Korean girls who would still be forced to play violin when her father granted her permission to stop. The party line being that Anna would miss her horses and dogs too much to tour.

On the red carpet, the cellist told her she had performed in Sweden over Christmas and Anna was relieved that she didn't feel even a single pang of envy. They went through the step-and-repeat as a group, but

Anna was pleased when the photogs singled her out and asked her to step forward, shouting out to her for her name. Once they figured out who her mother was, there was a bit of a stir, and even though Anna knew such attention was stupid, she also found it exciting.

While she waited to get checked in to the party, and every other girl was busy taking selfies, Anna looked around to see if she saw anyone else she knew. There, about ten people ahead of her, she spotted him. He was with a large group of guys and Beatrice, the most popular girl at her school. Beatrice and Anna had been closer friends in middle school, but once Anna started riding every day, she didn't have much time to socialize anymore, especially with Bea, who was a full-time party girl. Beatrice was always sweet to her and made a point to invite her to every party she had, but Anna had only gone to a few of them over the past couple years.

Anna couldn't help but feel a twinge of jealousy as she watched Vronsky put his arm around Beatrice, pretending to get her in a headlock, a brotherly sort of move that she had been victim to a hundred times with Steven. Suddenly she remembered, Beatrice had two male cousins, one of whom she was especially close to. That cousin was Alexia. Of course, now it made sense! Beatrice's father was Geneviève R.'s older brother. She watched with a bit of longing as Vronsky's group entered the club. They looked like they were having so much fun already.

It didn't take long for Anna to find her brother. She knew how Steven partied so she parked herself by the bathrooms and found him shortly thereafter. Anna had experimented with a few drugs here and there, but Alexander was very anti-drugs (except his precious Adderall) and it seemed too much of a bother to try to hide such things from him. Besides, she liked to keep a clear head, and found people who ended up sloppy drunk at the end of the night to be a little sad.

After her swig of booze, Anna decided she wanted more. "Brother, darling," Anna said with the lock-jawed voice she used when imitating her mother's way of speaking, "Can you be a dear and find me a real drink? Something delicious and worthy of my family name?" Steven, always happy to get everyone else drunk, loved seeing this playful side of his sister that she rarely showed in public. He gave her an exaggerated butler bow, accepting the challenge and saying he'd back posthaste. Anna stood with Lolly, and together they pointed out all the outfits they liked and hated. Kimmie arrived minutes later looking incredible and Anna gave her a warm hug hello. The two of them twirled for each other and kept shouting, "You look amazing." "No, you!" "You!" "You!" for a while until Steven returned holding three glasses. Anna took one and drank half of it immediately. She made a face, and yelled, "Uch, what is this?"

"Sugar-free Red Bull and vodka!" Steven yelled over the music. He handed the second drink to Lolly and gave up his own for Kimmie, telling her chivalry was not dead. Anna finished her drink, even though she found it revolting, and Beatrice, dressed in all Saint Laurent, appeared by her side moments later. The two girls hugged and went through the same you-look-amazing-no-you-do ritual she'd went through with Kimmie only minutes ago.

When Beatrice asked Anna to come dance with her and her friends, Anna declined. "I'm not much of a dancer. I'm more of a stand-around-er." But as soon as she said it, she spotted Vronsky heading their way. Desperate not to be present when he asked Kimmie to dance, Anna grabbed Beatrice's hand. "What the hell! This is a dance party, so let's dance." She pulled Bea away right when Vronsky arrived, barely even acknowledging him as she breezed by.

Kimmie noted Anna's slightly odd behavior but quickly dismissed it. Vronsky was now leaning over her to kiss her on both cheeks and whispering to her how amazing she looked. He then greeted Steven and Lolly, who decided it was time to hit the dance floor themselves. There was an awkward pause, and Kimmie held her breath because it seemed as if Vronsky wasn't planning to ask her dance. Her entire night flashed before her eyes at the thought, but then he smiled and said, "Come on, you and me?" Kimmie nodded happily and took his hand.

Over by the exit, Dustin watched the whole scene playing out. After hearing Kimmie express her love for another ten minutes ago, he felt ill and broke away from her, heading to the men's room where he splashed water on his face. He told himself he was feeling poorly because of the drugs, but he knew it wasn't that. When Dustin stared at himself in the mirror, he looked deep into his own eyes. He knew he had to put on a brave face, go back out and join the party, but he didn't think he could do it. He would never have come to a party like this if it hadn't been for Kimmie. Now that his dream of her was over, what was the point of him staying?

He was on his way over to say his good-byes when he noticed Vronsky heading toward their group. Like a glutton for punishment, Dustin stopped to watch. It wasn't as though he didn't feel like Kimmie was worthy of Vronsky. But a guy like Vronsky was likely to draw the attention of every girl in the world, so why did it have to be her? From his current vantage point, Dustin could clearly see Vronsky's face as he made his way over to where Kimmie and the rest of them were standing. Dustin recognized the expression in his rival's eyes, the same look he had seen in his own eyes for the last six weeks. Vronsky was a man in love, which meant it was game over for Dustin. His defeat was confirmed less than a minute later as he watched Kimmie taking Vronsky's hand, her face lit up with rapture.

In that moment, Dustin hardened his heart and decided it was time to go.

XXIII

Kimmie was now bouncing with Count Vronsky to the beat of Naughty by Nature's "O.P.P." She would have preferred a different song, once Vronsky explained what the Ps were in O.P.P, maybe one that wasn't about people wanting other people's Ps at all. But she made the best of the situation and tried to stay focused on the positives. She liked that he hadn't dressed in theme and instead wore black slim pants and a Gucci shirt and jacket she could tell was very expensive. His only hint at following the '90s theme was a thick gold clock on a gold chain around his neck.

This was the second time they had danced together, the first being a week ago when they were out getting dessert for their third date and he needed to stop by Le Bain to see one of his friends. They had only stayed at the club for half an hour, but when they were leaving the VIP area after meeting his friend, they had stopped to dance for a few songs. Kimmie suspected he was falling for her because his hands were all over her while they danced.

The two of them were out in the mob of the dance floor next to Lolly and Steven, but Kimmie had slowly edged to the right, wanting to be alone with Vronsky. She kept waiting for him to pull her in close like he did before, but for some reason he wouldn't. He seemed distant and she wasn't sure what the deal was. "Are you okay?" she finally asked, hating always having to yell over the din at nightclubs. He shook his head and apologized, saying he had been out all night two nights ago with his cousin Bea. And then pulled a repeat performance last night with his brother Kiril, who was home from college. He had only woken up a few hours ago to find he had slept through the entire day.

Kimmie forced a smile and nodded, but she couldn't help but ponder what exactly he and his brother had spent all night doing and who they were doing it with. Also, she couldn't imagine ever sleeping through an entire day. When the song ended, she hoped the next one would be better, and it was: Foxy Brown featuring Blackstreet, "Get Me Home."

"I love this song!" Kimmie lied, trying to sound cool. Vronsky nodded, took her by the hand, and walked her back over to Steven and Lolly, who had stopped dancing and were just making out.

"Thanks for the dance, Kimmie. Find me before you go," he said, and with that, Vronsky turned and pushed his way back through the crowd. Kimmie was gobsmacked. The whole thing happened so fast, she didn't have time to hide her feelings. Hot tears welled in her eyes, which she angrily wiped away with the back of her hand. She looked over at her sister, who had missed the whole thing, and Kimmie felt slight relief that at least there were no witnesses to her humiliation. One stupid dance where he barely even looked at her? That's what she had been waiting for all week? WTF?!

Not wanting to ruin her makeup, she knew she had to calm down, or better yet, find a way to forget. She moved toward Steven and tugged on his stupid track suit.

"I want to party," she said. "What do you have?" Steven looked at Lolly to see what she thought. "Don't look at her, she's not the boss of me."

Lolly shrugged, not wanting to deal with her right now.

"Sure, whatever. But if you drop it in the toilet don't come crying back to us for more." Steven pressed something into Kimmie's hand and nodded her toward the direction of the bathrooms. Kimmie nodded and made her way through the crowd, passing Anna who was still dancing in a circle of girls, including Vronsky's cousin, Bea.

While Kimmie waited in line for the bathroom she looked around to see if she could spot Dustin. She thought about texting him but knew she couldn't. Not now after she'd stuck him in the friend zone and told him she was in love with someone else. The fact that she had admitted her feelings so openly and had been so naive as to use the L-word made her feel like crying. But she didn't. She held herself together and patiently waited for her turn to go into the bathroom so she could see what Steven had blessed her with.

If she had texted Dustin, he wouldn't have received it anyway. He was currently on a Bronx-bound subway to see his brother. After leaving the club and walking aimlessly for a few blocks, Dustin had texted Nicholas and asked for his address. When his brother wanted to know why, Dustin simply replied: Because I'm going to get on the subway right now and we're going to hang. Dustin only had to wait a moment before receiving a pin for his brother's location.

Besides the zoo when he was younger, Dustin had never been to the Bronx before. He had no idea what kind of neighborhood his brother was living in, or whether it was safe to go there at this time of night.

Dustin had thought about whether he should text Kimmie and let her know he'd left, but ultimately decided against it. She was a smart girl who must have known what she was doing, and she had dashed all his hopes. Dustin knew he had to let his dream go now, because he was smart, too and knew when to cut his losses. The only problem he had now was how he could turn off his feelings with the flip of a switch. He wondered how long it would take to get over something that never really began. He hoped Nicholas might have the answer.

XXIV

Anna hadn't spent much time in nightclubs because they were not her boyfriend's scene. Sure, she had been to a few over-the-top bar mitzvahs and sweet sixteens like this one, but she normally stayed in the VIP area at such soirees where she sat and watched. She was astonished by how much fun she was having dancing with Beatrice and her friends. She liked being a part of something larger than herself, as if the thump of the music was the heartbeat of a bigger organism, and she was just one of the cells. She was getting sweaty and was certain her hair was now atrociously unkempt, but it felt so good not to care.

When Anna felt someone come up behind her and start dancing a little too close she let it go on for a few seconds before she turned and confirmed what she already knew. It was Alexia. A smile escaped before she could stop it and without a word Vronsky put his hand on her lower back and pulled her close. She let him. He smelled incredible, like the time she walked through Muir Woods on a trip to San Francisco with her parents and declared she had never smelled air so clean and piney pure. "Is this what the air is supposed to smell like?" she had asked. Her parents laughed in response. She echoed the same statement in her head now. *Is this what boys are supposed to smell like?* She closed her eyes and kept dancing, because it was as if she had no other choice but to do so.

She lost track of how many songs they danced to together, as each song kept bleeding into the next. She didn't notice when Beatrice and her friends left, but eventually she noticed the two of them were alone. They still hadn't spoken to each other, but really there were no words that could express what was going on between them. They were both sweating, but neither noticed or cared. At times, both of Vronsky's hands were on her back, and at times she ran her fingers through his golden hair. Sometimes he spun her around, spooning her and putting his face in the back of her neck, wrapping his arms around her waist. They moved together to the beat of the music. Either of them could only stand this for so long before one would pull back slightly, but it never lasted. Any amount of distance felt too far, and soon they were pressed up against one another staring into each other's eyes. Anna was desperate to kiss him, to have him kiss her, but she knew that was the line she couldn't cross. So instead she pressed her face into the side of his neck and breathed in his scent.

If someone saw them dancing together, they would just see two beautiful teenagers having a good time on the dance floor. There were hundreds of others around them in various states of intoxication and no one cared. What they cared about was feeling good, dancing with their friends, and the next song.

Lolly pointed them out to Steven, but they were rolling hard, so seeing Anna dancing with Vronsky didn't mean much. If Lolly were asked about it the next day, she wouldn't really be able to say what she had seen because while it looked like they were dancing a little too long and a little too close, all she could feel was happy about it. Steven was thrilled, too, not because Anna was dancing with Vronsky, but because his sister looked happier than he had seen her look in a long time. That was all that mattered, all that Steven wanted from a night on the town: everyone he loved reveling in the good life and saying fuck everything for the night, just like him.

While this was happening, Kimmie was in the middle of her own good time as she had met some bitchin' girls in the bathroom line and, using all the skills she had learned from her competitive ice dancing days, stuffed down her emotions, put on her game face, and decided to get into character. Performance was all about commitment, and tonight she was committed to acting exactly like what she appeared to be—the third hottest sophomore on this year's Hot List. And clearly it worked because she was noticed and a gaggle of other hot girls asked if she was holding. She nodded yes and said she was happy to share. And just like that, there were four pairs of designer heels standing around a dirty bathroom stall passing around a vial of cocaine. The trio were juniors at Nightingale and thanks to them, Kimmie had made a full recovery from her earlier rejection by Vronsky on the dance floor.

When the girls found out that she was Lolly's little sister, the same Lolly who was the boyfriend of Steven K., the girls were supes impressed. Only one of them out of the whole group had scored an invite to Steven's New Year's party this past year, so she and Kimmie took turns telling the other two all about it. Now completely zooted, Kimmie told them about her first time doing Molly when she ended up in Steven's mom's bathtub. Everyone screamed in delight over her story, and eventually the four girls hit the dance floor.

Kimmie realized she had been wrong about dancing in an all-female pack. It was way more fun than dancing with a boy because you were free to just rock out to the music without caring if you had never heard of the song before or if your hair was stuck in your lip gloss. They soon got into a pattern where they'd dance for five songs in a row, and then they'd march back to the ladies' room handicap stall.

When Kimmie next checked her phone, it was past three in the morning and she couldn't believe it. She decided she needed to go check in with her sister, and the vial was empty so her new friends started murmuring that it was time for them to head out. (Blow is better shared, while the come-down is best suffered through alone.) Kimmie found Lolly sitting at the main bar, posting a few pics from the night on her Instagram. The two of them hugged when they saw each other and even took a rare sister selfie, and then laughed, knowing their newfound sibling affection was absolutely the result of drugs.

Lolly said Steven wanted to eat, so the plan was to go find a diner. Kimmie said she wasn't hungry but was up to tag along for the ride. She began to tell her sister about the new friends she made and Lolly said she was pleased Kimmie had managed to have fun after all.

"What does that mean?" Kimmie asked. "After all what?"

Lolly squinted her eyes at her phone, distracted. "Oh, I thought maybe you left because of him."

"Him? Him who?" Kimmie asked, more than a little confused. "Lolly, focus."

Lolly looked up from her phone, now annoyed. "Kimmie, if this is what you're like after a few toots, I don't know if I like it."

"Sorry, I just don't know who you're talking about. Did something happen with Dustin?"

"Dustin?" It was now Lolly's turn to be confused. "God, we haven't seen him since we got here. I think he left ages ago. I meant Vronsky." Lolly pointed to the dance floor, and Kimmie turned and looked, immediately zeroing in on them. Anna and Vronsky were dancing together in the middle of the floor, not a millimeter of space between them. It appeared as if they both had their eyes closed.

Kimmie felt sick, but she couldn't tear her eyes away from them. They were dancing together like they were the only people in the club, oblivious to everything around them. But it was more than that—it was like they were magnetically attached, unable to be ripped apart. She tore her eyes away only when she felt her hot tears running down her cheeks. Kimmie grabbed a napkin off the bar, told Lolly she had to pee, and made a run for the bathroom. It was there in the same stall where earlier she had had so much fun that Kimmie let out everything she was feeling and cried and cried.

Lolly found her later and told her sister through the stall door that it was time to go. Kimmie couldn't bear to face anyone. She would find her own ride home. Lolly banged on the door and refused. It was much too late for that. Kimmie was to "get her shit together, get it all together and put it in a backpack, all your shit, so it's together," and meet them by the exit in ten minutes. As Lolly walked away she flippantly announced her quote was from *Rick and Morty*. This only added more salt to Kimmie's open wounds and she screamed back, "I hate you!" But her words were lost in the sounds of someone puking one stall over.

Lolly banged on the stall door fifteen minutes later, totally irate, and Kimmie saw she wasn't alone. She recognized Anna's go-go boots when she looked under the stall. Even though she knew she looked like a wreck, Kimmie opened the door anyway. Both Lolly and Anna were shocked at her appearance but neither said a word as she pushed past them. Kimmie heard them whispering to each other and turned back to them. "If we're fucking going, let's fucking go!" she hissed and then walked out of the bathroom, not caring anymore what they, or anyone else, might think of her.

XXV

Anna of course knew immediately when she saw Kimmie's tearstained face what had happened, and her guilt over her part in the matter came at her fast and furious. She had been astounded when she saw it was close to four in the morning, which meant she had been dancing for the last several hours with Vronsky. If someone had told her it had only been ten minutes, she would have believed it, their time together had flown by so fast.

Lolly, wanting to cover for her sister's behavior, blamed it on the fact that Kimmie was on coke for the first time and was probably suffering a harsh come-down. Anna didn't correct Lolly's assumption and instead told her she had just decided she wasn't going to go home with them after all but would shut down the party with Beatrice and then take the 5:45 A.M. train back to Greenwich. Anna asked Lolly to tell Steven and Kimmie good-bye for her. Lolly nodded and left, secretly excited she and Steven now had the entire apartment to themselves, since Steven's parents were in Greenwich for the weekend for a charity function at the country club. Steven had whispered something to her about "christening" every room, and Lolly was more than game to do so.

Anna spent a few minutes at the mirrors. She was completely devoid of makeup from all the sweaty dancing and her '90s crimped hair was all sorts of crazy, but when she viewed her reflection the girl looking back was not a hot mess. If anything, Anna looked more alive and jubilant than she had seen herself in forever. She reminded herself that she had been basically doing cardio for the last several hours, so that was probably the cause. But even as she thought this, she knew better. This look she had; it was something special.

She dawdled in the bathroom for a while, waiting for the others to leave. The last thing she wanted was to face Kimmie again, seeing her anguish and betrayal. Steven, Lolly, and Kimmie were gone by the time she exited, and the party was winding down. She found Vronsky talking to Jaylen, the birthday girl, sitting with her father and his celeb friends. She studied him for a moment marveling at how at ease he was, so confidently himself, no matter who he was with. He spotted her and waved her to come close, holding out his hand. She took it and slid beside him onto the couch.

The DJ announced they were playing the last few songs. Vronsky looked at Anna, and she nodded. She had never closed a bar down let alone an entire nightclub, so she was more than willing. Besides, she didn't feel tired at all.

The dance floor was alive again as revelers crowded the floor. They were all showing off for one another, dancing as a group. Vronsky whispered to Anna that seeing these basketball legends dance to "Rump Shaker" was something he would remember forever. When the last song came on, everyone screamed and threw their hands in the air. It was Heavy D & The Boyz' "Now That We Found Love," and Vronsky pulled Anna back into his arms, holding her close. He knew all the words, which made her laugh, and when the chorus started up she really took in the words, *Now that we found love what are we gonna do . . . with it?* There was no more perfect song for them than this one.

After the song ended, they walked toward the coat check hand in hand. Anna, still unable to forget Kimmie's face, grew somber, and Vronsky asked her what was wrong. "I'm sad the night is ending," she told him.

He nodded and said, "It doesn't have to end now. We could go get pancakes."

Anna shook her head and said in a quiet voice, "We can't. I don't even think we should leave together."

Vronsky frowned and said no way was he letting her go home alone at this hour. That was when she told him she wasn't going back to her New York apartment, but was heading back to Greenwich on the first train. Vronsky looked confused, but he didn't question her about it. Instead he told her he needed to hit the restroom and asked her to wait for him. She said okay and watched him walk off, all the while knowing that by the time he came back, she would be gone.

An hour later, all traces of the sexy party-girl version of herself were gone except the lingering sparkle in her eyes. She had planned to take a car back to Greenwich when she left the club, but instead she started walking. Her dad would have been ripshit if he knew she was walking around alone in the dark, but as it was five in the morning the streets were totally empty. She had never experienced the city this way before, and she found it quite beautiful in its silence. Bundled up in a Loro Piana cashmere coat, Anna was now on the first train of the morning, which was mostly empty. She picked a window seat, put her feet up on the seat across from her, and yawned. When the train emerged out of the tunnel into the early morning daylight, she found herself feeling a little blue. She pulled out her phone, which she had ignored all evening, and saw that she had several missed calls from Alexander and two voice mails, which quickly brought her back to reality. She texted Alexander to tell him she was on the train heading back to Greenwich to see her dogs and go to bed, letting him know she'd call him whenever she woke up. Normally she added a heart emoji to the texts she sent him, but this time she sent her text without one. Such a small detail, she was sure he wouldn't even notice.

When she looked out the window, she saw that it was snowing again. She leaned her forehead against the cool glass, watching the snowflakes until she fell asleep with a dreamy smile on her face.

She awoke with a start when the train jolted to a stop. Disoriented for a moment, Anna looked out the window to see the snow had turned to freezing rain. They weren't stopped at a station but were delayed on the track. Her car was empty except for one other person, who was asleep and snoring. She stood up, wondering what was going on, and decided to find out. In the next car over she found a uniformed employee who informed her that the heavy, wet snow had caused a tree branch to fall on the tracks ahead of them and there would be a slight delay while they waited for someone to clear the debris.

Anna walked back through the cars in a daze, yawning and sleepy. She was suddenly starving and decided to get a hot chocolate and a donut from the café car. Right as she was about to pay, someone put a fifty on the counter and said, "The lady's breakfast is on me." She whipped around to see Vronsky standing behind her. Her eyes widened in surprise, and she felt a rush of conflicting emotions. Of course she was happy to see him, more than happy, ecstatic even . . . but what did he think he was doing? He ordered himself a hot chocolate, too, and soon the two of them were seated across from each other in the first empty car they could find.

"What are you doing on this train?" she asked.

"I have to be where you are, so here I am. Plus, you didn't even say good-bye."

Anna blushed. "I didn't know what to say."

"Good-bye would have worked," he said teasingly.

"Alexia, this is madness. You have to go back to the city."

"I can't," he said, shaking his head. "I need to be here with you."

"I have a boyfriend. And everyone knows him in Greenwich."

"And I have an aunt and uncle there who are always happy to host their favorite nephew for as long as he would like."

"What about Kimmie?" Anna asked, as she was starting to feel a little panicky over the emotions swirling around her head. "She's so cute. You could be with her."

"Now you're the one being crazy," he said. "Kimmie's sweet, but I'm not interested. I'm interested in someone else." He was nothing if not direct, and it was sexy.

Anna's phone dinged, which she found odd given the early hour. It was a text from Alexander, asking her why her train was delayed. Staring at the bubbles on her screen, she was suddenly scared of what he was going to say next. The text that came in was the worst news possible. He said he was unable to sleep after their fight and decided to drive into the city to see her. He had stopped in Greenwich to get gas and breakfast when her text came in stating she was on the train. He said he was now at the station, waiting to pick her up.

"Oh god, Alexander is at the station. Waiting for me. He drove in because we had a . . ." She looked up breathlessly and met Vronsky's eyes. "Never mind, it's not important. What's important is you can't do this. We can't do this."

Vronsky reached across the table and took her hands in his own. "Anna, you know it's too late. It's happened already."

"What's happened? Nothing's happened! We danced together at a club, so what? We did nothing wrong." She pulled her hands from his and stood up quickly, accidentally spilling her hot chocolate. "Alexia, if you care about me at all you'll forget about this whole night." Anna started to walk off, but before she got to the end of the car, she stopped and turned around to face him. "I'm sorry I didn't say good-bye earlier. I couldn't bring myself to do it, because it meant our time together was over and I wasn't ready for it to be." She stood there staring at him staring at her and forced herself to continue. "But it's over now."

And with that she turned away from him and walked to the next train car. Count Vronsky sat very still, the only sound the dripping of her spilled hot chocolate, the only proof she had been there at all.

XXVI

Dustin awoke in the Bronx on a green pleather love seat in his brother Nicholas's tiny room in the Meyerson Halfway House above the taco shop before 6 A.M. on Sunday morning. The couch smelled of cigarette smoke mixed with sour mustard plus the collective stench of all the others who had crashed there before him. Three slashes of morning light shone through the broken plastic venetian blinds of an otherwise dark room. Dustin sat up slowly because he could hear Nicholas's raspy breathing.

When Dustin arrived the night before, he found his brother the sole employee of a tiny storefront called Taco Taco! When he entered the front door of the restaurant, if you could even call the dingy ten-by-ten room a restaurant, it was empty. The whole thing consisted of an orange counter and three sets of tables and chairs in varying degrees of disrepair. He checked his phone again, even though he knew he was in the right place. Dustin took a seat and his brother appeared moments later, smelling like cigarettes.

"Yo, what up?" Nicholas said as if Dustin weren't his younger brother by three years. "Ya hungry?" Dustin's stomach rumbled in the affirmative before he could open his mouth to speak. He nodded an emphatic yes.

"You still eatin' meat, right? You didn't go all hipster vegan on me, didja?" Nicholas chuckled glumly.

Dustin found his words. "Not me. I'll always be a carnivore." He added a few half-hearted wild boar–like snorts for a sound effect, but lost steam midway through the bit.

A half smile curling up his lip, Nicholas turned his back on Dustin and began to cook. He was making a taco platter because, well, that was all that was offered at Taco Taco! The silence continued through most of the meal, as Nicholas watched Dustin wolf down six soft tacos, barely pausing to chew. Only as Dustin was washing down his late-night meal with a Mexican Coke, did Nicholas finally speak. "Man, you're eatin' like y'got a hole inside that needs fillin'. I should know. Though, tacos wouldn't cut it for me. Hell, I'm pretty sure after working here I won't ever eat a taco again."

"How long have you been working here?" Dustin asked.

"Not even two weeks but it feels like two years. I work the late shift. Ten P.M. til five A.M. It stays kinda hoppin' til about three, but the last two hours are fuckin' killer."

Dustin nodded, even though it was hard to empathize with his brother. Dustin's only employment to date was tutoring rich kids in twenty-million-dollar apartments. "I thought you had another month in the program."

Nicholas explained he'd had another three weeks left in his three-month rehab stint, but he was released early on good behavior. What this meant for other people was they had excelled in the program and were granted an early exit, but Nicholas rarely behaved.

"So, you got kicked out?" Dustin asked, careful not to add the word "again" to the end of his question for fear of sounding judgmental.

"Uh-uh, took the fall for someone else." Nicholas said this in a way to show that was all there was to know for now. He grabbed Dustin's plate, heading back into the kitchen. "More?"

"No, thank you," Dustin replied, wincing at his own politeness. His mouth stung from the salsa, and he now hankered for something else to fill his void. "Anything sweet back there?"

"Nothing sweeter than me," Nicholas responded, laughing at his own sarcasm.

Dustin looked up to see his brother already returning with a paper plate of churros and a plastic honey-bear in his hands. Nicholas set the plate down in front of Dustin with a satisfied grunt. "Some things never change," he muttered.

Dustin grabbed a warm churro and bit into its sugary sweetness, pleased that his brother remembered his sweet tooth. "You bake these?" he asked with his mouth full.

"If by bake you mean I take them out of the freezer and fry the fuckers up in oil, then yeah. They're fresh, though. Someone called in a take-out but didn't show. Fuckin' tweakers, I should know better, right?"

Dustin squeezed honey onto the second churro and kept eating until they were all gone. His fingers were now sticky, but he stopped himself from licking them, remembering his long subway ride. "Can I wash up?"

His brother pointed him behind the counter, and Dustin went to the small EMPLOYEES ONLY toilet room that doubled as a supply closet. He avoided his reflection after he washed his hands, dried them quickly, and went back out to find his brother staring at his phone.

"Who'd you take the fall for?" Dustin asked, wanting to keep the conversation on his brother's life instead of his own. His brother was stingy with his words and was more the brooding silent type. He watched as Nicholas pulled out a bag of tobacco and rolled a cigarette at the table-top. Dustin's mouth twitched even though he didn't smoke often. He thought about how the only times he ever smoked were with his brother and at late-night study groups where students were open to anything to help keep them awake.

"Shall we?" Nicholas asked, holding up two perfectly rolled cigs.

They smoked out front on the sidewalk, Dustin leaning against the metal gate pulled down over the storefront, while his brother paced on the sidewalk before him. Dustin gazed out at the grimy street, litter trapped in the dirty melting slush. Fortified by nicotine, Nicholas told Dustin he had met a methhead from Arizona in rehab, Natalia, and she was the one who got busted with drugs. They were together when she got caught with them, so he took the blame. Nicholas added he had been clean for two and a half months already and was ready to get sprung anyway. Their dad had been informed and had shown up the next day and the two of them, father and son, had flown back East together in absolute silence. He tried to tell their dad that the drugs weren't his, but his words fell on deaf ears. "Never trust a junkie, I guess," Nicholas said, signaling his story was over by dropping his butt onto the sidewalk and stubbing it out with his shoe.

Dustin believed his brother's story, even though Nicholas was known for embellishing the truth for his own purposes. Dustin now understood the lengths a guy would go for the right girl.

"You going to see her again?" Dustin asked, hoping perhaps there could be a happy ending for at least one of them.

"She's supposed to text when she gets out. We'll see. Natalia ain't the most reliable chick I ever met," Nicholas replied, walking back into the restaurant.

"Never trust a junkie, I guess," Dustin added in an attempt to be jovial. He followed his brother and yawned, suddenly tired now that his belly was full. Nicholas pulled out a ring of keys from his jeans and handed them to Dustin, gesturing upward. "My room's upstairs. Can't beat the commute. Bathroom's in the hallway but be quiet in there because the guy next to the toilet is a real dickhead if you wake him up. He's got the morning shift here, so he's gotta get up at four thirty."

Dustin grabbed his paper plate and tossed it in the trash can on the side wall, trying to decide what he should do. He had texted his dad that he'd be home in the morning, so it was not like anyone was waiting up for him. Dustin took the keys from his brother and pulled out his wallet.

Nicholas shook his head. "On me, little bro. Go get some shut-eye, you'll buy me breakfast in the morning when I get up. Someplace that doesn't serve tacos."

Dustin had fallen asleep within minutes of curling up on the couch, his heartbreak covering him like a blanket. He didn't even remember hearing his brother come in several hours later.

The next morning, Dustin stood up from the couch and crossed over to the window to stare out at the soot-stained brick wall across the air shaft. It was a new day, and no one was more thankful that yesterday was over than he was. He thought about whether he would tell his brother about Kimmie over breakfast. He doubted his brother would be sympathetic to his plight, but Dustin didn't care. It wasn't comfort he was after. Dustin only wanted to purge himself of any remaining feelings for her, and then he never wanted to think about Kimmie again.

XXVII

The debris was cleared from the train tracks after twenty minutes, and the wheels slowly came to life and began to inch forward. Anna was relieved to be on her way again, but at the same time felt sharp pinpricks of anxiety, unsure of how she felt about where she was heading. She had taken the train to Greenwich thousands of times in her life, but this was the only trip she could remember where she was brimming with dread. *Funny how one night can change everything,* she thought to herself, but quickly followed it with a different reflection. *Nothing is different. I'll soon be at the same station where I always get off. My boyfriend will be waiting for me ready to apologize for our tiff with hot coffee and a chocolate croissant. He'll drive me home and my dogs will be waiting in the foyer windows, their wet noses smudging the glass. I'll have to brace myself against the door so they won't knock me over in their excitement.*

But even as she told herself what was to come, a secret part of her wondered where he was on the train. Did Vronsky clean up her spilled hot chocolate or did he just walk away from it? He cleaned it up; she knew he did. He was spoiled as they all were with money and servants, but when out in public his good manners would insist upon the cleanup of any mess he made. It was her mess technically, but it was because of him. He was the one who'd said all those things to her, sharing his feelings with no thought of consequence. Anna reminded herself she had never agreed, never said anything back to him. She had done nothing to encourage Vronsky to say those things; in fact, she had tried to make sure they were never said at all, leaving the party without saying good-bye as she did.

If she had stayed to talk to him at the club, what would have happened? Would he have been more understanding that she needed to go back to Greenwich? That she needed the peace of her own bed after a night of dancing with him? Anna couldn't recall the last time she had stayed up all night. Even at slumber parties as a kid, she was the girl who fell asleep first. She had no fear of missing out on anything and never hesitated to leave the other girls gossiping about cute teachers, new clothes, and all the parties they weren't old enough to attend.

In fact, this year she hadn't even attended her own brother's New Year's Eve party. Instead she had opted to stay in Maui with her parents and Alexander. The two of them rang in the New Year alone in the heated saline pool at the luxury resort near her parents' beach house. Now she remembered, Alexander had not even kissed her at midnight. A tropical breeze had blown a beach ball into the pool a minute before and Alexander had chased after it. He always did the right thing, her boyfriend. Picking up litter and throwing it away. Recycling to save the planet. He was the one who had made sure their school started composting in the cafeteria, just one of his many rulings as school president. When she had seen the beach ball land near them, her first thought had been what sound it would make if she popped it.

So when the New Year arrived, she was on one side of the pool and he was on the other. Anna thought about the maxim that it was bad luck not to kiss someone at the stroke of midnight, which she told Alexander later, when they walked along the dark beach back to her parents' place.

He had responded there was no such thing as bad luck, but then turned and asked in a teasing voice, "Does someone need a kiss?" Anna remembered she wished Alexander had just grabbed her and kissed her in the moment, as opposed to always having to discuss everything.

Anna was surprised Alexander had chosen to drive down from Boston to see her today. Being spontaneous was not his way, as he was usually scheduled down to the quarter hour. This impromptu road trip of his would surely disrupt his entire weekend. Anna wondered whether he'd detected something in her voice when he called before she had left for the party.

When the train screeched to a stop in Greenwich, the platform was empty, and Anna was hopeful that Alexander had chosen to stay in his car waiting for her. She hurried off the train, pulling up the hood of her coat so she wouldn't look around like a horse who needed blinders to be guided forward. She half ran, half walked in the direction of the parking lot when she heard Alexander call out her name. "Anna!" She bit her lip, and, keeping her face relaxed, turned.

There he was, her boyfriend, bundled in his navy Ralph Lauren parka over his pressed khakis, waving at her. Alexander wasn't wearing a hat, so his hair was wet from the snow and flattened on his head. *His ears . . .* she thought to herself, *have they always been so big?*

Alexander walked up and hugged her, kissing her still warm cheek with his cold, thin lips.

"You made it," he said, stating the obvious.

Anna fought to keep her composure. *Be nice,* she told herself, *this has nothing to do with him.* She grabbed his arm and tried to move him along, afraid to linger a moment longer than necessary.

"I brought you coffee and a croissant. Chocolate of course," Alexander said, not budging. *Of course you did,* Anna thought. *Never a surprise from you!* "Maybe that will make you happier to see me?" He was teasing her, but she couldn't help but feel like he was admonishing her for not appearing more pleased.

She forced a smile. "Thank you. Though I'm desperate to sleep, so you can have my coffee."

"What a surprise!" Vronsky's voice sounded from behind them. Anna shut her eyes, at once furious Vronsky would dare to do this right now and elated she would get to see his face again. She turned slowly and there he was, standing before her, his unruly scarf once again touching the ground. If she reached out her hand, she could touch his face. He was so close to her and yet there was a vast chasm between them.

Alexander looked confused at the young man standing before them and put his arm around his girlfriend's shoulders. Anna stepped to the side, shaking off his hand. "We were on the same train?" she said softly, framing her words as a question for her boyfriend's benefit.

"Alexander, this is Alex Vronsky. Beatrice's cousin from the city. Alex, this is my boyfriend, Alexander." Her words came out in a rush and she tried hard not to stare at Vronsky for too long, knowing she wouldn't be able to keep a smile off her face.

"Oh, yes. Pleasure to meet you," Alexander said, shaking Vronsky's hand after taking off his charcoal mittens. "What brings you to Greenwich so early?" His voice was low and serious as if he alone oversaw all who entered his city. Anna, normally not a catty girl, couldn't help rolling her eyes as she took in the scene before her. *What man wears mittens? Just because your half-sister knitted them for you, doesn't mean you have to wear them. Why must you always placate Eleanor like she's still a child?*

"I missed my uncle's birthday dinner a few nights ago and decided to surprise him," Vronsky replied, so casually that Anna herself had a moment of doubt wondering if perhaps this was his reason for being on the train, and not her. "He gets up early, my uncle." Vronsky proceeded to mimic a golf swing, which if he held a club would have conveniently brained Alexander.

"You left with the mother and came back with the son," Alexander reported with a tight smile, pleased at himself for his wit. He glanced at Anna like a proud dog that had just laid a stick at her feet.

Anna nodded and tightened her grip on Alexander's arm, suggesting it was time for them to leave. She was desperate for this torture to be over. If she didn't leave now she was afraid of what she might do. She was feeling so odd, so unlike herself. *You're just tired. You haven't had enough sleep. Everything is fine. Just say good-bye and then you can forget this whole ridiculous night.*

"It was nice seeing you again, Alex," she stammered. "Please wish your uncle happy birthday from me." Before she turned away, she allowed herself to look at him once more, full in the face, though she couldn't have resisted if she tried. Vronsky met her eyes with his own, and Anna was struck by their blueness against the overcast gray of the day. God, what she wouldn't give to dive into them and swim away.

Part Two

I

Valentine's Day is fraught with emotion for everyone, but for teenage girls it's the fucking worst.

It was a holiday with the sole purpose of shining a spotlight on romantic love, which tortured single people but also tormented those who were in relationships. In a way, it was almost easier to get through if a girl was single, because one could denounce the entire thing as a colossal waste of time, pointing out the fact that it was an arbitrary holiday made up by Hallmark to sell more greeting cards in 1913. This of course wasn't entirely true. St. Valentine's Day had much darker roots, originating in the third century A.D. in Rome as a day for matchmaking that involved the bloody sacrifice of animals, beating women to increase their fertility, and getting drunk and partying in the streets.

"Well, the getting drunk part will certainly be true for you and Steven," Kimmie said, after her sister Lolly read the Wikipedia entry out loud to her and their mother during breakfast.

"Bitter much?" Lolly quickly retorted, knowing better than to get into it with Kimmie before her mother finished her first Lavazza espresso of the day. Danielle, their mother, was not a morning person, and probably hadn't even heard Kimmie's dig anyway.

Kimmie didn't respond, mainly because her sister had spoken the truth. She was feeling incredibly depressed and had barely been able to drag herself to the breakfast table this morning, let alone change out of her pajamas. Kimmie had not gone to school for the last three days and was hoping for the same today.

Kimmie was never a kid who faked illness, and in fact had always been a paragon of health, so her mother had no reason to doubt her daughter's complaints of headache and general achiness. It also helped that Kimmie's mother was in a wonderfully distracted mood since returning Sunday night from her Saint Lucia vacation with her new boyfriend, David. Twelve days of couple's massages, romantic walks on the beach, and candlelit dinners were almost enough to expunge the bitter taste of her divorce, or so Danielle thought until her ex-husband Kurt answered the door on Sunday night when she came to pick up the girls. Just seeing her ex-husband's spray-tanned face smirking at her own freshly sunned face in the doorway was enough to make her clench her teeth. It was then that she heard from their father about her youngest daughter's illness, how she had been complaining all week of not feeling well, finally being sent home early on Friday. "Did you take her to the doctor?" she asked, knowing his answer already.

"Nope. She had no fever, so I figured it was just a virus. I let her sleep all weekend," he said.

Not wanting to ruin her relaxed island vibe, Danielle didn't press him further and instead took the girls back to her apartment on Beekman Place. Kimmie went straight to bed after her temperature was checked, not even feeling up to hearing one story from her mother's trip or seeing what goodies her mother had returned with. Lolly stayed up with her mom, oohing and ahhing over her pictures, all the while wondering if perhaps this would be the year she'd be invited to travel with Steven's family to their house in Maui for the Christmas holidays. After Lolly opened her gifts—a new bikini, a new bikini wrap, and two-hundred-dollar Swarovski crystal mermaid-blue Havaianas (to wear after pedis instead of the gross freebies they give out)—her mother inquired about Jaylen's sweet sixteen last weekend to find out if there was a connection to Kimmie's illness.

Lolly was no fool, as she knew she would be held responsible for any of her sister's questionable behavior, so she wisely hinted at boy troubles being the cause of the state of Kimmie's health. "She'll get over it, but it's the absolute worst timing ever. Valentine's Day is Thursday."

It was Thursday now and bad timing or not, Danielle knew she couldn't keep her daughter absent for one day longer without a doctor's note. "Kimmie, get dressed," Danielle said, not looking up from her iPhone. "Dr. Becker's office squeezed you in, so we can't be late."

"Do I have to?" Kimmie whined in return. "Can't I see him tomorrow?"

"No. You know I play doubles on Fridays and it's too late for me to find a sub. Now scoot." Danielle pointed to the door. After a big dramatic sigh Kimmie stood up and trudged out of the kitchen.

"Are you sure you want to take her out today?" Lolly whispered. "You can't go anywhere in this city without seeing a delivery guy carrying flowers or balloons."

Danielle grimaced, but then shook her head. "This whole thing can't be over a silly boy. I want to get her tested for Lyme disease. I never should have let her recoup from her knee surgery with your father at what's-her-tits's Vermont cabin this summer." Not wanting to ignore her other daughter, she asked, "So where is Steven taking you tonight?"

Lolly's face lit up, and a wide smile spread across her face. "It's a surprise. But I was hoping I could come home late tonight, please, Mom?"

Danielle nodded, knowing she'd be late herself from her own Valentine's Day date. "Okay, but you better be home by midnight. Devon's coming over to stay with Kimmie, so I'll call if I'm not home by then. On Devon's cell, not yours."

Lolly nodded, pleased with the midnight curfew as she had been hoping for eleven thirty. Lolly had lied to her mother's face, because she *did* know where she and Steven were having dinner: room service at the St. Regis hotel where Steven had booked them a room for the night. Their plan was to ditch school after fourth period and meet there by 2 P.M., which would give them a good ten hours of "celebration time." Lolly had a red lace bra-and-panty set on under her Alice and Olivia dress as part of her present for Steven. She was going to do an elaborate striptease to "Love" by Kendrick Lamar that she had choreographed with a red leather Agent Provocateur riding crop she had bought on a whim when buying her new lingerie.

She also got Steven a new Apple Watch since she'd smashed his last one to bits using the marble base of the towel warming rack in Steven's parents' bathroom. She bought herself one, too, but chose matching stingray ullu bands instead of Hermès. She was still a smidge conflicted about the present but reminded herself she had forgiven him and perhaps it would be an apt reminder he could wear every day.

Lolly gave her mother a big hug before she left for school, wishing her a happy Valentine's Day. "Text me after the doctor and tell me what's up with Kimmie, okay?" she added, genuinely concerned about her little sister, at least for a moment. Lolly suspected that there was no hope of Kimmie getting better until this day was over and done with. After all, what girl wanted to be reminded there wasn't a boy out there thinking of her the way Lolly knew Steven was thinking about her?

II

Anna was checking in at the front office of Greenwich Academy before homeroom because she had received an excused absence to attend the Westminster Dog Show in Manhattan. She had missed a half day of school the day before so she could see both her dogs show in their gender-specific Newfoundland breed groups. Gemma, failing to win top honors as Best Bitch, had received the Award of Merit, which, though still an honor, meant she wouldn't advance further. But her brother, Jon Snow, short for "Jon Snow of the Wall," had won Best of Breed. This meant he would advance and would be shown in the Working Dog group, which was to be judged at noon. If he won there, he'd advance to the main event of the evening, where he would compete for Best in Show on national television. Anna knew the competition was stiff and told herself she'd be fine if Jon Snow didn't win, and that she should consider herself blessed to have gotten this far. She planned to stay and watch the festivities til the final dog won the polished pewter gallery bowl and was declared Best in Show.

She turned in her homework to May, the front office secretary, who was dressed in red from her shoes to her velvet red headband. "Don't forget to check in at the theater . . ."

Greenwich Academy had instituted a new policy the Valentine's Day of Anna's freshman year that prohibited girls from receiving deliveries during classes. Being a school filled with predominantly wealthy girls, there was a lot of pressure on their boyfriends to send outrageously excessive gifts. It became competitive. (For years the Brunswick boys joked about V-Day having more casualties than D-Day, as some Academy girls broke off entire relationships if their beloved beaus didn't come through with something truly breathtaking, or worse presented a subpar gift that underwhelmed its recipient.)

It all came to a head three years ago when flying in Ecuadorian roses for your girlfriend had suddenly become de rigueur, unbeknownst to some of Brunswick's less attentive boyfriends, and Mavis C. called out Bridget B. on it: "Hey Bridget, I heard your roses aren't even from Ecuador!" The two girls went after each other with field hockey sticks in the hallway and the fight resulted in a bloody lip, a fractured collarbone, and fifteen stitches. (HEY BRIDGET . . . T-shirts and hats were later sold, raising two grand for the Senior Skip Day trip.) The school's Valentine's Day policy now dictated that deliveries could only arrive at 8 A.M., noon, and 2 P.M. and were sent to the school's performing arts center. Girls were permitted to see (but not post pics of) whatever was sent to them, but nothing could be removed from the theater until the end of the school day.

When Anna walked into the school's five-hundred-seat theater, she was overwhelmed by the smell of roses. As it was close to the first-period bell, the theater wasn't that crowded anymore. Anna walked up to Coach Sykes, who was on morning flower duty and wearing a lavender HEY BRIDGET T-shirt. Coach Sykes scanned her clipboard and told Anna she had two deliveries. Anna explained that she was leaving for the day so she'd be taking them with her now. She signed by her name and was told her gifts were in the number eleven section onstage.

For the past two years, Alexander had sent Anna a box of two dozen long-stemmed red roses, but she had specifically told him not to bother when they'd had dinner on Sunday night. She had taken the train to Westport to meet him at their favorite French bistro for a pre-Valentine's Day meal and they'd celebrate again in two weeks when she went to Cambridge to visit him. As usual they were the youngest people in the restaurant and Alexander had arranged for roses to arrive for her during dessert. Alexander was always thoughtful, but somehow his gestures never felt very romantic, which Anna couldn't quite explain.

The big fuss over Valentine's Day was not something Anna fully got. Sure, she understood the appeal of flowers and presents, but at the age of seventeen she had received more incredible bouquets than most women would ever get in their lifetimes. And the perfunctory formality of this holiday always made her feel weird and a little hollow at times. Also, depending on her mood, cut flowers made Anna feel melancholy. It seemed sad to watch something so beautiful die just for her own pleasure.

Anna's dad always sent her flowers, too, but this morning they had been waiting for her on the kitchen counter when she came downstairs. His card read: "For my lovely daughter, from the only man who will never disappoint you. Happy Valentine's Day, Anna! Love, Daddy." Her mother had given her a Day of Beauty gift certificate at the Four Seasons spa.

Anna walked up the stairs to the stage covered with dozens and dozens of vases filled with roses, at least forty giant teddy bears, and over a hundred boxes of chocolates. As she sifted through the deliveries, Anna wondered whether perhaps Steven had sent her flowers this year. It wasn't normal for them to exchange gifts, but given Anna's help this past weekend, she wouldn't put it past him. Her brother was an incredibly generous guy, spending money like a madman. Anna never asked her brother about the allowance he received from their parents, but she knew it was larger than hers. That said, she knew her wardrobe budget for the year was double her brother's, so it evened out. Steven explained away his excessive consumerism as being genetic; Koreans had a reputation for loving all designer goods and high-end electronics. Anna knew of this stereotype but never used it as an excuse when her credit card bills came in too high, which was rare for her and a monthly occurrence for her brother.

Her mother had been raised in typical old-money style, never in want of anything, but never ostentatious, though when she met Anna's father at Yale, she admitted he turned her head. Every year of school he showed up with a new fancy car, and by the time they were seniors and he was sporting an orange Lamborghini, she found herself dawdling after class out front, knowing he'd drive by and offer her a ride. She had been resisting his wily charm and refusing rides from him for two years straight. It wasn't that she wasn't interested in him earlier, but she was wise enough to the ways of rich boys to know he needed a few years to play the field.

Anna's mother was raised to care very much about her name and reputation so there was no way she was going to be just another crossed-out name on some rich boy's "fuck-it" list. When he pulled up that fall day of their senior year at Yale and asked her if she wanted to go leaf-peeping with him, she surprised herself (and him) by saying, "Only if you'll let me drive." Anna's mother was the first and only girl who had ever been allowed to drive his Lamborghini, which to this day remained her father's favorite car.

When Steven turned seventeen and got his license, their dad bought him a Porsche 911S with a glass top. Steven drove it for a month, received three speeding tickets, and then woke up one morning to find the car gone, replaced with a BMW M5. Anna drove a ten-year-old Mercedes station wagon, the hand-me-down "nanny's car," insisting she didn't want some flashy car for her sweet sixteen present. Anna knew there was no point in her driving anything nicer when it was only going to get covered in dog hair and slobber. Anna was only permitted to drive in Connecticut, her dad being much too overprotective to let his precious baby girl drive in bad weather or in the city. "Remember, you're still half Korean, which means everyone will assume you're at least half a lousy driver." Anna hated when her father joked about racial stereotypes, but as a good Korean daughter, she knew that correcting her father was impossible.

Finally she found a heart-shaped box addressed to her. She quickly opened the card to see her brother's serial-killer penmanship: "Happy V-Day, Sis. I owe you big! Love, Steven." She turned the box over and saw that he had sent her a dozen of her favorite chocolate mice from Burdick's. She slipped it into her purse and continued looking. Not finding anything, she nearly gave up when she noticed a plain square cardboard box with her name written across the top in Sharpie. She only had time to scoop it up, having just received a text from Thomas, her driver, who was out front waiting to take her to Westminster.

Hurrying down the empty hallway, Anna wondered what was in the box. She had a feeling she knew who it was from, and the thought of him made her heart pound. She almost hoped that it was just some routine gift from her boyfriend but she knew in her gut that wasn't the case. A twinge of guilt at how excited she was that it might not be from Alexander rattled her nerves, but only slightly, not enough to erase the giant smile from her face.

III

Kimmie stood outside the front of her mom's apartment building, waiting for their Uber driver to arrive while Danielle ran back upstairs to get her nearly empty bottle of under-eye cream. Her mom's itinerary was a trip to the doctor's office and then a little shopping at Saks, which was only an avenue away from Dr. Becker's office. Kimmie's plan was a trip to the doctor, a refusal to accompany her mom to Saks, then back home to bed to continue watching *My So-Called Life*, an old high school show she'd found after a deep dive on Netflix.

Kimmie had wanted to wear sweats to the doctor, but her mom wouldn't allow it. According to Kimmie's mom, drawstring pants were the top of a very slippery slope for any teen girl. Her mom had been hypervigilant about her diet ever since she came home, constantly reminding Kimmie that she could no longer eat like someone who trains seven hours a day. Without a word, Kimmie went to her room and changed into black leggings and her oversized black Skull Cashmere sweater, which fit her current mind-set. Her mother's response to her new outfit was not agreeable. "This isn't LA, this is New York. We don't consider SoulCycle tights proper attire. Go change. Maybe into something a little less gloomy?"

Kimmie stomped back to her room, hating her life just a little bit more than she did five minutes before. She replaced her tights with black jeans, but kept her skull-adorned sweater on.

"Seriously?" Kimmie muttered to herself as she saw her fourth Valentine's Day reminder in the two minutes she had been standing outside. There had been one flower delivery van, one bicycle messenger carrying a signature box of long-stemmed roses under his arm, a doorman signing for a basket of pink tulips, and the car that just drove by with a giant red teddy bear in the passenger seat. Staring at the stupid bear, Kimmie didn't know if she wanted to spit on the car window or sit down on the curb and cry. So far today, she had only cried twice, which wasn't bad.

What a difference two weeks could make. As much as Kimmie presently despised this ludicrous holiday, she had spent most of the previous month harboring major Valentine's Day fantasies. Her favorite involved Vronsky showing up at school for her at the end of the day, which of course would have been so delicious because her fellow classmates would have witnessed it. She imagined a scene akin to the last scene in *Sixteen Candles*, her mom's favorite movie from her own teenage years. Kimmie had never heard of it, of course, since it was from the century before she had even been born. (She loved to say this because it made her mother crazy.) But she'd learned about it several years ago when she was back in New York on break from training camp during the year after their dad had married their current Stepmonster. (Kimmie's mom had a rough six months following that unholy pairing.)

Kimmie had come home from the gym in the late afternoon to find her mom still in bed, watching the last minutes of *Sixteen Candles* over and over. But this wasn't a normal viewing; this was something else entirely. Kimmie watched her mom view it seven times in a row and then called Lolly at school. Her sister wasn't answering her cell, so Kimmie called the school's front office and asked them to find her sister in play rehearsal because there was a family emergency.

By the time Lolly got to the phone in the office, she was hysterically crying, assuming someone had died. Kimmie told her older sister to stop blubbering and just listen. Lolly yelled at her younger sister for scaring her and then gave Kimmie her first lesson on how to recognize an Ambien stupor. Lolly's theory was that sometimes when their mom couldn't sleep even after taking an Ambien, she'd take another one in the morning, but then forget. She would then have her usual Nespresso to avoid a caffeine headache and go back to bed. This would produce a weird, chemically induced fugue state where their mother looked like she was awake, but was actually asleep.

"Let me guess," Lolly said. "She's watching TV?"

"Yes!" Kimmie answered.

"What's she watching?"

"Some old movie called *Sixteen Candles*?" Kimmie said. "But she's just watching the last five minutes, and when it ends she lifts her arm up like Frankenstein's ex-wife and rewinds it to the part where the redhead walks out of the church in an ugly dress. She did it like seven times in a row. It's freaking me out."

"Been there, done that, own the T-shirt. Look, I wigged out the first time I saw Mom like that, too. It's totally *Stranger Things* meets *Paranormal Activity* in a four-hundred-dollar bathrobe!" Lolly whispered, because she could tell the nosy office secretary was trying to eavesdrop. "Don't sweat it, she'll stop eventually. But once, years ago, I sat with her when she was watching the Hathaway transformation montage from *The Devil Wears Prada* and she finally agreed to get me a navy Prada mini backpack. So there's bennies, too."

"What's a 'bennies'?" Kimmie asked. Nothing made her feel more like a little sister than not understanding her older sister's coolgirl slang.

"Benefits, dumb ass. Okay, gotta go. And next time, be a normal person and text me instead of calling the school and scaring the shit out of me."

Kimmie, now understanding the deal and feeling sorry for her mom, sat and watched the end of *Sixteen Candles* with her at least ten more times, later taking the DVD and watching the whole thing on her lap-top. Because of that day, those last five minutes of the movie were burned into Kimmie's brain forever.

In Kimmie's updated, Valentine's Day version, she'd be wearing dif-ferent clothes, of course, probably a pink dress, which sounded so basic, but Kimmie couldn't help it if she looked best in a cliché color. Even though Kimmie found the flower crown tired, she had one on like the redhead, only not in such disgusting colors and for sure with zero baby's breath. Once the street cleared, there he'd be. Count Vronsky was for sure her Jake Ryan, and instead of a red Porsche, he'd be leaning against a black Maserati. But Vronsky would do the exact same shy-smile-and-wave that Jake Ryan did. In Kimmie's version she wouldn't do whole "who, me?" thing and look behind her in shock, because Kimmie would *know* he was there for her. And he'd be holding a heart-shaped box of chocolate marshmallows, because it was Valentine's Day, after all.

Kimmie had honestly believed this was going to be the first Valen-tine's Day of her life to experience being in love and having a boyfriend. But that was before Sucky Saturday, which was what she was calling that agonizing night at the club.

"C'mon Kimmie, stop daydreaming. Let's go! We're running late." Her mother ushered her into the backseat of their Uber, which was waiting at the curb. Kimmie was horrified to discover it was the same car with the giant red teddy bear in the front passenger seat that had passed by her earlier. If she survived this ridiculously stupid day, it'd be an honest-to-god miracle.

IV

Anna held the cardboard box in her lap for a few minutes before open-ing it. She first exchanged pleasantries with Thomas, one of her father's regular drivers. She hadn't seen him in a while, so he showed her a few pictures of his new twin grandbabies born on New Year's Day in

Virginia. In return Anna explained the inner workings of Westminster to him, which reminded her that she had forgotten to bring the plush, heart-shaped squeaky toys she had gotten for her two dogs.

Lee Ann and Ali, her dogs' trainers and handlers, had picked up Gemma and Jon Snow on Sunday evening before Anna left for dinner with Alexander. She needed to get them used to being without her, and they would both be groomed first thing Monday morning in the city. Anna could have brought Gemma back to Greenwich last night, but she decided Jon Snow would be calmer with his sister around. This reminded Anna of her own brother, who got in less trouble when she was present, too.

Anna noticed her hands were shaking when she started to peel the tape off the box with her fingernails. She knew she was being silly, but there was nothing she could do to calm her nerves. She would never get a job with the bomb squad, that was certain.

Since they parted on the train platform eleven days ago, Anna hadn't seen him at all. Well, that wasn't exactly true. One day last week she decided to sit with Beatrice at lunch, where they talked about how much fun they'd had at Jaylen's party. And like a game of cat and mouse, neither girl brought up Vronsky's name. When Anna asked whether Beatrice had stayed in the city that weekend, she had told Anna she'd come back to Greenwich on Sunday to hang out with her fam. She showed Anna a picture of her mother's new custom Range Rover she had received as an early Valentine's Day gift from Beatrice's father. In the picture, Anna noticed Vronsky in the driver's seat, but he wasn't facing the camera. When looking at it, it took all her strength to not grab Bea's phone and enlarge the photo so she could study his profile. Instead, she commented on how she always loved the giant red bows that arrived on new cars and wondered where they were made.

"No doubt they were assembled by tiny hands in China," Beatrice said. Anna didn't react, though she noticed that Beatrice realized her error and didn't apologize, probably thinking Anna wouldn't be offended since she wasn't Chinese. This was exactly the kind of snarky comment Steven would make, so Anna was used to it even though she didn't approve.

"Was your mother happy with her new car?" Anna asked.

"Yes and no, she pulled me aside and asked me if I knew of any reason why my dad would feel guilty enough to buy her a new car. She just got a new car two years ago, and my mother barely drives herself as it is." Beatrice laughed, but again, Anna stayed quiet. She couldn't help but feel like Bea was testing her, so she wanted to be careful with what she revealed.

"Did your dad have a reason to be guilty?" Anna took the bait.

"Depends on how puritanical your values are," replied Bea breezily. "In my book, no. But does he probably have some new yummy twenty-something bouncing on his dick? Absoposilutely! My dad's no saint."

"I wouldn't expect so, with you as his acorn," Anna tossed out.

"Hot damn, girl! I always knew you had a little Veronica in there," Bea squealed.

Anna's first instinct was to apologize immediately, but before she could Beatrice placed her perfectly manicured finger over Anna's lips to stop her. "Don't you dare apologize. Bettys are *très* boring, and I know you're not that." Anna, pleased by the praise, spent the rest of lunch with Bea and her friends, a gaggle of popular girls whose topics of conversation hopscotched from fashion to boys to gossip with rapid-fire banter and lots of laughter. It was quite a fun change of pace for Anna, who sat with them a few more times as well. This year she had been spending her lunches getting a head start on her homework now that Alexander was in college and she no longer ate lunch with him at the Wick cafeteria.

In the car, Anna took the top off the box and stared at its contents. Inside were an envelope and two small gifts wrapped in red paper and white ribbons. Inside the larger of the two boxes, she found two gorgeous red leather dog collars. Each one had an engraved heart-shaped charm hanging from the silver ring with her dog's names on one side and her own phone number on the other. There was a small white card at the bottom of the box that read: "Best of luck for Best in Show!" Anna didn't even realize she was smiling until Thomas commented from the driver's seat. "Someone seems pleased. Gifts from Alexander W.?"

At the mention of her boyfriend's name Anna felt an immediate flood of shame. "It's from my brother. I did him a favor recently so he's just showing his thanks, I guess." Anna exhaled. *There it is. The first lie.* She dismissed her thoughts and opened the next box, which contained a small red velvet drawstring pouch. She pulled out what looked like a dog collar charm, but this one was heavier than the others. The charm was a thick shiny heart a little bigger than a quarter. She knew enough about jewelry to recognize this charm was more than likely white gold or platinum, as there was weight to it. Anna stared at it and saw that on one side of the heart the word YOU was engraved and on the other side, the word ME. Reading the words, she gasped.

"Everything okay, Miss K.?" Thomas asked.

She nodded quickly, unable to speak, her mouth suddenly dry. Anna quickly slipped the charm into her pocket, grabbed the envelope, and then closed the box, thinking that when she arrived at Madison Square Garden she'd store it in her overnight bag in the trunk. She had planned to sleep in the city that night. When she texted Steven of her plans, he'd told her about his V-Day, mentioning that since Lolly couldn't sleep in the hotel overnight, he planned to come home after he dropped her off.

Even though Steven probably didn't remember, he once drunkenly told her about their dad's standing hotel room at the St. Regis. It was a room rented by his company for any C-level executive who was working late and couldn't get home (her dad's office was two blocks away), but from what she gathered, the only person who had the key to the room was her dad. Steven had to have gotten permission from their father to use it for Valentine's Day, and she wondered whether Steven was going to share with Lolly that the suite may or may not be used by their father as a place to bring women.

When she had learned about the hotel room, Anna didn't know what to think. In her eyes her father was perfect, and she didn't like to think of him keeping secrets from her mother. She comforted herself with thoughts that her parents had been happily married for over twenty years, and perhaps her mom knew about the room. Anna wasn't naïve and had read enough books to know that marriage was complicated and some couples had certain "arrangements." But she had a hard time believing her mother would ever be the type of woman to turn a blind eye.

They were in Manhattan by the time Anna gathered the courage to open the last envelope. It was smaller than a regular greeting card and thinner, too. Inside the envelope, a postcard-sized ink drawing outlined four men wearing suits and sunglasses posing on a set of steps. The drawing was finely detailed, but there were no words on it, and Anna drew a total blank at who these men were or what they were supposed to represent.

Anna loved a good mystery, but she was irritated by the drawing. The fact that she didn't understand it made her feel stupid, and she racked her brain, going over everything the two of them had said to each other, which was very little. The most time they'd spent together so far was on the dance floor, but they had barely spoken for hours; their main communication that night had been through dancing.

Then, like a lightning bolt, she knew. She opened her phone and typed the words "Now that we found love." She hit search. Heavy D & The Boyz was the name of the group who sang the song from the club. Anna hit "images" and several pictures of the band came up. One of them was the exact pose on the postcard she was holding. She searched the lyrics and read them again, which brought her back to their last dance of the night.

Now that we found love, what are we gonna do . . . with it?

Anna smiled, her eyes sparkling with happiness at the secret message. She stared at the tiny work of art and thought about Vronsky hand drawing it for her while he listened to the song, thinking of her as he sketched. What a wonderful box of Valentines, each one more surprising and unique than the next. These gifts were *très* romantic! They couldn't have been given to any other girl; they were for her and her alone.

It was then that Anna finally admitted she had been thinking of him for the last week and half as well. She'd wondered if Vronsky remembered her dogs were competing at Westminster, and now she had confirmation he did. Her heart fluttered at the thought that maybe he would be there. *Would he dare? Could he be so bold?*

Anna grabbed her makeup bag out of her purse and decided a touch-up might be in order. As her mother always advised her, you never know when you'll get asked to go leaf-peeping in some cute guy's Lambo.

V

Kimmie hadn't seen Dr. Becker, her pediatrician, in a few years. Competitive athletes see sports-medicine doctors, and all last year she had only dealt with orthopedic surgeons because of her knee. But Dr. Becker had been her pediatrician since she was a baby. After a few minutes of catch-up with her mom in the exam room, Dr. Becker asked her mother to go wait outside while he examined Kimmie. As soon as her mother left, his demeanor changed. Dr. Becker was the doctor of choice for a lot of rich kids in Manhattan, so he was a guy who had seen and heard it all before. He was incredibly successful because he knew how to handle the parents of rich kids as well as the kids themselves.

Kimmie told her doctor how she'd started to feel mysteriously achy and tired a week and a half ago and then said nothing more. Dr. Becker gave her a look that said, "Cut the act and just tell me the real deal." There was something about his look that made Kimmie realize she needed to do exactly that, which is when she started crying . . . and blabbering. He listened for a bit, and then typed something on his iPad. Seeing him record her tale of woe made her incredibly self-conscious, so she stopped talking.

"So you started feeling bad after this sweet sixteen party on the second, but you really started to feel bad in the last five days? Is that correct?" Dr. Becker questioned.

Kimmie nodded.

"During this party, were you drinking or doing drugs?" Dr. Becker asked, prompting her to continue.

Kimmie, still crying, shook her head. Like she would ever dare admit such a thing to the man who used to give her lollipops after every visit.

"Kimmie, what we talk about in here is privileged, so I'm not going to tell your mom. The only time I have an obligation to tell her anything is if I think you're a danger to yourself or others. So tell me, did you drink or do drugs at the party?"

Kimmie decided she didn't care anymore what he thought about her and started talking, realizing that once she did, she couldn't stop. It felt good to finally have someone to confess to. Kimmie told him how she had been having a tough time now that she was a "civilian" again, no longer an Olympic hopeful but instead just a regular teenage girl. Who knew going to school at Spence would be way more challenging than waking up at 4:30 A.M. and getting to the ice rink for practice? She had never minded her early morning routine, mainly because when she was alone on the ice, she had a lot of time to think.

Kimmie admitted to suffering from insomnia for the first month of school because she hated how the other girls were whispering about her. And she felt too old to make new friends. Sure, she had it a little easier than most new students because of Lolly, but it was still hard. Lolly was often too busy with her upperclassmen friends. Kimmie liked her older sister, but their early tween years had been so different, with Kimmie always traveling for competitions and rarely spending time at home, that they weren't as close as they could be. Kimmie felt like she was woefully behind when it came to her social development and was struggling to catch up.

"I'm not used to being not good at stuff," Kimmie wailed pitifully. "Teenage girls are even judgier than ice dancing judges!"

"Never has a truer statement been made," Dr. Becker replied sympathetically.

Kimmie eventually told him that she tried Molly on New Year's Eve and she'd tried cocaine for the first time at the club, throwing her sister's boyfriend under the bus in the process as the one who gave her the drugs. She then listened as Dr. Becker explained what a coke hangover was like and how, by doing it, Kimmie had blown all the dopamine storage units in her brain. Which was absolutely the reason why she was so tired and needed a few days to recover.

"But if that really was only your first experience with cocaine, it doesn't explain why you're still feeling this terrible and crying eleven days later. I'm wondering if there's more to the story? I promise you I've heard it all before. Not to say your unhappiness isn't special, because it is. I'm just saying you need to trust me and tell me if there's more than you're letting on. Because if I had to make an educated guess, I'd say there may be a boy involved."

Kimmie nodded glumly and finally spilled the tea about her shameful abasement at the hands of Vronsky. "I thought he was into me!" she blubbered, looking at the floor. "And I . . . I loved him. Or at least I thought I did. He used me, and I feel so stupid!"

When Dr. Becker asked Kimmie if she'd had sex with Vronsky, or with any boy for that matter, she blushed crimson and emphatically stated she had not. "No way, I would never. We just did . . . other stuff," and watched as her pediatrician typed a sentence into his iPad. Hours later in the cab going home, Kimmie wondered what he had written, and if it was along the lines of "Thou doth protest too much."

After her physical exam was over and his nurse had drawn four tubes of blood from her arm for the slate of tests he had ordered, Dr. Becker handed her a red heart-shaped lollipop with the word LOVE printed on it in white. "Sorry, kiddo, these are the only ones I have today," he apologized. "I know you feel like crap about this Vronsky fellow, but I'm sure you'll have no problem finding someone more deserving of your affection."

Waiting for the elevator with her mom, Kimmie thought about her doctor's last words to her, which she knew he'd said to make her feel better, but instead made her feel worse. Because it wasn't true. Even though she hated Vronsky's guts right now, she honestly felt there was no one more deserving than him in the entire city. She stared at the word LOVE printed on the heart-shaped candy in her hand and her bottom lip started quivering. She threw it in the trash can next to the elevator, but it was too late, a storm of fat tears had already begun to fall.

Her mother made her walk to Saks anyway, and as Kimmie trailed three steps behind Danielle on the walk to Fifth Avenue, she blamed Lolly for her mother's inattention. Lolly was the queen of crying fits and had thrown so many tear-filled tantrums over the years that it had made their mother immune to Kimmie's own suffering. Kimmie stoically refrained from pointing out that in her fifteen years on earth, she had probably only cried in front of her mom a handful of times, and most of them had been out of anger over losing a competition.

What really pissed Kimmie off, though, was her inability to control her crying. She had tried and tried, alone in her room in the dark of night when she couldn't sleep any more. She'd command herself to "stop crying like a little bitch," but it didn't work. She knew she had every right to cry over what had happened to her at Jaylen's party, because she was heartbroken over her experience with Vronsky. It was hard to know what stung the most, the fact that he didn't share her feelings or that he had chosen someone else over her.

She had many hours to think about everything that had happened, and the only thing that had made her feel a little bit better was when she tried to step back and look at it all from a distance. Kimmie wasn't blind. Anna had things she just couldn't compete with. Anna's beauty was exotic, far more exciting than her own fake blondeness; Anna was older and more sophisticated than she was; and, most importantly, Anna wasn't available. Anna turned his head, and all guys love a chase. Plus, maybe competing with Anna's well-regarded college boyfriend made the situation too tempting for Vronsky to pass up. Poor Kimmie didn't stand a chance.

Sometimes Kimmie wanted Anna to suffer the same fate as she had, to be swiped left as soon as the next shiny object caught Vronsky's attention. But sometimes she hoped that Anna was the girl who had the power to take him down once and for all. If anyone could do such a thing, surely it was the perfectly enviable Anna K.

Kimmie knew these scenarios were pure speculation. She had only seen Vronsky and Anna dancing together at the club for a few moments and hadn't seen them make out. She had even asked her sister whether Vronsky and Anna had kissed at the club, but Lolly assured her they had not. Anna had a boyfriend and would never pull such a basic bitch move on the Greenwich OG. This didn't renew Kimmie's hope for her own chances with Vronsky, however. She had seen the way he was looking at Anna when they were dancing. He had never looked at Kimmie that way.

Kimmie was now at the point where she knew in her heart of hearts what she felt the most was self-loathing. How could she have fallen for Vronsky's charms so easily? How could she have believed that he loved her the way she loved him?

After a stop at the SK-II cosmetics counter, Kimmie tried once again to convince her mom to let her go home so she could sulk the day away. But once again her mom stayed firm and refused. "You need to eat lunch. Maybe your iron is low. I want you to eat some red meat. Are you on your period? How heavy is your flow?" her mom asked in her normal voice like she was inquiring about the weather.

"Mom!" Kimmie's bottom lip quivered in an effort not to cry yet again. "Could you be more embarrassing? As if my life isn't hard enough right now without you talking about my cycle in the middle of Saks!"

As Kimmie picked at the steak salad her mother ordered for her, she found out what Dr. Becker had told her mother in private after Kimmie's exam. Dr. Becker wrote her a note excusing her from school for the rest of the week, which made Kimmie breathe a huge sigh of relief. He thought that perhaps Kimmie hadn't fully processed her career-ending injury, and it was likely her current depression was her way of dealing with it. Dr. Becker had prescribed rest and recommended a few top therapists that specialized in adolescents.

"He thinks I need to see a therapist?!" Kimmie asked, her eyes wide with horror.

"Stop being so melodramatic, Kimberly, half the girls at Spence are in therapy." This was an underestimation on her mom's part, but that was beside the point.

"Please, please, please, can we not talk about this here? Let's just wait and see what my blood tests show. I mean, maybe I have leukemia and I'm dying. Then wouldn't you feel bad for making me go to a shrink? I'm sick, Mom, this isn't in my head!" Kimmie felt a little ashamed about saying such a thing, but whatever. She just felt so tired. Who knew you could feel so tired at the age of fifteen?

"Mom, are you even listening to me?" she whined when she noticed her mother was texting under the table. How many times had she heard her mother tell her and her sister how rude it was to be on your phone during meals, and now she was doing the same thing? Kimmie knew her mom was distracted by her own love life, and for a moment Kimmie indulged in the mean-spirited wish that her mother was still a sad-sack divorcée. Perhaps then she'd be more empathetic to her daughter's plight.

At the time Kimmie was holding her water glass, in fact squeezing it . . . hard. All she remembered was a pop, which sounded like it was coming from behind her. The next thing she knew, water was all over her lap and her mother had jumped up so fast she nearly toppled their entire table over.

Kimmie didn't feel any pain, but when Danielle grabbed her right hand and wrapped it in a napkin, the white cloth turned red incredibly fast. She was surrounded suddenly by the restaurant manager and two waiters, everyone freaking out over the amount of blood.

And just like that, Kimmie was back in Dr. Becker's exam room. As she stared at her gauze-wrapped hand, Kimmie noted that she felt a little better, though better might not be the right word. She felt calmer somehow. No, that wasn't it, either. What she felt was the momentary absence of misery, and the absence felt like nothing, which Kimmie more than welcomed.

Dr. Becker didn't think stitches were necessary. Instead he used some surgical superglue to seal the deepest of the three cuts on her hand and put Band-Aids on the ones remaining. He sent her mom off to the waiting room. He wanted to talk to Kimmie alone. For the second time in two hours, Dr. Becker stared Kimmie down, peering at her over his fashionable rimless glasses. "Was this really an accident?" he asked softly. "Look me in the eyes and tell me the truth."

"It was an accident. The glass was defective," Kimmie said. "It's not like I'm the female Hulk or anything. It just . . . happened, I swear."

Dr. Becker didn't respond right away and Kimmie panicked. "Oh god, do you think I'm crazy? I read how some people lose it after trying drugs once. Is that what's happening to me?"

"Kimmie, you're going to be fine," Dr. Becker answered in a calm tone. "You're a strong girl and I want you to know that given everything you told me earlier, what you're experiencing is normal. Teenage girls have a lot of social pressure these days, and it's perfectly healthy to have emotional outbursts and freak out. But when healthy crosses the line . . . that's when the blood shows up. Self-harm is not okay."

Kimmie met Dr. Becker's eyes with her own deadly serious gaze. "It was an accident."

"Okay, good. Accidents happen. I should know. Now, do you need another heart-shaped lollipop? Normally one is my limit, but it's Valentine's Day, so . . ." Dr. Becker smiled.

Kimmie didn't throw away her LOVE lollipop this time. Instead she opened it in the elevator with her teeth, spitting out the cellophane wrapper onto the floor. She suddenly felt hungry, ravenous even. She had barely eaten her lunch, and in fact hadn't eaten much of anything for days. But she felt different now. As soon as she put the lollipop in her mouth, Kimmie bit right into it, enjoying the crackling sound of the candy breaking apart, splintering between her teeth. She was so busy crunching the cherry-red candy, she hadn't even noticed there were two men her father's age in the elevator staring at her.

"What the fuck are you staring at?" Kimmie snapped. "Didn't you hear, it's goddamn Valentine's Day!"

VI

Dustin's brother and his mom hadn't spoken in half a year. Dustin blamed Nicholas for this. Six months ago, their mom had come home from the movies to find people in the apartment. Assuming she had just walked into a break-in, their mother rushed out and dialed 911 on her cell phone. But what his mom didn't know was that the break-in was being led by her oldest son, Nicholas, who was in the process of removing the Samsung 4K fifty-five-inch TV from her bedroom wall with a power drill. It was the very same TV Nicholas had installed only two months prior for Mother's Day. His mother had been so touched by Nicholas's gift that she had broken her own rule and given him some money afterward, which Nicholas used to buy drugs, breaking his four-month sobriety streak. Basically, the whole thing was a Greek tragedy of epic proportions as far as Dustin was concerned.

Dustin had missed the whole thing because it was his week to stay at his father's place downtown. But from what he'd heard, Nicholas and his friends bolted when they heard the sirens and ran right into their mother, who was standing in the hallway outside of her apartment. When she saw it was Nicholas, she grabbed him by the arm, but he roughly pulled away from her, causing her to knock her head into the wall and then fall.

To Dustin's brother's credit, he didn't leave his mother on the floor and flee like his two loser friends did. (They were apprehended outside the building.) When the police entered the apartment ten minutes later, they found Nicholas sitting on the couch next to his mother, administering a bag of frozen peas to the bump on the back of her head. Nicholas had begged his mother to lie for him and tell the cops he had been asleep in his room when the two men broke into her apartment, but she had refused. "I'd throw myself in front of a bus for you, but I won't lie." Dustin knew that statement was true because it was one of the things that both Nicholas and his mother mentioned in their account of the night's events.

By the time Dustin and his father arrived, his mom had taken a double dose of Valium, which had already started to kick in. She asked them to stay for the night, and neither could refuse upon seeing this shell-shocked and devastated woman.

That night provided the opportunity for the first heart-to-heart Dustin had ever had with his dad. Well, there had been one nonconversation about sex when Dustin was thirteen, but it consisted of his dad coming into his bedroom when he was studying and saying, "Your mom asked me to come over to have the sex talk with you. Do you need it?" Dustin responded in the negative, and his father exhibited visible relief. His father then informed his young son that he now had to hang out in his bedroom for the next half hour so he could report back to his ex-wife he'd done as he was told. Dustin and his dad watched *Game of Thrones* in Dustin's room, both staring in awestruck silence at the lesbian scene in Lord Baelish's brothel. It was one of the most awkward moments of his life.

This time, talking wasn't any easier, but far more necessary. The two of them sat on opposite sides of his mother's floral couch together, father and son sitting in the dark living room, lightless since the lamp had been broken in the chaos of the attempted robbery. There they discussed the elephant in the room that they had been ignoring for the past three years. They both admitted to feeling helpless over what to do and guilty because their inaction left Dustin's mother to do the heavy lifting when it came to Nicholas's drug problem. The issues had started the August before Dustin started high school, when he arrived home from robotics camp to find out that Nicholas had gotten busted with drugs at the Jewish summer camp where he had been working as a counselor. His parents sat Dustin down and told him that they'd checked Nicholas into rehab, though at the time they were both in the denial phase and didn't believe their son was an actual addict, just "needed to get back on track." But less than a year later the story changed completely and Dustin realized that things were escalating at an alarming rate.

Now it had been going on for almost four years with no sign of improvement and had become common knowledge, whispered about behind their backs: *"Oh them? Well, the parents are divorced, Jewish, and get this, they have an adopted black son who is incredibly accomplished academically while the older son, the biological child, is a drug addict."*

Clearly tonight's incident meant it was time for Nicholas to go to rehab again, his fourth go-around. Dustin told his dad that from what he had read online, twenty-eight-day rehab treatment programs weren't effective for long-term results and to get better ones, a three-month stay was needed. His father agreed but explained the huge financial cost of rehab. Insurance paid for some, but the good places, the places where people in their family's tax bracket sent their children to kick the habit, didn't usually take insurance for any stay longer than a month. His father explained he had a new wife to consider, and that he'd happily spend his retirement savings if he believed for one second that his eldest son would come out of rehab and stay clean forever.

This was when Dustin heard his father cry for the first time. Thankfully he didn't see it. Hearing his father cry as opposed to seeing it was far less uncomfortable for Dustin, but at the same time no less upsetting. Dustin wondered if it was the darkness that allowed them to talk so openly and honestly. Dustin took a deep breath and said he wanted to use his own college fund to pay for Nicholas to go to rehab for a three-month stint at a reputable facility. He had already received a partial scholarship to MIT and he could take on a loan for the rest. The money would be better spent getting his brother the help he needed.

"He tried to steal Mom's TV," Dustin began, feeling relieved to share the emotions that were filling him up. He had no choice but to say what was on his mind or risk exploding. "The same TV he gave her for Mother's Day, which I know you paid for, too, Dad. Do you get how twisted that is? She cried that night in my room after Nicholas left, but they weren't sad tears for once. They were happy ones. You should have seen her at dinner, so happy and smiley. She actually believed he was gonna stay clean. Like she really believed it. She kept saying to me: 'He knows how to use a power drill; he didn't even chip the paint; he used one of those leveling things just like a professional!' She thought he could get a job at Best Buy and be one of those guys who installed TVs in people's homes. This was what her happy mom tears were about. Think about it, Dad, if I came home and said I got a job at Best Buy, she'd take my head off with a soup spoon. She acted like she was prouder of Nicholas's fictional employment at the Geek Squad than when MIT called me and basically told me I was accepted before I even applied." Dustin's voice rose with anguish, but he didn't care and couldn't stop his words anyway. "And to think that dumb ass then came here tonight to steal that very TV back? Who does that? There's no way he didn't understand what he was doing. I mean, Mom never stays out late, so he probably came here knowing he was going to get caught. If that's not a cry for help, then I don't know what is."

It was then that Dustin cried in the dark, sitting two feet from his father. Later, the two of them searched through the kitchen looking for booze. They eventually found a bottle of Prosecco that his mom had under the kitchen sink, and father and son, neither of them big drinkers, gamely polished off the entire bottle together. They drank it warm at first but later added ice, cracking jokes like they were two Real Housewives sitting poolside on a hot summer day, and later tossing the bottle down the hallway trash chute to hide the evidence.

Dustin's father said he'd call his accountant to figure out a plan about rehab for Nicholas. Dustin made his father swear to never tell his brother or mother they were using his college fund, because Dustin had brought this idea up before, after he'd learned that Nicholas's own fund had been depleted, and his mother interrupted him before he even got his thought out and said that Dustin's money was for him and him alone. And if he didn't need it for his education then he could put it toward buying his first home. "Dad, don't feel guilty about it. We both know it's the right thing to do. Please, let me help." His words brought tears to his dad's eyes again, but neither of them acknowledged it.

The next morning Dustin woke up in his room to the smell of pancakes and coffee and the surreal noise of his parents laughing. His mother was making a big breakfast to thank him and her ex-husband for staying the night. The three of them ate together, which was a rare occurrence since the divorce ten years prior, talking about everything except for the reason they now sat together. At the end of the meal, his mother announced that she needed a break from her oldest son. She didn't want to know when Nicholas got out of jail. She didn't want to know where he went afterward. Her heart was broken, and she needed time. Dustin and his father agreed to step up and take care of things, which had been their plan all along. Dustin wished they had been able to tell her their plan first, which would have probably alleviated at least some of her guilt in having to take a breather from mothering.

Months later over a different pancake breakfast at a diner in the Bronx, Dustin finally sacked up and asked his brother Nicholas if he was still clean despite having been ejected from rehab early. The amount of relief that he felt when his brother told him he was still hanging on was enormous. His exact words were, "Dude, you think I'd be working at a taco shop if I was using?" Dustin's second question was whether Nicholas felt like he was ready to see their mom, and Nicholas said he'd be open to it if she was, but he needed Dustin to be there, too. Dustin agreed to talk to their mom about it when he took her out for V-Day dinner, not wanting her to be alone for the holiday, or himself for that matter.

Dustin was in the denial stage of his grief over Kimmie. He had decided that Valentine's Day morning at the florist, when he was picking up flowers for his mother, that it was ridiculous to have become so obsessed with a girl he barely even knew. He felt even more ridiculous for having convinced himself he was in love with her. Dustin soothed himself by saying that Kimmie's purpose in his life was not so that he might experience romantic love for the first time, but perhaps to be a distraction from endlessly worrying about his brother and whether he had given up two years of college tuition for nothing.

These were lies Dustin told himself standing before all the red roses that filled the store. But sometimes he knew it was best to believe the stories you told yourself in order get through a day. After all, didn't the cornerstone of sober living preach getting through life one day at a time?

VII

Lolly knew there were haters out there who wondered how she'd managed to land a hottie like Steven. Well, it wasn't luck, because Lolly worked very hard to get one of the most eligible boys in the city. Lolly knew she wasn't naturally beautiful herself, but what she lacked in nature's gifts, she more than made up for in effort. Lolly was "money pretty," and she knew it. Her hair had four-hundred-dollar highlights and was cut every eight weeks. Her nails were always perfect and done in the latest fashion. She had gotten a nose job during middle school and even though she requested Reese Witherspoon's nose and ended up with Michelle Williams's slightly thinner nose instead, she accepted it gracefully. Lolly had been on a diet since she was thirteen, went to SoulCycle three times a week, did a hundred sit-ups every night before bed, and even secretly bought some waist-shaping bodywear she saw advertised on Instagram that supposedly tightened her core as she slept.

Every compliment she received about her looks, from her mother's friends, her pear-shaped grandmother, or even sketchy men who whistled at her on the street, Lolly appreciated. She drank up compliments like a camel, storing them up for later, because only she knew just how hard she had worked to get them. So when she caught the attention of Steven at SoulCycle one afternoon two years ago—his bike had been behind hers—she had never felt more glorious in her entire life.

"Damn girl, you rocked it today on those hills." Those were the first words Steven had ever spoken to her. Well, that's not true, because two weeks previously he had said, "Yo, wrong bike, Ponytail," at which point Lolly was so embarrassed she almost fell trying to unclip her shoes and move over for him. To her, those words didn't really count, because he would have said them to anyone, and so they shouldn't count as his first words specifically to her.

Of course, she already knew who he was, noticing him months ago in class and carefully noting what times and teachers he preferred. She was a motivated exerciser already, but a little eye candy never hurt anyone, right? Steven was one of the best-looking guys at Collegiate—he was six feet tall, had an eight-pack from lacrosse and tennis, and looked like a studly mashup of John Cho and Ryan Gosling—and if that weren't enough, he also had this New Year's Eve party that was so notorious it made him famous throughout almost every high school in the tri-state area. Lolly, not knowing how she found the nerve, replied to his compliment by asking him if he wanted to stay for a double ride with her.

"Damn, you can do two classes in a row? Hashtag ballerbitch," he responded. Steven had only been doing SoulCycle for the past three months and still couldn't believe how difficult it was for him.

"I don't do them all the time, but I've done a few. It's easier than it sounds. It's an endorphin thing, I think." Lolly was sure her voice was shaking as she spoke to him, but luckily the music was loud enough to drown out any tremble in her tone. "Wanna try?" she added, praying this unbelievably cute boy in front of her said yes.

"Hellz yezz, let's do it," he said. Steven prided himself on being up for anything and everything, and he seized any opportunity to try something new if it gave him bragging rights. Also, he had just spent the last forty-five minutes staring at Lolly's ass in the last class, so he was pretty gung-ho.

The entire time during their impromptu second class together Lolly didn't feel any pain at all. In fact, it was probably the easiest class she had ever done, because she was on cloud nine over the whole "seat-cute meet-cute" situation. And as fate would have it, Steven had just recovered from a particularly epic coke bender a few days prior and had decided to chill with the drugs for a bit and start taking better care of himself. The timing was perfect all the way around. Steven was good at excess, but not with excess free time, and so he asked Lolly if she wanted to see a movie that weekend. Lolly knew this was her best shot at Steven, and she took it with gusto. Every time Lolly saw Steven over the next month, she spent at least ninety minutes getting ready, sometimes a full two hours. She had already read every fashion magazine, but during that time she stepped up her already high-maintenance beauty routine. She watched every contouring tutorial on YouTube and agonized over each and every outfit she wore in front of him. And all her efforts paid off beautifully, because Steven, witnessing her transformation, found Lolly to be better and better looking each time he took her out, which tricked him into believing that this was a result of his growing feelings for her.

Steven told her that Korean women who lived in Seoul would spend hours getting ready before going to the supermarket, and that outward appearances were of paramount importance. He worked hard to keep his body in top form and dressed impeccably, and Lolly felt it was only fair of him to expect the same of his girlfriend. When Steven told Lolly she was practically Korean in her hard-core type-A diligence when it came to her looks, it was the highest compliment he had ever paid her and he meant it. Lolly adored how often Steven told her she was beautiful, but she fell in love with him because he was honest enough to tell her when he thought she had made a misstep with her outfit or hair. Her best friends, Miley and Hannah, thought this made Steven an asshole, but Lolly defended him and fully admitted that every single time he said something like this he had been right. Lolly was proud of Steven's eye for fashion and for being a stickler when it came to details. He could even tell the difference between when Lolly had synthetic eyelash extensions versus when she splurged and got the mink ones. It had taken Lolly three months of backbreaking work, but when Steven K. finally asked her to be his girlfriend, it was the proudest moment of her life.

She didn't admit any of this superficial stuff when she talked to Anna last week, but that was only because Anna was naturally gorgeous and seemed to achieve her own beauty effortlessly. The one thing that hurt the most after she found out about Steven's cheating with "Brad" was not that he stuck it to some other girl, but that he hadn't had the decency to have sex with someone who was prettier than she was; at least *that* she could understand. Lolly had a good visual memory and had seen enough naked pics of "Brad" on Steven's Apple Watch to see her rival was no size zero. But the pics had given her hope because she knew Steven valued a woman's looks. Perhaps the only thing he saw in the ho-bag was that she was DTF, and sex was something Lolly had been withholding.

So the morning after the "Brad incident," when Lolly spent five minutes staring at her sleeping soon-to-be-ex-boyfriend, in a surprising twist, she did a total 180 and decided she was going to have sex with him. Lolly had really wanted her first time to be with someone she loved (ideally someone who hadn't slept with someone else!), but now she had a new plan. She would turn the tables on her philandering scumbag bf, give him exactly what he desired most, and then take it away forever. "Hump him and dump him!" as Miley liked to say.

Lolly had been the star of every school play for the last five years and knew she was a fine actress. That morning in bed with Steven, she gave the performance of a lifetime. She stripped down and slipped into bed with her sleeping beau, waking him up with a gentle kiss on the neck. Sure, Lolly liked fooling around with Steven, but she was always a little self-conscious about how she looked in the moment so she could never fully relax and enjoy herself. This time, however, Lolly came alive, like something woke up in her, and she found herself for the first time in a long time having fun. She didn't give a single thought to how she looked or even how Steven thought she looked. She didn't care if he was enjoying himself, either. She just felt free, and in doing so she started to get super turned on herself. Afterward, Steven was blown away by Lolly's turnaround and started crying, begging Lolly to forgive him and promising he'd never cheat on her again.

Looking into her boyfriend's eyes, Lolly remembered Anna's final piece of advice from the night before. The only chance they had at a future was if Lolly loved him enough to find it in herself to forgive Steven for what he did to her. Trusting Anna's wisdom, Lolly felt she did love him enough, and she forgave him. Ever since then Lolly and Steven had never been happier together.

A week and a half after her decision to stay with Steven, Lolly was at lunch with her two best friends, who were pestering her about her and Steven's Valentine's Day plans when the idea of the holiday blow job came up. "My mom was in such a foul mood this morning because she had a root canal scheduled and said it was bad timing because of the BJ my stepdad is expecting for Valentine's Day," Miley announced out of nowhere. Miley was one of those girls who liked to say things just to get a reaction. "Everyone knows that all boyfriends and husbands expect an extra-special blow job on major holidays. Their birthday blow job is probably the biggest deal of the year, but Valentine's Day is probably second since usually it's the man who must do most of the heavy lifting when it comes to V-Day gifts and such. I mean, it's only fair they get rewarded for good behavior. And since I know you're not gifting Steven your cherry anymore for Valentine's Day as punishment for his very bad 'Brad' behavior, I guess you're still on the hook to give him his celefellatio! You know, since you're still his girlfriend. And no doubt Moneybags is getting you a killer gift."

"Uch, why do we always have to talk about this stuff?" Hannah, who was still a virgin, asked Miley, whose V-train had long since left the station. "I mean, just because me and Lolls are still virgitarians doesn't mean we're like these pathetic repressed creatures who need to constantly be bombarded by the sexpertise of the one and only deflowered member of our trio." Hannah winked at Lolly, who had confided in Hannah, but not yet Miley, that she'd lost her virginity to Steven on the snow day after the "Brad" debacle. Lolly and Miley had been best friends since kindergarten and had always maintained a strict pact that they would tell each other everything first, before they told Hannah. This was the first time Lolly broke the pact, knowing Hannah would be way more supportive in her decision to stay with Steven. Hannah was a theater geek like herself, who knew the words to every Broadway musical, which meant she was better equipped to understand that love and relationships were complicated, and that happy endings were made even better with a few power ballads of despair thrown in for good measure.

Miley rolled her eyes at Hannah. "Whatevs, just trying to help my bitches out, but if my help's not wanted, then lots of luck, ladies . . ." She stopped for a moment, but then couldn't help herself and went in for the kill shot. "I just don't know how you could take him back after what he did! I mean I know you love him, but we all know he's gonna do it again. My mom always says: once a cheater, always a cheater."

Lolly remained calm even though she had told her friend earlier that morning she didn't want to hear any more of her Steven bashing, but Miley was obsessed with her alpha status, which meant she had to have the last word. Right now, however, Lolly just didn't want to get into it. It was important to keep at least one area of her life running smoothly, and since her home life was currently tension-filled she really needed her school life to stay chill.

But that didn't mean she was going to share with Miley that she'd crossed the Rubicon with Steven and gone from virgitarian to carniwhore. What she was going to do was make sure she was as good in bed as any bf-sexting ho-bag from the South Bronx, if not better. So in preparation for Valentine's Day, Lolly hid in her closet when she should have been doing homework (although couldn't this be called homework?), put on her new gold Beats headphones, and typed the words "best blow job ever" into the search bar.

VIII

Steven's dad had called him from Singapore and asked him to deliver his Valentine's Day gift for his mother to the apartment. Well, "asked" was the wrong word; Steven's father didn't ask things from his only son, he demanded them. Steven, who couldn't say no to his father, promised he would, but he knew the only way he could do it and not be late for his rendezvous with Lolly at 2 P.M. at the St. Regis was if he ran his father's errand at lunch. So, Steven had Van Cleef & Arpels messenger his father's gift to his school and then picked it up before leaving for the day.

It never once occurred to Steven that he should text his mom before showing up at the house, because, why would he? When he walked in his front door, he noticed a pair of size-thirteen limited edition Big Baller Brand sneakers by the door. Thinking about it later, Steven wondered why the shoes didn't give him pause but for some reason he had just assumed they belonged to one of the many workmen who were installing the new cherry wood bookshelves in the library. This made no sense though, because Steven knew the designer kicks retailed for six hundred dollars at Barneys.

"Mom! Hey, Mom!" he called out, heading into the kitchen to see what he could find to eat for a quick lunch since he was missing pizza day at school.

When his mom didn't answer, he put two Hot Pockets into the microwave and went looking for her. In the hall, he heard music coming from his parents' bedroom. When Steven opened the bedroom door, his mother was lying on her back in bed while being attended to by some naked guy with an enormous winged dragon back tattoo. Steven's first thought was he must be experiencing his first acid flashback, because there was no way what he was seeing was real.

Luckily his mom and Mr. Back Tattoo were so caught up in the throes of passion that neither of them noticed his presence in the doorway. Seconds later Steven was back in the hall with his forehead pressed against the wall and his mouth still hanging open. He just stood there listening to The Isley Brothers' "Between the Sheets" playing loudly through the door. Steven instantly recognized it as the melody that The Notorious B.I.G. had sampled for "Big Poppa," one of Steven's all-time favorite rap songs, making the whole thing ten times worse. Dumbstruck was the only word that could properly describe Steven's state of mind. Actually, flabbergasted and gobsmacked would also have worked. His bewilderment quickly turned to nausea, and he barely made it into the foyer bathroom before he threw up the chocolate Muscle Milk he had just downed minutes before.

Steven, shaky and sweating, paced around the foyer trying to decide what to do. Eventually he landed on a plan of action, which was to flee the scene of the crime he had just witnessed. He left his mom a Post-it

Note on the front hall table along with her Valentine's gift from her husband and took off.

Steven asked the doorman to hail him a cab as he felt unable to work his phone and order an Uber. Soon he was in the backseat heading toward the hotel. What struck Steven the hardest was his inability to process how he was feeling, besides being in dire need of mouthwash. Steven reminded himself that his dad regularly cheated on his mother, so it shouldn't be surprising to find out his mother was doing the same, but it was. It just seemed so wrong and disgusting to him, mainly because this was his mother. He couldn't really think of her as a woman, let alone a sexual being.

His mom was elegant and regal, which certainly didn't correlate with what he had just witnessed. She had gone to the best schools, debuted in Greenwich and New York society, and was a very powerful woman in the highest social circles. So what the hell was she doing with some guy who had a tattoo of a clichéd dragon on his back? Also, the guy had to be young, like in his twenties, because no dude over thirty would know about the sneakers he'd seen in the hallway. That meant his own mother was banging some guy who wasn't that much older than he was.

His mom received handwritten Christmas cards and fruit baskets from Anna Wintour. She'd stopped wearing skirts above the knee at forty, never showed cleavage unless the designer she commissioned a dress from demanded it. When she warned him to be careful and use birth control with Lolly and he confessed to her that she was making him wait, she praised Lolly for her proper upbringing and ladylike traits.

What he had seen a half hour ago was not ladylike behavior.

Steven thought about calling Anna to tell her. Anna had texted him earlier, thanking him for the Valentine's Day chocolates and reminding him she was on her way into the city for the dog show. Steven, of course, had forgotten all about it. He felt momentarily better knowing his sister was probably in the city right now, and that he could tell her in person later, if he chose to tell her at all.

Steven arrived at the St. Regis a bit early, which meant Lolly was probably not waiting for him yet. He wanted desperately to go to the King Cole Bar for a drink, but he knew they probably wouldn't serve him. On the other hand, it was still early in the day and perhaps the bartender wouldn't think a teenager would have the audacity to order booze in the middle of the afternoon. He wished he could tell Lolly what he'd seen, but he knew it was impossible. He couldn't talk about his true feelings about people cheating so close to when he had just gotten busted himself. It hadn't even been a week yet.

Sitting in the lobby, his right knee shaking nervously, Steven texted Dustin: Dude, it's a no go this afternoon w/ V-Day. Tomo?

A reply from Dustin came in immediately. Figured as much. Yes re: tomo.

Steven texted back, You around late tonight? After midnight? Am having a thing.

Yeah, hit me up later. Happy V-Day.

Same 2 u bro.

Doubtful. Love sucks. Dustin's last text made him wince, as Steven had forgotten about his friend's own girl troubles. When Dustin had showed up on the Monday after the party for their tutoring session, Steven didn't know whether his friend would want to talk about Kimmie. When Steven opened the door, Dustin's first words had been, "Let's never speak of her again, okay?"

"I don't even know what her you're referring to, bruh," Steven replied, abiding by the bro code. If Dustin didn't want to talk about Kimmie, then who was he to go against his wishes? Steven wondered whether Dustin might be interested to hear that the Count was out of the picture when it came to Kimmie, but at the same time he had heard from Lolly that Kimmie was still wigging out over the whole thing, so perhaps he needed to let things cool down.

Even though Steven had been warned by both his parents not to talk about private family affairs with outsiders, he knew he could trust Dustin to keep what he'd seen a secret. Steven also knew Dustin had family drama of his own. Everyone knew Dustin's older brother, Nicholas, had been in and out of rehab for years, and as far as he knew that's where he was right now. Heroin was something Steven had never tried, mainly because he was afraid he'd like it too much. He hadn't tried meth, either, but that was more due to his misguided notion that meth was the drug of choice for the poor.

Steven considered the possibility of his father knowing that his wife slept with other men, but dismissed the notion quickly. Steven's father was proud, as many Korean men were. It seemed a man would lose face immediately if he had a wife who had lovers on the side. His parents were certainly not the type to have an open marriage. Not a chance. Privacy, the protection of the family name, and Anna were his father's top priorities, and Steven experienced firsthand how angry his father could become if anyone jeopardized those things. Steven shook his head, pissed with his mother for putting him in this terrible position. This was exactly the kind of shit Steven didn't like to think about. *Above my fucking pay grade*, he thought to himself.

Steven knew exactly what would get his mind off his troubles: cocaine. But he didn't have any on him, and he didn't have any weed, either. Lolly was insisting on a drug-free Valentine's Day, telling him she had special things planned that would make Steven high without the use of mind-altering substances. Steven smiled for the first time since the whole thing went down. Lolly had surprised him by being pretty wild in the sack right out of the gate. He had high expectations for the day's festivities and had splurged on her Valentine's Day gift, getting her a Cartier Love bracelet in rose gold. He had gotten his dad's permission to charge it, and his father had said no at first, but Steven alluded to a little trouble in paradise and that he really needed to make up for some misdeeds on his part. Steven's father liked when his son owned up to his mistakes and agreed, though Steven knew his father would probably use the nine-grand charge against him at a later date.

Steven's stomach rumbled, which was when he decided he would wait upstairs in the room for Lolly and order room service. He needed food and fast, which was precisely when he remembered the two Hot Pockets he'd left in the microwave at home. Steven slammed his fist into his thigh over the error. Now his mother would know he had been home for longer than his note suggested. Steven briefly considered going home and getting rid of them, but that seemed too risky. The last thing he wanted was to run into his mother, or worse yet, Mr. Back Tattoo.

If his mother brought up the Hot Pockets, he'd play dumb and hope for the best. Yes, what more could he do?

Damn, he thought, *Valentine's Day is one crazy fucked-up day.*

The Westminster Dog Show was one of the few remaining benched dog competitions left in the country, the idea being that each dog waiting to be judged was given a designated spot in a holding area so that attendees could walk around and view the dogs up close while their owners, handlers, and groomers gave them last-minute touch-ups. Anna had been a dog lover her entire life and had attended Westminster many times as a child. Her favorite part was walking around and looking at the dogs before they entered the ring.

Her father had always taken her, and it was here at the show when she told him that one day when she was grown up, she would have a dog win a ribbon at Westminster. Anna's father told his daughter that he was positive if she put her mind to it, then she would surely make it so. Now, ten years later, Anna had accomplished half of her goal, and though she didn't know it, she was the youngest owner in the arena.

Her father was in Singapore on business and wasn't able to be there with her, but he had woken up in the middle of the night and FaceTimed her to wish her and Jon Snow of the Wall the best of luck. The Working Group was due to be judged within the hour.

Anna loved her father and knew how much it pained him to not share this moment with her, but he assured her she had more than earned her place as one of the twelve hundred owners showing their dogs in this world-famous competition. She was touched to have received his call.

Her father had raised her to be grateful for the important moments in life, and she made a point to savor today.

As much as she enjoyed her close relationship with her father, she saw it came at a price, which was the effect that it had on their family as a whole. The way her father spoke to Steven, his tone so stern and demanding, was shocking to her. It was true that Steven had started getting into trouble as early as the fifth grade, but even before that, Anna couldn't help but notice how differently he treated them.

Anna's Korean grandmother once commented on it as well, telling Anna over lunch one day how lucky she was to be treated like gold by her father. She explained in her halting English that in Korean culture, daughters were considered expendable and were never valued as highly as the sons. The sons had the family name and it was their duty and honor to take care of the parents, while daughters would grow up and marry, joining their husband's family, which meant all praise or shame they garnered in their lives would be reflections not on their father's good name, but their future husband's.

"My daddy doesn't think that way. Probably because he's more American than Korean," Anna had responded without thinking about her audience.

"Your father is Korean first, and will always be," her grandmother said with a ferocious scowl. "You'd do well to follow his example!" And then her grandmother reached over with her long red nails and pinched Anna's arm. Anna, only ten years old at the time, cried out, more from surprise than pain. She didn't shed tears in front of her grandmother, not wanting to give her the satisfaction. Instead she excused herself and wept alone in the ladies' room.

Anna had no intention of telling her father what had happened, but when she knocked on his study door to say good night, as she did every night, he pulled her into his lap. He asked about her visit with her grandmother and Anna, not wanting to lie to his face, buried her face in her father's shirt and said it was fine and how much she liked her truffle French fries, which was the only thing she had enjoyed about the visit.

Knowing his daughter well, he pressed her for details, and reluctantly, Anna told him everything her grandmother had said. Emboldened as she went along, Anna showed him the faint pink mark that remained from her grandmother's pinch. Anna's father's face went stone cold as he listened to her story. He then told her, using a tone of voice that he promised wasn't because of her, that he was displeased with his mother; her views, he said, were from another time and place. What he didn't share with Anna was that it was his mother's old-fashioned thinking that had caused her to have a terrible relationship with her own daughter. His mother and his younger sister Jules hadn't spoken in years and had left him stuck in the middle of an unflinching standoff.

"You, my lovely daughter, are not expendable. You're the most precious thing I have in the world, and I'm never giving you up to another family. All your accomplishments will be for your own name when you grow up." He then kissed her head and finished by saying: "But for now, you're mine, and mine alone!"

Anna giggled, happy to hear her father's words match everything she had thought herself. "Does that mean you'll never let me marry?" she asked, half teasing and half serious because some of this talk was a little over her head.

Her father laughed, not a sound she often heard. He told her no, but she should know that he'd never allow her to marry someone who wasn't worthy of her. And so far in all his years on the planet, he had never met a person who fit that description.

Anna threw her arms around her father's neck and declared she loved him best. No one made her feel as safe and loved as he did. She knew she was lucky to have him for a father, so she told him she would always make sure she was a good girl he could be proud of.

"You'll soon find that doing the right thing is rarely the easy choice. But I promise you'll sleep better at night because of it." And with that, he kissed his favorite child good night and sent her to bed.

Anna thought about that evening often over the years, because the whole incident left her with so many conflicting emotions. The next day her mother came into her room and sat her down for a talk. Anna had expected her to be supportive in the same way her father had been, but that's not what happened.

Her mother told her that her father had called her grandmother and yelled at her for pinching Anna, using a voice that she had never heard him take before. Obviously, her grandmother was not pleased to be talked to that way by her favorite son, so she hung up the phone on him. Anna's mother had always suffered a strained relationship with her Korean mother-in-law, who would never quite look her in the eye, because she deemed her unworthy of her son. Anna's mother told her that her father was an important and very busy man and that these small matters would be better kept from him in the future because now it was going to take a while for everyone to get past what had happened.

Anna was so surprised by her mother's reprimand that she just nodded mutely. After her mother left her room, Anna cried, and wrote in her diary that she loved her daddy more than her mommy because he was nicer and better and obviously loved her more, too. Ashamed at putting her feelings down on paper and afraid they would be found out later, she tore out the page, ripped it up, and flushed the torn scraps down the toilet.

Anna hadn't thought about that second part of the memory in a long time. She and her mother weren't very close, and if she had to say why, it was probably because of this very incident. In that moment, it was like her mom had declared her allegiance and shown where her true loyalties lay, not with her daughter but with her husband. Sometimes she wondered whether her mother was jealous over how her father doted on her. She and her father had far more in common, similar in so many ways. They were both quiet and calm, though socially adept, calculating but not cold. And of course they shared a love of dogs, admiring them for their simple natures and unconditional love. Anna checked the time and hurried back to find Lee Ann, her dog handler, and wish her well before the judging . . . and to give Jon Snow a good luck kiss on the snoot, for good measure.

X

As Anna made her way through the large backstage area, a familiar voice called out to her. "Darling girl, is that you?" Anna stopped in her tracks and turned around to see Geneviève R., Vronsky's mother, standing near the bench of a majestic Russian wolfhound named Tolstoy, who had won Best in Breed and was waiting to go before the judges in the Hound Group, which would start right after the Working Group. Anna smiled and greeted the lovely woman warmly, taking in her incredible Tom Ford slate-blue pantsuit.

"Hello, Mrs. R. It's wonderful to see you again," Anna said happily. She was pleased to see Vronsky's mother, but the reason her heart started beating rapidly in her chest was because she now had even greater hopes her son would be here as well. Geneviève introduced Anna to Tolstoy's owner, explaining that he was going to be the stud for next year's litter and she was promised one of the puppies. Anna congratulated the owner for her win and was pleased when the woman knew exactly who she was, and her not-so-little dog, too.

"Speaking of, I need to get back to him. Again, it was so lovely to see you." But Anna couldn't make herself leave quite yet.

"You know, I was just asking Alexia about you," Geneviève said, as though divining Anna's thoughts. She waved her hand in the air and continued with a knowing smile. "He's around here somewhere."

Anna asked Geneviève to say hello to her son and then started to head off. Geneviève wished Anna good luck. "I'll be keeping an eye out for Jon Snow."

He's here. He's here. He's here, Anna thought as she quickly made her way toward her own bench. She felt foolish for being so happy about it, but she couldn't help it. She had felt his presence and was glad to know she could trust her senses when it came to such things.

An hour later Jon Snow placed second in his group, which meant he would not be advancing to the main event where Best in Show would be crowned. Anna was disappointed, of course, but she reminded herself that Jon Snow was only two and a half years old, which was much younger than most of the other dogs he competed against. The dog who had won Best in Show the previous year was four years older than him, so he had plenty of time to become the one true king of Westminster. Second place would bring a ribbon home, which meant she had now achieved her goal of showing a dog and winning a ribbon.

During the competition, she had scanned the crowd hoping to spot Vronsky and his mother in the stands, but she never located them. Anna knew Geneviève would tell her son they had run into one another, so she forced herself to remain patient and let him find her. Tracking him down herself would give the wrong impression, something she was already worried she had done at the dance club.

Anna left her seat in the main arena and started to make her way back to the bench area when she received a call. It was Alexander. She was about to answer it, but as she stared at the picture of her bf's face on the screen, she couldn't make herself accept the call. Instead she ignored it, quickly texting him her second-place news and telling him she'd call him later. He immediately texted back: CONGRATULATIONS!!!!!!!! with balloons, but she had put her phone back before seeing his message.

When she arrived at Jon Snow's empty bench, Alexia Vronsky was waiting for her. He was standing there admiring the next dog over, a feisty tri-colored corgi named Scribbles. Vronsky was wearing perfectly fitted jeans, a slim-cut T-shirt, and a navy Thom Browne sports coat expertly tailored to his build. His blond hair looked shorter than it had when she last saw him, but it was still long enough to hang slightly over his eyes. She watched as he brushed his hair out from his face. His baby blues were just as dreamy as she'd remembered them.

Anna stood there and admired him from a slight distance unnoticed. Just before she was about to walk up out of the crowd and say hello, she felt something goose her in the backside. Jon Snow's favorite greeting, for dogs and humans, was nudging his giant snout into a butt. He had just arrived from the winner's circle and was amped up from all the excitement. Twin four-inch strands of drool hung from his jowly mouth. Anna turned around and crouched on the floor, wrapping her arms around his big furry neck, and he returned her enthusiasm by knocking her over. This was a common occurrence in their owner-pet relationship as Jon Snow outweighed Anna by sixty pounds. Very much accustomed to such things, Anna laughed and inspected her outfit for the inevitable splotch of drool.

After she untangled herself from Jon Snow's mane, Anna looked up to see Vronsky gazing down at her, flashing a smile as he offered her a hand to help her to her feet.

"Are you sure you can handle the slobber?"

"I'd love to handle any slobber associated with you," Vronsky replied in his most charming voice.

Anna laughed at his response and took his hand, his palm warm, his grip firm. He helped her up and soon they were standing face-to-face where they struggled through the motions of an awkward half hug, some-how managing not to touch at all, betraying every instinct and desire to do the opposite.

"Count Vronsky, meet Jon Snow of the Wall, second best of the Working Group, though I disagree," Anna said. "Jon Snow, meet Count Vronsky, best in his breed. Shake." Her Newfie did as he had been taught and held out his paw, which Vronsky shook with a smile. He then took a knee and gave the giant dog a proper greeting.

Anna watched the whole thing with a huge smile until she remembered where she was, rushing over to Lee Ann and congratulating her on a job well done. Lee Ann handed Anna the large sea foam–green ribbon, which she took happily. Her plan was to have it framed for her dad when he arrived home from Asia.

Jon Snow was exhausted from his big day and rightly so. He made an anxious whimper that probably meant he wanted to see his sister, Gemma, and curl up with her for a much-needed nap. After Vronsky took a few pictures of the happy occasion, Lee Ann's assistant led Jon Snow away to her hotel room. Lee Ann said good-bye and rushed off to watch the dogs being judged in the next group.

And just like that, Anna and Vronsky were alone together. Even amongst the swarms of people, it felt like they were the only people in the Garden.

"Can I take you to a late lunch?" Vronsky asked, the din of the crowd fading around his voice.

"Yes, sure, sounds fun." She knew she should feel somewhat guilty, but all she felt was hungry, thirsty, and happy. What was the big deal? It was just one little lunch.

XI

Anna had never been to Keens Steakhouse before, but she knew it was a place her father and brother frequented after taking in a game at the Garden, where her father had four courtside seats. At one point in time, Keens, which was over one hundred and thirty years old, had a strict policy that barred women from eating there. When she walked into the large bar area and took in the masculine décor—lots of wood and leather—she noted that the place still didn't seem to court a female clientele.

"Are you sure you're okay with it here?" Alexia asked. "We can go somewhere else."

"No, this is great. I've always been curious about this place," Anna replied, suddenly nervous. She had been expecting to go to a much more casual place for lunch, but when Vronsky suggested Keens she jumped at the idea. "Your mother didn't want to join us?"

"My mother only eats breakfast and dinner. She finds lunch 'pedestrian,'" he said with a smile. "Give me a moment, I'll grab us a table."

Before Anna could tell Vronsky she'd be fine at the bar, and might even prefer it, he was gone, appearing again moments later with the maître d' by his side, a short man in a brown suit with a comically large mustache. Anna gamely followed him out of the bar through the first-floor dining room, past the maître d's podium, and up a wooden staircase. Once on the second floor they crossed through a larger dining room and headed up a short flight of stairs that ended in a small hallway near the restrooms. Eventually the maître d' gestured Anna through an open doorway, and they were in a small private dining room with only four tables, none of which were currently occupied. Anna turned around in confusion to face Vronsky, but before she could ask what was happening the maître d', whose lapel pin read REMI, spoke, his voice low and booming. "Welcome to our Lillie Langtry room, named after our very first female customer in 1905. Ms. Langtry sued to gain access because she was tired of hearing about our famous mutton chops and wanted to try one for herself."

Anna laughed in surprise and sat down in the chair at a four-top table that he'd pulled out for her. Vronsky sat in the chair across from her, as the mustached man cleared off the other two table settings. He handed them each a large menu and informed them their waiter would be in shortly. Before leaving the room, he stopped, turned back as if to tell them something he had forgotten to say, and declared: "If I had a girlfriend as beautiful as you, I'd want to keep you all to myself, too. Happy Valentine's Day." He exited with a wave.

Anna stared at Vronsky, her mouth open in surprise, but received only a shrug in response from him. "I only paid extra for the private room, not the compliment. That was all him. Though he does make a good point."

Ann looked around the quaint room in silence. She really didn't know what to say. She was flattered by all the fuss, but this was followed by a nagging worry that being hidden away seemed to imply they were doing something wrong.

"You're uncomfortable. I'm sorry. I know the main dining room gets loud, and I wanted us to have a chance to talk without shouting. This place has several private rooms; the one I thought we'd be in is much larger and I've eaten there a lot of times with my brother and his friends. I didn't even know about this room," he said, standing. "I'll go ask for another table."

"No, don't. It's okay. I like this room. And good for Lillie Langtry for standing up for what she wanted. It's just . . ." Anna trailed off.

Vronsky reached across the table and took Anna's hand. "Tell me what you want. I'll do whatever makes you happy."

At his touch, Anna blushed. Lunch in a private dining room was fine, but holding hands was definitely not. She pulled her hand back out of his grasp. "I am happy," she said. "Happy that Jon Snow won second place. It's nice to have someone to celebrate with."

She was about to tell Vronsky that her father would have been here with her if he could, but their waiter entered at that moment, a lanky man as tall as the maître d' had been short, and as surly as the other was friendly. Anna decided to wait to thank Vronsky for his Valentine's Day gifts, and instead the two ended up discussing every family animal they'd each had the pleasure of knowing. Vronsky was a skilled story-teller and captured his mother's voice in a way that was accurate, but not disrespectful. His best story was about the time he and his older brother, Kiril, were charged with looking after one of his mother's lap dogs, who they had managed to let wander off in an airport in Italy. The two of them searched everywhere, frantically trying to find the Yorkie, which they did only minutes before boarding their plane. Or so they thought. After they had taken off, they realized they had the wrong dog.

"How did you find out?" Anna asked, her face bright from laughing.

"When the dog lifted his hind leg and peed on the man's shoe across the aisle. You see, my mother's dog was named Petunia. She was a girl!"

Anna then shared the history of how she came to love Newfound-lands, which she followed by telling the story of her six-year-old declara-tion of having a dog at Westminster one day when she was grown up.

"Well cheers to you being all grown up!" Vronsky said, lifting his glass of sparkling cider to toast her. They clinked glasses merrily and moved on to the next animal they had in common: horses. Vronsky had ridden a lot as a child, in fact it was possible they crossed paths at Stau-gas Farms when they were both much younger. But when he rode a mo-torbike for the first time in Italy at the age of eleven he found himself less impressed by the speed of four legs, and hadn't ridden a horse since, though his thrill-seeking tendencies made him a big fan of the Mary-land Hunt Club timber race. Anna told Vronsky she was less attracted to the danger of horses and instead adored the companionship and con-nection they provided. She had two horses, both of whom were sure to be wondering if she was dead because she couldn't recall the last time she had let an entire week go by without riding them. "I just don't understand where the last two weeks have gone," she said truthfully, then added, "Well, now that Westminster is over with, I suppose I can go back to my boring old ways."

"Boring? You? I highly doubt that!"

Anna smiled and locked eyes with him. "You may be projecting, Alexia. Because from what I've heard, you're the one at the table who has an exciting life. I'm sure I'm far less interesting than the many, many girls you normally run around with."

Alexia grinned and shuffled uncomfortably in his chair, but before he could respond she leaned in and continued.

"Can I ask you something?"

"Anything."

"Why do they call you 'the Count'?"

"Do you really want to know?" he asked.

"I don't know, do I?"

"When Bea and I were toddlers, she had this purple blankie I used to tie around my neck. Her favorite color was yellow and she wore this yellow dress all the time. So our parents nicknamed us 'Bea Bird' and 'the Count.'"

"You mean, like, from *Sesame Street*?"

"Go ahead . . . laugh."

"It's adorable. But you do know . . ." Anna trailed off, not wanting to be the one to repeat the rumor.

"People think it's because I've slept with too many girls to keep count. I do know and I'm fine with it. It's far better than the truth."

"Not to me."

"Well good, because you're the only one I've ever told."

Anna was thrilled that he'd confided in her something so embarrassing, but she was also alarmed. This was a crossroads, and they both recognized it immediately. They could keep up the pretense of a friendly meal filled with light chatter and family stories, or they could move on to more serious fare: talking about the undeniable chemistry between them. Vronsky would have liked to broach the subject, but there was no part of him that wished to talk about his reputation with Anna, and he couldn't talk about the one without bringing up the other.

This wasn't out of fear that Anna would discover all the girls he had wined, dined, and 69'd before her. That was common knowledge he was sure she had heard. No, he strongly felt his past no longer mattered. His view since he met her was that Anna was his only future and no other girl mattered to him. Every moment he spent in her presence felt dreamlike and came with a beautiful yet disconcerting need to feel powerful in her eyes. Every single thing about her he found enthralling: the way she twisted her napkin while she talked, how she covered her mouth with her hands when she laughed too loudly, the way she leaned ever so slightly forward when he told an entertaining story. Against all these things he was powerless.

"I was wondering what your thoughts were on whether we should return his dog," he said in a quiet but firm tone. Anna was confused and her face showed it. Vronsky continued. "The homeless man from the train station. He's posted a few lost dog signs. I found one the other day and was planning to call you about it." Vronsky reached into his inside jacket pocket and removed a folded-up piece of paper. He handed it across the table to Anna.

She took the paper and opened it, finding a crude homemade LOST DOG flyer with a hand-drawn charcoal sketch of a dog with a large square face that looked like a cross between a pit bull and a Rottweiler. The dog's name was Balboa. There was no phone number listed, only the name Johnson listed as the owner and Grand Central Station as the address.

"This is the dog you rescued . . . on the day we met?" Anna asked, sad to remember the other one who had died by her train on the night of their first encounter. She looked up to meet Alexia's eyes and he nodded.

"He's still with my mom's dog walker," Vronsky reported. "I've taken him to the vet and he's had a full checkup. I had them scan to make sure there wasn't a previous owner before Johnson, and Balboa didn't have an ID chip." Vronsky reported these facts in a tone that was hard to read, though it softened as he went on. "It's funny his name is Balboa, because I had been calling him Rocky since I found him."

Anna nodded, her smile withering and her mood now matching Vronsky's. "So you're asking whether we should reunite the dog with his homeless owner?" Anna paused, thinking. "I would need to talk to him. The man. I can't decide until I meet him. Maybe I'll see if I can find him." Anna folded the paper Alexia had handed her and put it in her purse. She then pulled out her wallet.

"Whoa, whoa. You mean to do this right now?" Vronsky asked, more than a little surprised by Anna's decisive nature.

"This sign is the saddest thing I've ever seen. He must be out of his mind right now. I'd go insane if one of my dogs went missing for two minutes; I don't know what I'd be like after two weeks. Do you know how happy he's going to be to get his dog back? And if we have it in our power to bring a happy ending to this story, why wouldn't we do it on a day that's all about love?"

Vronsky found Anna's passionate outburst captivating, though he wished she would be a bit more realistic. "Anna, everything you just said may be true, but that doesn't change the fact the guy's homeless. Shouldn't we consider the dog's welfare first?" Vronsky asked this in a way meant not to challenge Anna, but to better understand her.

"Alexia, most people don't choose to be homeless. I know my dogs would rather be with me on the streets than in a home with someone else. But I also concede that I'm a crazy dog lady so maybe I am jumping the gun. Look, I'll know what to do when I find Johnson."

"That's fine, but what's not is you tracking down some homeless dude by yourself."

"Well, then I guess we need to get the check, because I only have a few hours before the Best in Show judging starts."

Vronsky shook his head in wonder. Perhaps winning that ribbon and fulfilling her childhood goal had catapulted her into adulthood after all. He stood up from the table. "I'll go get the check, but you owe me a dessert." Anna looked up at the beautiful boy standing before her and nodded.

XII

The pair, one blond and blue-eyed, the other raven-haired with charcoal eyes, made a striking couple as they walked lockstep into Grand Central Terminal together. First, they had surveyed the streets around the entrance, showing the poster to every homeless person they found, like two TV detectives looking for a lead on a missing person's case.

"Excuse me, sir, do you know a Johnson? He's a man who lost his dog," Anna asked. Her questions were almost always met with blank stares, but Vronsky followed this up by holding out cash, which really opened the dialogue. From what they could gather, Johnson was a regular in the neighborhood, usually sleeping on the benches inside the station. No one had seen him in the past day or two.

A determined Anna took the news in stride and headed inside the station with the intention of exploring every train platform until they found him. Together they crossed through the grand hall. Anna had decided they should start with the track where Johnson's other dog had died. If she were bereft and desperate, that's where she would be.

"Track twenty-seven," Vronsky volunteered, not caring that he was showing his sentimentality by remembering their first meeting place.

Before they went down the escalator leading to the track, Anna stepped to the right and turned to face Vronsky. "Thank you for coming with me," Anna said.

"Are you kidding me? There's no one else I'd rather be spending my day—"

"Stop. You didn't let me finish."

"I'm sorry. Go on," he added quickly, again in awe of the dazzling beauty before him.

"I also want to thank you for the . . ." She paused, looking for the right words. ". . . very thoughtful gifts you sent me earlier today. I appreciated all of them, but I can't keep them. My bag is still at the Garden, so I can return them to you when we get back later."

Vronsky frowned, unprepared for this. He was careful to keep his voice casual and calm. "But I don't want them back. They're for you, Anna. Each one was for only you."

"Alexia, I know you know this, but right now I think we both need to be reminded: I have a boyfriend. It's not right for me to accept gifts from another guy." She took a breath and forced herself to just say it. "Especially today of all days. I'm sorry."

"No, no, don't apologize, Anna," Vronsky responded, reaching out to touch her arm but then stopping himself. "It's me who should be apologizing. I didn't mean to upset you. I just had to let you know how I feel. You're all I've been thinking about since we first met. And I promise I've never felt like—"

"Alexia, stop," Anna interjected. "Talking about it will only make it worse, okay?" This wasn't going at all how she wanted it to. "Can't we just be friends? Friends who look for homeless people together?" Anna tried to keep her voice light and airy.

"Yes, of course," Vronsky replied, not looking at her. He said the words because he had to, not because he believed them. Alexia Vronsky didn't, couldn't, wouldn't view Anna as a friend, and frankly he didn't want her to see him that way, either.

Anna nodded, relieved to have done what she knew was right. She stepped forward and went down the escalator. She wasn't sure whether he'd follow her, but she hoped he would.

Vronsky stepped onto the escalator two steps behind her, continuing their odyssey together.

Anna's intuition was quickly confirmed. They found Johnson lying down on a bench at the far end of the platform. He looked to be in his forties, but his stringy hair and beard, both fully gray, gave him the appearance of someone much older.

"Johnson?" Anna asked. "We want to talk to you about Balboa."

The man sat up so fast, Anna startled and stepped backward, while Vronsky stepped forward, putting his arm out to shield Anna.

"Where is he?" Johnson asked, his eyes wild. "Did you find him? I've been scouring the whole damn city . . ." His anguish was evident.

Anna, unafraid, sat down next Johnson and looked him in the eye, explaining how they were there the night he was arrested. Vronsky had rescued Balboa and taken him to a safe place. Johnson's relief at the news was clear and he excitedly told them how he had found Balboa three years ago when he was a puppy, abandoned and bleeding in a dumpster. He had nursed the dog to health and Balboa had repaid his kindness and protected him when he was once attacked by a group of drunken college kids. Clearly the memory upset Johnson because he grew agitated. "You're going to give him back. He's my dog. Mine! He's all I have now that Scottie's gone."

Vronsky bristled, but Anna kept her cool. "We are. We will. I needed to meet you first."

"Are you sure you're able to take care of him?" Vronsky added.

"He eats before I do. I treat him good," Johnson said defensively. He was growing more anxious by the second. He kept rubbing his dirty jeans with both hands and then whispered, "He's mine and I need him. He needs me, too!"

Anna, now satisfied, gently told Johnson they'd return Balboa to him.

"Now! You do it now!" The man jumped up and grabbed Anna's arm.

Vronsky stepped in quickly, pulling Anna away from Johnson's grip in one swift motion. "Sir, you need to calm down right now! If it weren't for her, you'd never see your dog again. I, personally, wonder if Balboa wouldn't be better off where he is."

Johnson apologized immediately, assuring them over and over that he was able to take care of the dog. "I miss him so much. Please, he's all I have. I love him and he loves me. We should be together."

Anna promised Johnson they would return, and she and Vronsky left together. They took the subway to the dog walker's apartment, then shared an Uber back to Grand Central with Balboa sitting in between them, and then watched the reunion between Johnson and Balboa that even Vronsky had to admit was touching. Afterward they passed the time conversing on safe subjects: the classes they were taking, the friends they had in common, and the TV shows they both watched. Neither mentioned the holiday again, though there were signs of Valentine's Day everywhere. As the sky darkened into night, they saw dressed-up couples heading into restaurants holding hands. There were women on the street proudly carrying the flowers they had received at work from their lovers. They even watched a man crossing the street in front of them holding a giant bouquet of heart-shaped balloons flapping around in the breezy twilight.

Anna and Vronsky had spent half the day together, hours of walking close, their hands inches apart, itching to reach for the other. In the cab back to Madison Square Garden, they were quiet at first, both lost in thought contemplating their weird and wonderful day. A few blocks away from the Garden, Anna turned to Vronsky. "If you think I didn't notice you giving Johnson money for Balboa, you'd be dead wrong."

Unable to deny it, Alexia looked Anna in the eyes. "And if you think I gave him the money just for Balboa's sake, then you'd be wrong. Anna, I wanted you to see it, but it wasn't a ploy. I don't want to play games with you." He knew this was the moment to kiss her, but he didn't want to overwhelm her with his intensity, even though he was already overwhelmed himself. "Anna, have dinner with me tonight, right now."

Anna shook her head. "You know I can't." She met his eyes. "Alexia, I'm not saying no because I don't want to go. I'm saying no because it isn't right."

The cab ride was silent after that, and when they pulled up to Madison Square Garden, Vronsky got out and held the door open for Anna, who got out, but not before asking the cab driver if he could wait. "I'm coming in with you," Vronsky said.

"You can't. The show's televised; what if we're seen together?" Anna didn't say her boyfriend's name, but it was obvious that's what she meant.

"I have to get the box back," he reminded her. "You're the one who said you wanted to return my gifts."

Anna knew she was caught. "Fine, I'll keep them. But you should go. Now." Anna wasn't sure she could handle being near him for a moment more.

He didn't press her on the matter. "Happy Valentine's Day, Anna," Vronsky said, embracing her before she had a chance to refuse him. Anna inhaled his heavenly scent even though she knew she shouldn't.

"Happy Valentine's Day, Alexia," she murmured back, before pulling away from him and running into the Garden.

When Vronsky climbed back into the waiting taxi, the driver glanced at him in the rearview mirror. "Man, how did you let that pretty thing go?"

"I haven't," Vronsky replied, speaking the only truth he knew. Vronsky pulled out his phone and texted his cousin Beatrice his next move, hoping it would be checkmate. Need assistance. Need house party ASAP. Maybe country house?

Her reply was immediate. No doubt, Boy Scout. Costume party?

He replied, You're the boss.

How was V-day?

Vronsky sighed, more like a groan, and sent his cousin one last text. Woof!

XIII

Although Kimmie had now spent an entire week in bed, she still didn't feel better when she and Lolly arrived at their dad's brownstone on Sunday night. Her father took one look at his pale, skinny, youngest daughter and immediately pulled out his phone, calling his ex-wife to discuss what was going on. Kimmie sat on the steps, her chin propped up on her hands, listening to the conversation start to get heated between her parents, her mother blaming him for not taking her to the doctor earlier. She stood and went upstairs to her room, not caring that her parents were fighting, not caring about anything at all.

An hour later, her sister knocked on the door and asked if she could come in. Kimmie didn't answer, so Lolly entered. Seeing Kimmie was already in bed, Lolly walked over and climbed under the duvet. "Mom hung up on him twice, but he called her back both times," Lolly reported. "She answered, which means she's really worried about you. You know how one of Mom's favorite things is to ice Daddy out."

Kimmie just nodded, too tired to care about her parents' squabbles, even when she was the topic of discussion.

Lolly was worried about her little sister, too. At first, she felt it was an attention-seeking, oh-woe-is-me move on Kimmie's part, and she was too busy with her own life to get involved. But Kimmie did look pretty gnarly, and now that it was hitting week three Lolly had changed her mind. "Kimmie, do you want to talk about it?" Kimmie turned away, not wanting to show the tears that were now falling down her face. "Please," Lolly pleaded. "It might make you feel better." More silence. "Look, I know I haven't been a great big sister lately, and I'm sorry. But I'm worried about you." Lolly reached out and touched her little sister's hair, which she used to be jealous of because it was so much thicker than her own. Now Kimmie's hair was limp and needed a good shampooing. "Hey, if you take a shower, I'll give you a blow-out with my new Dyson Airwrap. I'll beachwave your whole head and then we can take dope slow-mo videos to post. Or how 'bout I give you a mani? Steven got me some fire nail art stickers from Korea and you can have first pick."

"No thanks," Kimmie said, sniffling. "I just want to sleep."

Lolly was now officially concerned. She had apologized, a rarity for her, and even offered Kimmie access to her mani/pedi kit, which her little sister always pestered her for. "Name it, Kimmie, and I'll do whatever you want. Or better yet, ask me anything, and I promise I'll answer truthfully. Seriously, the more embarrassing the better." Lolly almost burst into tears with relief when this finally got her sister to flip back over and face her. She gave Kimmie a big smile of encouragement. "I'm glad that worked, because if it didn't, I was gonna have to remove the X-Acto knives from your art box."

"Is Vronsky with Anna now?" Kimmie asked, hating herself for wanting to know.

"What? No! Of course not!" Lolly replied sharply. She knew her tone was too strong, so she continued more gently. "I mean, as far as I know they haven't seen each other since that night at the club. I asked Steven about Anna yesterday, and he said she was in Boston this weekend seeing her boyfriend. She goes up once a month."

Kimmie digested the news but said nothing, annoyed she had even asked. It's not like she really cared what Vronsky did anymore. The last few days she hadn't even thought about him that much. She had pinched a few of her mom's Ambien when Danielle was off at her Bar Method classes. She had only been taking a half at a time, but she liked that they gave her dreamless sleep.

"I'm sorry he hurt your feelings, Kimmie, but that guy is so not worth all this misery." Lolly handed Kimmie a Kleenex to wipe her runny nose. "Are all your tears really just for him?"

"What does that mean?" Kimmie asked. "Just say it, Lolly."

Lolly took a deep breath, careful to keep her voice calm and nonjudgmental, theorizing that perhaps part of Kimmie's misery stemmed from a second boy besides Vronsky. She knew from Steven that Dustin had planned to ask Kimmie out on the night of Jaylen's party, but his end goal had been to ask Kimmie to his senior prom, which despite being a tad cliché, she found endearing. Dustin left the club so early that night that she and Steven both assumed something had happened between him and Kimmie. It had only occurred to Lolly in the last day or two that perhaps part of Kimmie's misery was wrapped up in the fact that she had rejected Dustin's advances for Vronsky, only to get dissed by Vronsky immediately afterward. This one-two punch of bad timing was enough to knock anyone on their ass. Perhaps Kimmie was rueful over her lost opportunity with Dustin, who wasn't as babe-a-licious as Vronsky but was vastly superior in intellect and character.

Kimmie listened to her sister's theory with interest, surprised that Lolly had spent so much time pondering her well-being. Lolly usually spent all her free time thinking of how to make herself look better and which perfumes would make her smell better for her dumb boyfriend. Kimmie wondered if there was a scent that stopped your boyfriend from cheating. "Hey, can I ask you another question?" Kimmie asked.

"Sure," Lolly said. "Go ahead."

"What happened on Valentine's Day? You came home so early that night."

It was now Lolly's turn in the hot seat, and she wasn't pleased one bit. Lolly wanted to tell Kimmie it was none of her business, but she knew that she couldn't. She had agreed to answer any question, so she had to stay true to her word. "Let the record show I know you're changing the subject because you don't want to admit I'm right about the Dustin thing." Lolly sat up and fluffed her pillow for a moment, stalling as she decided whether to tell her sister the truth. She hadn't even told Miley and Hannah the real story, but she thought perhaps she should take her own advice and air her problems. "Okay, Steven rented us a room at the St. Regis for Valentine's Day so we could have a super romantic night together. But when I got there, he wasn't feeling well. I was disappointed, but what could I do, you know? We rented a movie on pay-per-view, ate room service, and just cuddled and stuff." Lolly stopped, not really wanting to recount the rest of her story.

"And then what?" Kimmie asked, showing the faintest spark of her old self.

"And then we started fooling around . . . one thing led to another and in the middle of his special V-Day present he lost it." Lolly said the last part in a rush, her cheeks flushing in embarrassment.

"Lost what?" Kimmie asked, innocently.

"Think about it, Kimmie," Lolly urged. "He lost it . . . as in . . ." Lolly held her index finger straight up in the air and then let it drop slowly down.

"Ohhhhhh," Kimmie said. "Ewwwww."

"Don't say 'Ewwwww.' It wasn't his fault. I read about it online and apparently it's a thing that sometimes happens to guys. He was probably freaked out from all the pressure of Valentine's Day."

"Well, it wasn't your fault, either."

"I never said it was! Of course it wasn't my fault. Why would you say that?"

"I don't know, because you were the one . . . it doesn't matter, I'm sorry."

"Because I was the one what? Giving it? You think it's my fault?"

"No, no, no, I was just making sure Steven wasn't blaming you, because if he did I'd be pissed and kick his ass." Kimmie regretted displaying her newfound hatred of men in front of her sister. She had been flip-flopping between abject sorrow and man-hating rage for several days now.

The last thing Lolly wanted was to start a fight, so she gathered all her strength and reined herself in. "Kimmie, no, Steven didn't blame me. But he did get all weird and locked himself in the bathroom for a long time complaining about his stomach, but I think he was hiding in there."

"You mean he was crying in the bathroom like a girl?" Kimmie snorted. This was the closest she had come to feeling joy since the downward spiral of her life had begun.

"Kimmie, stop being a psycho meanie! I don't know what he was doing in there, but the whole night was ruined. I tried to talk to him about it but he refused. So, that's why I came home early! Now I'm upset, too, but I guess that's what you wanted. Are you happy now?" Lolly didn't mean to yell at Kimmie, but her Valentine's Day shit show was something she desperately wanted to forget. She kept telling herself that it wasn't her fault, but how could she know for sure? Even though she tried not to think about "Brad," she couldn't help wondering if Steven had ever had this problem with her.

Lolly watched as her little sister's bottom lip started to quiver and a new flood of tears streamed down her cheeks. *Good God*, Lolly thought to herself, *and I always thought I was the biggest crybaby of the family!*

"I'm sorry. I'm sorry," Kimmie wailed. "I swear I wasn't trying to make you miserable, too. I'm sorry I'm such a bitch. I just feel so . . . so . . . wretched." Kimmie rolled herself over onto her stomach and gave a half-hearted scream into a pillow.

Lolly rubbed her little sister's back and told her it was all going to be okay. She knew Kimmie didn't mean to make fun of Steven, and it was common for someone who was hurting to lash out and hurt the ones they were closest to. "Well, you're lucky you still have time before you have to deal with stupid penis problems," Lolly offered, trying to find something to lighten the mood. "Seriously, you should put off having sex as long as you possibly can. It's just so complicated and confusing. I mean, like, don't we have enough to worry about as girls without adding sex into the mix?"

Lolly felt Kimmie's back grow stiff below her hands. She wasn't exactly sure how she knew, but she did. Lolly was aghast and unable to hide her horror. "Oh god, Kimmie, you didn't!"

Kimmie flipped over onto her back, still covering her face with the pillow and nodded her head up and down. It was true, her sister had guessed the terrible dark secret shame that was ruining her life. It wasn't just the regret of dissing Dustin moments prior to being rejected herself. It was also the regret of losing her virginity to Vronsky the week before the party where he dissed her for Anna K. Kimmie would have done anything to take it all back if she could. Anything at all.

Lolly wished she had never gone into her sister's room. She was totally shocked over Kimmie's revelation and had no earthly idea what she was supposed to do or say now. This was when it sucked to be the older sister. Sure she had a few years on Kimmie, but she absolutely did not have more experience in the sex department. In fact, now that Lolly thought about it, it seemed that her little sister had lost her virginity before she did. This made her feel both worse and better in alternating waves, an emotional seesaw she wanted to get off of as soon as she possibly could.

How lame that your little sister lost her V-card before you did!

How sad for her that she lost her V-card to Count Vronsky of all people! Though Lolly knew of at least four other girls who were in the same boat.

Meanwhile, still hiding beneath her pillow, afraid to look her sister in the eye, Kimmie's thoughts were also cycling through a Ferris wheel of anxiety.

She thinks I'm a slut.

She's probably going to use this against me forever; I shouldn't have told her.

She's going to tell Steven. He's going to tell Anna, and hopefully she will find it so disgusting she'll never speak to Vronsky again.

Steven's going to tell Dustin to prove that I was never good enough for him. I'm a fallen woman. A fallen woman is a slut, right? I don't even know what a fallen woman is! I'm so dumb!

Lolly bit the bullet and broke the silence. "Kimmie, we need to talk about this." Lolly watched as the pillow now shook from side to side. Lolly grabbed the pillow and ripped it from her sister's clutches in one fast yank. Kimmie was so surprised she yelped, making a noise so silly that the two sisters looked at one another and immediately burst out laughing. Once their giggling fit got going, they couldn't stop, and soon they were both rolling around on the bed laughing so hard they were clutching their stomachs. Lolly got the hiccups and started coughing, and Kimmie had to jump up and run to the bathroom before she peed the bed.

When Kimmie returned, she brought her sister a Dixie cup of water from the bathroom. Lolly normally wouldn't drink tap water, but her throat hurt from her coughing fit. Or maybe it hurt from her activities of last week . . . served her right for listening to some online sex guru about practicing her knobjob technique with a carrot. It was now imperative that she deal with the issue at hand, which in the wake of their laugh attack they could do openly and honestly. This was by far the closest the two sisters had ever been in their lives.

"Did you tell him you were a virgin?" Lolly asked.

"No. I thought he would ask. Or he would know, but he didn't realize until it was too late and then he sounded freaked out about it, and so I lied and said I had done it once before. Last year while I was in Nevada. With my coach."

"Kimmie! You said that? Are you crazy? Holy shit, is it true? That was a lie, right? I don't think I can take it if you tell me your skating coach molested you."

"No, gross. Of course not. Coach Paul is so gay. I lied. I don't even know why. It just came out."

"Well, thank god for that at least, I mean, not about you lying, but whatever, what's done is done. Jesus, Kimmie. Technically you got your cherry popped before I did," Lolly said, looking down at her nails. She had picked the nail polish color Like a Virgin Pink yesterday at the salon. This made her smile in a sad way.

"Shut up! You're lying."

"Why would I lie about something like that?"

Kimmie was shocked, having assumed that Lolly and Steven had been having sex regularly for a year now. Unable to stop her meanness, Kimmie thought: *Why else would a catch like Steven still be with her if she wasn't putting out?*

As if reading her sister's mind, Lolly said, "I know it's weird, but it was just easier to let people think we were boning. I would have told you the truth but you never asked."

"Is it too late to ask now?" Kimmie quietly questioned.

Lolly told her she had been waiting to "do the deed" until she knew she was emotionally ready. She had wanted to be certain she was madly in love with the guy before she went all the way. Basically, she wanted it to be special, since it was a one-shot-once-in-a-lifetime kind of thing. She watched Kimmie's face as she told her all these things and was secretly satisfied to see her sister's eyes grow wider and wider in surprise, but once Kimmie got over the shock of it all, it sunk in that her own experience was as far from Lolly's as one could possibly get. And if Lolly's first time having sex was all about love, then what did that mean about her own first time?

XV

The Greenwich Academy library was the last place Vronsky expected to find his cousin Beatrice after school on a Monday, but when he rounded the magazine racks, he saw her sitting at a table against the wall, clacking away on her gold MacBook.

Sensing she was no longer alone, Beatrice looked up from the essay she was plagiarizing from her stepbrother's theology paper. "Of all the libraries, in all the towns, in all the world, he had to walk into mine," she said to her cousin. "What up, cuz? Nice helmet head."

Vronsky ran his fingers through his hair and flipped her off in jest, then sat down across from her, placing his motorcycle helmet on the table between them. "Naughty girl not answering your favorite cousin's texts after posting a Close Friends InstaStory about sneaking out at two A.M. last night. I had to ride out here to make sure you weren't floating facedown in some drug dealer's hot tub."

"Please, I could snort the whole school under the mirror-topped table," Beatrice quipped. "And you only texted me, like, a few hours ago. I'm a busy bee, V, you know that."

Vronsky reached across the table, flipped Beatrice's laptop around in one quick motion, and stared at the screen. "Impressive. I was positive you'd be on some gossip site checking out Kendall's latest lip gloss release."

"Kylie's the makeup mogul, you numchuck. Kendall's the model!" Though as she was saying this she realized her cousin was purposefully teasing her.

"'So while God distinguishes himself as cause separate from effect, the metaphysical division between Cain and Abel (antediluvian/ postdiluvian) illustrates the effect preceding the cause for the reader . . .'" Vronsky recited. "My, my, my! There may be a brain under all those hair extensions, after all." Vronsky closed the laptop and slid it back across the table. He knew he could only tease Bea so much before she'd go for the jugular. He needed her, and he knew she knew it.

"What's happening with the party planning? Is she coming?" he asked. "I was thinking maybe you could have a slumber party and invite her to sleep over?"

"Yes, maybe if we were twelve years old." Beatrice rolled her eyes at her younger cousin. She had never seen Vronsky desperate over a girl before. Normally she'd roast his nuts over an open flame for being so pussywhipped, but there was something about his ardor for Anna that she found rather sweet. This was the first time she'd ever seen him sweat someone like this. Bea was rarely surprised by people, but she wondered if perhaps Vronsky really was in love with Anna as he claimed. She had seen him infatuated with so many girls over the last two years, and there wasn't a lion on the veld who could bring down a gazelle faster than him, but as soon as he made the kill he'd be off chasing the next piece of tail. She was so curious to find out if a similar fate would befall Anna.

"V, I'm handling it, okay?" she warned. "I heard she went to Boston last weekend, so she should be free this upcoming Saturday night. My Cambridge spies are keeping tabs on the OG to see if he's coming to town first. It's his half-sister's birthday soon, so who knows when her sad little soiree will be. Last year she had an art critic come and give a lecture on Byzantine mosaics . . . at her birthday party! What dwanky boof plans that?!"

Vronsky listened to his cousin in silence, relaxing a little because it was clear she had everything under control. It wasn't that he doubted her puppet-master skill set, but the suspense of it all was driving him mad. He hadn't seen Anna for almost two weeks, and he already knew that she'd gone up to Boston for the weekend. He had been tempted to follow but decided that showing up on another train with her might make him look like a stalker. Also, Boston wasn't a city he was too familiar with, and he didn't want to deal with the headache of tracking her down. If he was being brutally honest with himself, he questioned his ability to stomach witnessing her with her boyfriend firsthand. "Beautiful Bea, have I told you how much I worship you and everything you're doing for me lately?"

"I gotta finish my paper, so you need to run along." She waved him off like a bothersome fly. "Go to the house if you want. Mommy's having twenty people over for dinner, so there should be plenty for you to snack on." She then added, "Though, if you're looking for another kind of goodie . . . I believe you'll find her at Staugas Farms finishing her riding lesson in half an hour."

"Can I borrow one of the horses?"

"You're going to ride?" Bea snorted. "Desperate, much?"

His eyes clouded over at her comment, and he frowned. His cousin was in rare form, so he wasn't sure whether he should try to be serious or not. He had hoped to get her honest perspective, because he had been feeling so unlike himself lately. All these emotions were making him cagey. She was the only person he trusted to talk to about his real feelings, but even still, he was reticent to open up to her completely. While she was a master of manipulation and social climbing, she rarely if ever shared her innermost hopes and dreams, assuming she had any at all.

The only time she had ever bared her soul to him was three years ago when their families vacationed together in Bali. They had tried ayahuasca together, so it's hard to know if that even counted. It hit her first, and he held her hair back while she threw up on the beach. Afterward, Beatrice started to cry and laugh at the same time, then she got up and stumbled into the warm waves. Vronsky, afraid for her safety, even though he was tripping his very own face off, managed to pull her back before she got too far out and before the naturally occurring hallucinogenic completely obliterated his concept of reality.

She started sobbing in his arms then and confessed she wasn't supposed to be an only child. Her mother had had difficulties getting pregnant, so her parents had turned to IVF. After several tries her mother became pregnant with triplets but was aghast at the idea of having three babies simultaneously. Undergoing a risky procedure where one of the embryos would be extinguished, leaving only twins, she suffered a complication and two were lost, leaving Beatrice as the sole survivor.

"My mom is a selfish murderer!" she cried. "It's like a part of me is missing. I should have had two sisters, but no, she couldn't ruin her fucking figure, so she killed them in the womb!" Then she turned to Vronsky and, in all seriousness, said, "While I watched!"

Vronsky wasn't sure if Beatrice remembered confessing this to him, because they never spoke of it again. To be honest, he hadn't remembered it when he woke up twenty-four hours later in a stranger's hammock two miles from the beach house they were renting. But when the memories of that night came back to him on the flight home, it was her inconsolable sadness that hit him like a flash flood.

She had cried for a long time as they lay on the beach looking at the stars. Eventually Beatrice announced in a pitiful voice that she, too, was a murderer because she had already had two abortions. "I hate condoms. Can't stand the smell of them," she said. "Oh my god, that makes me a selfish spoiled brat just like my mom! Do you think I'd be different if I had sisters, Vronsky? Do you think I'd be . . . happy?"

"They missed out on not having you for family," he told her. "I know I'd be lost without you." Beatrice was like a sister to him.

Vronsky thought of this sentiment as he grabbed his helmet off the table. He walked around Beatrice's seat and gave her a warm and loving hug from behind. "I adore you, Bea, I hope you know that." Beatrice tensed up at his touch, but then relaxed into her cousin's embrace.

"Back atcha, handsome; you're my favorite person in the world," she murmured, not taking her eyes off her computer screen. "I'll text you when I talk to your bae tomorrow. If you see her tonight, don't mention the party, okay?"

Vronsky gave her a wink as he walked off, but Beatrice didn't see. She was already busy on thesaurus.com, trying to figure out the minimum number of words she'd have to change to make the stolen paper her very own.

XVI

Vronsky pulled up to a four-way stop on his way to the stables where Anna took her riding lessons. Across from him a blue 2010 Mercedes wagon yielded at the stop sign, and he waved it ahead, despite his right of way. Bikers made other drivers nervous, and his mother warned him that his first accident, even if it was tiny, would be the last time he ever sat on a motorcycle. (Most mothers have jurisdiction over their children until they hit eighteen or so, but rich kids whose families have teams of lawyers to draft their trust funds can get all sort of pesky provisions slapped on their freedom, if they're not careful.) So Vronsky kept his daredevil nature in check when riding in the city.

As the station wagon made a right turn in front of him, Vronsky revved the engine of his red Ducati Monster, lost in thought. It was now his turn to make a left onto the road leading to Staugas Farms, where

Anna stabled her horses. There were no other cars waiting, so he idled for a moment, unsure of what to do.

You're going to look like a total swimfan showing up at a horse farm on a ten-thousand-dollar motorcycle. Everyone knows her there and you can't show up expecting no one will notice. What are you gonna say if you run into her? "Hi there. I just stopped by because I missed your face"? Don't do this. Don't be this guy. You hate this guy. You're the guy who hooks up with this guy's girlfriend. You're the guy who sleeps with this guy's girlfriend and then his sister.

You're also the guy . . . who needs to be where she is . . .

Vronsky gunned the engine and turned left. It was as if the hands of fate punched the throttle, willing him toward his destination. Two minutes later he pulled into Staugas Farms and parked his bike between two Range Rovers. When he took off his helmet, he ran both hands through his hair a few times, took a deep breath, and headed to the stables.

It had been five years since he had ridden a horse and being back around them made Vronsky realize he didn't miss it one bit. There were only two things that had ever appealed to him about riding: the nobility and magnificence of the horses, and the attraction he felt toward the girls who rode them. He found everything else abhorrent. He hated the smell, didn't like the mud, and it turned out he didn't like the look he got from the extremely tall stable hand when he asked if Anna K. was back from her lesson.

"Who wants to know?" He sneered. "I'm not allowed to just give information out about our clientele to any pretty boy who walks in off the street." The guy spoke with an exaggerated slang that sounded false to Vronsky. On further glance, Vronsky was pretty sure the guy in front of him wasn't that much older than himself, even though he towered over him and had the facial hair of someone much older.

"I'm a friend of hers," Vronsky said. He now fully regretted not going straight ahead at the four-way stop when he'd had the chance. "From the city."

"Oh, am I supposed to be impressed? You coming to the country from the big bad city?"

Now Vronsky knew the guy was taking the piss out of him, and he wasn't amused by it. "Look, dude, my Uncle is Richard D. on Pear Lane. He plays golf with Mr. Staugas. Like every week."

"Ohhhhhh, well I guess that makes your uncle the fag on Pear Lane I've heard so much about."

Vronsky moved fast, his fist cocked and ready to pound on the homophobic guy who dared besmirch his uncle's good name, but the dude easily ducked the blow. He doubled over and bellowed with laughter. Confused by the familiar sound, Vronsky turned to find the guy smiling and holding his arms out wide.

"Damn, bruh! I punk'd you good, son. You shoulda seen your face. I'm surprised smoke didn't come out of your nose like that cartoon dragon you loved so much. What was his name, again? Toothy?"

"Toothless," Vronsky corrected him. He shook his head in wonderment. He was so focused on his quest to see Anna, he hadn't recognized Murf, one of his old teammates from when he played Little League in Greenwich. "What the fuck, Murf! The last time I saw you, you were the size of Kevin Hart but now you're as tall as Draymond Green!"

"Yeah, I grew. But I'm only six-three, my boy Green is six-seven."

The two boys embraced in a good old-fashioned bro-hug.

"Sorry I didn't recognize you," Vronsky said, feeling a bit humiliated that he had name-dropped his uncle like a d-bag. "It's been a long time."

"Too long, City Boy," Murf replied. "Let's go catch up over a cold one, aight? And before you tell me you can't 'cause you gotta 'hashtag: go see about a girl,' Anna left five minutes before your goldilocks ass darkened my stable door."

Ten minutes later the two were sitting on bales of hay drinking ice-cold tall boys like Wild West cowboys. Murf and the other Staugas Farms workers hid a big cooler filled with beers for when they needed a break from "the rich twatches we work for," as Murf so eloquently put it. Murf tipped an imaginary cowboy hat at Vronsky. "When I say rich twatches, know that I ain't talking about your boo, Anna. She's not like the others. She's everyone's favorite. Hell, I've got kin in Buffalo where it's cold as a witch's tit in winter and I'm pretty sure she'd melt the whole damn town in January with that smile of hers."

Vronsky raised his can in agreement. As much as he was dying to talk about her, he knew he needed to be careful with what he said about Anna and who he said it to.

"Aww man, you catchin' feelings for her? 'Cause you know she couldn't be more taken. Spill the tea."

"There's no tea to spill," Vronsky said. "I've just taken a number to get in line, so I can admire her along with everyone else here." Vronsky grabbed a beer for himself and tossed another to his friend, who caught it one handed. Murf had been picked for all-stars when they played together and Vronsky had not—well, not until Murf got him on the team by telling the coach he wouldn't play unless his friend did, too. Vronsky smiled at the memory. "Hey, by any chance does Anna drive an old blue Benz wagon?"

"Yep, that's her. Everyone else shows up in this dusty-ass place in brand-new, perfectly washed limited edition Range Rovers, but she shows up in that. Normally she's got those humongous dogs that look like bears in the back, but I didn't see them today. Why do you ask?"

Vronsky drank his beer and shook his head. "No reason." So that was her, at the four-way stop before he got here. She was right there in front of him and he didn't even know it. *I wonder if she knew it was me on the motorcycle?* He hoped not, because if she did know and didn't come back, that might mean he was right about being a fool to come here.

"Okay, if you say there's no reason, then I guess there's not one. But I gotta tell ya, it's pretty whack, you showing up out of the blue when I've never seen your ugly mug around here before, and I've worked here for years now. Now that I'm thinking about it, Anna and I started coming to Staugas Farms the same week. Of course, she was here to ride five-hundred-thousand-dollar thoroughbreds while I was being paid minimum wage to pick up their shit."

"I didn't know you liked horses," Vronsky said, hoping to change the subject.

"I didn't. Still don't. Well, some of 'em are cool," Murf admitted. "I got this job because that's where the judge sent me after I got caught shoplifting. Second offense. It was either this or juvie, and the judge was a friend of Mr. Staugas's and asked if he had any work for a wayward kid. He said yes and set me straight. He even fostered me when my mom went to rehab. Now this stinky mudhole feels like home. Funny how that happens, right?"

Something clicked in Vronsky's head when Murf said it. It was like this little wheel in his head had been spinning and spinning, around and around, making him crazy. But Murf nailed the essence of what he was feeling. Home. The reason he needed to be near Anna was because something about her felt like home. "Murf, she's killing me." Vronsky spoke the words so softly he wondered if he had even said them out loud at all. "I've never felt this way about any girl before. I rode a motorcycle here for chrissakes. To a horse farm. What's happening to me?"

"I know I've got a big mouth, but I'm not a bad listener when you catch me in the right mood." Murf moved around a few bales so he could put his feet up.

Vronsky started talking, and Murf listened. It didn't matter that the two boys hadn't seen each other for half their lifetimes, or that they came from opposite worlds, Vronsky from the one percent and Murf from the poor part of Greenwich that no one even knew existed. For an entire season on the Greenwich Blue Jays they were inseparable: they shared the same team bench, shared a double-cheese pepperoni pizza after every game, cracked jokes, told secrets, and developed a friendship that could bridge any superficial gap between wealth and status. And this meant something to both of them, so it wasn't such a stretch that they could share this here together again.

XVII

When Anna pulled into the stately circular driveway at the front of her house, her stomach slipped into a knot at the sight of Eleanor's custom-hued, baby-blue Mini Cooper blocking the view of the garden. She racked her brain wondering if she had forgotten plans to meet her. She was admittedly distracted these days, so it was possible something had slipped her mind. She checked her iPhone calendar and was relieved to find nothing. Since missing Eleanor's tea party after her all-nighter at 1 OAK, Anna hadn't seen much of her boyfriend's younger half-sister. Anna knew that Eleanor told people Anna was her best friend, but Anna had never once referred to Eleanor in that way, for the simple reason it wasn't true.

What was true was that Anna spent way more time with Eleanor than she preferred, but as Alexander's father's daughter from his second wife they were together for every family occasion. So when Alexander was still at Brunswick (the brother school to Greenwich Academy) Eleanor would somehow always try to tag along, never thinking to ask if she was intruding. And now when Alexander came home once a month for the weekend to see Anna, it was oftentimes hard to find time alone together. Alexander stayed at his dad's house when he came home, and Eleanor seemed to always be there.

On those weekends, if Anna's father was working in the city or out of town and her mother had decided to stay in the city for the night, Anna would sometimes spend the night there. Her father frowned on Anna spending the night at her boyfriend's house, one of the many things he was strict about. Her mother tended to look the other way, which was mainly because she held Alexander in such high regard. When Alexander was invited to vacation with them, they had to sleep in separate bedrooms, which meant if Steven was along, the two boys bunked up. Because of this, there was no way Anna would let her boyfriend sleep over at her parents' house for fear of getting caught. On the weekends Anna went to Boston, her father expected her to stay at his company's corporate apartment in Copley Plaza, but she never did. And thankfully, her father never asked, nor did he seem to check up on her the way she knew he checked up on Steven.

"Finally, you're home! I've been waiting forevs," Eleanor called out as soon as Anna walked through the front door. Eleanor was sitting in the formal living room and stayed put because she wasn't a fan of Gemma and Jon Snow. Whenever Eleanor came over, Anna had to bar them from whatever room Eleanor and she were in, which drove Anna crazy, because the dogs simply didn't understand why. Eleanor claimed she was slightly allergic, but it wasn't true. She found their drool gross and unsanitary, and since she was borderline OCD, it was just easier for Anna to keep them separated when Eleanor did a "pop-by," which was Eleanor-speak for an unwanted intrusion. Anna loathed Eleanor's pop-bys. Why couldn't she just announce her intention beforehand by text like every other teenager in the world?

"Hey Eleanor," Anna said, making sure her voice didn't reflect her current feelings. "To what do I owe this pop-by?"

"I feel like I haven't seen you in forever, and it was making me boo-hoo, so I said to myself, 'Ellie, you turn that frown upside down and scoot your cute B-U-T-T on over and tell Annie you miss her!'" Eleanor's voice was sweet and saccharine. "Is it time for the dogs to say bye-bye, yet? I'm feeling very neglected sitting here all by my loney-lonesome. Plus, my nose is starting to twitch like a bunny's."

Anna sighed inwardly. Normally the dogs knew to make themselves scarce when Eleanor showed up, making a run for the large doggie door in the mudroom, but they must have refused this time as they were still awaiting Anna's arrival. "Gemma! Jon Snow! Backyard!" she commanded, and the giant snootbears got up and headed toward the kitchen. Anna followed them in case Magda, the head housekeeper, had already started cooking dinner. Jon Snow was a notorious counter thief who once savagely destroyed the Christmas turkey, which Anna swore he had learned from watching *A Christmas Story* on TV. She let the dogs out the French doors, and they galloped out onto the back lawn, turning around sadly when she shut the door and they realized she wasn't coming out to play. *Sorry guys, blame Eleanor.*

Anna had planned to read through dinner, but now she had a feeling Eleanor would invite herself to stay, so she texted Magda that under no circumstance could she serve a multiple-course meal. Later, as the two girls ate a vegetable lasagna in the dining room together, Eleanor finally brought up the real reason for her visit. "Annie, can we real-talk now?" Eleanor asked, using her best grown-up voice, which sounded like a talk-show host on a heavy dose of Adderall. "Pweease?"

Anna hated that Eleanor called her Annie and had asked her several times not to, even once enlisting Alexander to make her stop doing it, too, though that didn't work, either. And if that wasn't enough, Eleanor held at least half her conversations in baby talk, which was like nails on a chalkboard to Anna's ears. "Sure thing, what's up?"

"I'm still undecided about what I want to do for my birthday. I mean, besides spending it with my BFF, obvi! Mommy wants to throw me a family dinner at the club, so I'm supposed to find out what works best for you and Alexander. Is he coming down this weekend?"

Anna shook her head. "Nope, I was just there and he has a paper to write."

Eleanor's face fell at the information, landing on her most annoying pouty look.

"Well, I guess we could do my b-day family din-din the weekend after, but that's a little sad for me. You know, because my birthday is technically one day closer to this weekend than the next." This was Eleanor's specialty: passive-aggressive pouting until she wore you out emotionally and got what she wanted. "Maybe Alexander could write his paper here? I just think my birthday family dinner would be so much better if it was this Sunday night at the club."

"I thought your mom talked about doing a brunch this year." Anna knew this would never happen, but sometimes it seemed only fair to torture Eleanor since she was always torturing her and Alexander. Well, she couldn't speak for her boyfriend, because he never complained about Eleanor. "She's my sister, Anna," was his refrain on the few occasions when she let her annoyance with Eleanor show. "Family is family."

"No way, Sunday birthday brunches sound like something old people do. Plus, there's always too much syrup around a brunch for me to ever relax. You know how much I detest—"

"Sticky things, yes, I know. Have *you* talked to Alexander about doing it this Sunday night already?"

"I've left him several messages about it, three today, even. But he still hasn't called me back. I know you two talk every night, so I was kinda sorta hopin-n-prayin you'd talk to him for me. He'll do it if you ask him since he lurrrves you. Please, Annie-pie, Ellie's asking so very nicely."

Anna agreed, giving in to avoid the headache she now felt radiating up her neck, and reminding Eleanor that Alexander said no to her plenty. She knew he'd be annoyed at her for getting involved when he was probably avoiding Eleanor's call on purpose, but she just didn't have the patience for Eleanor's whining right now. The headache crept behind her jaw, making her ears hurt. Less than two hours ago she had been so calm and centered, cantering with Marc Antony, who had jumped particularly well during her riding lesson this afternoon.

Her memory traveled back to when she left Staugas Farms and was at a four-way stop across from a guy on a motorcycle dressed all in black with a red racing stripe on his tinted helmet. Seeing a motorcycle while driving always made her nervous, so she paid special attention to the red shiny bike before her. Her mom called them "donorcycles" and refused to let Steven get one, even though he had begged for an entire year. He gave up after he got his driver's license, though Anna knew her brother rode his friend Kaedon's bike at their house in the Catskills.

She had been surprised to learn on Valentine's Day that Vronsky's mother even allowed him to ride one, and without a proper license, which, even though he had just turned sixteen, he still hadn't bothered to get. (In France when Geneviève was growing up every fourteen-year-old had a moped.) *Ah, there it was!* These days every single thought she had seemed to lead right back to Vronsky. The sleek Ducati bike made her nervous, bringing up thoughts of a motorcycle accident, which made her think of how terrible it'd be if Vronsky ever crashed his motorcycle.

"Annie-hoo, are you listening? I asked you a very important question. Do you think we should have a funfetti cake for my family dinner, or for my actual birthday dinner, you know on the actual day I was born? You've got to be there for that, too. We're having lobster rolls flown in from Maine, I think. Well, at least that's what I told Daddy I wanted . . ."

"Funfetti cake for your actual birthday dinner," Anna said on autopilot. "Vanilla ice cream on the side." She was barely listening, because she was now fantasizing that the motorcyclist she had seen earlier was Vronsky, and that he'd ridden all the way in from the city to see her. He was turning in the direction of Staugas Farms; she had seen so in her rearview mirror as she drove away from him. Wouldn't that have been so lovely? If he had come to see her?

"Annie! Annie!" Eleanor snapped her fingers. "Are you even listening to me?"

Yes, Eleanor, unfortunately, I am. . . .

XVIII

Dustin was surprised when Steven had texted that he should bring his brother over for their tutoring session. He had tried to reschedule their session for the following day since he had plans to spend the afternoon with his brother, but Steven said it was imperative that he see Dustin today, so he and Nicholas came over.

When Nicholas walked into Steven's apartment, he whistled at the fancy digs, which embarrassed Dustin, even though Steven didn't seem to notice. Steven suggested that Nicholas play his PS4 while they did their schoolwork, directing him to a shipment of advance copies of new games that wouldn't come out until next year. Steven's dad was tight with one of the head honchos at Sony's gaming division, so these boxes would arrive every few months with the latest video games.

Just another perk of the superrich, Dustin thought to himself, whereas his brother Nicholas had to comment out loud about it: "No shade, but you one-percenters got some sick-ass perks."

Steven nodded and agreed. "Hells yeah we do." (Comments like this should have made Steven an asshole, yet somehow they came across as charming, which Dustin found to be both disturbing and fascinating.)

Once Nicholas was settled into the living room playing Fortnite, Steven motioned for Dustin to follow him instead of going to their usual workplace in the dining room. Dustin walked down the hallway behind his friend, and Steven led the way into his bedroom and closed the door. Dustin had never been in Steven's bedroom before, and as he entered, he understood why Steven hadn't even clapped back over his brother's lack of filter . . . because it was true. Everything in the lavish, professionally decorated bedroom was top of the line. Dustin felt like a character in a Hollywood movie. Steven turned on the massive flat-screen TV that hung on his wall and commanded Siri to play Lost Boyz' "Lifestyles of the Rich and Shameless."

"Sorry for being so mysterious, bro," Steven said. "But I really need to talk to you and only you."

"Sure thing," Dustin replied, suddenly growing anxious that somehow he had done something wrong.

"I wanted to talk the other day, but I couldn't because of Lolly." (Lolly had been there for their entire homework session two days earlier.)

Dustin was now more nervous, saying a silent prayer that Steven wouldn't mention the very name that he had been avoiding like the plague.

"Stop with the face, dude, this isn't about Kimmie," Steven said.

And there it was: the DJ in Dustin's chest made the vinyl of his heart skip a beat.

"I've been trying to forget the whole thing, really. But I can't. It's impossible. I have to tell someone, and you're the only one I trust with this secret. . . ." Steven was pacing back and forth on the high-end shag carpet in front of the TV as the opening strains of "Renee" bumped out of the special-edition Bose surround-sound speakers.

"Steven, just say it. You'll feel better."

"You can't tell anyone. Not a soul. Cone of silence, but you gotta swear first. This is some fucked-up repugnant shit that cannot leave this room."

"Are you high?" Dustin asked. "Because you're acting like it. And I should know, I've got an addict in your living room right now." Dustin couldn't help but wonder if Steven's dad had a lock on his liquor cabinet.

"No, I'm not high, I had one bump, but it was just to calm me down."

Dustin thought about telling Steven that cocaine was a stimulant, but he didn't want to get off topic or risk losing his friend's confidence. "Steven," said Dustin in his calmest and most trustworthy voice. "I swear I won't tell a soul."

Steven stopped pacing and stood in front of Dustin, who was sitting at Steven's desk in a silver mesh Herman Miller chair. "My mom . . . The other day I . . . fuck! I can't do it. I can't even make myself say it."

"Steven!" Dustin said sharply.

"On Valentine's Day I walked in on some dude with a back tattoo going down on my mom."

Dustin heard the words, but they didn't really register. "Come again?"

"Dude, not cool, not cool at all," Steven said, even though Dustin wasn't trying to make a pun. "It was a dragon."

"What was a dragon?" Dustin asked.

"The tattoo on the dude who was downtowning my mom!" Steven gagged a little. "It had wings on it. It was kinda baller, I mean out of context. It had these iridescent silver eyes that looked—"

"No one cares about the tattoo!" Dustin started pacing. "Did they see you?"

"Nah man, he was deep in there and my mom was staring at the ceiling. I had to come home and deliver a V-Day gift for my dad and there was music playing and I opened the door. God, why did I open that fucking door? My whole life would be different if I didn't open the motherfucking door! Fuck! It even ruined my favorite swear word!"

Steven's bedroom door swung open. Dustin and Steven stared at Nicholas, who was standing in the doorway. "Dude!" Steven said. "Don't you knock?" Dustin saw the irony in this but kept silent.

"Yo, just got the final skin, Entropy, and it's dope AF!" Nicholas declared. "I saw Hot Pockets in y' fancy-ass fridge, can I snag a couple?"

"Nicholas," Dustin said. "We're eating dinner with Mom right after we're done here."

"Have as many as you want," Steven said quickly. "Sorry, we're just talking about my history paper."

"No doubt, stay nerdy," Nicholas said with no judgment whatsoever. "Nicholas out." He shut the door.

Once Nicholas was out of earshot, Steven relayed to Dustin the whole episode in all its gruesome detail. It was obvious that Steven had been bursting at the seams to get this off his chest for some time, and the more he talked the calmer he became. Dustin, on the other hand, got more and more animated as the conversation continued. It was as if

Steven had passed his psychological baggage off onto Dustin like a flash drive planted on an innocent bystander in a spy movie.

"Dude, I can't even imagine . . ." Dustin said to his friend, even though he would still trade Steven's mommy drama for his own if it meant Nicholas and his mom would mend their relationship. Actually, he'd have to think about that one.

"No, you can't," Steven agreed. "I've been avoiding her for days, but she's starting to sense something's up. You think it's the Hot Pockets that fucked me? I left two in the microwave on Valentine's Day. What if my mom knows I know about the dude with the dragon tattoo and his Big Baller shitkickers?"

Dustin was barely following the words coming out of his friend's mouth.

"Dustin! Tell me what to do."

Dustin thought about the Hot Pocket situation. His own mother would notice, but that's because she was obsessed with having a spotless kitchen and would have found the forgotten Hot Pockets immediately. She also wasn't the type of mom to get head from men with back tattoos. These were key differences. "No way your mom saw them. Don't you guys have a cook? A chef, or whatever you rich people call your staff?"

Steven stared at Dustin in awe. "Duuuuuuuude. Why didn't I think of that? I could have asked Marta last week and then I wouldn't be brickin' it nonstop. This is why I'm friends with you, you smart son of a . . . really nice lady."

"I got you man," Dustin said. "And besides, even if your mom did find out you knew, she's not gonna ever bring it up." The relief was now apparent in Steven's face and Dustin was pleased that he could be somewhat helpful.

"One problem down, one to go," Steven said. "How do I un-remember this shit? It's like burned into my brain."

"*Eternal Sunshine of the Spotless Mind*," Dustin said.

"The what of the what now?"

"It's this Charlie Kaufman movie with Jim Carrey and Kate Winslet and there's this company that can erase your memories if you really want to forget something."

"Holy shit," Steven said. "That's not a documentary, is it? Can they do that?"

"Please, if they did I'd have already been there," Dustin said. "You'll just have to forget the old-fashioned way. Booze and drugs, or *GoT* for the third time in my case."

Steven laughed. "You're a good friend, Dustin," he said, clapping his hands on his friend's shoulders and looking him straight in the eye. "Thank you. I feel better."

"Better enough to do homework?" Dustin asked.

"Nah, but better enough to play a three-way FIFA tournament with your bro?"

"Let's do it," Dustin said. It was obvious his friend was in no condition to study, and Dustin was nervous about his mom-brother reunion dinner so he was all in for the distraction, plus he knew Steven would still pay him for the tutoring.

When the two friends walked into the hallway, the smell of Hot Pockets wafted from the kitchen but neither one of them said a word about it.

XIX

Every weekend, all over the country, teenagers are having house parties.

But what is typical for 99 percent of teens was quite different from a Beatrice D. shindig. Her parties started out as ragers and always went well into the wee hours of the morning. The cops were never called, the reason being that her favorite house-party location was a fifteen-thousand-square-foot country home on sixty acres, just over the New York border. It was probably misleading to call it a house party, but an estate party didn't exactly have the same ring to it.

Normally Beatrice sent out her invites on perfumed stationery, but because this party was so last minute, she was forced to send an Evite. She chose to send it while she was at school, wanting to have eyes on her guest of honor as she received it. Though the girl in question had no clue she was the sole reason for the hundred-plus-person get-together, that's exactly what she was.

Beatrice located Anna sitting on the steps in the winter sunshine, bundled up in her white Moncler coat with the fur trim reading *The Bone Clocks*, and hit send. Bea checked her own phone and saw the new email with the subject line: IT'S MY PARTY AND I'LL DRUNKCRY IF I WANT TO! She smiled at the line; not her best creative work, but it amused her.

Bea looked back up at Anna, who had stopped reading and was now checking her phone. Bea had to move quick.

"Hey, Annacakes, can I count on your presence?" Bea asked, joining her on the steps even though she detested sitting on the ground. "I want you to spend the night. Like officially, as opposed to the rest of the drunken animals who will no doubt crash there, too. We have eight bedrooms and you can have first pick, because your pores are so tiny."

"Me and my pores totally want to come," Anna said. "But Eleanor's birthday is next week and it's turning into a scheduling nightmare. I'm still waiting to hear when the family dinner will be."

"Family dinner? Good lord, don't tell me you ran off and secretly married the Greenwich OG without telling anyone. Think of all the expensive gifts you'd be missing out on!"

Anna laughed. Bea was probably the funniest person she knew, though she'd never tell her brother this. "No, of course not!" Anna responded even though she knew Bea was only teasing her. "You think I'd willingly become sisters-in-law with Eleanor?" As soon as the words came out of her mouth, Anna regretted it. What was it about Beatrice that brought out her catty side? "That was mean of me. I take it back."

"There are no takesie-backsies in life, babe. You've got kitten claws anyway. Trust me, that wasn't mean. Allow me to demonstrate mean: Eleanor is a blandiose slunt whose skanctimonious drama-dialing must be a real thorn in your pretty French-manicured paw."

"Bea, stop!" Anna stifled a laugh. "She's Alexander's little sister."

"Half-sister," Beatrice corrected. "Look, I'm a stepsister, which is even lower than a half-sibling, but if my older stepbrother Royce's girlfriend didn't come to my birthday party, I'd get over it and we're supes tight. Eleabore is your bf's problem, not yours. And remember, everything can be solved if you throw enough money at it. Get her a PEGG." Anna looked at her, confused. "A preemptive guilt gift . . . My dad's the king of such things. I knew exactly when he was gonna miss one of my birthdays because I'd get some super-mongo gift ahead of time. He bought me an alpaca when he was gonna miss my tenth birthday. Hell, I was hoping he'd have to go to London for my sweet sixteen so he'd buy me a Bentley."

Anna's father didn't do the pre-emptive strike thing but would instead show up with a GGAF, guilt gift after the fact. When he came home from Singapore two days ago, he brought her a new orange ostrich Birkin bag because he felt bad for missing Westminster.

"I'm not taking no for an answer. You deserve to have your own life, too. I know there's way more to Anna K. than being Alexander W.'s perfect girlfriend, hell I danced with her just the other night. Dig deep and rescue your inner party-girl, 'cause my bash is gonna be fun as fuck. I'd tell you what Vronsky's planning to wear, but he'd Marie Antoinette me in a flash." Beatrice dropped an imaginary guillotine over her neck and made a cartoonish dead-queen-walking face.

At the mention of Vronsky's name, Anna's suspicions were confirmed. When she first opened Bea's Evite, the first thing she thought was that the timing seemed odd. Beatrice was known for her parties, but they were usually planned far more in advance than this one. *Alexia asked his cousin to throw a party so he could see me!* She couldn't be certain, but she knew it was true.

"Okay, okay. I'll be there. I just have to figure out how to deal with Eleanor," Anna said. Bea was right, it's not like she was married to Alexander. She was only seventeen!

"God help me for saying this, but you can bring the hand-washing Jesus freak if you must."

"That won't be necessary," Anna said, holding up a stop-palm. "She's the worst at parties. My brother calls her a fun-Roomba. Speaking of, did you . . ."

"Invite your brother? Of course I did," Bea purred, happy that everything was going exactly as she knew it would. "You know . . . if you and my cousin end up together, I'd be thrilled to have you and your hunky soupdumpling big brother in the fam."

Anna blanched at Beatrice's directness, but she didn't let on as she found her place in the book she was reading.

"Okay, gorgeous, get back to geeking out, I'm going to lunch," Beatrice said, and strutted off quite pleased with herself. Though she was still uncertain whether Anna was ready to quit the zero and get with the hero.

"Hey, Bea, wait up!" Anna called out. "Can I joinsie? I'm ravenous, too."

Oh me, oh my, Bea thought to herself as she waved Anna to come with. *Vronsky may have caught a pretty little fly in his web after all.*

XX

On the day of Bea's party, there was a 70 percent chance of snow. Anna's father insisted she and Steven take the Cadillac Escalade, which was the safest of all his cars (since Anna refused to drive the Hummer). Anna, Steven, and Lolly planned to leave Greenwich in the afternoon and would arrive at Bea's family estate well before sundown. Bea was hosting a pre-party catered dinner for her A-list friends, the three of them plus twelve others who were all invited to spend the night.

"Kimmie isn't coming?" Anna asked when she saw Lolly and Steven arrive from the city by themselves. "I had Bea send her an invitation."

Lolly shook her head. "Kimmie's been a little under the weather lately."

Anna frowned. She had been hoping Kimmie would come so Anna could clear the air between them. Anna hated the idea of girls letting boys come between them. But after Kimmie had confessed her feelings for Vronsky and then seen Anna dance all night with him, Kimmie probably thought the worst of her. And Anna didn't blame her. "Is it because she hates me?"

"Don't be silly. Kimmie could never hate you. That whole Vronsky thing was just a dumb crush. I never wanted or expected it to amount to anything. They had only gone out a few times before Jaylen's party, so she had no right to get that upset."

Anna wasn't aware that Kimmie and Vronsky had spent any real time together, but she didn't let on that the news bothered her. "Would it help if I called her? She still has time to make it. We don't have to go up early for the dinner."

"Oh no, Anna, you're too sweet," Lolly responded. "Kimmie's actually been sick for a few weeks now. In fact, my mom is taking her out West to see a specialist and spend a weekend at a spa. They're leaving tomorrow morning, so even if she wanted to come, she couldn't."

Satisfied by the excuse, Anna dropped the subject.

Lolly was of course concerned about Kimmie, but she truly believed her younger sister would be fine, and she was super excited to be included in Beatrice's A-list inner circle, which she knew was only because of Anna. She had seen pictures of Beatrice's country house in one of her mom's back issues of *Architectural Digest*, and the property was incredible. Each of the eight bedrooms were decorated in the style of various historical decades, starting with the roaring twenties and including all the fun decades—the Stepford Wife fifties, the groovy sixties, the disco seventies, the feather-haired eighties—but skipping the depressing ones that involved the Great Depression and those world wars. Every room contained a custom jukebox that supplied a soundtrack of music from that decade in time.

Normally, Beatrice assigned everyone a number, and that was the order in which the guest got to pick their bedroom. Lolly had her heart set on getting the sixties "make love, not war" bedroom, which would be the best fit for the costume she had chosen for herself, but she didn't know what number they would get. She was going as young Cher, and she had found a Bob Mackie–inspired jumpsuit with a zipper that went all the way down to her crotch. She had wanted Steven to go as Sonny, of course, but he thought the big pornstache made him look ridiculous. He was going as John Wick, in a Luca Mosca skinny black suit (the same one that Keanu wore in the movie), complete with bullet holes, blood splatter, and a stuffed beagle puppy.

During the car ride, Lolly finally summoned the nerve to ask Anna what she was wearing to the party. She didn't know why she felt weird about asking, but she did. Perhaps it was because Anna was effortlessly chic and didn't have to try hard to look beautiful and cool. Anna confessed she still hadn't decided, but she had a few different options and would decide when they got there. It was exactly this casual confidence that blew Lolly away. Lolly hoped that Anna might volunteer the options she was mulling over, but she didn't. Anna seemed unusually quiet, but then, Lolly hadn't ever been on a car trip with her longer than a taxi ride, so perhaps this was what she was always like.

Lolly's mind now drifted to Steven, who was also unusually reserved, but he had been acting weird ever since Valentine's Day and Lolly was growing used to it. At first, she pestered him to talk to her and tell her what was wrong. He kept insisting that nothing was wrong, he was just distracted by his heavy course load and his dad was cracking the whip about getting serious about his P.G. applications. (It had been decided by his father that Steven needed one more year to shore up his transcript to get into an Ivy, especially with the blowback from the Varsity Blues scandal.) Lolly wasn't sure whether to believe him or not, but he told her he was going to increase his tutoring sessions with Dustin from three times a week to five, which seemed to back up his story. This bummed Lolly out because the other two afternoons of the week they usually spent together going to SoulCycle or catching a movie.

She worried that perhaps "Brad" was back in the picture, but when she asked Steven point-blank about it, he swore up and down that he had never texted or seen her again. He even offered up his phone so that Lolly could see for herself, and though she knew she should refuse and tell him that she trusted him, she didn't. She took his phone and read all through his texts and emails, discovering only that boys were super-boring texters. She had noticed that his text strand with Dustin was only a day or two long, but when she asked Steven about it, he said he had accidentally deleted it. This sounded plausible to Lolly, knowing that out of all of Steven's friends, Dustin was the least likely to be a troublemaker. Lolly was happy that Steven and Dustin were becoming closer of late. Dustin was a good influence on him, and she knew that Dustin was fond of her, which made her feel good.

"Steven?" Lolly asked. "Did you invite Dustin?"

"I did," Steven replied, eyes on the road. He was driving up to Bea's house while Anna was in charge of driving home, the logic being that Steven would be hungover in the morning, as he always was after a big party.

"Well? Is he coming?" Lolly asked, annoyed at the one-sided conversation, though she would never dare to snip at him with his sister in the car.

"He was supposed to be driving up with his brother tonight, but he texted me this morning and said something came up and he couldn't make it."

"I wonder if something happened with Nicholas?" Lolly mused. "I hope not, Dustin told me the other day that he's been clean for almost three months now."

"You should tell Dustin to take the train," Anna piped up from the backseat. "I like Dustin; he's a good egg."

"That's what I always say!" Lolly exclaimed, happily.

"That's because we're good eggs, too, Lolls. Takes one to know one." Anna sat up and put her arms around the passenger seat, giving Lolly a friendly hug. "Hey, Steven told me you have your heart set on the sixties room, and since Bea gave me first dibs, I'll be sure to snag it and then I'll take whatever number you guys get, okay?"

Lolly was so overcome by Anna's show of generosity, she teared up. Not only that, she found it so comforting to know Steven had been listening to her when she voiced her desire for that room in particular. His putting in the extra effort to make sure she got what she wanted delighted her. All Lolly's paranoid thoughts vanished and she let out a deep sigh of relief.

Ava Max's "Sweet but Psycho" bumped on the satellite radio but before Steven could change the station, Lolly and Anna both squealed, "OMG! I love this song!" right at the very same time. The two of them laughed, and Steven called jinx, then turned up the volume and smiled, happy that his girlfriend and his sister were getting along so famously.

Steven was driving away from his troubles, looking forward to one of Bea's infamous parties, observing the speed limit because of the eight ball he had in his hip pocket.

This night away was going to be what the doctor ordered for all three of them.

XXI

The sixteen teenagers were seated at a long table with three Christofle silver candelabras set in the center. Beatrice sat at the head of the table. On her right were Anna; Vronsky; her best most loyal BFF, Adaka, who happened to be actual Nigerian royalty; Murf; Daler and Rowney, fresh off a flight from Milan; and Addison and her twin brother, Benjamin, the teen stars of the biggest Disney Channel show since *Hannah Montana*, who were in town from LA. On Beatrice's left were Steven; Lolly; Rooster, the Wick's star quarterback; Brayton, a ballerina from Stockholm and the daughter of Beatrice's mom's best friend; LiviX2, a pop star duo whose real names were Olivia and Livingston, second cousins who recently inked their first record deal and were playing at Coachella in a few months; and last but not least, Dandy Zander, who went by DandyZ, Beatrice's gay CrossFit-junkie bestie.

An A-list such as this only worked because no one had to compete with anyone else. Each and every one of them had won the lottery, except for Murf, but that was what Bea liked about having her cousin's old baseball buddy in the mix. She kept an eye on him to make sure he didn't appear to be uncomfortable, but he was seemingly at ease in the present company.

When Murf had walked into the dining room and saw that he was sitting between a Nigerian princess and a pair of runway models, he turned to Vronsky and said, "After tonight you should kill me, so I can die a happy man."

"I'm the one who's happy," Vronsky replied. "Really pumped we got back in touch."

"I wish I could take all the credit, but I have a feeling the real reason you're so stoked just entered the room." Murf lowered his voice as Anna K. glided toward them.

Anna's eyes grew wide at the sight of Murf and she hurried over to hug him. Vronsky couldn't help but feel a mild twinge of jealousy seeing her in another guy's arms, even though he knew it was nothing more than a friendly embrace. "You know my boy Vronsky, I assume," Murf said, detaching from Anna's hug.

Anna smiled at her blue-eyed suitor. "I believe we've met once or twice."

"How do you do?" Vronsky asked formally and made a show of taking her hand and placing a delicate kiss on it as he bowed.

Murf chuckled to himself. "If you'll excuse me, I need to go elucidate my tablemates as to the myriad counterintuitive benefits of polyamory. Yeah, Mr. S. got me one of those word-a-day vocab calendars."

Anna and Vronsky both laughed as Murf strutted off.

"So, how do you know Murf?" she asked.

"He was a power hitter shortstop when I played first base for the Greenwich Blue Jays," Vronsky told her. "When we were seven years old. We lost touch for a long time, but recently reconnected."

"Do you know he works at Staugas Farms?"

"Yes, I think I may have heard that . . ."

Anna subdued her excitement, as now she knew for certain that the boy on the motorcycle had been him, but before she could respond, a bell sounded and Beatrice called out, "Dinner, my darling dearhearts, is served!"

Anna and Vronsky headed to the table, and she was pleased (though not surprised) to find that they were seated next to each other. Anna glanced around the room, wondering if anyone was watching them, but no one seemed to care. The only person Anna had to be a bit cagey around was Lolly, but Lolly was busy fawning over LiviX2, telling Olivia and Livingston how much she loved their newest single, "You Only Liv Twice," and that she was dying to go to Coachella and hear them perform live, and of course get the chance to see her current fav Ariana Grande who was headlining this year. They offered to hook her up with some VIP artist guest passes (which were one step higher than the regular VIP passes anyone could purchase) if she was willing to trek all the way out West, to which she asked if they were serious, to which they said, "Yeah, no biggie," to which Steven said he was sure that that could be arranged for Spring Break, to which Lolly threw her arms around her boyfriend's neck and shouted how much she loved him to the rest of the room.

Anna told herself to relax: *No one here cares about your secret crush.*

After everyone sat down, Beatrice tapped her glass with a fork. "Before we eat, I'm going to start by introducing everyone, but I'm not going to name the person. It's your job as guests to guess who I'm talking about." It was games like this one that gave Beatrice her reputation for being the life of every party. Those who knew Beatrice well might have worried about what she would say, but Beatrice was on her best behavior, for she knew the key to a good party was getting everyone loosened up and feeling good.

"Number one: we met naked in a bubble bath," she began, waiting for the first guess.

DandyZ sat up in his seat and shouted, "Your delectable cousin, Count Vronsky!" DandyZ made a kitten claw and growled a little rowr Vronsky's way.

"You are correct, lovey," Bea said. "Now don't be jealous, girls, but as babies Vronsky and I were bathed together countless times." She paused for a moment. "Number two: we met and bonded over our fondness for the Fresh Prince."

Anna knew this one, but she could tell Lolly knew it as well, so she let her call out the answer. "That would be none other than the Fresh Princess," Lolly said and bowed toward Adaka, who gave the table the queen's wave.

"Very good, sweet Lolly, very good," Beatrice said. "Now, for number three: we met when I 'accidentally' wandered into the Wick boys' locker room by mistake. I didn't get in trouble because I told him my eyes were dilated from my optometrist appointment." She covered her mouth for a second like she was telling a secret. "It was a total lie! I just wanted to see how everyone was hanging . . ."

Murf's hand shot up.

"We're not in school, Murf, no need to raise your hand," Beatrice said.

"Oh word, my bad," Murf said. "I bet that's my boy Rooster right there."

"Correct!" Beatrice said. "And quite the package he is. Upstairs and down."

Vronsky fired a look at Murf. "How'd you know that?"

Murf shrugged. "Honestly, he's the only one of y'all who looks like he plays sports."

"Number four!" Beatrice commanded the attention back to her. "We met in the Valentino showroom in Milan, but we bonded in the bathroom ten minutes later when we . . . ahem . . . powdered our noses together."

Daler's lanky runway model arms extended over her and Rowney, pointing down at both of them. "That was us! But we weren't putting on makeup, we were doing blow . . ."

Rowney jabbed her pointy elbow into Daler's exposed rib cage. "You're not supposed to guess if it's you, and FYI, she wasn't being literal when she said 'powdering our noses,' she was being euphorical."

"God, I love you, beauties." Beatrice blew them a kiss and continued. "Number five: we met at a Little League game when he came up to me and said, 'Your cousin was too embarrassed to tell you this but you've got birdshit in your hair.'"

Now Anna chimed in, "That's got to be Murf!"

"Correct! You guys are too good at this game!" Bea laughed.

"No fair," Murf said. "That clue was way too easy!"

"My apologies, Murf," Beatrice said. "I may be perfect but I'm not infallible . . . Number six! We met at a Bergdorf shoe sale, when we were both holding the same shoe and we had the same size feet. Lucky for us they had two pairs left so we both got them, otherwise we'd both have matching scars."

"Lolly!" Steven called out.

"Steven!" Lolly nudged her boyfriend. "You're not supposed to . . ."

"What?" Steven said. "You're not me!"

"All's fair in love and guessing games," Beatrice quipped. "Number seven: we met at the 'kids' table' at Chelsea Clinton's wedding. After we ate all the chicken fingers we stole a bottle of champagne from the bar and got drunk by the pool. Hint: I wasn't the one who threw up in the shallow end."

The twins, Addison and Benjamin, broke out in a tandem laugh, giving away the answer.

"Addison was so hungover the next day, I got the headache!" Benjamin said.

"Okay, number eight!" Beatrice kept the game rolling. "We met because our superficial mothers dragged us to Canyon Ranch instead of Disneyland."

"Brayton!" Adaka said. "Everyone knows your moms are joined at the hip . . ."

"Number nine!" Beatrice said. "We met backstage at a Justin Bieber concert. We broke in and stole a pair of his boxer briefs from his dressing room, which we now FedEx back and forth like the Sisterhood of the Traveling Underpants."

"Process of elimination," Vronsky said. "Must be Olivia and Livingston."

"Speaking of," Olivia said. "Keep an eye out for a FedEx package in the next couple days."

Livingston smirked and said, "Every time I wear them to bed, I have a Bieber sex dream."

"TMI, Livi," Olivia said to her cousin.

"Oh don't be such a prude, Olivia," Livingston said.

"Number ten! We met when I drunkenly grabbed his dick and he politely informed me that we weren't playing on the same team, and he told me that if I angled the arch in my eyebrows differently it'd really make my eyes pop."

DandyZ took a sip of champagne, stood up, and curtsied. "Guilty as charged."

"Number eleven!" Bea said. "We met at a sandbox in the Hamptons when we were five years old. She showed up with the bucket and I showed up with a shovel."

"My sister, Anna!" Steven said. "I was there, too. I destroyed their sand castle and sent them both running off, crying!"

"Yes you did, you big meanie," Anna joked.

Bea made a face. "That was number twelve. Steven destroying our sand castle. But you do remember he got in trouble and we got banana splits from the snack bar. Game over!"

Everyone cheered and toasted Beatrice, to which she raised her glass and told them it was time to go around the table and say something nice about her.

"Oh come on, Beatrice, don't make liars out of us!" At this, everyone roared with laughter and after that, the entire meal was punctuated with delighted banter and the clink of champagne flutes filled with Veuve Clicquot.

The mood was set for one hell of a night.

XXII

After Anna checked out Lolly and Steven's swanky sixties-themed room, she walked down the hallway to her room, her Louis Vuitton suitcase rolling behind her. She was lost in thought trying to decide which costume she was going to wear. She had narrowed it down to three different ideas: black leather pants, a black shiny latex bustier, sunglasses, and slicked-back hair in the vein of Trinity from *The Matrix*; a platinum-blond wig, black silk slip dress, and a white mini trench coat with stiletto boots, à la *Atomic Blonde*; Mrs. Smith from the Angelina/Brad Pitt movie, for which she would wear one of her dad's white button-down dress shirts and a pair of knee-high red Wellington boots. Each of them was distinctive, and she was very much in the mood to channel a cool ass-kicking movie heroine who didn't take an ounce of shit from anyone.

When she reached the last door at the end of the hall she found Vronsky leaning against the wall, waiting for her.

"Hey you," Vronsky said. "Just making sure you didn't get lost."

Anna held up the map that Beatrice had drawn for her on a cocktail napkin. "I've got a map," she said, immediately on guard. "Though I've never needed one in a private residence before. This house is insane."

"Yeah," he conceded. "Kiril, Bea, and I used to play hide-and-seek but we would never find each other, so it wasn't much fun. Can I show you around your room? I told Bea she should put you here. It's my personal favorite."

Anna nodded as Vronsky opened the door and held it so she could go in ahead of him. Anna entered the room and looked around at the over-the-top, yet still tasteful eighties décor. There was a lot of bright neon, and she loved it immediately. Vronsky followed her in, careful not to let the door close for fear of seeming less of a gentleman.

"I wouldn't take you for a guy who's into eighties music," Anna said. She started to lift her suitcase to place it on the king-size bed that was covered in a shiny satin hot-pink bedspread, but Vronsky rushed over and helped her. "It's not heavy, I got it."

Getting the hint, he took two steps back. "Sorry. I'm just happy you're here, that's all."

Anna didn't respond, mainly because the only thing she could say that wasn't a lie was that she was happy to see him, too. She had just had one of the most fun dinners of her life. During the meal, she kept wondering if she had wasted years being with Alexander, because with him, meals were totally different. All Alexander and his friends talked about was schoolwork, politics, and the environment. Her boyfriend was very active when it came to environmental issues and political activism. But tonight's dinner conversation was more about art, creative pursuits, fashion, and celebrity gossip, which she knew her bf would have found frivolous and lowbrow. *I'm only seventeen . . . isn't it my time to be silly?*

"Anna?" Vronsky said, interrupting her thoughts. "Earth to Anna, come in, come in."

Anna laughed, embarrassed to have spaced out in front of Vronsky. "Sorry. I'm just not used to this kind of party. It's like we're all playing dress-up in some crazy castle. Dinner was so, so . . ." She hesitated, not wanting to sound like a wide-eyed simpleton in front of him. "It was just so fun. I loved it. Beatrice is incredible."

"That she is," he replied. Vronsky was now sitting on the bed. "She's like Vegas: all fun, all the time. But you've got to know when to leave, or you'll end up in rehab or the subject of a true-crime podcast."

All Anna wanted to do was take a running leap and flop down onto the bed next to Vronsky, but she knew she couldn't. That's the kind of thing one did with a boyfriend, and she already had one of those. She wasn't sure what her next move should be.

"Should I leave?" Vronsky stood up and smoothed the wrinkles from her bedspread.

"No!" she cried. "I just . . . don't know what I'm going to wear tonight. Any interest in judging a costume fashion show?" She was tired of worrying so much about what was proper and what was not. She wasn't doing anything wrong; she'd told him that she just wanted to be friends. Friends can ask friends to help them decide what to wear to a costume party, right?

"Nothing would make me happier," he said, his face glowing. He waved Anna to the door that led to the bathroom and commanded, "Go on, let the show begin!"

"We need music, please. I heard from Lolly every room has its own jukebox?"

Vronsky rolled across the bed to the other side and stood up. "As you wish," he said. "One eighties dance track coming up!" He walked over to what Anna thought was a wacky robot sculpture in the far corner of the room. "Do you recognize this guy?"

"No," Anna said. "Should I?"

"Anna K., let me introduce you to Johnny 5 from the movie *Short Circuit*. Beatrice became obsessed with this movie when she was seven, and always said she wanted Johnny 5 for a best friend. When her dad was trying out a trial separation from her mother, he did what any rich father does . . ."

"I know! I know!" Anna raised her hand like an overeager student. "He PEGG'd her!" She covered her mouth with her hands. "Oh, that didn't sound right at all. He Pre-Emptively Guilt Gifted her with Johnny 5!"

"Very good, young lady. Someone's been studying their Bea-speak vocab list. Gold star for you." Vronsky pushed a button in the back of the robot's head and Johnny 5 came to life. "Bea was sad when the prop arrived and didn't talk or move, so her father had someone convert it into a stereo system and added a few lights. Johnny 5 plays eighties tunes via a well-hidden iPod."

"Amazing!" Anna clapped her hands in awe as Madonna's 1983 classic "Holiday" filled the room and she spontaneously started dancing. Vronsky waved her off and she grabbed her suitcase and skipped into the bathroom to change.

After Vronsky made her show him every outfit twice, he finally cast his vote that Anna should go as the star of *Atomic Blonde*. "With your face and that wig, you could have single-handedly brought down the Berlin Wall!" Anna agreed that the blond wig made it feel more like a costume. She stared at herself in the full-length mirror, almost not recognizing herself as the sexy secret agent looking back at her.

"I know how to make sure," Vronsky said. "We have to test it out." He hopped off the bed and started dancing toward Anna, and soon they were both showing off their best eighties dance moves in the middle of the room to Whitney's "I Wanna Dance with Somebody." The next song that played was Foreigner's 1984 slow-dance hit "I Want to Know What Love Is," and the two teens froze momentarily, like a couple of nervous sixth graders at their first school dance. Vronsky recovered quickly, and pulled her into his arms before she had time to object. Anna closed her eyes and thought about resisting, but instead she nestled in even closer to him. When he put his hand on the small of her back, he shocked her, such was the electricity between them.

They danced for only ten seconds before a light knocking interrupted the moment. Anna turned her head and saw Lolly, dressed as a twenty-something Cher, standing in the open doorway holding a large makeup case. Anna and Vronsky separated quickly.

"Sorry!" Lolly squeaked. "I just came by because you asked me to help you with your makeup? I didn't mean to interrupt . . ."

"You didn't!" Anna said. "We were just goofing off. This song came on and . . ."

"And I was showing Anna how I danced at my first school dance in fifth grade. I asked the prettiest girl in class, not realizing she was a full head taller than me," Vronsky said, coming to Anna's rescue. "Her name was Sally W." Anna stared at Lolly, wondering if she believed Vronsky's story, a little unsettled at how seamlessly he could spin a lie and come up with an excuse.

"OMG," Lolly responded sympathetically. "I was the tallest girl in fifth, too! Of course, then, I had no idea I'd stop growing the next year." Lolly entered the room, smiling. "Your room is so cool, Anna! And, you look incredible. Charlize would be jealous if she saw you. I'm thinking a smoky eye and a pale lip would be the perfect touch."

Anna finally found her words. "No, you look gorgeous, Lolly. That pantsuit is to die for. You know my mom has an original Bob Mackie buried somewhere in her closet? I'll have to show it to you."

"Well, ladies, I'm off," Vronsky said. "It's my turn to go get dolled up. Anna, I leave you in good hands." He waved and made his getaway right as Soft Cell's "Tainted Love" started to play. *I've got to get away from the pain you drive right into the heart of me. The love we share seems to go nowhere . . .*

XXIII

Dustin scrolled through Lolly's Instagram and looked at her most recent posts. He could now see for himself the many debaucheries he would miss by bailing on the party. He could probably still go if he wanted, but it would involve a lot of transportation logistics that he wasn't up to dealing with. Today had drained him, and where a party might help some people feel better, Dustin was positive it would only further deplete him. Plus, he was feeling cranky, which wasn't the best vibe to bring into a party. The only thing that really wowed him in Lolly's pictures was the motorcycle from *Easy Rider* parked in the corner of their sixties-inspired bedroom. Dustin had seen the movie for the first time at Film Forum with Nicholas. And the second time by himself during Nicholas's second stint at rehab.

Steven had invited Dustin to the party two days ago. Dustin said no as soon as he heard it was out of town, but eventually Steven persuaded Dustin to come, telling him he could bring Nicholas, and that they were welcome to borrow his Beemer and drive up from the city together, because Steven was going early with Anna and Lolly in one of his father's cars. What finally sold him were three things. One, Steven told him Kimmie wouldn't be there. Second, when Dustin googled the house at Steven's insistence, he saw that it looked like a movie museum filled with tons of props from famous films, including a Johnny 5 from *Short Circuit*, which was one of Nicholas's favorite old movies. Lastly, Dustin liked that he and Steven were becoming friends, not childhood friends, and not friends out of convenience, but friends who wanted to spend time together because they actually wanted to hang out. Dustin and Steven were opposites in many ways, but the differing perspectives they offered each other were no doubt positive. Steven was one of the few people able to get Dustin out of his own head and stop obsessing about everything, and Dustin felt he was useful in teaching Steven to be more thoughtful when it came to his actions.

On the morning of the party, Dustin woke up to a phone call from his dad, asking him to meet him for breakfast. He didn't explain why they needed to meet since it was Dustin's weekend at his mom's place, but his dad told him it was important. Dustin took the subway downtown and met his dad at the Silver Spurs diner near Houston. As soon as he slid into the booth, his father told him he had received a call from the Bronx halfway house this morning informing him that Nicholas had not showed up for work. Full-time employment was a mandatory condition for Nicholas being able to reside there. "I told them Nicholas was sick. But the max he can miss is two days." His dad flagged down the waitress, pointed to the domed donut display case on the counter, and ordered two chocolate glazed. Dustin and his father shared the same sweet tooth. Some of Dustin's favorite early childhood memories were from going with his dad and Nicholas to get bagels on Saturday morning. His dad would always buy two black-and-white cookies for the three of them to share and as childish as this sounds, Dustin always felt like the famous New York cookie represented his family life: he was the needed chocolate part to balance out the vanilla. He smiled ruefully at the memory of his childish innocence.

"When's the last time you spoke to him?" his dad asked.

Dustin checked his phone. "Two days ago. It was just a text about why he thought today's rap is stupid, because all those guys do is repeat stuff and rhyme words with the exact same word, which isn't really a rhyme at all. And don't even get him started on mumble rap."

"Did he tell you he was leaving town?"

"No," Dustin responded. "Dad, you're jumping the gun. Maybe he is sick."

"I went there this morning, and it looked like he didn't sleep there last night."

Before Dustin could respond, his dad received a phone call from Marcy, Dustin's stepmother. Jason excused himself from the table and went outside to take the call. While Dustin waited, the waitress came by and placed the two donuts in front of him. Dustin nervously picked one up and bit into the chocolatey cake.

When his father returned, he didn't sit down, but placed a twenty-dollar bill on the table. "That was Marcy. She was going to visit her sister in Jersey today until she found the car missing from the garage. C'mon, we have to go back to the house."

As the two walked west, Dustin's dad continued with his story. Marcy had assumed they had parked the car in the wrong space again, which had happened before, but when the guy who worked there checked the log it said it was taken out the day before yesterday.

"You mean it was stolen?" Dustin asked.

"It wasn't stolen," his dad continued. "The person who took it had the spare key and a note. Marcy and I are the only two people who are permitted to take it without one."

When Dustin got back to his father's place the pieces slowly clicked together, one by one. Marcy was upset because she had to admit the whole thing might have been her fault. Nicholas had shown up unannounced when his father was at work telling her Dustin had said he could borrow some clothes. Nicholas had spent a few minutes in Dustin's room, but before he left she made him a sandwich and soup for lunch. While he was eating, Marcy got a call from her sister and had left Nicholas alone in the kitchen for five minutes. When she came back Nicholas had been sitting in the same place and had just finished eating. He thanked her and left. Dustin's dad asked Marcy why she hadn't told him about it and she said she'd meant to, but she was asleep when he came home from work that night and then he was already gone before she got up the next day. After that it slipped her mind.

"He seemed completely normal," she added. "In fact, it was the best I've ever seen Nicholas. It was the most talkative he's ever been. With me, at least." As the new wife, Marcy had a good relationship with Dustin because he lived with them part time, but she barely knew Nicholas.

The spare car key had been hanging on a hook by the door, and it seemed Nicholas had used one of the many free pharmaceutical notepads lying around the kitchen to forge a note for the garage to make it look legit. Dustin went to go check through his room. It was hard to tell what was missing since Dustin's clothes were scattered between his parents' apartments, one of the downsides of being a child of divorce. The only things Nicholas had taken were the clothes Dustin had worn to the hip-hop party and maybe a backpack. Though, when Dustin opened the Band-Aid box in his sock drawer his heart sank. He'd had over three grand in cash stuffed in there, but it was now empty except for a folded-up piece of paper. This note was written on paper advertising a new heart medi-cation and had the faded illustration of an anatomical heart at its center. Nicholas had written his words inside the heart: "D, I had to go see about a girl. N."

Dustin smiled, but it was bittersweet. The note his brother left him was a movie reference from *Good Will Hunting*. It was Nicholas who had shown him that movie three years ago on the first night of Chanukah at their grandparents' house in Boston. It had been the last Chanukah Nicholas and Dustin had spent together, and it had been a great time. Nicholas had never been very vocal when it came to their relationship, but that night he did say that Dustin was the Matt Damon character and that he was the Ben Affleck character. He didn't elaborate, but Dustin knew that Nicholas was saying he admired Dustin for his smarts and knew he'd go out into the world and do amazing things. Wanting to play it cool, Dustin didn't say anything back except, "Yeah." But because of this moment Dustin loved the film and had seen it probably fifty times by now. Whenever he pulled all-nighters for school he'd put the movie on in his room for comfort while he studied.

Dustin stared at the note and everything became clear. Last week, during the reunion dinner with their mom, Nicholas received a call in the middle that he said he needed to take. Dustin was annoyed at the time, mostly because his mother was worried, and when Nicholas hadn't returned after five minutes she sent Dustin to go find him. His brother was outside smoking a cigarette and talking on the phone. When he finished, Nicholas told Dustin it was Natalia, the girl he had met at rehab. She had just left the facility and gotten her phone back. At the time, Dustin was happy for his brother, because he could tell by Nicholas's face how thrilled he was to have heard from her. *At least one of us still has a chance at love*, he thought.

When Nicholas returned to the table, he apologized to their mother, but when she asked him about the call, he lied and said it was a work thing. Dustin said nothing, of course, but he assumed his brother didn't tell their mom the truth because he knew she was a stickler about following the rules of sobriety, and one of the big ones advised not to get into a romantic relationship in your first year on the wagon, especially with another addict.

The dinner ended well even though it was tense at times, and Dustin walked Nicholas to the subway station afterward, which is when his brother told him Natalia was in Arizona. She was going to some wellness center affiliated with their program. It was for an outpatient program designed to help her get back on her feet. She had asked him to come and visit, but Nicholas told her it wasn't doable until he saved enough money to get there. Taco Taco! didn't offer paid vacation. Dustin told Nicholas he would be happy to accompany him out West, once he graduated in a few months. He even offered to pay for the plane tickets and the hotel with his tutoring money. His brother answered saying he'd rather drive cross country, like how Matt Damon did in *Good Will Hunting*.

Dustin was touched by his brother's shared reverence for the film, which they had never really spoken about before. But now, he was less pleased, since his brother had obviously decided to rob him and leave him behind.

XXIV

At the same kitchen table where Nicholas had sat three days prior, Dustin filled in the blanks for Marcy and his dad: the rehab girl, the stolen money, the *Good Will Hunting* reference. His father listened to the tale without interruption, just letting his son talk until he was finished, something his mother never did. Jason was relieved that they had a lead as to where Nicholas was going; stealing a car and money to drive across the country to see about a girl was far better than stealing a car and money to buy drugs and get high. Having been an ER nurse, Marcy said she was positive Nicholas wasn't high when he came over.

Marcy apologized over and over for forgetting to tell them about Nicholas's visit, but his father comforted her by explaining it wouldn't have made any difference. He was positive that when Nicholas left the apartment, he had walked straight to the garage and embarked on his cross-country road trip right then and there.

The next decision was whether to tell Dustin's mom what was going on. Dustin voted no, reminding his dad they had agreed to be the ones to step up and deal with Nicholas's care for a while. Sure, the reunion dinner had gone well between mother and son, but it would be a shame to demolish the rebuilding of their relationship over this latest development.

"I'm sorry, Dustin, but I don't agree," Marcy said. "I know it may not be my place to get involved, but as a woman who's going to be a mother, I would want to know."

It took Dustin a moment to understand that Marcy was pregnant.

Dustin had had no idea his father had planned to have children with her, but it made sense. Marcy was only in her late thirties, so why wouldn't she want to have a family of her own? Dustin offered his hearty congratulations to them both, although the joyful news was overshadowed by the current Nicholas fiasco.

Dustin's father cast the deciding vote, saying he understood both his son's and his new wife's reasoning. Dustin's mother had a right to know, but he thought it best to wait until they had more information. "Call him," Jason said. "See if he picks up. If he tells you the truth, we'll go from there." Dustin would have preferred to make the call alone but could tell his father wasn't going anywhere. Nicholas didn't answer anyway, so Dustin left a simple voice mail and asked that his brother call him back. He tried to keep his voice neutral so his brother wouldn't think he was angry about the three grand. Honestly, Dustin didn't care about the money at all, but he was freaked out that his brother took the car. Nicholas had done some really crazy things while under the influence of drugs, but as far as Dustin knew Nicholas was sober when he did this, which made Dustin wonder if love was the most powerful drug of all.

Since the Kimmie debacle, Dustin had made a point to shut down his interest in romantic pursuits. It seemed like so much drama and pain, and he wasn't quite sure what the point was, though if things had turned out differently between him and Kimmie, he would probably be dancing in the streets and shouting the exact opposite from any and all rooftops.

Dustin thought about his brother driving twenty-seven-hundred miles in a stolen car for a meth addict named Natalia and wondered whether his journey would end in disappointment and disillusionment like his own quest for Kimmie had. He eventually concluded that every man needed to find out the truth about love for himself. Dustin loved his brother and wanted to believe in the fantasy that perhaps this girl was what his brother had been looking for his whole life, and that she might fill the void that he'd once filled with drugs.

Dustin stared down at his phone and saw the newest selfie Lolly had posted. She and Steven were dressed up for the party as Cher and John

Wick. They looked so beautiful and happy together. More than that, they looked like their lives were better than everyone else's.

Dustin had read that there had been a growing trend of anxiety and depression in teenagers who had grown up with smartphones. Everyone was addicted to gawking at the endless photo stream of beautiful people living fabulous lives. It seemed the only reason for doing anything these days was just to post pictures of all the fun you were having, just like Lolly and Steven were doing.

But Dustin knew the dark underbelly to the picture. He knew Steven was torn up over his mother's recent infidelity, and possibly had a drug problem himself. And if recent events were any indicator, he was following in his father's footsteps of betraying the woman he was supposedly committed to. And though Lolly had taken down the post of her wearing Steven's mother's fur coat the night she found out about "Brad," Dustin had taken a screenshot of the picture. He didn't do this with any creepy intentions. In fact, he wasn't sure why he had done it at all. Perhaps it was a reminder to himself of the many startling faces of humanity. She had looked like a demon from a Japanese horror movie, eyes rimmed in black, makeup smeared, her expression frozen in pain.

It reminded him of *The Scream*, the popular Edvard Munch painting that so many books and movies referenced. When he was younger he always wondered why that particular painting had captured the popular imagination. Now, having witnessed his mother's suffering over his brother, his own suffering over Kimmie, Steven's suffering over his mother, and Lolly's suffering over Steven, Dustin understood why people liked the painting. It was comforting to know there were others who had suffered like you had.

He scrolled through his photos and found the screenshot of Lolly, mesmerized by the stark contrast between the Lolly he knew, the Lolly dressed as Cher, and the fur-clad Lolly in the photograph. It was almost unimaginable that they were the same girl.

XXV

At Bea's, a large tent straddled the lawn from the back patio made of stones imported from Scotland, to the Japanese Zen garden designed by the world's best Japanese Zen garden architect (oddly, an Argentinian man named Manolo). This was not your standard white tent used for outdoor weddings or high school reunions. Bea had rented a grand red-and-white-striped circus tent that could easily accommodate an elephant dancing on its hind legs. When Anna had first walked into it, she half expected to see a circus in full swing.

The tent was divided into separate areas. A black-and-white-checkered dance floor took up the center right, with a raised DJ booth in the corner and a full-service bar in the other. On the opposite end of the tent there was another bar and a seating area with high-top tables and red leather spinning bar stools. Several large couches formed a square around a huge full-size Persian rug that had colorful tuffets and Moroccan pillows flung about. Three large hookahs and a bowl of California's finest Kush that LiviX2 had bought for the occasion sat on a low table next to the sofas. Basically, this party had an option for everyone.

By midnight, attendance had swelled to a hundred guests. Due to the size of the tent and the whole property in general, it didn't feel crowded, and the party maintained an intimate, relaxed vibe. Various groups of colorfully costumed people scattered through all the areas, but the beating heart of the party was Beatrice, who was now decked out in a white bikini and red angel wings, a scantily clad Cupid holding court on the Turkish gabbeh rug in the couch area. Beatrice wasn't a hostess who liked to circulate, mainly because she was either barefoot or in five-inch heels. She much preferred to sit and have the party come to her. Sitting with her now were Adaka, dressed as Serena Williams (though it was doubtful the tennis legend ever wore a hot-pink thong under her tennis skirts); Livingston, whose costume consisted of an eclectic mix of random accessories: a top hat, a leather tool belt, a vintage Sex Pistols T-shirt, and a tutu (she was her own version of Wonder Woman, as in "I wonder who she's supposed to be?"); Rooster, sorely lacking in the imagination department, who wore his football jersey; and a couple dressed as a fire emoji and a poop emoji signifying that they were "hot shit."

John Wick and Cher were on the dance floor with two dozen others showing off their fancy footwork to Twenty One Pilots' "Tear in My Heart." Lolly, already drunk from whatever was in Beatrice's punch bowl and high from a no-nonsense whack off the hookah, spotted him first. Her first thought was, *Wow, that guy over there is dressed like my dad*, which made her start to giggle, and the woman he was with was wearing a long sleeve Alessandra Rich polka-dot dress, making her the only female at the party trying to cover up her goods rather than flaunt them. This reminded her that she wanted to sneak back into the house and go peek in all the other bedrooms before they were filled with drunken couples making out.

"Steven, doesn't that guy look like my dad?" Lolly said, still giggling. "Sorry, sorry, I mean, John Wick, doesn't that guy look like my dad?" She turned Steven around so he could see the man she rudely pointed at.

Steven stopped dancing, his face serious. "Fuck!" he said in a low voice. "That's Alexander and Eleanor."

Lolly danced in a circle with her hands in the air, not processing what Steven had just said. He put his arms on her shoulders and leaned in close, so she assumed he was about to kiss her and tilted her chin up in anticipation. "Babe," he whispered. "You need to focus. We need to find Anna before they do. I'll go talk to them and you go find Anna. Can you do that for me?"

Just then Mariah Carey's dance mix version of "Dreamlover" bumped through the speakers and Lolly bopped off to join a triad of gays with DandyZ at the center who were screaming their approval at the song choice.

Steven swore, angry with himself for wasting precious time. Lolly was in no condition to handle her assignment, but then Steven spotted Murf, dressed as Kanye West, sandwiched between Daler and Rowney, the only two girls at the party tall enough for him. (Daler and Rowney were in all green, a pair of Versace and D&G green beans.) Steven danced over to Murf and grabbed him by the arm, pulling him away from the dancing models.

"Dude," Steven said. "I need an assist." He pointed at Alexander and Eleanor, who were now standing by the bar.

"Fuck a duck, that's no bueno," Murf mumbled, and pulled out his phone. "I'll text the Vronsk, but I dunno if his kilt's got pockets."

The boys quickly decided Steven would run interference, while Murf went in search of Anna and Vronsky. Before they could separate, a bare-foot Beatrice was by their side. "I spy with my little eye . . . trouble with a capital T."

"We're on it," Steven replied. Murf nodded and started making his way through the dance floor.

"Mr. Wick, shall we?" Bea asked, placing her hand on Steven's arm. The two of them left the dance floor and walked together right into the lion's mouth, approaching Alexander and Eleanor, who were both hold-ing glasses of sparkling water.

"Dude, what's up?" Steven said to Alexander, keeping his voice casual. "Didn't know you were in town this weekend. Hi, Eleanor."

"Hello, Beatrice." Alexander ignored Steven to say hello to Beatrice, which was what proper etiquette demanded in mixed company. The lady must be greeted first. "You know my sister, Eleanor, right?"

"Of course," Beatrice replied snippily. She hated people who stated the obvious like it could pass as conversation. Beatrice leaned in to give Eleanor an air kiss, but Eleanor took a step back.

"Ooh, sorry," Eleanor said, not sounding sorry at all. "I'm not good with touching a stranger's bare skin. Aren't you cold? Why are you so shiny? Is that glitter?"

"Body glitter," Beatrice said. "The kind strippers use."

"Where's Anna?" Alexander asked, as uncomfortable with Beatrice's outfit as his half-sister was, though he was better at hiding it. "She's here, right?"

"Of course," Beatrice said. "She's probably flitting around some-where. It is a party, after all." She didn't bother keeping the edge out of her voice, which was probably due to the three fat lines of blow she had done already.

The foursome was so busy rubbing one another the wrong way, they didn't notice when Anna and Vronsky entered the tent with Ben and Addison, whose access to Disney's costume department had them dressed as Chip and Dale. They hit the dance floor immediately, oblivious to the fact that many of the other partygoers had already heard about the situation playing out twenty feet away. There were many people at the party who hadn't met Anna before, but everyone there knew the Greenwich OG on sight.

Anna and Vronsky were grinding to Lizzo's "Truth Hurts." They only had eyes for each other, which everyone had noticed all evening, but these were Beatrice's and Vronsky's friends, so no one really cared. Nearly everyone in this bunch had cheated on their bfs and gfs before, or at least seriously thought about it. Anna had lost the white trench coat an hour ago and her black silky slip was sticking to her in the most appealing way. One of the tiny straps had fallen down her shoulder, and Vronsky couldn't help himself, punch drunk as he was. He leaned forward, took the strap between his teeth, and pulled it up and back over her shoulder. His warm breath on her bare skin made Anna shiver, even though she wasn't cold inside the heated tent.

"Hey, Anna!" Lolly hollered. She was standing by the speaker, but from her acting classes she knew how to make her voice carry to the back of the house. Half the party craned their necks to Anna and Vronsky. Enthralled by her dance partner, she reacted to Lolly's call a few seconds later than she should. Lolly pointed and continued, "Alexander is here. I thought he was my dad at first. They wear the same khakis!"

Anna and Vronsky stopped dancing. Anna crossed her hands over her chest and stared across the dance floor. Alexander, Eleanor, Steven, and Beatrice stared back. Lolly noted Steven's face, and she knew he wasn't happy with her. *Oopsie*, she thought to herself as she watched Anna leave the dance floor, alone. Lolly looked around and noticed many of the guests were watching, too. It was only when Alexander clasped Anna's arm and ushered her out of the tent that Lolly had a flash of clarity. She would have hung her head in shame, but a DJ remix of Miley Cyrus's "Wrecking Ball" distracted her. "Ooooh!" she cried, moving her feet to the beat again. "I loooooove this song!" She threw her head back and started singing along, "I came in like a wrecking ball . . ." oblivious to how appropriate the lyrics were to the current drama afoot. *I never meant to start a war . . .*

XXVI

Anna wore Alexander's Burton ski jacket over her tiny dress, unsure where she had left her white trench coat. Her legs were cold, but she walked across the dark lawn toward the pool, Alexander following close behind.

"Where are you going? Why aren't we going into the house?" he asked, crossly.

Anna didn't answer, because she couldn't without lying. She didn't want to go into the house with Alexander, because it was now the setting of some of her newest and best memories, which she didn't want to spoil with the ugly ones she was sure were about to come. "There's a heat lamp. And privacy." Walking faster, she reached the high hedges that surrounded the oval black-bottomed pool. "What are you doing here?"

"I came to drive you home," Alexander said. "It's supposed to snow tonight."

"We're in Daddy's Escalade, it has four-wheel drive. But that's not what I meant. I didn't know you were coming in this weekend at all."

"Eleanor's dinner is tomorrow night now," he answered. "She kept calling and begging me to come down, Anna. You know how she gets. What else was I supposed to do?"

"Tell her the world doesn't stop and start just because it's her goddamn birthday." Anna had meant to stay calm, but she couldn't. She was pissed.

"Anna," he said.

"Don't 'Anna' me, Alexander. You're not my father. I can say what I want. There have been ten thousand emails about this stupid dinner. You do realize I'm not the one related to her, right?"

"Have you been drinking?"

"Yes, I have. You know why? It's a party! That's what people do at parties, drink and have fun. But maybe you don't know that, because we never go to parties."

"Why are you talking to me in that tone? I'm not sure I understand what's going on with you. What have I done to make you like this?" His voice was now a little bit louder.

"Like what?"

"You're barely wearing any clothes and it's freezing. Did Steven give you drugs?"

Anna ignored his question and continued. "Did you know it was a costume party? Why aren't you wearing one?"

"I'm not here for the party; I'm here for you."

"But why? I told you I was spending the night, and I'd be back tomorrow."

"Eleanor was worried you'd get snowed in and Steven's not the most responsible—"

"I'm not your responsibility. I'm your girlfriend!" Anna yelled.

"Anna." His voice was calm now. "You are my girlfriend and I love you. That's why I'm here."

"Excellent. Then let's go join the party and have some fun."

"Anna." Alexander looked at his gold Rolex. "I can't. It's getting late and my paper's not going to write itself."

"Oh my god! If you want to stay, great. If you want to go write your stupid paper, then go do that." Anna stood. "Because I'm going back to the party." She really needed to leave because she had no idea what she might say or do if she didn't. It was like the barn doors had been thrown open and all the horses were running free, trying to escape a terrible fire.

"The fellow you were dancing with?" Alexander asked and Anna stopped. "Is he the guy I met at the train station?"

Anna couldn't turn around to face her boyfriend, so instead she talked to the hedges in front of her. "Vronsky. He's Bea's cousin."

"I trust you implicitly," Alexander began. "But I couldn't help noticing that people seem to be talking about you two in a way that is . . . disheartening."

"Are you accusing me of something?" Anna asked, whipping around in the dark to face him. "People gossip, Alexander. This is Bea's crowd, it's like a sport for them. I've done nothing wrong. We were dancing, so what? I've been dancing with lots of different people all night." She looked Alexander straight in the eyes for the first time since he arrived.

"You're beautiful," Alexander said in a soft voice. "So beautiful that when you walk into a room, every boy can't help but notice. Clearly, Vronsky is taken with you, and I don't blame him. I'm not saying you're purposefully leading him on, but what I am saying is if you do so, even by accident, it would be untoward. To him, and to me. You should be careful not to let him misinterpret your overtures of friendship as anything more. I don't like to be the subject of gossip."

Anna closed the gap between them in four steps, now inches away from his face. "Then you should have worn a costume," she said. "I'm going back to the tent, or we could go skinny-dipping together. C'mon, I'll even strip first." She knew her challenge would be met with silence, which it was. "Figured as much." Anna turned and headed back toward the house. Alexander's exasperated sigh made a cloud in the chilly air and then he followed her.

When they were halfway up the grassy lawn, a figure approached them in the dark. "Alexander? Annie?" Eleanor's voice cut shrilly through the darkness. "Where have you been? Aren't you cold, Anna? I'm freezing. I should have worn my long coat like Mommy told me to. Some weirdo dressed like the Cookie Monster spilled his wine on my dress and now three of my polka dots are burgundy!"

"I'm going back to the party," Anna said as she passed Eleanor in the dark.

"But, but . . ." Eleanor whined, giving Alexander a confused look. "It's almost one in the morning, shouldn't we leave? You know I'm prone to dark circles when I don't sleep enough."

"Anna's staying," Alexander said, putting his arm around his sister's shoulders. "C'mon, I need to get a cup of coffee to warm up before we head out."

Eleanor held her ground. "What do you mean, she's staying? We drove all this way to get her. This is so not fair to me."

"It was a mistake. My mistake," Alexander responded. He waited for a moment longer, and then he, too, continued walking toward the tent.

"Alexander!" Eleanor cried out, stomping her foot in the wet grass. "Wait for me!"

When Alexander and Eleanor entered the tent, Anna was sitting on the floor next to Beatrice, who was in Rooster's lap. Surrounding them were Olivia, Brayton the ballerina (who was dressed as Belle from *Beauty and the Beast*), and Adaka. Alexander walked past them to the coffee station by the desserts, and fixed himself a double espresso, which he needed before he made the long drive back to Greenwich, especially with an unhappy Eleanor in the passenger seat. He walked back to the couch area and stood behind Anna. Anna didn't turn to greet him.

"Beatrice, thank you for the lovely party, but Eleanor and I are going to head out now," he said in a subdued voice. He was about to turn and go, as he had fulfilled his duty by thanking the host, but he stopped. "Also, I apologize. It was rude of me to not show up in costume."

"No apology necessary," said Beatrice, who had just taken a hit from the hookah, which contained a purple budded hybrid called Crunchberry. She exhaled a huge plume of smoke that rose and shrouded Alexander in a momentary fog. Beatrice smiled, the squinty-eyed smile of the super-stoned. "If anyone asks, just say you came as a giant dick."

XXVII

Vronsky and Murf were perched on two different sturdy branches of a hundred-year-old oak tree in the center of the circular driveway. It hadn't been an easy tree to climb, but they managed it by carrying over a large decorative urn from the front steps of the house. The urn weighed at least two hundred pounds, but between the two of them, they beasted it to the base of the tree.

Murf was rolling a blunt in his lap while Vronsky stared off, looking dejected. "You goin' true Scotsman under there, flying commando?" Murf asked, nodding at Vronsky's kilt.

"No freeballin' tonight," he said. "Gotta keep it classy. Anna's here, I mean . . . she was."

"Well, good then, we already had one dickhead pop up at this party," Murf chuckled. "Except it wasn't yours; it was your girl's." He lit the freshly rolled blunt then passed it to Vronsky, who took a drag and held in the smoke for as long as he could, hoping to ease his troubled mind. Tonight was his big chance with Anna, and it hadn't gone well. "Alexander . . ." he muttered disdainfully, exhaling the smoke.

Murf took the blunt from Vronsky and shook his head. "That guy is everything I hate about Greenwich. I don't know how you didn't put hands on that chump waltzin' up in here acting like he owned Anna's ass."

"The thought crossed my mind," Vronsky said.

"If I were you I'd've shown homeboy some manners, but if my black ass so much as looks at a guy like Alexander the wrong way, shit, I can hear the police sirens just thinking about it . . ."

"So you're calling me a pussy then."

"Yeah, basically."

Vronsky laughed and shook his head. "This girl's in my goddamn head, man."

Murf took huge rip off the blunt and let out an enormous amount of smoke drift up into the branches. "Maybe you wanna drop this whole Anna K. obsession you got going on. I ain't ever seen so much talent in one place as there is here tonight and I'm sure all these little shorties would happily line up to make your pretty ass forget your troubles. I mean, Anna's great, but she's just a girl."

"I wish it were that simple."

"Tell me why it's not."

"How can I explain it to you when I don't even understand it? It's like whenever I see her, nothing else matters except for her, like I just wanna be around her all the fucking time and I'm obsessed with everything she says and does and when she's away from me, I feel completely and utterly empty, like I'm a ghost or something."

"You know what you sound like?"

"What?"

"Every single girl who's ever been in love with you." Murf laughed. "Kidding! But real talk, you, my friend, are in hella deep," Murf said. "Which means you got one play left."

"What's that?"

"You gotta go after her with everything you got. No more of this bullshittin' around, having your cuz throw big-ass parties just so y'all can be in the same place."

"I know, I know, I just wish she didn't leave with that asshole . . ."

Murf cut Vronsky off and put his finger to his lips with a quiet shush, stubbing out the blunt on the tree bark as none other than Alexander and Eleanor burst through the front doors of the house and hurried down the steps. Up in the tree, Vronsky and Murf could hear them clear as day.

"This is ridiculous!" Eleanor's whiny voice cut through the cold winter night. "Just go back in there and make her come home with us."

"And what do you propose I do? Club her over the head and throw her over my shoulder like a caveman?"

"She's your girlfriend!" Eleanor wailed. "You shouldn't leave her here with all these drunken idiots frolicking around like they're at some bacchanal in ancient Greece!"

"Just get in the car. I want to go home." Alexander opened the passenger door of his hunter-green Range Rover for Eleanor, but she didn't get in.

"I'm going back in to get her," she said, and her half-brother grabbed her by the arm.

"No, you're not," Alexander said sternly.

Still listening breathlessly up in the tree, Vronsky and Murf both looked at each other with raised eyebrows.

"Let go of my arm," Eleanor said, her nostrils flaring.

Alexander released his grip and Eleanor got into the front seat, slamming the door behind her. He walked around the back of the Range Rover and grabbed both sides of his head before composing himself and getting in on the driver's side.

"Damn." Murf finally breathed as the SUV trundled away down the long driveway. "At least that white girl showed some fight, which is more than I can say for his sorry ass. You know what I say, he's canceled. Anna deserves better."

Vronsky remained silent, his head spinning as much from the new development as the pot. "She's still here . . ."

"Looks like it's your lucky night . . . hopefully both our lucky nights. Those two model chicks your cousin's friends with been clockin' me since dinner." Murf hopped down out of the tree and looked up at Vronsky. "You wanna go hit the dance floor, let old Murf show you how to tear it up?"

"I have to find Anna," Vronsky said.

"Hells yeah y'are," said Murf. "Time to go out-gangsta the OG." Murf danced around in the frozen grass like a prizefighter warming up for the ring.

Vronsky hit the ground beneath the tree with a soft catlike plunk. The first snowflakes of the night began to drift in the frigid night air. "Hey, Murf."

"Whatup, bruh?"

"What if she doesn't feel the same way about me?"

His friend stopped jumping about and thought for a moment. He walked over to Vronsky and put a hand on his shoulder and looked him square in the eyes. "Then at least you'll know . . ."

Vronsky exhaled deeply, the high from the marijuana enveloping him and shielding him from all thoughts of his feelings for Anna going unrequited. In his mind, that was an impossibility. "Yeah," he said. "I guess."

"Come on, Romeo. Last one to the tent is a no-ass-gettin' chump," Murf said and took off running.

Vronsky broke into a sprint.

XXVIII

After putting Lolly to bed, Steven found his sister in the chef's-grade kitchen, sitting on the pantry floor, stabbing at a five-gallon tub of strawberry ice cream with an oversized spoon. It hadn't taken him long to find her in the enormous house, because he knew exactly where to look. Many times, he had found his sister sitting in the pantry of their own house, eating a snack. She did this out of necessity, unable to enjoy her food while two drooling dogs stared at her. She would find a small space with a door where she could hide and eat without distraction. The pantry door in their Greenwich house had been painted twice to remove the scratch marks.

Anna, no longer wearing her platinum blond wig, looked up at Steven expectantly, as though she had been waiting for him the whole time. The pantry was bigger than most Manhattan studio apartments and could easily fit a bedroom set. He entered and closed the door behind him, joining Anna on the floor. She reached over and handed her brother a second spoon, which confirmed she had been expecting him.

Steven, wired from all the coke he had done, seized the spoon and dug in. "Lolly's passed out. She's going to freak when she finds out what she did. By accident, of course."

"Don't say anything," Anna told him. "It wasn't her fault. I only have myself to blame. Well, and Eleanor."

Steven agreed. As much as he wasn't a fan of Anna's boyfriend, he despised Eleanor's self-righteous brand of brattiness even more. It was spoiled whiny girls like her that gave rich kids a bad name. He had once witnessed Eleanor pitch a fit at a country club Sunday brunch when they hired a new pastry chef who added raisins to the carrot cake. "Who fucking shows up like that? Normally party crashers come to have fun, but they were more like party crushers."

"She was worried we'd get snowed in and I'd miss her stupid birthday dinner tomorrow night." Anna didn't see the point in telling her brother that her boyfriend had also felt Steven would impede her punctuality, as Steven was forever running late.

"It's snowing now," Steven reported. "But we're only supposed to get a few inches."

Anna nodded distractedly.

"I heard from Bea that Alexander left right after your talk?" he said, fishing for more information, but not wanting to press her.

"You mean after our fight?" Anna corrected. "How dare he show up here to retrieve me like I'm some child? Though in his defense, I'm sure he wouldn't have come if Eleanor hadn't pushed him."

"Maybe he did it to shut her up. I'd drive to Brazil if it kept her trap shut," Steven said. He was positive Alexander had put some of the blame on him, too, as if he wasn't trustworthy enough to get his sister home in a few inches of snow. He knew Anna would never confirm his suspicions. "How did you leave things with him?"

Anna shrugged. "I don't know. He came in and said good-bye to Bea, but I refused to look at him. I didn't say good-bye to either of them." Anna pushed the ice cream away, suddenly sick of the sweetness. "He had the nerve to warn me about leading on Vronsky. He said he didn't like to be the subject of gossip and it was obvious people were talking about us." Anna watched her brother as she said this, studying his reaction.

Steven blew the hair out of his eyes and shook his head. "That guy," he said, "is such a toolbag, the granddaddy of tools."

Anna couldn't help but laugh. She knew her brother didn't like her boyfriend, but Steven had never once spoken ill of him in front of her. "I don't know if he's the granddaddy of tools, but he really can be difficult," she agreed. "Were people talking about us, Steven? I mean, before Alexander showed up and got everyone talking about us?" She watched her brother nod his head.

"People talk shit about everybody, Anna," he said. "What you and Vronsky are doing is nobody's business except your own."

"That's nice of you to say." Anna shook her head sadly. "But we both know it's not true. Sure, my life is my own, but I am also Alexander's girlfriend. So the company I keep *is* a little bit his business, too. Like how Lolly had every right to be upset over Marcella."

"That was different," Steven said, choosing to defend his sister's honor instead of his own. "I was guilty of being a scumbag. You and Vronsky were just dancing."

Anna grabbed her brother's hand. "I adore you for defending me, but it was more than dancing. I mean, not more like *that*. But, more like . . . well, you know."

Steven looked away, not wanting to let Anna see his face. Of course Steven had noticed the way Vronsky and Anna had been looking at each other throughout dinner, like they were the only two people at the table. Lolly had told him earlier about showing up to Anna's room and finding Vronsky there. Lolly made a point to say the door had been wide open, so it wasn't like they were hiding. Lolly's exact words were, "I felt like I walked into the falling-in-love montage of a rom-com. He's such a smitten kitten!" Lolly had found the whole thing innocent, which is what Steven loved about her. Sure, Vronsky was gorgeous and all, but Anna had a boyfriend, and was in no more danger of straying than Lolly was herself.

"Anna, you know you're only seventeen, right?" Steven said, finally deciding his sister needed the tough love advice she always extended to him. "If you like Vronsky, and yes, it's obvious you guys are stupid for each other, then go for it. Dump the OG and be a normal teenage girl and date boys, go to parties, cut loose. We have our whole lives to get married and be perfect society couples, so why start now? For god's sake, you met Alexander when you were fourteen, which I personally have always found more than a little suspect on his part. What sixteen-year-old dude macks on a fourteen-year-old girl?"

"Two of the girls in my quartet were his age so he just assumed I was—"

"So he says, but whatever. I don't give a fuck about him," he replied. "All I'm sayin' is why not act your age and see how you like it? Look, I don't know what to make of this Vronsky fellow, because he's a straight-up hound dog, but I know you can handle yourself around bad boys. Dealing with me all the time must be good for something. I see how Vronsky looks at you, and it's not the typical hit-it-and-quit-it look. I know these things."

"Steven!" Anna squealed. "Please stop."

"You know what I'm trying to say," he replied.

Anna nodded, because she knew exactly what he was saying. She had had the very same thoughts. In the beginning, she did think Vronsky was only interested in her because he wanted to sleep with her. But now that they'd spent more time together, Anna believed Vronsky's feelings were far deeper than a passing fancy fueled by base desire.

"The ice cream's melting," Steven said and stood up. Anna took her brother's hand and got back on her feet. Together they exited the pantry and were back in the dark kitchen.

"Is the party still going on?" she asked. She looked at the kitchen clock and saw that it was past two in the morning.

"Yeah," he said. "I gotta tell you, this Bea chick is giving my host-with-the-most rep a run for my money. I may have to step my game up next New Year's. I'm gonna go back out to the tent, want to join me?"

"I do." Anna wasn't sleepy at all, so why let Alexander ruin her good time? "Thank you, Steven. You're a great big brother." She stepped forward and hugged him. "I'm going to keep hugging until you hug me back!" she warned, grinning.

Steven wrapped his arms around his sister and kissed her on the top of her head, something he had watched his father do to her a million times. It used to make him a little jealous when he was younger, if he was being honest with himself, how much his father adored Anna, but he'd learned to let it go and not let it get under his skin too much. Anna really worked to be the best person she could be. If anyone was the best of Greenwich, it was his sister, and not her blowhard boy-friend.

Steven's eyes grew misty, as sibling affection overwhelmed him. He knew he was lucky to have a sister like Anna, and all he wanted was for her to be happy. At dinner, Anna had glowed with joy like he had never seen. And if it was Vronsky who made her this happy, then so be it. Besides, he was confident he could give Vronsky a proper beatdown if he ever dared to hurt his little sister.

XXIX

When Vronsky and Murf had returned to the party after seeing Alexander and Eleanor drive off, Anna was nowhere to be found. Vronsky went back to the main house to look for her and had even knocked on her bedroom door, but when he opened the door, the room was empty. Luckily, the Tahoe Alien Indica he'd smoked with Murf helped him stay calm about her unfindability, a word he decided was an actual word even though it wasn't. He was really fucking stoned. What he needed to do was grab a couch in the tent, rest his eyes, and wait for her. Since meeting Anna, whenever he closed his eyes, he saw her face. She was haunting him, but Murf was right that it was time for him to go big or go home as there would be no peace of mind for him until they were together. When he heard Anna's voice calling his name, floating above him, he assumed he was dreaming. He smiled at the heavenly sound, enraptured to hear his name on the lips of his love.

"He's not asleep because he's grinning like a twonk." Beatrice's voice rang out. "A beautiful blond twonk. Wake up, V!"

He opened his eyes and saw Anna standing above him, staring down at him. She was truly the most beautiful girl he had ever seen.

"Alexia, we have to finish our dance," she said in a quiet voice. "Our last one got interrupted."

He sat up immediately and rubbed his eyes to make sure he was indeed awake. Anna held out her hand to him, and he took it quickly. They walked back to the dance floor, hand in hand, oblivious to everyone watching them. When they started dancing, the floor only had a few people on it. Rallying around Anna and Vronsky in a show of support, every member from the party still able to stand joined them on the dance floor.

Like a dormant volcano erupting without warning, the party came alive again in a matter of seconds. A mighty second wind blew through the tent whether they were ready for it or not. The dance party went on for many songs, but at 3 A.M. the DJ packed up and went home happy with his five large, plus the eight ball Beatrice slipped into his jeans pocket for a tip, and soon there was only one couple left on the dance floor, holding each other close.

In Vronsky's arms, Anna felt like she could stay up forever. She was so focused on him—his breath, his hands, his smell—that when she finally looked around she was surprised to find they were alone dancing to the songs from a playlist he had secretly compiled in her honor. She honestly didn't even remember the DJ leaving or when Vronsky had placed his iPhone into a large glass, which served as an amplifier so they could continue dancing.

Only when a big gust of wind blew in at 4 A.M. did Anna shiver a little, which made Vronsky stop dancing, though what they had been doing was more like two people clutching each other desperately as they swayed back and forth.

When they opened the tent flap door, they saw the ground was covered in two inches of snow. Anna had cast aside her heels hours ago and was barefoot, so Vronsky picked her up and carried her across the yard, one pair of footprints in the snow displaying their newfound union.

He carried her all the way through the dark house without running into a single person though the vast place was littered with others also wide awake behind closed doors. Lolly had woken up, thrown up, and brushed her teeth, and, upon opening her door to go find Steven, she found him on his way in holding a bottle of vintage Cristal he'd pilfered from the wine fridge. They were now having the romantic night she had wanted to have with Steven since Valentine's Day.

Beatrice had grown bored of Rooster's dumb jock antics and now had one of the bartenders, Dahlia, a former student of the French clown school Ecole Phillipe Gaulier, in her bed. Meanwhile, the DJ, who everyone thought had gone home, was actually blowing lines with Adaka off an antique mirror that cost more than a car. One of the Livis was painting Rooster's toenails Russian Navy, her signature color nail polish, while composing a new pop song in her head. Murf had scored big-time, sharing a king bed with Daler and Rowney. Clement and DandyZ were hosting a small dance party in their seventies disco bedroom. They had shared their stash of Ecstasy with Ben and Addison and the second Livi, and the five of them were dancing to Hot Chocolate's "You Sexy Thing" like their parents once had at the Limelight. Brayton had discovered the ballroom on the far side of the house, turned on the chandeliers, and was performing a private ballet for a few party stragglers who couldn't go home because they hadn't yet returned from their trip to shroom-land.

In this one glorious moment in time, every teenager in the house was happy making memories they would never forget, but no one more so than Vronsky. When he opened the door to Anna's room, he paused for a moment at the threshold, giving her an opportunity to turn him away. Instead Anna burrowed her face into his neck, and he crossed the threshold into her room, kicking the door closed behind him.

He didn't want to let her go, but he put her down gently on the bed.

Anna was now the one who felt as though she was waking up from a beautiful dream. Worry flashed on her face.

"What's wrong?" he asked her gently.

"I don't want this night to be over. I don't want you to go. I don't want to fall asleep because I don't want to wake up to tomorrow." Where she once had control over her words in his presence, this was no longer the case. Anna felt compelled to tell him everything, how me made her feel, how he excited her and frightened her at the same time.

"Anna," he said, taking her face in his hands. "My Anna, the night's not over, and I'm not going anywhere." She looked at him, her dark eyes sparkling with hope, like he was the only boy in the world who could nourish her back from the brink of starvation. He couldn't hold himself back anymore, he couldn't be patient, or slow, or careful, one moment longer. It was he who was the one who was starving, and it was she who could save him.

Vronsky kissed her soft lips, gentle and slow at first. But she responded immediately to him, and soon the two of them were kissing hungrily, the truth now finally clear: this, them, here, now, was the only thing that mattered, the only thing that had ever mattered.

Anna broke away, her heart pounding in her chest, her eyes wild with want. She hadn't even realized they were lying in each other's arms on the bed.

"We have to stop," she gasped, sitting up. "It can't be like this. It's not right. I want you, but you're not mine to have."

"That's not true," Vronsky said quickly, sitting up and kissing her again. "I'm all yours."

"No," Anna said, and pulled away, now standing up and straightening her dress. "I can't think straight, I meant I'm not yours to have. We can't do this now. It's not fair to him. I'll feel terrible tomorrow." She looked out the window. The sun would be coming up soon and tomorrow would be upon them.

"Don't make me leave," Vronsky said in a husky voice. "I can't. I won't. I'll sleep on the floor."

Anna knew it would be impossible to watch him walk out the door without running after him. "I know it's up to me now," she said. "I need to do the right thing. Give me some time to handle things properly, okay?" When Vronsky didn't answer right away, she went to him and kissed him. She wanted to prove she was telling him the truth and to remind herself why she wanted him so bad. Vronsky nodded, resigning himself to obey her every word. He had hope now, hope that they would soon be together, as she tucked him in on the window seat cushion under the pink bedspread. She wasn't sure she would be able to fall asleep with Alexia lying ten feet away, but eventually she did.

She awoke with a start, totally disoriented, to someone banging on the door. It opened and Beatrice entered wrapped only in a bedsheet, looking a little groggy herself. Beatrice sized up the situation immediately, seeing Anna still in her dress from the night before, and Vronsky, kilt-clad, on the window seat running his fingers through his hair.

"I'm sorry to wake you like this," Beatrice said, her face a somber mask. "Your mom just phoned the house because you weren't answering your cell. It's Alexander. There's been an accident."

Part Three

I

Life's not a bitch, it's actually a dick.
You've got to go out and kick it in the balls.

These were Kimmie's thoughts when she woke up in the morning. It was a revision of a longer quote by Maya Angelou, *"I love to see a young girl go out and grab the world by the lapels. Life's a bitch. You've got to go out and kick ass,"* which was printed and framed above Kimmie's bed in her private room at the Desert Vista Wellness Center. She shortened it and added the expletive to give it some oomph when she wrote it on a pink Post-it and stuck it to her bathroom mirror. She stared at the Post-it every morning while she brushed her teeth. It was supposed to be inspiring, and it was: it inspired her to keep the fires of her man-hating anger burning brightly.

When Kimmie arrived at the Desert Vista Wellness Center in Arizona with her mom three weeks ago, she thought the place was a spa where they would be getting beauty treatments and lounging in the sun by the pool. What she soon learned was that while the wellness center did have a pool, there were no beauty treatments to be had. This spa was more for the mind than the body.

Kimmie did not object or even cry when she learned her mother had brought her there under false pretenses, but instead found it validating. Something had to be wrong with her for her mom to do something so drastic. What she didn't know, and what her mother didn't tell her, was that the weeks after the party when Kimmie was depressed and refused to go to school had set off some red flags at Spence. The only way for her to get back the semester's tuition was if Kimmie was put on medical leave and enrolled in a program. Danielle worried the school might think Kimmie had gotten into drugs or alcohol, but Dr. Becker and the new therapist, whom she had visited at Dr. Becker's suggestion, alerted the school that Kimmie's issues were emotional, not behavioral. Kimmie had exhibited all the classic signs of depression: crying, loss of appetite, sleeping her days away. There was talk of putting her on medication right away, but Kimmie's father refused and demanded to hear other options.

The wellness center's program was nothing so intense as drug rehab. She wasn't locked in a ward at night because her enrollment was voluntary. But she was part of the inpatient clinic, which meant a much steeper price tag than the teenagers who only came a few times a week to participate in the local outpatient program the facility offered as well. Kimmie's days were packed with private counseling, group therapy, art therapy, and exercise. Kimmie felt numb at first, just going through the motions of her daily activity schedule that was printed on a little card and slipped under her door. But there was something about the anonymity of the place that appealed to her. No one knew her, and she didn't know anyone else. Also, she was happy to be almost twenty-five-hundred miles away from New York City.

They had taken away her phone, which she was fine with, not wanting any reminders of whatever was going on with the girls from school, or even with her sister. The last pictures she had seen were on Lolly's Instagram at the airport on the morning before she and her mother left. She had received the invitation to Beatrice's costume party via Anna, but there was no way she would have ever gone, certain that Vronsky would be there. Lolly knew better than to post any picture with him in it, but there were plenty of pictures of Lolly, Steven, and Anna all dressed up in costumes and having what looked like a glorious time with a lot of other beautiful teenagers, a few of whom Kimmie recognized from TV and magazines.

She kept flipping through the pics over and over in the airport, but they started to stress her out, so she turned off her phone and put it in her purse. She decided right then and there she was going to delete all her social media accounts. She wasn't particularly active on social media, mostly because she'd never had the time when she was training, and when she moved back home after her knee injury she never really wanted to post pictures of her boring shut-in life of physical therapy. Once she started school, though, she became obsessed like everyone else and was soon following hundreds of people: girls at school, celebrities, even her old friends from the ice dancing world, but eventually staring at other people's posts started to make her feel weird. She kept wondering if everyone was really having as much fun as they seemed to be. #YOLO #FOMO #JOMO #IDON'TCARE-O

Having to turn her phone in at the wellness center was her first clue that her mother had deceived her. Her second clue was when they got to their room there was only one single bed in it. That was when Kimmie's mother confessed everything, having been too chicken to do it earlier on the plane like she had planned. She was enormously relieved when Kimmie walked over to the little framed quote over the bed, read it, and said, "It's okay, Mom. I like this room." Her mother started to cry and hugged her daughter, telling her that everything was going to be better soon. Danielle explained she was staying at a nearby hotel and would be coming to visit every day, even sitting in on the first few therapy sessions to make sure Kimmie liked her new therapists before heading to Canyon Ranch to meet some of her friends.

"You need to know you're not a prisoner here, Kimmie," her mother explained. "If you want to go see a movie or eat at a restaurant you can just take an Uber and go. You'll just need to sign out and be back before your curfew." She pulled out the booklet about the Desert Vista Wellness Center and left it for Kimmie to peruse at her leisure. "Dr. Becker said this is a wonderful program, and the patients he's sent here always came back rested and ready to tackle life again." Kimmie nodded and reassured her mother once again she wanted to feel better and was ready to work toward that goal. The last week at home, she had been feeling so low she had even googled "cutting." The videos she saw online were very upsetting, and what disturbed her even more was that when she read the blog posts of girls who were cutters, a lot of them said they did it to stop feeling pain, as opposed to inflicting it. When Kimmie thought about how she was feeling, it wasn't pain exactly, but more a fuzzy numbness, like she was underwater, or trapped behind thick glass.

"Does Lolly know I'm going to be here for a month?" Kimmie asked. Her mother said she hadn't yet told her sister anything but would explain everything to her once she returned home. Kimmie's only request was that she tell Lolly not to update her on gossip from home. Her mother agreed that Kimmie needed a total break.

During her first week of therapy Kimmie learned she had most likely been suffering from low-grade depression ever since returning home after her career-ending injury, and that the first time she felt any sense of joy was when Vronsky kissed her at Steven's party, which she latched onto like a drowning person to a life preserver. Desperate to keep the good feelings coming, she had become wrongly convinced that he was the sole reason for her happiness. If this were true, then what she had thought was love wasn't love at all. Her brain was just trying to find a way to make her feel better.

This revelation was a great relief to Kimmie. Maybe she wasn't to blame for her error in judgment in rushing into sex with Vronsky. If anything, he was the one who had unfairly taken advantage of her delicate mental state. She was the victim in the whole thing, the same way all the girls he had seduced before her were victims, the Little Red Riding Hoods to his Big Bad Wolf. In her second week of therapy she jumped at the chance to change the narrative. If she didn't want to be the victim, then it was within her power to do something about it. Life had been a dick to her, but not anymore. It was time for her to take action and kick it squarely in the balls.

II

Kimmie attended group therapy once a day, usually in the morning, but sometimes she went to a second session in the evening, as well. There was something about listening to the troubled lives of other teenagers that made her stop analyzing her own problems. All she had been doing was dissecting her own psyche for weeks now and frankly she was sick of herself. Plus, there was a girl who often attended the evening group sessions who Kimmie had a crush on. When Natalia had caught Kimmie's attention last week, Kimmie had an intense feeling of admiration for her, a feeling not dissimilar to how she felt around Anna the first time she met her. It wasn't romantic, this longing she felt, but a different beast altogether. She didn't "want" her. She wanted to be her.

Natalia was probably the same age as Lolly, but she could easily have passed for someone much older. Kimmie knew Natalia couldn't be older than eighteen, because if she was, she'd have to attend a different group. Even though she was tall, skinny, had no hips and two puffy bee-stings for breasts, she exuded a raw sexuality that exploded out of her like a Roman candle. Kimmie hated short hair on girls, but Natalia had an artfully disheveled mop of bright green and blue hair that perfectly accentuated her wide-set emerald eyes. Perched on her metal folding chair, she was like an alien cat creature sent down to Earth to let the human race know exactly what was what.

During the five times she had spoken in group, Kimmie had ascertained the following: Natalia had grown up in Vegas with a single mom who worked as a cocktail waitress at an off-strip low-rent casino and dabbled in a little light prostitution when money was tight; Natalia was twelve when she tried meth for the first time (given to her by her mom's on-again/off-again drug dealer boyfriend); the only thing she knew about her dad was that he was a degenerate gambler who had no interest in his daughter other than sending cash whenever he won big (which wasn't that often). Natalia said she had tried a lot of other drugs, but what she liked about meth was the invincibility it made her feel. She had once run the Vegas marathon high on meth in four hours wearing Converse high tops, jeans, and a bikini top.

She had just gotten out of a fancy rehab facility (one of her mother's old rich dude regulars got her in as a charity case, and she had been selected to enroll in an outpatient research study of meth addicts, which is how she ended up at Desert Vista) and she was now two months clean, a record for her since she had started using. What Kimmie liked best about Natalia was she didn't seem to care what people thought of her and spoke about whatever happened to be on her mind when it was her turn to share. She found being sober boring AF, and the only thing keeping her from using again was her new boyfriend who she had met at rehab. "I wake up and think about meth, but I go to work instead. After work I think about meth, but I come here instead. After group I think about meth, but my bf picks me up and we go get dinner. After dinner I think about meth, but we go home and fuck until we're both asleep. Oh, and if the craving gets particularly bad, I get pierced or add another tattoo to my canvas."

Kimmie normally preferred to sit across from Natalia in the semicircle so she could stare at her, but when she showed up to group today, the only seat available was next to her.

"Hey, you," Natalia whispered. "Smelly Pits tried to sit there, but I told him I was saving it for you. Thank god you showed up!"

Kimmie blushed with excitement before Dr. Rodriguez started the session. She could barely concentrate as Dime Bag Dougie complained about his tortured high school experience, because she was so elated at Natalia enlisting her as an ally. Kimmie's mother had given her the advice that she was here to work on herself, and not to make friends. "Misery loves company, and I don't want you getting sucked into someone else's problems, okay?" At the time, her mother made sense, but now that Kimmie had learned more about psychology, she thought her mother was wrong. If anything, listening to the outside perspectives of others was helping her better understand herself.

When she was a competitive ice dancer, Kimmie had had no time to analyze herself, concentrating instead on her footwork and focusing on the next competition. But after it was over, she had been left with a huge void of unmanaged time and energy. Kimmie's one-on-one therapist, Dr. Park, told Kimmie she needed to explore things she was interested in.

"But how will I know?" Kimmie asked. "What if nothing interests me?"

Dr. Park assured her that the big struggle of one's teenage years was figuring out those things for oneself, and not just going with the pack. "Trust me, you'll know what you like when you see it," Dr. Park said. "And it's okay to try things out and experiment, so if you try something and realize you don't like it after a while, then that's okay, too. You're in charge of who you want to be, Kimmie."

These were the words that Kimmie thought of when she turned to Natalia after group ended and said, "Hey, can I grab dinner with you and your bf? I'll pay for it, and we can go somewhere totally expensive. I've got my mom's platinum card."

"Hell, yeah," Natalia answered. "We should slut up and really raise some eyebrows at this snooty French place where my boyfriend is a dishwasher."

Natalia texted her bf that she'd be out soon then accompanied Kimmie to her room so she could get her purse. Kimmie hadn't brought any dressy clothes, but Natalia said she had a few pieces she could loan her. "Have you ever thought about dying your hair?" Natalia asked as Kimmie signed out. Kimmie hadn't gotten her hair done in a month and was currently sporting gnarly dark roots, but where she'd be shunned in Manhattan for it, no one here had seemed to care.

"I know, my roots are the worst, right?" Kimmie began, but was interrupted by Natalia.

"No, no, sorry, I wasn't root-shaming. I meant, have you ever thought about dying your hair a different color? You're already a smokeshow, but a little pop of color would make your hotness otherworldly."

Kimmie had never considered dying her hair a color other than honey blond in her entire life. But that was the old Kimmie, a person she desperately wanted to bury. "I'd be down to go for it, if you know someone who could do it for me."

"You're looking at her," Natalia boasted. "I've changed my hair color every other month for the last two years so I'm a pro, if you're up for it. I swear you'll love it."

Kimmie nodded happily. "Yeah. But I want something fierce. Maya's got me in a ball-kicking mood."

It didn't matter to Kimmie that Natalia had never heard of Maya Angelou; in fact, she found it refreshing. She was sick to death of snooty private school girls who pretended to read *The New Yorker* for the articles and not just the cartoons; what she liked about Natalia so much was that she was just so real.

Natalia's bf was leaning against a maroon Volvo SUV smoking a cigarette when the two girls exited the building. There was something familiar about the black hoodie he had on, but Kimmie figured it was a popular brand.

Natalia gave her boyfriend a deep tongue kiss, and Kimmie watched as he grabbed her ass in return.

"I'm Kimmie," she said, once the lovebirds came up for air.

"Cool," the boy said with a grin. "Call me Nick."

"Hey, Nick," Kimmie said, returning his grin. "You have the same taste in cars as my dad."

Nick and Natalia cracked up over her comment, and when Kimmie asked what was so funny, Natalia said she always made fun of Nick's "dad car," too.

Natalia pulled a pack of cigarettes out of her denim jacket and offered one to Kimmie. Without hesitating, Kimmie grabbed one, knowing she may make a fool of herself. Deciding to own her truth the way her new friend always did in group, Kimmie announced, "I've never smoked before so . . ."

"Don't you worry. I've got your back." Natalia hooked her arm in Kimmie's, something Lolly often did when they were younger. "Let me show you how to smoke like a badass."

Kimmie couldn't remember ever wanting anything more.

III

When Anna arrived at Alexander's parents' house after school, she was told by their housekeeper that his private nurse had showed up late so he would be "indisposed" for another half hour. Anna couldn't help but be irritated that he hadn't texted her, since he knew she had a riding lesson that afternoon. She felt ashamed at her annoyance, reminding herself that she was lucky enough to still enjoy such things, while her boyfriend was on bed rest recovering from a fractured pelvis and a broken left leg.

She told the housekeeper to let Alexander know she'd be back that evening after dinner. Walking out the front door, she sighed. After-dinner visits were open ended, which meant she would have to stay longer. For the last week, she had been visiting him after school, knowing she had a perfect out in her riding lessons or dinner plans.

"Annie!" Eleanor yelled from the front door. "Where on earth are you going?"

Anna's hand was on her car door handle, but she pulled it away and turned around. "Hi, Eleanor," she said, but didn't make any move to go back to the house. "I'll be back after dinner."

"Just because Alexander's busy doesn't mean you should leave," Eleanor responded. "You know, maybe I could use some cheering up, too?"

Eleanor had come out of the accident with a sprained wrist and a few facial lacerations, one of which was still taped by the orders of her plastic surgeon. But because she was Eleanor, she was still milking sympathy from the traumatic event. When they were only five miles from home a deer crossed the road, and Alexander hit the brakes. Because the road was slick from the snowfall, the car skidded, flipped on its side, and slammed into a tree. Eleanor had been asleep, so she missed the whole thing, which was probably why she hadn't suffered as many injuries, since she didn't brace against the impact.

"I'm trying to get in a riding lesson. It's too late to cancel," Anna said quickly. "Before I come back tonight, maybe I'll pick up some froyo for you, okay?"

"How nice for you," Eleanor snipped. "Getting to go on with your life, while my poor brother is bedridden and in lots of pain."

Anna had been dealing with these passive-aggressive comments from Eleanor for long enough. "Eleanor, if you have something you'd like to say to me, I'd love to hear it."

Eleanor didn't bat an eyelash and met Anna's gaze head-on. "We wouldn't have even been on that road so late if it wasn't for you. If you would have just come with us in the first place, we would have missed the snow entirely."

"Really?" Anna said, coolly. "Correct me if I'm wrong, but Alexander told me it had been your idea to 'pop by' Beatrice's and pick me up because you were worried about *your* birthday."

Eleanor gasped at Anna's directness, opened her mouth to respond, but then closed it again, unsure of what to say.

"Tell Alexander I'll be back to visit him later," Anna said. "Or don't." She climbed into her car and drove off, as Eleanor stood in the front yard staring after her.

Anna's elation over her victory was short-lived, and by the time she arrived at Staugas Farms, she regretted it. She knew Eleanor would complain to Alexander, and the last thing he needed during his recovery, which was already causing him to miss six weeks of college, was to play referee between his sister and his girlfriend. She really felt for him and of course wanted to help him get through his recovery in any way she could, as she would for any of her close friends. But Alexander wasn't just a friend, he was her boyfriend. And she was his girlfriend.

Girlfriend, Anna thought to herself. *I'm still his girlfriend, even if I don't feel like it anymore.*

The morning when Beatrice woke her up with the news of Alexander's car accident was a total blur. Vronsky wanted to accompany her to the hospital, but she refused. Instead she woke up Steven. Lolly, who was too hungover to go anywhere, would stay behind and get a ride back to the city from Vronsky. Anna and Steven drove back to Greenwich in silence, though when Steven saw the remnants of the accident on the road, a demolished tree and tire marks in the mud, he said what they were both thinking: "This is how accidents happen . . . when people go where they shouldn't be."

Anna hadn't responded at the time, but she shared her brother's sentiment fully. She stared down at her hands in her lap, the same hands that had run through Vronsky's golden locks only a few hours before. She thought about telling her brother that she had decided to take his advice and break up with Alexander, but she didn't see the point. Her mother assured her that Alexander and Eleanor were both going to be fine, but Alexander was going to have surgery as soon as Yale's finest surgeon drove down to handle the VIP case. Anna knew her plans to break up with Alexander would have to be put on hold indefinitely. Until she had more information, there was no alternative.

She did feel weird about her role in the accident, because Alexander and Eleanor would never have been out driving if it weren't for her, although Anna took comfort in the fact that Eleanor had been the one to push Alexander to come for her on that snowy night. While she absolved herself of that particular guilt, she couldn't so easily forgive herself for what had occurred between her and Vronsky. Calling it a harmless kiss would be like calling the *Titanic* a boating accident.

Vronsky, still wearing his kilt, had carried Anna's bag for her to the Escalade. Steven didn't question why Vronsky was up that early. He just got into the car and set the GPS to guide them to Greenwich Hospital.

"Please text me later, okay?" Vronsky pleaded softly.

She couldn't do more than nod at the time for fear she might start crying. And she didn't want to cry because she wouldn't have known why. Would her tears be for Alexander or for herself because everything had just become infinitely more complicated? She did hug Vronsky good-bye though, even sneaking a quick kiss onto his neck before she pulled away. She didn't want to do to Vronsky what she had done to Alexander the night before, which was let him leave (though this time she was doing the leaving) without him knowing where he stood with her. She may not have spoken her words aloud, but she was in love with Vronsky, and there was no turning back.

By the time they reached the hospital Alexander was already in surgery, so Anna, Steven, their mother, and Alexander's dad sat together in the waiting room. Eleanor had already been discharged from the emergency room and she and her mom were in the city at Lenox Hill Hospital, where the plastic surgeon, who had handled her mother's chin augmentation, worked to make sure the five cuts that Eleanor suffered were stitched up to minimize any scarring. After Anna and Steven told their version of the events from the night before, everyone took a seat and stared at their phones.

During that time, Anna received a notification that a new player,

HeavyV, wanted to start a game of Words with Friends with her. She almost refused the invitation, but there was something about the timing of the request that gave her pause, so she accepted. When she opened the app, she smiled for the first time since she had left Beatrice's house. She stared at the two-letter word US that he had played and saw there was a message: ME + YOU = US. Anna messaged him back: ME—YOU = :(

Now, weeks after that moment at the hospital, Anna pulled up to the stables and cleared her head of the confrontation with Eleanor. She tapped the WWF app, selecting the only game she had going. Without even glancing at the board (which had built up to a crisscross of low-scoring words: US, YOU, LOVE, ME, SEXY . . .), she went right to the messages. But before she had tapped out even two words there was a knock on her window. Startled, she looked up at Vronsky smiling down at her through the window.

Vronsky and Murf hung out in the stables while Anna rode Mark Antony, but every few minutes he checked his phone to look at the time.

"Maybe you should get a little practice in," Murf said. "Or are you cocky enough to assume that riding a horse is like riding a bike? Bicycles can't sense nervous energy, and real talk: every horse in here is buggin' out with all your pacing."

"Okay, okay," Vronsky replied, trying to sound casual but failing. "Beatrice promised me Bunny Hop is the calmest of her mom's horses, so I'll be okay."

"You better be, 'cause the last thing that girl needs is to run around having to take care of your skinny ass, too." Murf walked out of the stable into the afternoon sun, waiting for his friend to follow. As the two of them walked to the next stable where Beatrice's mom kept her horses, Murf whistled a tune that Vronsky couldn't place.

"What song is that?" he asked. "Sounds too upbeat for the likes of you."

Murf shook his head in embarrassment then admitted it was the new single from LiviX2. Daler and Rowney had gifted it to him on iTunes, and he was surprised by how much he liked it. "When I asked Mr. Staugas if I could take Spring Break off to go to Coachella, he faked a heart attack, then laughed his ass off at me when I was about to dial nine-one-one. In all the years I worked here, I never asked for days off."

"He said yes?" Vronsky asked, pleased to hear about someone else's less complicated love life.

"He not only said yes, he told me he wanted to pay for my plane ticket. It's hard to see a black man blush, but I did when I told him it wasn't necessary because I was flying private. You're coming, right?"

"Don't know yet," Vronsky replied. He wanted to join, but there was no way he was going unless, by some miracle, Anna was able to go, too.

"Look, I know it's coldhearted to kick a dog when he's down with a broken pelvis," Murf said. "But all this waiting until he's better is bullshit. He's not gonna be cool either way, at least if she kicked his ass to the curb now he'd have Percocet to ease the pain."

Vronsky didn't answer, because he didn't want to speak out against Anna, though he was in complete agreement with Murf's assessment of the situation. Every time he tried to bring up Alexander with Anna, she bristled and refused to discuss it. These days he barely got to see her, though they were texting all day every day, so he wasn't going to waste the precious minutes he had with her talking about her busted-up bf. The fact that he was getting on a horse so he could spend some alone time with her showed the lengths he was willing to go.

Riding a horse was much scarier than riding a bicycle, because you were so high up. Bunny Hop was a six-year-old gelding but had been around long enough to recognize an inexperienced rider. Vronsky pulled out his most soothing voice, the one he used to use to sweet-talk girls back to his house, but Bunny Hop was having none of it. He couldn't get her to go faster than a leisurely stroll, so by the time he arrived at the apple tree where they had arranged to meet, Anna had fed Mark Antony two apples and eaten one herself. As soon as he arrived, he slid off Bunny Hop before she came to a full stop, took Anna's face in his hands, and planted a kiss on her. "You taste like apple," he murmured.

She laughed and pushed him away, handing him an apple that he took gratefully and bit into with a crunch. "That's not for you," Anna said, pointing to his horse. "It's for her." She took the apple out of his hands and gave it to Bunny Hop. The horse chomped it delightedly, then nuzzled her giant snout against Anna's cheek.

Anna and Vronsky had exactly twenty-three minutes together under the apple tree, and when they sat up after minute twenty-two, they were both breathless and hornier than a herd of antelopes. Anna had never been kissed the way Vronsky kissed her, and she had never wanted to kiss someone so badly herself. She knew she had said she'd visit Alexander later, but when she stood up, brushing the dirt off her backside, she had changed her mind. Maybe it was time to stop putting everyone's needs in front of her own.

"I want to see you tonight, but we can't have you and that motorcycle roaring through the neighborhood. Can Murf drive you somewhere?" she asked. "Or could you borrow his truck?"

"What do you have in mind?" Vronsky asked, not daring to get his hopes up too soon.

"My mom went back to the city and I have the house to myself tonight, so maybe you can come by later when it's dark?"

Vronsky agreed immediately and promised to be discreet. He let Anna head back to the stable first, not taking his eyes off her until she and Mark Antony were just a tiny speck galloping off into the distance.

The combination of Percocet with a Soma muscle relaxer is known on the street as a Las Vegas cocktail. Alexander knew this because he was not a fan of taking any prescription medication (not including Adderall, of course) and wanted to do some online research about the numerous pills he was prescribed after his surgery. He discovered that the pharmaceutical cocktail recommended by his surgeon was quite popular. He hated to admit it, but he liked it. Maybe a little too much. It made him forget about the fact that he was falling behind in his studies, that he had a broken leg and may always have a slight limp, that his girlfriend had been moody and distant, and, most importantly right now, it kept him composed in the middle of his seventeenth game of Scrabble with Eleanor.

"G-I-V-E-T-H, triple word score on the H . . . so that's . . ." Eleanor paused, counting her score on her fingers.

"That's not a word, Eleanor."

"Sure it is. *The lord giveth, and the lord taketh away.* Job 1:20. That's twenty-one points for Eli-corn! Ooooh, I'm winning now."

If Alexander wasn't floating on a lazy river of opioids, he would have definitely challenged her, but instead he just said, "If you say so." He rearranged his own letters, studying them. He noticed he could spell Anna if he wanted to, though of course proper nouns weren't allowed, but if Eleanor was cheating, so could he, right? Alexander connected two Ns and the A to the last word he'd played, HOAX.

"Uch. Not funny." Eleanor immediately started picking up his letters to hand back to him.

"Stop! If you can break the rules so can I," he said in a whiny tone that sounded foreign to his ears.

"Whatever has gotten into you, I don't like it," Eleanor said in a voice that matched her mother's intonation. But she put his letters back on the board.

"Is she coming back?" he asked.

"Who?"

"Anna."

Eleanor sighed. "Don't you find her weird lately? It's like she's a totally different person."

"Please, not this again."

"All I'm saying is that if I was your girlfriend, I would never, ever leave your side when you're helpless like this," Eleanor cooed.

"I wouldn't say I'm helpless."

"You know what I mean! This was her! She did this. Your poor leg, my face!"

"Your doctor said you won't have any scars that anyone can see."

"But I see them. I'll always know where they are. She could have killed us both."

"You're exaggerating. Besides, Anna wasn't driving the car. We hit a deer on a snowy night. It was an accident."

"Was it? Why didn't she leave with us? That blond guy she was dancing with. Don't pretend you didn't see them. I assumed he was gay because he was so pretty but one of my friends told me he is very much not gay and in fact is a very well-known fuck-boy around town."

"Eleanor!" Alexander didn't know if he had ever heard Eleanor swear before, and there was something so comical about hearing his devout little sister say the word "fuck-boy" that he started to laugh. It was absurd. Everything was absurd. Eleanor's rage. The fact that he'd almost lost his spleen. That when he closed his eyes he could still see the haunting image of a deer bursting out of the woods and running into the street. The brightness of the pupils glowed in the headlights and the poor creature's eyes grew so big in fear that for a moment he felt like they were a portal to another dimension, like a tunnel that he could drive through. He could still remember the crunch, though the doctor said it might have been the sound of his leg breaking, not the sound of an innocent animal's death.

Anna used to remind him of an innocent fawn with her big eyes and her sweet face. But not lately. What Eleanor was saying wasn't untrue, even though he refused to admit it to himself. Anna had been aloof and distant, her visits perfunctory, and she always wanted to read to him instead of talking. Though, in her defense, it's not like he was able to keep up his side of the conversation high on pain meds, with the most exciting part of his day being when Jimela brought him his bowl of lime Jell-O.

"I need to sleep, Eleanor. Can you wake me when she comes over? Jimela said Anna told her she'd come back later."

"I said that," Eleanor retorted. "Because that's what Anna said earlier. She said she'd bring over frozen yogurt for me. Do you think she'll remember?"

"Yes, I do," Alexander replied softly. "You need to stop being angry with her, Eleanor. Think of all the wonderful things Anna has done for you in the past; don't you always say that all your favorite headbands are gifts from her?"

"No one's disputing her fashion sense. Look, I get it. She's beautiful and perfect and blah, blah, blah, but she needs to do right by you. She needs to understand how lucky she is to get to be with you, that's all. Please, I hate when you're cross with me. I promise that when she comes over tonight I'll forgive her and we can all move past it, okay?"

"That's very noble of you." Alexander said this half in jest, but he knew Eleanor would take it seriously as sarcasm always went over her head.

"I think we're out of the whipped cream I like. Should I text Anna and tell her to get some? Or maybe Jimela could run out and get it for me?"

"I think Jimela has been working hard enough. Perhaps you should go out and get your own whipped cream?"

"See?" Eleanor cried. "This is exactly what I mean. You're so good, Alexander. Of course, I should go myself." She came over and adjusted the cashmere throw covering him and leaned over, giving him a kiss on the cheek. He hated it when she did that. She did it even in public, little pecks hello and good-bye. She did it in front of his friends, too, and in turn they mocked him and called him Jaime Lannister. As Eleanor walked away, the smell of her vanilla perfume made him gag slightly, or was the Las Vegas cocktail making his stomach feel like a hollow pit?

VI

Vronsky parked Murf's truck with the farm's logo by the side of the house instead of in the circular drive. It was still visible, but looked like a workman's vehicle, so any neighbors who noticed it wouldn't find it odd. Not that neighbors could even see down the long, gated driveway to the house. Vronsky didn't get out of the truck right away, but instead gave himself a moment. Murf hadn't been thrilled to offer up his new but used truck to someone with no driver's license, but Vronsky kept throwing out numbers of how much he'd pay him until Murf relented, though not before calling him a privileged white rich kid who was out of touch with the real world, and agreeing to rent him his truck for a Benjamin.

Vronsky thought about the emergency spliff that Murf had hidden away in a Dr. Dre *The Chronic* CD jewel case stored in the truck's glove box and wondered if he should take a hit to calm his nerves. He had kept waiting to receive a message from Anna that she had changed her mind and he shouldn't come, but no such text arrived. He opened the Words with Friends app, staring at his letters. He could play the word HERO, with the H on a double letter score square.

Some hero I am, he thought to himself. *Too chicken shit to get out of the truck.*

In his entire sexual history, and his list was long and impressive for someone his age, he had never felt this nervous. Sure he'd been over-the-top excited before, but a teenage boy going through puberty could get excited over just about anything.

He and Anna had never discussed their sexual histories, though she had teased him about all his past conquests on more than one occasion. She did this out of insecurity, probably because she had only been with one person. But in all his sexcapades he had never been in love before, and now that he knew what love was, all his past hookups paled in comparison.

Anna had seen the truck pull down the driveway, but he hadn't come inside the house yet. She had left the mudroom door unlocked like she'd said she would. She was alone, which was rare because Magda and her husband lived in a small house on the property, and when her husband was out of town, Magda slept in a room off the kitchen. She did it for Anna's benefit, or so she said, but Anna knew that Magda was the one who got scared alone at night. Anna was never worried because of Gemma and Jon Snow. There was no chance anyone they didn't know could get past three hundred pounds of Newfoundland coming at them from both sides.

Anna dismissed the notion that Vronsky was nervous and sitting in Murf's truck, too scared to come in. If anyone needed to be nervous, it was she. *What am I doing? Why did I invite him over?*

She asked herself these questions to salvage her pride, because her secret self knew exactly why she had asked him to come over. The house was empty, and she had never wanted anything the way she wanted Vronsky. For the last several weeks she had been walking around in a state of constant irritation, like her skin was too tight. She was overly sensitive to the slightest touch, and she noted how every texture she came into contact with gave her new sensations she'd never experienced: the way clothes draped over her body, or the way her high-thread-count sheets felt extra smooth and cool to her skin. She was taking long showers these days in hopes the hot water would somehow desensitize her. But nothing had been working. All she pictured when she closed her eyes was his face, and she could summon the fragrance of Vronsky without even concentrating. When Vronsky kissed her, all she wanted was to sink to the floor with him. Earlier today, out in the field when they were making out, her shirt had come untucked and when he slipped his hand underneath it and she felt his hands on her bare skin, she had to bite her lip to keep from moaning.

That was when she decided she needed to see him. If she didn't spend more time with him, she'd go mad. She couldn't concentrate in school. She was distracted at home. This morning she had poured grapefruit juice into her cereal thinking it was milk.

Anna knew what she was doing was wrong. Alexander was still her boyfriend, but somehow, she didn't care anymore. If it weren't for his car accident, she would have broken up with him, which meant she would be free to love Vronsky and to be loved by him as well.

The dogs were barking, howling with excitement and scrambling around the slick marble floor of the foyer. She wondered if she should go rescue him from their slobbery kisses. No, it would be good practice for him. They were child's play in comparison to what she planned to do to him. She wanted to eat him like a bowl of ice cream. She wanted to put her fingers in his mouth and make him suck the tips. She wanted to get him into her childhood bed and scare all the monsters hiding under it. An earthquake, they would think. The end of the world, they would think. That's what she wanted most of all, to be loud, unbridled, with no one in the house. Anna was tired of being quiet and polite and demure.

She couldn't hear him climbing up the steps, but she knew he was coming because the dogs were bounding thunderously up the stairs. She looked up, and he was standing in her doorway. Was there a nervousness about him? If there was, it was gone in an instant. He crossed the bedroom and joined her on the bed. Their kissing was like breathing for her, as though she had been holding her breath whenever they were apart, and now that he was with her, she had to gasp and take in as much of him as she could.

Her robe was on the floor in a manner of seconds, her bra forgotten, her panties kept on as a mere formality. She laughed, trying to unbutton the tiny buttons on his shirt, kissing him hungrily as she went. He smelled so good, a mix of wild lilac and freshly chopped wood. She could tell he was hard, could feel it pressing against her. She wanted to see all of him, wanted to taste every square inch of him.

Afraid he might explode early from her naked body grinding against him, he knew he had to slow down the pace. "Anna . . . Anna," he purred as she unbuckled his belt. He grabbed her hands to stop her, and she looked up at him, wild-eyed, animalistic, and now he understood. He was the prey. He was the fish who had seen the shiny object twinkle in the water, and she had hooked him through the heart with such precision that when he burst to the surface he felt as though he was being lifted by the hands of God herself . . . *look at me, I can fly!*

She had him in her mouth, and he gripped the duvet, clutching it as if it could save him. It was too late for him, he had gone over the cliff like a cartoon cat, holding onto a daisy at the edge for dear life, plinking the petals off one by one. *She loves me, she loves me not, she loves me, I love her, I will love her forever . . .*

She was above him now, her face hovering close to his. As she lowered herself slowly upon him she stared into his eyes, and he could tell she was lost in ecstasy, too. Now that he was fully inside her, she halted for a moment, this beautiful, mysterious creature who had caught him, and he knew the second she started again, he would burst.

In one quick motion, he rolled her over onto her back, thrust his hips forward, and she moaned his name, "Alexia!"

That was his undoing, his name on her lips. He thrust again and again, and she cried out loudly as he brought them both to the brink, gasping her name. "Anna!"

If this was what it meant to be the prey, then he wanted to die by her tooth and claw over and over again. Vronsky rolled off her and stared at the ceiling, little shiny dots flashing in his eyes like he'd just looked directly into the sun.

"Alexia . . ." she whispered, rolling onto her side so she could observe him, her hands tracing the soft blond hair running up his belly.

He rolled onto his side so that they were facing each other. Words no longer mattered; nothing mattered except for them right now basking in the afterglow of their first time. He touched her face and kissed her, because that was the only instinct he possessed.

She loved the way he kissed her, his hunger everpresent, and she felt the same hunger when she kissed him back, as if she had no idea which of them was devouring the other, so equal was their passion for each other. She had had sex before, but not like this. She didn't even know where her boldness came from when she climbed up on him, the throbbing ache of her desire was so great. It was the purest form of lust she had ever felt, and the wave that followed when he rolled her over, thrusting into her, releasing everything she had ever held back was like a tidal wave obliterating her life into two separate time periods, B.V. (Before Vronsky) and A.V. (After Vronsky).

And then he reached for her again.

#

Dustin wanted to go to Arizona with his father and help bring back Nicholas, but his father said no. There was no way Dustin could miss school without his mother finding out about Nicholas's disappearance, which they had managed to keep secret from her. "But if we split the driving, we could drive all night and make it back in two days," Dustin said. "It's my senior year. I could easily make up the work."

"I'm not driving the car back. I'm flying home with him," Jason said even though he had no idea if he could convince his eldest son to return home at all. "I can ship the car back."

Dustin didn't argue his point any longer, because it was obvious his father's mind was made up. He had called and texted Nicholas numerous times but never got a response. This worried him, but he hoped that his brother's radio silence meant he had caught up with the girl, Natalia, as opposed to his other love, heroin.

Dustin was also relieved not to leave Steven in the lurch with his schoolwork. These days Dustin was tutoring him every day because midterms were fast approaching. Lolly often joined them, but she never mentioned Kimmie's name, probably because Steven had told her not to. He still thought about her, even though he wished he didn't. The pain of her rejection stung less with the passage of time, but when she popped into his head, he still felt a hollowness inside him, as if all the rabbits of his infatuation had burrowed through him and fled, leaving behind an abandoned warren where his heart once thumped for her. (He briefly tried journaling and writing poetry to get her out of his head, but so far it wasn't working.)

He let out a big sigh over the sound of pencils scribbling and pages flipping, but neither Steven nor Lolly seemed to notice. Dustin was doing his own homework, and he had just read the same paragraph of *Wuthering Heights* three times. Why was it when he worried about his brother that Kimmie always appeared in his head?

"Lolly, can I ask you something?" Dustin's voice sounded strange to him in the grand dining room of Steven's apartment. "Never mind, forget it."

Lolly put down her pencil and pulled the band out of her hair, retying her ponytail again. She had arrived twenty minutes ago from a SoulCycle class, and her cheeks were only now losing their pinkness. "Just ask me, Dustin."

He shook his head, already regretting the can of worms that he had meant to keep closed.

"What's your sister been up to?" he asked, unable to speak her name. "Last I heard she was sick. Is she feeling better?"

Steven stood up abruptly. "I'm hungry . . . who wants a snack?" He saw Lolly and Dustin raise their hands without looking at him, as they were focused on each other. Steven knew that Dustin wasn't going to like what he heard, and he didn't want to be there when Lolly spilled the beans. Steven had finally found a little peace these days after the drama of V-Day and the hubbub surrounding Anna's boyfriend's car accident, so he left in search of comfort food.

"Kimmie's been away, Dustin," Lolly reported. "My mom took her to a wellness center in Arizona. I thought it was a spa trip, because she had been so . . . under the weather. But then my mom returned alone and told me Kimmie was in a program to get help."

Dustin nodded even though he didn't really understand what Lolly was talking about. He was confused, concerned, and cursing himself for letting his curiosity get the better of him. "What kind of program?" he asked. "I mean, obviously it's none of my business, so if you don't want to tell me, that's fine."

"My mom said Kimmie's depressed. My dad was against putting her on medication, so this program is pretty intensive, I think. Honestly, I don't know. My mom told me Kimmie didn't want to hear about anything, so when I talk to her, we really only discuss how she's feeling. I spoke to her yesterday and she sounds better. Stronger." Lolly was speaking the truth, because Kimmie had sounded more confident and self-assured on the phone, but she still seemed weird to her. Kimmie told Lolly that she had dyed her hair purple, but she couldn't send a picture because she wasn't allowed to have a phone. Lolly was shocked to hear this, but her mother told her to be positive when she spoke to her little sister, so she'd said, "That sounds awesome, Kimmie. I'm sure you look amazing."

Kimmie had told her that she'd met a friend in group therapy, and the two had become besties. She also told her not to tell her mother, because Danielle would not take the news of her youngest daughter hanging out with an ex-methhead very well. The other thing that Lolly noticed about Kimmie was there was a steely edge in her voice, and her sentences were peppered with therapy-speak. Empowerment. Victimhood. Emotional highways. Honestly, it all sounded like nonsense to Lolly, so she kept up a steady refrain of positive adjectives and eagerly anticipated the moment when she could get off the phone. The most disturbing thing was when Kimmie said she intended to confront Vronsky for what he did to her. "He needs to take responsibility for his actions, and I can't let go of my pain until he gives me the apology I deserve."

It made no sense, what Kimmie was saying. Yes, Vronsky was guilty of a pump-and-dump, but it's not like he forced Kimmie to have sex. She was the one who'd lied to him pretending she wasn't a virgin, so how could she blame him for being insensitive when she was so insecure? The whole thing made Lolly uncomfortable, but she was powerless to express her feelings. Maybe this anger was part of Kimmie's therapy process, one of the stages she had to go through. This girl on the phone sounded nothing like her little sister, and it made her sad. "I'm worried about her, Dustin," Lolly said, her voice trembling. "I hope those doctors know what they're doing."

"I'm sorry, Lolly," Dustin said, his voice barely above a whisper. "I had no idea you were dealing with so much. And I'm sorry Kimmie has been having a hard time."

"Should I tell her you said so?" Lolly asked. "I mean, when I talk to her next? I could tell her you were asking about her."

Dustin hated himself for his coldness, but he needed to stay in survival mode when it came to Kimmie. He already knew more about her than he was comfortable with. He shook his head. "No, please don't. I'm trying to put all that behind me. I've moved on."

Lolly knew he was lying to himself, and, unable to help herself, decided it was time to tell Dustin the truth. "I know something happened between you two the night of Jaylen's party, but Kimmie's never told me what it was about."

"It was nothing. I asked her out and she said no," Dustin said, speaking more harshly than he meant to. "She chose Vronsky. End of story."

"Dustin, c'mon. Don't be like that. It's true, back then she had eyes for Vronsky, but he wasn't interested in her. Nothing happened between them that night." Lolly wasn't exactly lying, because nothing had happened between Vronsky and Kimmie the night of the party. Their unfortunate hookup was the week before and was none of Dustin's business.

"She said she was in love with him," Dustin said. "That doesn't sound like nothing to me. Please, Lolly. I don't want to talk about this. I just can't go there."

"I'll just say one more thing and then I promise this conversation is over, okay? Please?"

He sighed and nodded, knowing he deserved this since he'd brought it up in the first place.

"Kimmie is very young and because of her skating, she was far more naïve than most girls her age. She didn't know what she was talking about when she said she loved him. She had a crush. Love isn't a light switch you can just flip on and off. It's not fair of you to hold her inexperience against her. You're too smart for that. C'mon, I know she thinks highly of you, so perhaps if you saw her again . . ."

Dustin stood up so abruptly his chair flew back and hit the floor with a bang, which brought Steven running back into the room. Dustin scrambled to pick up the chair and then immediately started tossing his books into his backpack. He needed to leave. He felt like there wasn't enough oxygen in the room. He needed air. "Sorry, guys," he muttered. "Steven, I'm heading out. Text me if you need me to proofread anything for you. Lolly, I know you mean well, and I'm sorry I'm acting like a baby, but I can't talk to your sister ever again. I do hope she feels better, and of course, I only wish her the best."

Dustin ran out the door and suffered a mild panic attack in the elevator. He used the inhaler that he always carried, the first time in months. He took two big puffs, and it helped him catch his breath, but it did nothing for his heart, which ached for the girl he loved, who hadn't loved him back.

VIII

It had been fifteen days since Kimmie shed a tear and she felt like she deserved something to commemorate the occasion, like how Natalia got her thirty-day orange chip from Narcotics Anonymous and how her bf, Nick, had a ninety-day red medallion that he kept on his key chain. Since their first outing a little over a week ago, the three of them had been seeing each other almost every day. Kimmie and Natalia had bonded that first night over their fancy Italian meals, after Nick put the kibosh on them eating at Raoul's, where he worked. Nick said he liked to keep the different parts of his life separate and felt that showing up as a patron would send a weird message to the guys he worked with.

After dinner, true to her word, Natalia spent the next two hours dyeing Kimmie's long blond hair an electric purple ombre that faded into lavender at the ends. Kimmie loved her new hair and told Natalia that she wanted to get a tattoo, too. Natalia said she knew a guy who'd give her one, even though legally she had to be eighteen. Nick, who had been playing Fortnite on the secondhand PC they had in their tiny one-bedroom apartment, spoke up sharply and said no.

"What do you care if Kimmie gets a tat?" Natalia asked her boyfriend.

"She's too young," he said. "Tats are forever, not the same as changing your hair color."

"I got my first ink when I was younger than her," Natalia said.

"That's because your mom sucked and didn't look after you properly," Nick said, his eyes fixed to the computer screen. "You want her mom raising holy hell with the program? Those people have been good to you."

"Oh, please," Natalia shouted. "You don't know! What, you got some sort of crystal fucking ball where you can see the future and shit?"

"Trust me, I know her type. I grew up around rich girls just like her."

The fight escalated quickly from there. Kimmie thought about intervening, but she didn't dare speak up, mainly because everything Nick was saying was spot-on. If she came home with a tattoo, her mother would lose her mind. It wasn't just because she was Jewish and a tattoo would prevent her from being buried in a Jewish cemetery, but because her mother always said tattoos were low class and trampy. Two months ago, if you had asked Kimmie if she would ever get a tattoo, she would have scoffed at the notion. But that was two months ago, and Kimmie was hell-bent on going back home a totally different girl. It was just like Taylor Swift's hit song: *"I'm sorry, the old Kimmie can't come to the phone right now. Why? Oh, 'cause she's dead!"*

The most fascinating thing about watching Natalia and Nick fight was the escalation and sudden drop-off. At its peak the two of them were standing up facing each other dropping f-bombs like two nuclear powers at the end of days. They were so loud Kimmie was afraid someone might call the cops. At one point Natalia shoved Nick in the chest with both hands and he looked pissed enough to hit her. But he didn't. Actually, it was her push that seemed to snap him out of it and the very next words out of his mouth were, "Baby, I'm sorry. I'm such an asshole. I straight-up love you." Natalia followed suit and then the two of them started making out like crazy, which did get a little physical when he picked her up and sat her down on the kitchen counter, a shower of empty Red Bull cans raining to the floor. Kimmie was mesmerized by the spectacle and was sad when they carried their lovefest into the bedroom, returning ten minutes later as if nothing had happened at all.

The only thing Natalia said about the whole thing later was that maybe Nick was right and Kimmie should wait on getting a tattoo because she had some she regretted herself. Kimmie nodded and thanked her for the new hair and said she was going to Uber back before her curfew. Natalia gave Kimmie a fierce hug good-bye and slipped her a half pack of menthols and a lighter so she could practice her technique. She made a point of saying good-bye to Nick, too, but he was back to playing his video game again, and only gave her a cursory nod farewell.

While she waited for her Uber at the front of their tiny apartment building, Kimmie leaned against Nick's Volvo and lit up. She couldn't help but dwell on Nick's statement about growing up with girls like her. He'd said it so contemptuously, she would have ordinarily been offended, but on this particular night she wasn't. She was currently hating on the type of girl she used to be, too. Natalia and Nick seemed so cool and real to her, saying whatever they wanted whenever they wanted at whatever volume they pleased. She especially admired how Natalia didn't let Nick tell her what to do or think and how she was willing to get in his face and let him know he wasn't the boss of her. Natalia was the ultimate badass, and Kimmie couldn't get enough of her.

After that, Kimmie and Natalia were attached at the hip. Once, when Nick took a double shift at the restaurant, he gave Natalia the keys to the car, and the two girls went to the local mall, got pizza, and ended up piercing each other's ears with ice and a needle that they sanitized with a Bic lighter, using a technique Natalia's Vegas bestie, Sarah, had taught her. Kimmie now had three piercings going up her right earlobe, while Natalia had seven.

It was on that night that Kimmie finally confessed to Natalia about what had happened back in New York and how she ended up in Arizona. Natalia was a good listener and after hearing the story, she agreed that Kimmie should go through with her plan to confront Vronsky and give him a piece of her mind. Natalia told Kimmie that she loved being a girl, but that she often felt like boys had it way easier. They could screw around all they wanted and be lauded by their friends as a true hero. But if a girl fucked around and, God forbid, enjoyed sex, then she'd be labeled a total whore. It wasn't fair. The only way to fight back against gender inequality was to not give a shit and not apologize. "If Nick yells at me, I'm gonna yell louder. If he hits me, I'm gonna hit him back harder."

"Holy shit, has Nick hit you?" Kimmie asked. "Because that's really not okay, Natalia."

Natalia swore Nick had never laid a finger on her, which made him her first boyfriend who hadn't. "Nick's been clean for a while, but junkies are unpredictable. So who knows what he's like when he falls off the wagon. No way I'm letting my guard down. But something tells me he doesn't have that in him."

"He seems like he really loves you," Kimmie said, not caring that her voice sounded dreamy and wistful. She had seen the way Nick looked at Natalia and even though she had been making a real effort only to move forward these days, there was something in it that reminded her of the way that Dustin had looked at her when they went to Serendipity 3 for hot chocolate. It seemed so long ago, but the memory of it was as clear as a church bell on a quiet Sunday morning.

Her therapist had told her that it wasn't good to label your memories as either good or bad, but to be able to see them from an objective viewpoint where something could be positive and negative at the same time. So even though she had been lumping that hot chocolate night with Dustin as a bad memory because of Vronsky, she was now able to see it was okay to remember it as good memory, too. She then told Natalia about Dustin, marveling at how she had been so clueless when it came to boys, but knowing it was pointless to want a "do-over."

"Don't beat yourself up. You don't even want to know the number of dickheads I've been with. And I've had tons of boys tell me they loved me, but Nicky's the only one I've ever really believed. I wake up in the middle of the night and catch him staring at me. It's sweet, but also a little psychotic. I find it hot AF. You can't blame a girl for whatever rando thing she finds romantic. Some girls like flowers and chocolates, while others get off on having their bf get the high score on Ms. Pac-Man at a shitty pizza place and putting in NLN, for 'Nick loves Natalia,' instead of his own initials."

Kimmie laughed with Natalia, and she realized how long it had been since she laughed with a friend and how much she missed it.

IX

Kimmie's father was supposed to fly out, pick her up, and bring her home, but the night before he was set to leave, Kimmie's Stepmonster broke a heel coming out of a restaurant and face-planted into the sidewalk, busting her collagen lips and breaking several teeth.

"I wish I could come out and get you, darling, but I can't very well send David to go see Guns N' Roses on his own when I'm the one who gave him the tickets," Kimmie's mother told her over the phone. "You understand, right? I booked you on a red-eye that leaves tonight at eleven P.M. Daddy will pick you up at the airport. You were supposed to be with him for your first week back, but now that your Stepmonster broke her face, you'll be here with me instead."

Kimmie stood in the front office of Desert Vista talking to Danielle. She hadn't officially been discharged, so she didn't have her phone back yet. "Mom, can't you get me a hotel room and I'll just hang out here until Dad can fly out and get me? I hate red-eyes."

"Everyone hates red-eyes, Kimmie," her mother replied with an unwavering tone. "But I upgraded you to first class so I think you'll survive. Text me later from the airport. Love you."

Kimmie handed the phone receiver back to the secretary and went to pack. She finished in a hurry, dropping her one suitcase off at the front office and letting them know she'd be back in the evening to catch a cab to the airport. She had already said her good-byes to Natalia and Nick the night before, but now that she had six free hours to kill she had something she wanted to do. The other night when she and Natalia cruised the low-rent mall, Natalia had seen a black leather motorcycle jacket she loved in a store window. She was so taken with it, she had pressed her whole body against the windowpane and made out with the glass, leaving smeary wet tongue prints on it. "If you love it, just buy it," Kimmie had told her.

"Yeah, like I could ever afford a jacket like that," Natalia said. "Please, that baby's gotta be at least two hundo, if not more. That's more money than all my clothes combined."

Kimmie wanted to buy the jacket for her friend right then and there. Two hundo was so not a big deal in Kimmie's world, Lolly spent more than that on eyelash extensions every month, but she wasn't sure if Natalia would take offense or not. Natalia's moods and opinions seemed to fluctuate by the minute. The jacket was three hundred and twenty dollars and Kimmie charged two of them to her father's credit card, one for Natalia, the other for herself. The leather jacket wasn't exactly Kimmie's taste, but she knew Natalia would wear it all the time, so she wanted one to remember her friend by.

Natalia had just gotten a new job working at a discount tire store, so Kimmie didn't want to bother her at work. She knew they left the sliding back door unlocked as Natalia was always losing her house keys. Kimmie's plan was to drop the jacket off in their bedroom with a note and her phone number. She didn't want to be so presumptuous to think that Natalie and Nick would drop their own plans to hang out with her at the airport, especially since the two of them threw her a surprise farewell dinner at their apartment the night before. Nick had made these amazing tacos (though he weirdly didn't eat any himself) and Natalia made them fun cocktails out of Hawaiian Punch, Red Bull, and wine coolers. Kimmie was surprised about the wine cooler part because they weren't supposed to drink. But Kimmie didn't say anything about it, and neither did they.

Kimmie had just left Natalia's jacket on the bed and tucked the letter into the pocket when she heard Nick shouting from the living room. Panicked, Kimmie ran to the closet to hide. After a few more seconds, Kimmie realized it wasn't Nick and Natalia fighting but Nick and someone else, a man, someone older.

The walls were thin and cheap, and Kimmie could hear pretty much everything they were saying. Listening, she put together that the second voice was Nick's father. Now she knew why Nick drove such an expensive dad car: he had stolen his dad's and driven it across the country. Nick kept shouting for his dad to take the damn car, that he didn't need it anyway. His dad asked if he even had a job. Yes. Was he using drugs? No. And who's this girl, Natasha? Natalia, and there's no way I'm leaving the love of my life to go back to New York when there's nothing for me there.

New York? Kimmie thought. *Nick never once mentioned he had lived there.* Nick's father told him the only thing he should be focused on right now was his sobriety. Nick swore over and over he wasn't doing drugs, but his father must have found the wine cooler bottles in the kitchen because now they were fighting about that. The whole thing was awful and Kimmie was desperate to leave, but she knew she had no choice other than to wait it out. She tried to stop listening to them and think about something else, but it was hard to do so. Nick's father kept saying he was done, and that if Nicholas didn't come back with him now, he was going to wash his hands of him, that he could forget about calling for money or asking for help ever again. Nick told his father to fuck off, which was when Nick's father really lost it and screamed at him that his last stint in rehab had cost one hundred thousand dollars that came out of his brother Dustin's college fund, and "Do you know why?" he asked Nicholas, his voice nearly cracking. "Because your younger brother loves you, Nicholas. Dustin loves you so much that he'd rather waste his money trying to save you than go to college for free!"

Not only did this news shut Nick up, it made Kimmie gasp loud enough that she had to slap her hand over her mouth to keep herself quiet. *Nick is Dustin's older brother, Nicholas!*

This revelation rocked Kimmie so hard, she knew she couldn't wait around to see what happened. She needed to get out right now. She crawled out of the closet, opened the window in the bedroom, kicked out the screen, and climbed out. Her feet hit the pavement of the driveway and she took off running. And she didn't look back.

X

When Anna arrived at the annual Greenwich Ride for Charity horse event and heard from Murf that Vronsky had signed up to be one of the Staugas Farms riders, she assumed he was joking. Vronsky had met her at their apple tree after her last three lessons, but four horse rides through a flat grassy field hardly made him qualified to race against riders who had been training for the event for months.

"It's crazy. He can't do it." Anna looked at Murf, who was trying his best to fix a lopsided bow tied to the side of the metal bleachers. She nudged him out of the way and retied the blue satin ribbon perfectly.

"That's what I told him!" Murf said. "And he's not doing the track, oh no, not that crazy white boy. He had to be a baller and sign up for the timber race."

Anna was shocked to hear this. Timber racing was the American version of the steeplechase, which was a very rigorous and dangerous sport that had been going on for the last one hundred years, though it originated and was far more well-known in Ireland and the UK. The Maryland Hunt Cup was basically the Super Bowl of the sport and consisted of a four-mile course with twenty-two hurdles (fences usually made of timber) in varying heights, the highest being five feet. But this timber race was a much smaller event that was held annually in Greenwich to raise money for the children's hospital. It was a quarter the length with only seven hurdles, the highest being two and a half feet. It was designed with teen riders in mind, but still, every year someone seemed to get hurt.

Anna's overprotective father had barred her from participating in the Greenwich event, saying it was ridiculous that any idiot could sign up and that most accidents happened not because of trained equestrians like Anna, but because stupid boys were looking to impress long-lashed girls. Anna was so upset over the news that she phoned Vronsky, something she had never done before. Their only form of communication remained texting via Words with Friends, though Vronsky often joked about buying them burner phones.

Vronsky didn't answer her call, which annoyed Anna, and even though she wanted to leave a message urging him to pull out of the race, saying his horse would have to jump over her dead body if that's what he intended to do, she refrained. Instead she hung up the phone and deleted the call record from her phone. She thought about changing Vronsky's name in her contacts to something else, but that made her think of her brother and the infamous "Brad," so she couldn't bring herself to do it. Not knowing what else to do, she opened up the WWF game and texted him that he needed to call her immediately. She then asked Murf if he wouldn't mind finding him for her, but when he asked where he should tell Vronsky to meet her, she had no answer. Everyone attending the event knew who she was, which meant everyone also knew that she was Alexander's girlfriend, which meant that she couldn't be seen with Vronsky without arousing suspicion.

Now what am I going to do? she thought. *This is what you get for lying.*

Anna knew she was having a full-fledged affair behind her boyfriend's back, but she continually justified it by telling herself she was going to break up with Alexander as soon as he was off bed rest, less than a month away.

She had often chastised herself for not telling Vronsky they had to wait. But every time she thought about nixing the affair she found herself unable to. The flame of their desire wasn't that easy to extinguish, like a trick candle that couldn't be blown out.

She believed with all her heart that the reason they were having such incredible sex was because they were so madly in love. It was as if the chemistry between them needed to be mixed and compounded, lest it settle and turn toxic. She had never felt so alive and happy as when she was wrapped in Vronsky's arms. If there was any downside at all, it was the fact that the more they hooked up, the more they wanted it, as though they were junkies for each other. Every morning when she reached for her phone and checked WWF for messages, she'd see his text: Good morning, gorgeous! I want you, I want you, I want you. Vronsky was careful never to speak of his past with other girls, but he told Anna, in no uncertain terms, that what was happening between them was like nothing he had ever experienced before. These were no lines that Vronsky was feeding her. It was true—his love for Anna was unprecedented.

Since their first time at her house, they'd managed to see each other almost every single day, even if it was only for an hour in the early morning before school. Vronsky had taken to sleeping over at Beatrice's house, heading back into Manhattan on his bike after seeing her, while Anna was telling her mom she was going to school extra early to catch up on the homework. She'd swing by and pick him up at the end of Beatrice's long driveway. Since they couldn't be seen in public they drove around Greenwich looking for a secluded place to park.

The first time, they parked in the back of a church, which Anna wasn't thrilled with, but she soon forgot where she was when Vronsky's hand slipped down her jeans. Yesterday Anna picked him up and they ended up pulling into an underground parking lot, driving down to the lowest level where she climbed across the gearshift before the headlights had even turned off. She'd planned better this time by wearing a skirt. Anna confessed she had never in her life walked out of the house without underwear on, explaining she had a clean pair stuffed in her backpack.

The fact that Anna wanted him so badly filled Vronsky with a lust he couldn't hold back. Normally he'd have been mortified at being what his friends would call a one-pump-chump, but Anna found his inability to control himself intoxicating. And because of his age it didn't even matter. She would just stay on top of him and in a few minutes, he'd grow hard again inside her, the second round lasting much longer than the first. Loving the exquisite torture of riding him slowly, she would try to hold out for as long as she could, but she often found herself crying out his name sooner rather than later. They went three rounds and Anna ended up late for Latin. *Coitus, coituum, coitibus . . .*

"Anna, stop checking your phone," Beatrice said, with a sly smile. "If I had known that being all ooey-gooey-lovey-dovey would make me look as dreamy as you, I'd have tried it long ago."

They were sitting together in the bleachers set up for spectators of the timber race, which was due to start any minute now. Anna flushed with embarrassment at Bea's words. "Sorry," she said softly. "I just don't know why he hasn't texted me back. Don't you think he's crazy for entering the timber race?"

"Don't fret, my pet," Beatrice said. "My cousin was quite the jumper back in the day. His mother always says that his instructor told her Alexia had the confidence and talents of a future Olympian. Now if this were a motorcycle race, I'd be nervous. Sure, he's crazy for entering, but he's always been an adrenaline junkie. If we should worry about anything it should be for my mother's quarter horse. Vronsky's in it to win it, and he's gonna ride Frou Frou harder than she's used to. But I'm sure you know all about that . . . when it comes to V."

Anna tried not to react to Bea's comment, which was a little too sharply pointed for her taste. Perhaps Bea didn't even realize she was being prickly with her. She was probably feeling a bit jealous of Anna's happy glow. Vronsky had told her on the DL that Bea's secret love affair with Dahlia, the circus girl from her costume party, had ended abruptly, when after a night of clubbing in the city she found Dahlia showing off her acrobatic skill set to Bea's stepbrother, Royce, whose apartment they had crashed at the night before. Bea didn't take it well, and Dahlia was kicked out onto the streets of SoHo, Porky Pigging it with only one shoe.

Without giving away what she knew, Anna grabbed Bea's hand and said, "I'm so happy we get to spend the day together. I'm sorry I've been a little MIA lately, but please know I'm so grateful for all your help with . . . well, you know."

Beatrice, happy at the show of gratitude that she felt she deserved, smiled at Anna. "Aww, you're such a doll. I'd do anything for V. If he's happy then so am I." Bea hugged Anna, but when she pulled back her smile was gone, replaced by a frown. "Well, so much for our funderful day," she muttered. "Don't look now, but you've got double trouble at six o'clock."

Anna waited for a moment and then slowly turned her head to look behind her. Her heart clunked like a clock striking midnight, signaling the end of Cinderella's magical evening. Eleanor, in a ridiculous pink hat, was pushing Alexander in a wheelchair. As wheelchairs were not designed for grass, it was a pathetic sight to see. Everyone in town had heard about Alexander's accident, and soon there was a large crowd rushing to their aid. Moments later a few of the larger men in attendance were carrying Alexander across the field like he was a king.

A warning horn sounded, and for a split second Anna wondered if she'd imagined it, but then realized it was a man using an air horn to signal that the race was beginning in ten minutes.

Anna's phone vibrated with a text from Murf. Anna, I told him you didn't want him to race, but he said that you shouldn't worry about him. And I quote, "'cause I got this" and he wanted you to know

She stared at the incomplete message bubble, waiting for the rest, but nothing came. She texted back, Know what? What did he want me to know????? Bubbles appeared and Anna wanted to shake her phone as if that would do anything. While she waited she used her binoculars to watch the starting line, and she spotted Vronsky mounted atop Beatrice's mother's horse Frou Frou, trying to steady himself in the saddle. *Oh, my baby*, she thought, *why, oh why are you doing this?*

Anna's phone vibrated and she saw Murf's text. Sorry, dropped my phone! He wanted you to know he's gonna get you that trophy! *black thumbs-up emoji* *black bicep muscle emoji* *trophy emoji*

XI

Not wanting to leave her seat next to Beatrice, Anna pretended for as long as she could that she hadn't seen Alexander's arrival. She stared out onto the field with her binoculars, hoping that the race would start and she could go deal with him afterward. It seemed like some draconian form of punishment that she would be expected to tend to her boyfriend-in-name-only while her true love was about to try and clear seven hurdles on an unfamiliar horse.

She grabbed Bea's hand and gave it a nervous squeeze.

"Just breathe," Bea whispered to her friend. "Adaka's little brother is competing today and he's only eleven. Vronsky'll be fine." Bea sat contentedly, relishing the tension of the moment, always composed in high stress situations.

Anna lowered her binoculars and saw her brother standing in front of the bleachers. She wanted to signal him that danger was nearby, but before she could, she watched as Lolly rushed over and whispered something in his ear. Anna could tell by Steven's face that Lolly had just informed him that Alexander and Eleanor were in attendance. He looked up at Anna and she gave a quick nod to tell him she knew. Steven grabbed Lolly's hand, and the two of them started making their way into the bleachers. They only made it up two steps before Eleanor was behind them, tapping Lolly on her back. Poor Lolly had no choice but to turn around and play nice. Anna lowered her binoculars and put on her sunglasses, thankful it was a sunny day and no one would be able to make eye contact through her Oliver Peoples Benedict aviators.

Lolly pointed up at Anna and Beatrice, and Eleanor waved up at them enthusiastically. "Anna!" she yelled out, her high-pitched voice an arrow shooting straight through Anna's nerves. "Come down! Alexander's here."

"Do you think I can pretend I didn't hear her?" Anna asked through gritted teeth, trying to wave Eleanor to come up to them.

"Sorry, babe," Bea replied. "I think you have to go down there because I'm not gonna sit next to that dumb thot with a hat."

Anna knew Bea was right. The crowd waited for her to make a move. She stood up and began to make her way down. When she passed Steven and Lolly, she offered them her seat, and Steven gave her hand a quick sympathetic squeeze. Alexander was back in his wheelchair, and someone had brought over a bale of hay for him to prop up his leg, which was encased in a fiberglass boot. He was wearing a Harvard baseball cap and a placid smile on his face that Anna recognized as his opioid grin. By the time she reached his chair she was seething, but greeted him with a smile, knowing everyone was watching.

"Hey you," Anna said. "I thought you decided this was too much trouble for your first public appearance."

"It was my idea," Eleanor said, her voice like nails on a chalkboard. "Everyone has been calling the house and asking to see him. I figured why not just bring the mountain to them? Besides, we've barely seen you in days, and my brother misses his girlfriend. So here. We. Are."

"Eleanor, I stopped by this morning," Anna said. "When you were at Zumba class."

"Yes, but Alexander said you stayed for five minutes and then flitted off, like you've been doing all week."

Before Anna could say another word the starting shot sounded, and the race began. Anna peered through her binoculars. There were twenty-five horses participating in the event, staggered in groups of five for five seconds. Anna knew that five seconds was no time at all for a fast horse and soon they were all clumped together in a pack. Her heart started beating as fast as the hooves that thundered through the grass.

"Anna, Anna?" Eleanor whined. "I forgot my binoculars, can I use yours?"

"No," Anna replied. "You should have brought your own." She heard Eleanor stomp off in search of someone else to pester.

"Anna?" Alexander said, quietly. "Can I use your binoculars? I had given mine to Eleanor, but I guess she left them in the car."

Wordlessly Anna handed her binoculars to Alexander but didn't take her eyes off the horses, which were now rounding the first flagpole and would soon be heading back in front of them. From what she could tell, Vronsky had made the first three jumps easily. Maybe Beatrice was right, and Alexia was a natural. The horse he was riding was an experienced jumper and knew what to do.

Seconds later the first three horses were in front of them, all of them taking the low wooden fence with ease. The crowd cheered, as Anna did, delighted to see that her Alexia was in fourth place and gaining on the horse and rider ahead of him. Anna wished she could scream out Vronsky's name loud enough for him to hear, but it was impossible. Alexander had grabbed her hand and pulled her close so she was standing right next to his chair.

"Can I have the binoculars back?" she asked, knowing she shouldn't. "Please."

"Of course, I'm sorry. You must have so many friends competing."

Anna was watching the race, but she noted the displeasure in Alexander's tone.

The crowd gasped as one of the horses knocked down the wooden beam in front of them, but since it was one of the last horses, there was no collision and the rider corrected the horse, able to continue much to everyone's relief. Anna noticed Murf run out to set the pole back in place. She looked away from the finish line for just a moment, when she heard the screams.

The binocular's lenses magnified the chaotic scene. Anna could see that at the last jump, the highest jump, at least three horses had tumbled in an ungainly heap of twisted equine legs. Anna gasped, scanning all the horses, hoping desperately that Vronsky's horse wasn't in the melee. Unable to contain herself, Anna jumped the partitions of hay and bolted out into the field.

"Murf!" she screamed. "Was it him? Is he okay?"

Murf, already running toward the chaos, stopped at the sound of Anna's voice and turned around to face the lone figure standing in the field, her face stricken.

"Go back, Anna!" Murf yelled. "I'll let you know as soon as I do."

Steven, who had seen his sister run out into the field, pounded down the bleachers himself, vaulted over the partition, and was by her side in seconds. He put his arm around her as he escorted her back to the stands. Anna hid her face, but it was too late; everyone had already witnessed what she had done.

"Bring her here," Alexander called out, his voice stronger than it had been since his accident. Unsure of what to do, Steven thought about whisking her away, but knowing she'd never leave until she knew Vronsky's fate, he ushered her back to the Greenwich OG.

Anna sat on the bale of hay where Alexander's leg was propped, and promptly pulled out her phone, waiting for news.

Her phone dinged, and she saw Murf's message. He's okay. But Frou Frou is ducked. Ducking autocorrect! Anna started to cry happy tears that Vronsky was all right.

"What did you hear?" Alexander asked sternly.

"One of the horses that fell is badly hurt. It's terrible. I'm going to go down there."

"You'll do no such thing," he replied. "I want to leave right now, and you're coming with me."

Anna glanced at him in shocked amazement. "As if I'm some kind of pet to be ordered about at the whims of my master?"

"Anna," Alexander said in a low voice. "I don't feel well. You're obviously upset, and everyone is watching. We're going home now. Steven, can you help me with my chair?"

Steven looked at his sister, and she nodded for him to go ahead. Anna knew she would have to go with Alexander. Her only consolation was that in all the hubbub and rush to get Alexander home, they had forgotten Eleanor, and Anna smiled thinking of her bf's half-sister looking all over for them in her ugly pink hat.

XII

A hospital bed had been installed in the sunroom since Alexander couldn't yet navigate the stairs to his bedroom. Anna sat in the rocking chair by the window and stared out into the grand backyard. The car ride had been silent, and after the servants helped Alexander to bed, Steven left to pick up Lolly. Before he left, he gave his sister a big hug and told her he'd wait at the house until she returned. Anna just nodded, knowing if she were to speak, she'd start to cry.

Alexander knew he had to ask the question, but he didn't want to. He wanted to wait until his leg stopped throbbing and the Percocet kicked in, but he knew the pill would be no match for the pain to come. So, they sat in silence.

Eleanor had been suspicious for weeks now, but Alexander had shut her down every time she brought up Anna's recent misguided behavior. Yes, he had been doped up, but he wasn't a moron. He had noticed everything that Eleanor had griped about but just couldn't and wouldn't believe it to be true. The girl he knew and loved, the girl he had planned to marry, had grown cranky and aloof during her visits, yet he couldn't bring himself to ask her why. The simple reason was that he feared an honest answer. But now things were different. She had shown her cards in front of the entire town, and all he had was regret. Regret that he hadn't dealt with the situation earlier. Regret that he had agreed to go to the horse race. Regret that he had driven to the party to get her that snowy night. And regret that he'd left without her when he knew he shouldn't have.

He just couldn't believe that Anna could fall for a guy like Vronsky. It seemed impossible that a doe-eyed, blond-haired pretty boy was causing him so much misery. Laughable even. But no one was laughing now, especially not Alexander.

"Anna?" he said, his voice hoarse and cracking. "Do you want to start, or shall I?"

"It's true," she said quietly.

"What's true?" he asked.

"Your suspicions about me and Vronsky. We've been . . ." She hesitated. "I've been unfaithful. I should have told you earlier. I had every intention of telling you about my feelings for him, but . . ." Anna's mouth was dry with shame. She couldn't go on. She was desperate for the floor beneath her feet to open up and swallow her whole, chair and all. *Why, oh why didn't I just break up with him beforehand? Now everything is a disaster. And I have no one to blame but myself.*

"But . . . ?" he asked, refusing to make it easy for her.

"But you had a car accident and so I waited. But then I couldn't wait with him, so I . . . so we . . . please don't make me say it."

"You owe me that much," he said, his voice now steely and ice cold. "Go on."

"I slept with him!" she cried out, angry at him for making her say it, even though she knew she had no right to be. "I cheated on you behind your back while you were laid up in a hospital bed, okay? It was wrong and I did it anyway. I knew better, but I couldn't help myself. I had no choice."

"No choice?" Alexander shouted. "Did he hold you down? Did he threaten you? Of course you had a choice! Everyone has a choice. What you had was a grotesque lapse in judgment, a . . . a . . . moral black hole that sucked up everything that was good and decent about you."

It took everything in her power not to jump up and run away, never to look back. Anna felt like she might cry but refused to shed a single tear. Instead she bit the inside of her bottom lip until it hurt. "I was wrong. You deserve better than what I did. But it's too late now. It happened. I did it and all I can give you is my confession."

"Do you have feelings for him?" Alexander asked, knowing he needed to learn as much as he could about the situation before deciding how to proceed.

"Of course I do," she said. "Or were you hoping I was just doing it for the sex? Do you think I'd do this if I didn't care for him? Do you think so little of me?"

"That's not fair, Anna. I didn't know you were so unhappy. Is this because we didn't go to my prom?"

"What?" Anna tried to hide her exasperation but failed. "You think this is about a prom? That's absurd."

"Is it?" he asked, his voice now sad. "Because maybe if we went and you danced with me like . . ." His voice faltered, and he couldn't go on. He had seen the way they looked at each other on the dance floor at Bea's party, and he'd chosen to try to forget it. To tell himself it didn't mean anything when he knew it did. "I'm tired. I need to sleep," he said. "My leg is killing me. Can we talk tomorrow?"

"Alexander, I don't think there's anything left for us to talk about. I'm sorry it had to end like this, but it did. It's over." Anna stood up, relieved that she'd said her piece and could now leave. She wanted to go home, curl up into a ball, and sleep.

"No, Anna," Alexander said. "You don't get to throw away our last three years like it was nothing. We had plans, a future together. Are you not going to give me the courtesy, the decency to talk this through? Help me understand what happened! You can't possibly think you have a future with him! He's a child, for fuck's sake."

Anna sat back down. The grief in his face pained her. He looked so helpless in the hospital bed, his leg broken, in a room surrounded by ugly vases and cheap baskets of wilting get-well flowers. Alexander's last words really hit her hard, and his tone reminded her of her father and how he sometimes spoke to Steven when he was disappointed with him. She shut her eyes as the enormity of the situation pelted her like rain pouring down without warning. Her mother and father were going to find out what she had done. Alexander's dad and stepmom would also be told. Anna had a great relationship with his parents, and his dad had always told her he loved her like a daughter. Their lives were totally intertwined, as close to marriage as two teenagers could get, really. She was a fool to have thought she could just tell him it was over and walk out the door like some stupid movie where the guy doesn't get the girl and just accepts his fate.

"Okay, you're right," she conceded. "Why don't you take a nap and I'll come back tomorrow?"

"Don't see him," Alexander said, looking her straight in the eye. "Can you do that for me? Don't see him or talk to him until we have time to talk tomorrow. You owe me that at least."

Anna was not a liar, and in fact had taken great pains never to lie in the past few weeks, even if she had been vague and told half-truths about her plans and whereabouts. So when Anna told Alexander that she wouldn't see or talk to Vronsky until after she and Alexander spoke in the morning, she meant it. They had spent three years together as boyfriend and girlfriend, and she did love him, or at least she had thought she did. Only now, after falling in love with Vronsky, did she understand the difference between being "in love with someone" and "loving someone."

Anna kept her word to Alexander and didn't answer Vronsky's texts, nor did she answer the phone when he called her. She didn't answer Beatrice's calls or texts, either, not wanting to exploit the loophole of honesty and make her the go-between. Instead she just went to bed and slept longer and harder than she had in weeks.

The next morning, she drove back to Alexander's house and they talked for hours, going around and around, crying and yelling at various times. Alexander told Anna he still loved her and wanted to work things out. He believed that even though Anna said she loved Vronsky, it wasn't true, that she'd been taken in by his looks and fun nature. But he was wrong for her in so many ways. Alexander shouldered some of the blame. He had been too wrapped up in his own life and of course she deserved fun and dancing and he wanted to be the one who gave it to her. He begged Anna to take some time, at least a few weeks, to really think things through and consider giving him one more chance. If she would do this for him, and if she decided that she still wanted to end things, then he'd do everything he could to make sure her reputation wasn't harmed and would never speak ill of her to anyone. He'd even go so far as to deny the truth and tell people that Anna had not betrayed him with Vronsky.

Half-heartedly, Anna agreed to take a few weeks, but she told Alexander that she would see Vronsky at least once to let him know her plans, though nothing would happen between them. She said that during the next two weeks Alexander could no longer consider her his girlfriend. She was free from all obligations. Alexander agreed to the terms but urged her to avoid spending time with Vronsky alone as it would only cloud her judgment. By the time they had finished wheeling and dealing in heavy emotional currency, it was dark out and pouring rain, but it didn't matter. She was too drained to give a damn.

XIII

Kimmie spent the morning with her mom at PS 137, a public school where she was enrolling as a new student. Danielle wasn't happy about her daughter's decision to leave Spence, but she was too afraid to argue against it. Kimmie's return home, with her new purple hair, black leather jacket, Doc Martens, and dark nail polish, had set her on edge. Kimmie had heard her parents fighting the morning her father picked her up from the airport. She went straight to her room, and her dad stayed with her mom to talk in the kitchen. She'd told her father in the ride over about her decision to leave Spence and asked him to tell her mother about it. He didn't want to do it, but Kimmie forced his hand, casually reminding him he never once visited her out in Arizona and hadn't even bothered to pick her up. "I'm fifteen, Dad, you really want me to blame you for everything when I'm your age?"

Her parents agreed to enroll her in public school, though they warned she may have to repeat her sophomore year, but Kimmie would take the necessary tests to see if she could get into Stuyvesant or Bronx Science for next year, two of the most competitive public schools in the city. She remembered hearing from Dustin how much he loved his time at Stuyvesant, and though she wasn't sure if she was as smart as Dustin, she wanted to try.

She had thought about Dustin nonstop on her sleepless red-eye flight back East. She couldn't get it out of her head, hearing his father tell Nicholas how Dustin had given up his own college tuition for his brother's rehabilitation. She doubted Lolly would have done the same for her, and she knew the old Kimmie might not have done it, either. Kimmie wished she could go back in time and ask Dustin more about his relationship with his brother, and while she was at it, ask him more about what it was like to be adopted. On appearances alone it seemed like Dustin had a good life because he was smart and already poised for success after getting into the college of his choice, and sure, his parents were divorced, but so were everyone's, though it must have been hard for him to be one of the only black members of his temple. But she knew why she didn't ask any of these questions: she had been selfish, only caring about stupid things like parties and if the wrong boy was going to text her.

Kimmie couldn't believe all that had happened during her month away: Alexander's car accident, dead horses, and broken hearts. But instead of feeling like she had missed out, she was happy she had been away, which furthered her resolve to walk away from all this rich-kid private-school nonsense. If public school was good enough for Natalia and Dustin, then it was good enough for her.

At the end of their meeting, when her new school principal, Mr. Kriesky, said he'd see her tomorrow, Kimmie was shocked. She'd assumed she'd have to start that very day. He told her public school was a little more relaxed and that he thought it'd be better if she started fresh in the morning. When he said, "Go out and get a Mister Softee, spring has sprung!" Kimmie smiled, knowing she'd made the right decision about school.

Afterward, her mother went off to take an Orangetheory class and asked Kimmie if she wanted to join her. Kimmie declined, wanting to go to Central Park and enjoy her last day of freedom before starting another new school. Her mother looked relieved at her answer, and Kimmie knew it was because her mother wasn't comfortable with the "new Kimmie" yet. She almost called her mom out on it but decided to let it go. Sure, she was more empowered and in touch with her anger these days, but it's not like she wanted to turn into a total bitch. As hardcore and badass as Natalia was, she was also incredibly thoughtful. Before Kimmie left, Natalia had shoplifted herself a pair of cheap gold hoop earrings from Walmart and had also snagged a pair for Kimmie. Kimmie touched her purloined earring and thought of her friend.

Natalia had loved the leather jacket that Kimmie left as a present for her, and Kimmie had several pictures of Natalia wearing it. It looked better on her, but Kimmie always knew it would. They had texted back and forth several times a day for the first day or so after her return, but suddenly the texts dwindled in number, and three days later their long-distance friendship had fallen into radio silence. Kimmie briefly wondered if this was a bad sign but decided to be positive, thinking instead that Natalia and Nicholas were busy planning their new careers as Insta influencers. During Kimmie's farewell dinner, Nick revealed the couple's new plan, where Natalia would be featured in cool hair-coloring videos for anyone interested in obtaining the alternative rocker chick look. Nick planned to direct and shoot the videos in their apartment and knew a lot about filmmaking from his extensive reading about famous directors. Apparently, the idea was hatched by Nick after he watched Natalia dye Kimmie's hair that first night they all hung out. Later in bed, he told her that not only was she wildly charismatic (she was), but she was also a natural born instructor, which he'd noticed as she explained her technique in a clear and concise step-by-step manner to Kimmie.

He had it all worked out. He was going to take on some extra shifts to make some extra cash, or hell, maybe he'd become an Uber driver, with plans to buy some secondhand lighting equipment and a dope digital camera, so he could properly capture his girlfriend's hotness. "None of this iPhone filmmaking shit" would fly with him. Kimmie thought the idea was brilliant and volunteered to be one of Natalia's "Before and After" hair models. She said as soon as they were set up, she'd fly back out for a week to help, maybe for summer vacation. Natalia and Kimmie toasted Nick for his brilliant idea, and he did that guy thing where he told them to fuck off, though it was obvious he was pleased. It was the one time Kimmie had ever witnessed Nick excited about something other than Fortnite and Natalia's ass. Kimmie wasn't paying him lip service, she truly felt like it was a great idea.

When she lay in bed her last night at Desert Vista, she had thought how great it would be to have a bf who believed in her the way Nick believed in Natalia, a goal Kimmie wrote down in the "long-term future life goals" section of her journal.

It was these long-term future life goals that Kimmie thought about as she walked through the park on a mission, because she only had one more thing to cross off on her "deal with past bullshit." Kimmie had almost given up on her idea of calling out Vronsky, thinking maybe it was better to leave the past in the past. All she wanted to think about was the future, but then Lolly told her about the whole Anna/Alexander drama, and Kimmie's anger at Count Vronsky renewed. Not only did he almost take her down, but now he was dragging down Anna.

When the doorman rang up, and the housekeeper answered, Kimmie explained she had Vronsky's homework, taking a chance that he was at home recovering from his accident at the horse race. She was immediately buzzed up and she wondered if the housekeeper had announced her arrival. But when she walked into the apartment and the uniformed housekeeper was talking on her phone, Kimmie figured she was on her own.

She found his bedroom and knocked, announcing herself through the closed door. He called out that he needed a moment, and a few moments later he opened his door, pulling on a sweatshirt over his taped up torso. Vronsky was clearly surprised to see her, and she was about to apologize for not calling first, then bit her tongue, remembering what Natalia had said about apologies being the last refuge of spineless pussies. Kimmie was no pussy, at least not today.

Kimmie entered Vronsky's dimly lit bedroom and flipped his desk chair around to face him as he sat on his unmade bed. Vronsky offered her a beverage and suggested they talk in the kitchen, but she refused. What she had to say to him wouldn't take long. He gestured for her to begin and she did.

She told him about her time in Arizona and her many exhausting therapy sessions. She told him how she had learned a lot about herself and explained that when she got back to New York after her ice dancing dreams were dashed that she never properly grieved for her loss. Her therapist's theory was she had been suffering from low-grade depression because of it. She then told him that when he kissed her on New Year's Eve it was the first time she had been happy since coming back to New York.

She went on to say that she didn't have much experience with guys and she used to be ashamed to admit this, but now she no longer cared. She was only fifteen years old, a baby really, and she now knew it was dumb to pretend she was worldlier than she was. She then told him how he had really hurt her feelings when he didn't call her the day after they had sex for the first time, and admitted to him that she had lied about sleeping with her coach and she had been a virgin, which made their first time her "first time."

"Did you know?" she asked. "Did you know I was lying?"

To his credit Vronsky admitted he'd suspected as much, but he'd ignored it. He asked if she'd felt pressured into having sex, and she told him while he didn't pressure her physically or verbally like in a creepy way, she had felt a kind of pressure, because she was so desperate for him to like her back. She really felt like she had no choice but to give it up, so to speak. He had asked her to come back to his house, and they had sat in the living room where he made a point of saying there was no one home. Clearly, he wanted to fool around, and at the time she had wanted it, too.

But he moved so fast, and she was shocked when he stripped her down and took off his own clothes. He had seemed so matter of fact about it all, so confident that her legs would part for him, that she followed his lead and figured that was just how these things went.

There was no question of consent, but when she had cried out in pain, she wanted to know why he didn't ask her if she was all right, why he didn't ask . . . if it was her first time. Instead he had acted horrified and made her feel like a total fool. Maybe if he had been sweeter about it she would have found the strength to tell him the truth, and then maybe they would have decided it wasn't a good idea. But that hadn't happened. The fact was now that night on the couch with him would always be her very first time. And as the saying goes, you never forget your first time, even if you want to.

She demanded again to know why he didn't call her the next day, and he sheepishly claimed he thought he had. But Kimmie showed him the screenshots of her phone, proving not only that he didn't call, but also that he didn't even bother to text her. She asked him how he'd feel if someone he really liked fucked him and then never called him. She told him how she waited for him at the ice rink, but he never showed up. She reminded him how they'd texted the day of Jaylen's party and he'd said he was excited to see her, but that clearly was a lie. She told him that she had bought a new outfit for the party because she had been delusional enough to think he was going to ask her to be his girlfriend that night. But he barely looked at her on the dance floor, busy as he was trying to find his precious Anna.

Vronsky, face cast to the floor, started to say how sorry he was, but Kimmie said she wasn't looking for an apology from him. She was taking full responsibility for the part she'd played in all of it. She shouldn't have gone to his house. She should have been more vocal that she was in over her head. She had chosen to tell him the truth about how much he hurt her, and that his behavior proved he wasn't the nice guy he pretended to be. But in a twisty, screwed-up way, she was almost fine with how it all went down, because the young woman standing before him today was stronger and much less naive than the insecure little girl he deflowered on his mother's expensive Italian leather couch.

She told him he didn't need to worry because she wasn't going to tell anyone about coming over here today. She was doing this for herself, and he no longer mattered to her in any way. She didn't care if she ever saw him again, but given the likelihood that she would, she'd be polite and hoped he could respect her enough to do the same. Kimmie said coming over here to tell him all this was her way of moving forward, of saying good-bye to her past, of taking the sheep mask off the wolf and revealing him for what he was.

She hoped that from now on, because of her, he would treat girls with a little more respect, because pretty girls, even if he viewed them as personal playthings, had feelings, too. She asked him if he wanted to say anything back to her now that she was done, but all he said was how sorry he was that he had hurt her feelings. He said that in the past he was guilty of being selfish, but that these days he was a changed man, though he offered no explanation.

"A real man wouldn't have treated sex as a sport; and a real man doesn't go around stealing other people's girlfriends."

His nostrils flared as he stood up to walk her out, but she stopped him. She was more than capable of finding her own way. As she rode down the elevator, she wasn't sure if she felt better, but she did know she felt proud of herself for living up to her new code of not taking shit from anyone, especially not a guy.

XIV

Vronsky sat on his bed in silence, shell-shocked from the Kimmie bomb that had exploded in his face. He didn't know what to do with himself, so he just lay back on his bed and stared at the ceiling, trying to absorb everything that had been said, not just by Kimmie but by Anna, who had shown up twenty minutes before Kimmie to tell him what had happened with Alexander.

Then Anna stepped out of Vronsky's closet, and as she did, he remembered how he'd once hid in his brother's closet, which he considered his sexual awakening. But now it occurred to him that watching his brother have sex was what started his own sexual odyssey and was not as cool as he'd once thought it was. Maybe that was where he learned to treat women the way he did.

Anna's face was hard to read, but her shock and dismay were obvious. She'd had no idea that Vronsky had had sex with Kimmie and overhearing her pain about it broke her heart and left her feeling sick in the pit of her stomach. Sitting in the closet listening, she wondered if perhaps Alexander was right, that she didn't know Vronsky as well as she thought she did. How could he have treated a sweet girl like Kimmie so cavalierly? What kind of guy would take a girl's virginity and not even contact her the next day? Sure, she realized she was in no position to judge after what she did to Alexander, but she knew she was in the wrong over her actions and was deeply remorseful. That didn't seem to be the case with Vronsky when it came to Kimmie.

Anna told Vronsky she was going to do what Alexander had asked of her. She needed time to think things through and their intimacy was clouding what was left of her good judgment. Anna was particularly pained because prior to Kimmie's intrusion, and despite the fact that she had told herself and Alexander she would refrain from having sex with Vronsky, she had been on the verge of sleeping with him again. "I told you I made a promise to Alexander and I want to keep it," she said in a voice so quiet he had to lean forward to hear her. "It was only two weeks that we had to wait, but still you tried to have sex with me anyway. Am I not worth waiting for?"

Vronsky slid off his bed and got on his knees. He begged Anna not to leave him this way. He told her he was sorry, that she had to forgive him. He could hardly resist her the same way she could barely resist him. He loved her, would always love her, only her, forever. He admitted he'd treated every girl before her like dirt, and he now saw the error of his ways. She was the most precious thing to him in the world. He pleaded for a second chance.

"You know me, Anna," he said, pitifully, not even bothering to wipe away the tears falling down his beautiful face. "You know you do. Just like I know you."

"I don't know anything anymore, Alexia," Anna said, involuntarily reaching out to touch his face, but then stopping herself. "Actually that's not true. I do know one thing, Kimmie's got a right to be disappointed in you, and now I know exactly how she feels. I'm going to leave now, and please don't contact me."

Anna walked home from Vronsky's house in a daze. She was beside herself and had no idea what to do about it. How did life get to be so complicated? And how did it happen so fast? The last few days were a nightmare, but things had been insane for months now.

Anna heard a familiar jingle and turned to see a Mister Softee truck parked up ahead. Breaking into what was probably her first smile in days, she quickened her step and went to get a cherry-dipped cone. She and Steven were obsessed with Mister Softee as kids and even put together a business plan for their father, called "Why We Need an Ice Cream Truck, and How to Get One!"

Anna sat on a bench and took a picture of her half-eaten cone and texted it to Steven with the message: I wish we were little kids again! Life was so much easier! She watched as bubbles appeared and then her brother's text came in: Where Are You? She texted back that she was wandering around aimlessly through Central Park. Come home, he texted.

When Anna entered the apartment, Steven was waiting for her and without even saying hi, she beelined right toward him, clutched her brother, and cried. Steven hugged her back and told her everything would be okay. "Everything is a mess," she said, wiping away her tears. "I don't know who I am anymore."

"Welcome to my world," her brother replied. "Maybe we should go see a Marvel movie."

"Which one?" she asked.

"I don't know, but there's always one playing somewhere."

Then Anna's mother came home and told Steven she needed to speak with Anna alone. Anna shook her head and said that anything her mother had to say, Steven could hear, too.

Anna's mother reluctantly agreed, then started to speak, telling them she had received a call from Anna's school that Anna had skipped classes and that her normally perfect grades had plummeted in recent weeks. Without giving her daughter a chance to respond, she continued that she had also heard the rumors about Anna and Vronsky and Alexander and demanded to know what was going on. Anna told her mother what had been happening, leaving out the sex stuff, and admitted she was absolutely in over her head and honestly didn't know what she should do.

"Well, I do," Anna's mom replied curtly. "You're going to stop wasting your time with that Vronsky kid and beg Alexander to forgive you. Really Anna, I don't know exactly what went on and I don't want to know, but I'm very disappointed in your actions. Alexander has been so good to you and he deserves far better than he got. I just hope your father doesn't hear about it; he'd be crushed to know his precious daughter isn't everything he thought she was."

Anna blinked her eyes rapidly to keep the tears of shock at bay. Her mother rarely took such a vitriolic tone with her. Telling her how disappointed her dad would be was a no-holds-barred kill shot. Anna hung her head and watched as two tears fell in tandem and soaked into the black denim of her designer jeans. She wanted to say something, but she didn't know what.

Anna needn't have worried over what to say because her big brother had plenty to say in response.

"Are you fucking kidding me?" Steven said, his voice trembling with fury. "Anna's worth ten million Alexanders! Beg for that douchebag's forgiveness? Over my dead body she will. Whatever Anna did is her own goddamn business and nobody else's."

Their mother was never a fan of the clapback, but this was something else entirely. "I am the parent here and I can talk to my daughter however I please. Do you know what it's like to walk into the salon and find out that people are whispering about your daughter? How she cheated on the favorite son of Greenwich when he was laid up with a broken leg? She's not some regular high school girl who gets to act a slut like it doesn't matter. She's the daughter of this family, and she has to know her actions affect everyone, the same way yours did when you got kicked out of every school in town!"

"You think I'm a slut?" Anna asked, unable to hide the hurt in her voice. "Mom, I was going to break up with Alexander, but then I couldn't because who can break up with a guy who needs a bedpan? I . . . I . . . I'm not just with Vronsky for fun. We love each other!"

"Oh Anna, grow the hell up. I've heard all about that boy. He's been in love with half the girls in Manhattan, the same way his mother 'loves' every rich man she can lay her manicured hands on. Of course he tells you you're special, that's what every guy says when he wants to get into your panties."

Anna pulled her knees into her chest and pressed her face into her knees. *What is happening? How can she talk to me this way? Isn't a mom supposed to protect you?*

"Tell me, Mom," Steven began, his voice no longer trembling, but extremely measured and calm. "Is that what the Dude with the Dragon Tattoo tells you when he wants to get into your panties?"

Anna lifted her head up and gazed at her brother. She had no idea what he was talking about.

"That's right, Mom," Steven continued. "I know how you spent your Valentine's Day. Dad buys you a forty-thousand-dollar diamond necklace, but I guess you wanted a pearl . . . Is that how you show your respect to Dad?"

Their mother stood up, her face blank with shock. She smoothed the wrinkles from her black pencil skirt and without saying a word grabbed her alligator Birkin bag off the table in the foyer and walked out the front door, closing it behind her.

Anna looked at her brother in wide-eyed amazement. "What the holy hell just happened?"

Steven sat down on the couch next to his sister and just shook his head. He opened his mouth but before he could speak, his phone started buzzing in rapid-fire succession.

Steven pulled his phone out of his pocket and answered. "Oh my god," he muttered. "When?"

"What happened? Who is it?" Anna grabbed Steven's arm. "Tell me." Even though she was currently pissed at Vronsky, the thought of something bad happening to him filled her with terror.

"I'll call you right back." Steven hung up and sat back down on the couch again.

"You're scaring me, Steven!" Anna cried. "What happened?

"Dustin's brother, Nicholas . . ." Steven said blankly. "Heroin overdose. He's dead."

XV

Dustin didn't have a black suit to wear to his brother's funeral, so Steven and Anna took him to Goodman's Men's and bought him one. Dustin stared at himself in the three-way mirror wearing the black Theory suit and gray shirt that Steven had picked out for him. Over his shoulder in the reflection, he saw Anna and Steven standing in the doorway behind him, each of them holding a different dark tie option. Seeing the brother and sister standing together cemented his cold new reality, and he started to sob.

Two days later the funeral was held in the same temple where Dustin and Nicholas had been bar mitzvah'd and the place was again packed. Dustin was not a fan of public speaking, but on the morning of the service he told his parents that he wanted to say a few words. His father said he didn't have to, but Dustin insisted.

Staring out at the sea of black-clad mourners, Dustin took a moment before he began his speech. This wasn't because of his grief, though he was chock full of it, this was because he'd spotted Kimmie in the crowd sitting next to Lolly, who was sitting next to Steven and Anna. And even though Kimmie looked pale and sad and had this crazy, wild, purple hair, and even though his brother had overdosed three days ago and would be gone forever, his heart still skipped a beat for Kimmie.

"Nicholas was my older brother by three years. Everyone who met us always commented on how different we were, not just because I'm black and adopted, but because of our personalities. But today I'm here to tell you how similar we are, too. It was my brother who instilled in me my love of cinema and for that I am eternally grateful. I saw my first R-rated movie with him when I was nine. *Old School* was playing on HBO and my parents had gone to some wedding, so we were alone for the entire day. I didn't understand a lot of the movie, but we had a great laugh at the part where Luke Wilson gets drunk at his friend's wedding after catching his wife cheating on him, and he starts to give a hilarious speech about why love sucks, but his other buddy Vince Vaughn stops him. None of this is important, but what does matter is that my brother and I spent the rest of the afternoon making up funny speeches that we would give at each other's weddings when we grew up.

"Nicholas told me that he'd announce I used to sleep with a fork under my pillow because I was more scared of cutting myself than having an efficient weapon against the monsters that I thought were under my bed. And I told him that I would tell everyone that he wore these green Tigger footy pajamas until his dirty toenails burst through the seams like he was the Hulk.

"As we got older that was something we would always threaten each other with. We'd say, 'You better watch it or I'll tell everyone what you did when I give your wedding toast.' I know it's an absurd thing, the two of us so young talking about our future weddings, but it's just something we did and it's important for me to let all of you know my brother was more than just some junkie who OD'd in Arizona.

"I had a whole speech prepared that I wrote the night I found out that he died. It was pretty epic, if I do say so myself, but I've decided not to give that speech today. Because it was far too angry, because I am so incredibly pissed at my brother for letting his addiction get the better of him. It was far too self-pitying, because I'm even more incredibly sad about my brother being gone. And it was far too preachy about the perils of drugs. If you want more info about the opioid crisis you can read about it in *The New York Times*. But you don't come to a funeral and talk about the tragedy of a life. You come to a funeral to talk about the beauty of it.

"The other reason I'm not giving that speech is because this morning I received a letter from Nicholas that he wrote to me before he died, and I'm going to share that letter now. . . ."

Dustin took a folded piece of paper out of his inner jacket pocket, unfolded it, and began to read:

"'Dear Baby Brother AKA Dickweed, I am writing you this piece of snail-mail on a sheet of Holiday Inn's finest stationery with a very cheap ballpoint pen that I stole from the front desk. I know that these days no one writes letters anymore because of email and texting, but you know

I hate all that technology shit so I'm doing the retro thing and mailing this to you instead, though I don't even know where to get a stamp or even how much they cost.

"'Why do I have Holiday Inn stationery you ask? Good question, smartypants, you always were the genius of the family. Well, it's because I'm using the last of the money I stole from you (sorry 'bout that, you know I'll get it back to you, bro) to celebrate my one-month anniversary with my gf, Natalia. Yeah, the girl I met at rehab. She's currently in the shower and I expect she'll be enjoying it for a while because the water pressure at our place sucks ass.

"'I have something very important to tell you. Remember that pancake breakfast we had in the Bronx when you came to see me? Well, I told you about Natalia, though back then I didn't know if she'd call me, so I was playing it cool. And you told me about how a girl broke your heart. You were angry and hurt and told me that love was overrated and a waste of time, and I agreed and then tried to make you feel better by saying that any girl who didn't see you for the great guy you are is obviously stupid and you'd be better off without her.

"'Well, I'm writing to tell you I couldn't have been more wrong that day. Love is not overrated or a waste of time. I think everyone says that when they're not in love, never been in love, or were in love and it didn't go their way. Why? Because a life with no love is, in my humble opinion, no life at all. I was a shitty kid and Mom and Dad deserved better than me, but thank god, like literally thank God for delivering you to them, because you're the son that any parent would be so lucky to have. You're like the son in a movie who's wiser than his parents and smarter than all his stupid friends. We should write a movie together, bro! I got so many ideas . . .

"'Anyway, I know I've been a fuckup and I want you to know your tuition money wasn't a total waste, yeah, Dad told me what you did for me, spending your college savings to send my dumb ass to rehab again. It means a lot to me that you believed in me, and I love you for your optimism. Which brings me to my next point. I'm totally gonna get fucked up tonight, I've already got it on me. Sorry dude, but I need one last hurrah before I go on the straight and narrow forever. You see, I couldn't remember my last time . . . the last time I used, and that seemed weird to me, and so I wanted to make it an event. I know this sounds like I'm rationalizing, and maybe I am. Remember what they say, never trust a junkie, but that's my fucking story and I'm sticking to it.

"'Here's the plan. I'm gonna party with my girl in a hotel like a true pimp 4 realz, but before I do I'm gonna tell her, like I'm tellin' you, that it's my last time because I want to marry her and spend the rest of my dumbass dish-washing days with her forever. You'd totally dig her, man. She's hot, sexy, funny as hell, and best of all she calls me on my shit, which you know I need. I love her. She's made me a believer that there is something better out there for me than drugs. I can't wait for you to meet her. She and I have some big plans, which include buying a junker and driving cross-country to see about a boy . . . and that boy is you. My kid brother. Because I love you and if I've learned anything at all about life from the movies, it's that when you feel something big and know something bigger you share it with the world.

"'Your brother forever, Nicholas.

"'P.S. Oh yeah, start writing your wedding toast 'cause I'm pretty sure I'm gonna be the first of us to need one. Knock that best man speech out of the fucking park!

"'P.P.S. Memberberry how I said I wasn't feelin' Kendrick Lamar? Natalia likes him, so I'm givin him another go. If that don't prove my love than nuthin' will.'"

Dustin folded the letter and put it back in his inner pocket, and when he looked out at the crowd he saw that people were crying but people were smiling, too.

"Well, that was all Nicholas had to say, and so that about sums it up. Nicholas, it was an honor to be your brother and I'm gonna miss you every day. Okay, Rabbi Kennison, take it away . . ."

XVI

True to her word, Anna had not texted Vronsky for over a week now. It wasn't as difficult as it could have been because after Nicholas's memorial service, Dustin's family sat shivah for seven days, alternating between his mother's and father's apartments. Anna and Steven went on the first day and ended up going every day for all seven days. Their friend clearly needed their support, and truth be told, they both needed the time to reflect on their own screwed-up lives, too. Luckily there were no mirrors to reflect their sadness back to them, since it was a Jewish custom that when sitting shivah all the mirrors in the house had to be covered. The mirror was a means of accepting social importance through appearance, and during a time of mourning, such superficial thoughts were frowned upon, so all mirrors remained hidden to dissuade one from getting distracted with their own self-importance, when they were supposed to be using the time to reflect upon the loved one who had passed.

Dustin stayed mostly silent, but here and there he'd express his feelings out loud, alternating between deep sorrow over never seeing his brother again and anger. "It doesn't make sense," Dustin said. "You find a girl who you love and want to spend the rest of your life with, and that girl actually loves you back, then why do the most addictive drug on the planet again? Didn't he think that maybe his last hurrah could be his literal last hurrah of his actual life? Fucking idiot."

"He didn't know," Steven said gently. "He probably misjudged the amount he took, since he had been clean for a while. He made a mistake. People make mistakes."

"And now he's dead," Dustin said. "Some mistake."

"Have you heard from her?" Anna asked. "Nicholas's girlfriend?"

"No," Dustin replied. "We got her number from my brother's phone but it's no longer in service."

"If she loved him, why wouldn't she come to the funeral?" Steven asked. "Guilt?"

"It's not her fault," Anna said quickly. "It was an accident. Maybe she's just afraid everyone blames her."

"My mother does," Dustin said. "She also blames my dad for not bringing him back. She's also mad that we didn't tell her about spending my college fund for Nicholas's rehab, or the stolen car, or any of it. She pretty much hates everyone right now. She might be stuck in the Kübler-Ross 'anger' stage for a while."

"Dustin, your mom will come around," Anna said. "I mean, I know you lost your brother, too, but a parent losing a child is supposed to be the worst thing ever. But what do I know? I know nothing about anything." Anna looked down at the floor.

Steven put his hand on his sister's back and gave it a rub. "Everything is fucked," he said. Steven and his mother had barely spoken in days, and he was at a loss with what to do about it. Luckily his father was on an extended business trip so he wasn't around to notice that his wife was no longer acknowledging either of her children. For Steven, the only saving grace about Dustin's brother dying was that it gave him a chance to worry about someone else's problems, troubles that were far bigger than his own.

Two days after Nicholas's memorial, Steven appeared in Anna's bedroom doorway. He told her he was going to pick up Lolly and head downtown to Dustin's dad's apartment for the second day of shivah, and that she she should come, too. When they were outside Lolly's mom's place, Anna wondered whether Kimmie would be coming along, but Lolly came down by herself. She was dressed in a simple black Prada dress, holding two foiled bundles.

"Hey guys," she said as she got in the backseat. "I baked Dustin's family some banana bread. One gluten-free and one regular."

"That's nice of you, Lolls," Anna said. "Kimmie didn't want to come?"

"She said she'll come over when she's ready," Lolly told them. She had tried to explain to her younger sister that being a good friend to Dustin in his time of need was far more important than the stupid stuff that had transpired between her and Anna and Vronsky. But Kimmie said that wasn't what it was about.

Lolly was just happy that Kimmie had stopped crying all the time and that her sister had returned looking much healthier, though at the same time she was worried that Kimmie seemed to have swung too far to the other side. Lolly's mom had told her they needed to be nonjudgmental and simply offer their unconditional support until Kimmie settled down. According to her therapist, Kimmie was working through some tricky emotional issues, and her new look and attitude were part of the process.

Anna nodded but didn't speak. She had been thinking about Dustin's eulogy nonstop for two days. His brother's letter about love being the meaning of life, and how he had finally learned this because of a girl who he randomly met in rehab, was just so mind-blowing. It was terribly tragic that Nicholas found the one thing he had been missing in his life but died right afterward. Anna couldn't help but think that if things had gone differently for Vronsky during the timber race she could be the one in mourning. *I found the love of my life but right now I'm choosing not to be with him. Why? What am I trying to prove? And to whom am I trying to prove it? I still love him; I wonder if he still loves me.*

"Have you talked to your mom yet?" Lolly asked. Steven had come clean about what had happened on Valentine's Day, as well as the reason he'd chosen to keep it from her. Lolly wasn't happy he'd withheld the truth, but she understood why. It was a relief to know that it was his mother's affair that was the cause of her boyfriend's weirdness for the last month and a half and not something else. In a strange way Lolly felt as though everything that had happened with Steven's mom benefitted her, though she'd never say this to him. They had had a very long talk about Steven's feelings on cheating, exploring why he felt it was more wrong for his mother to do it than it was for his father. Lolly pointed out that it was a total double standard, which he fully admitted and was working hard to understand the root cause of his sexist thinking. He also admitted he would be devastated if he found out Lolly was with another guy behind his back and asked her, no begged her, to let him know if she was unhappy in the relationship or with him before she found herself tempted by another guy. Lolly didn't tell him that she had literally never once found herself thirsty over another guy since she'd been with him, but she didn't.

What was even more shocking to her than Steven's mother's affair was that Anna had cheated on Alexander with Vronsky. This revelation rocked Lolly's world. When she watched Anna, beside herself with grief, run out onto the field after the horse accident like a lunatic, Anna's face had shown such fear over Vronsky being hurt, it was like she was possessed. It was like those urban legends of adrenaline-fueled mothers lifting two-thousand-pound vehicles to save their children. Lolly had never seen Anna lose her cool before, and she found it wildly romantic. It wasn't right what Anna did, cheating on Alexander behind his back, but Lolly understood Anna's decision to wait until Alexander was better and back at college before she broke it off with him. Lolly knew if she was in a similar position, she might have done the same. Or would she?

Lolly found one day of sitting shivah to be plenty for her. Seeing Dustin's mom barely holding herself together was too much for Lolly to take for four hours, let alone days on end, as Steven and Anna were doing. She could tell that Steven and Anna had both been in denial about their own troubled lives, and it struck her as sad that it had taken someone's death for them to reflect upon themselves at all.

XVII

When Vronsky walked out of school, he was surprised to find his mother's longtime chauffeur, Leonard, sitting on his Ducati parked in the back of his school.

"This is a sweet ride," Leonard said, as Vronsky walked over to greet him. "How fast does she go?" Leonard had been his mother's chauffeur since before Vronsky was born and so he felt like family. Vronsky was careful with his words around Leonard though, because he knew his mother paid for Leonard's loyalty with the signature on his paychecks (she also had paid for Leonard's children's college educations).

"From what I hear, easily one-forty," Vronsky answered with a grin. "But I've never gone over the speed limit, personally."

Leonard laughed heartily and threw his leg over the seat and sat down on the bike. He then told Vronsky his mother wanted to see him, and he was to go to the Pierre Hotel for afternoon tea. Vronsky politely told his mother's driver he had other plans and asked that Leonard send his apologies to his mother.

"No can do, Mr. Vronsky," he said. "She's not asking this time."

"Fine," Vronsky said casually, careful not to let his annoyance show. "I'll go there right now." He stepped toward his bike, but Leonard made no move to get off.

"You're supposed to ride with me, or if you've got another helmet I'll ride with you," Leonard said. "Don't fight it. You know how she can get." Leonard carefully stepped off the bike.

Vronsky was pissed and was tempted to jump on his bike and tear out of the lot, the hell with Leonard and his mother. But he had seen how difficult his mother made his older brother's life when he didn't fall in line. After one semester of college, Kiril told his mother he was going to drop out, because he felt college was a waste of time. He woke up the next day to find his credit cards cut off and his bank account empty. He had lasted two days before calling his mother, asking her opinion on whether he should take macro- or microeconomics for his upcoming semester; she said macro, and Kiril got an A in the class as an apology.

In the backseat of his mother's silver Mercedes Maybach, Vronsky kept silent. Normally he wouldn't have held his mother's bullying against Leonard because he knew the man was just doing his job, but he wasn't in the mood for small talk. Vronsky had been waiting for his mother to drop the hammer for weeks now, surprised it had taken her this long to summon him. Ever since he became obsessed with Anna, he knew he had ignored every other area of his life. He had canceled on his mother half a dozen times in the last month alone, and each time he did it he expected a call from her, but none had come. Vronsky figured his mother was wrapped up in some personal drama, and considered himself lucky she was otherwise occupied.

It had been over a week since he had heard from Anna, and he was barely holding it together. Every day after school he rode the forty minutes to Staugas Farms in hopes of seeing her, but Anna had been a no-show all week. So instead he hung out with Murf. At first they drank beers and Vronsky sulked, but after two days of bitching and moaning, Murf put his friend to work. A new storage shed had just been built, and Vronsky helped Murf get it organized properly. Vronsky's back was still bruised from the timber race fall, but his bruises were now yellow and green, versus the angry purple and red they had been. Murf taught Vronsky how to handle a power drill, patiently walking him through how to put together the first of the eight ten-by-ten industrial steel shelves that would line two walls of the unit. Vronsky found the monotonous work relaxing, though it didn't free him from his constant roiling thoughts of Anna. The labor gave him something to do, and it would be a good way for him to get back in Mr. Staugas's good graces after the whole timber race debacle.

What had happened arguably wasn't his fault. It was the horse in second place, whose front hoof clipped the plank and caused it to fly in the air. Frou Frou misjudged the jump due to the flying plank and tumbled onto the fence, bringing the whole thing crashing down. Frou Frou's fall caused a collision of the two horses behind him. Fortunately, Vronsky had been thrown off Frou Frou's back before the horse landed on top of him and crushed every bone in his body. If he hadn't been so lucky, he could have ended up like Frou Frou, thrashing on the ground with a broken back, shrieking and whinnying, his nostrils flaring, his eyes wild and black. The sight of that magnificent beast writhing in pain shook Vronsky to his core. He couldn't shake the memory of the horse's final minutes of life since it had happened, and he suspected the image would haunt him forever. He'd felt so helpless during the whole thing and refused to get himself checked out by the EMTs until he found out his horse's fate. When Dr. Khurana, the large-animal vet on hand, arrived at the scene seconds after the fall, he took one look at the animal writhing on the ground and shook his head. It didn't take a trained veterinarian to see that Frou Frou would never stand again.

Vronsky wanted to comfort the poor creature, but he couldn't get close until after the doctor shot Frou Frou with the tranquilizer dart. Frou Frou's shrieking stopped almost immediately, but his breathing remained loud and labored, and his eyes grew dull from the heavy sedative.

Eventually Vronsky approached the giant beast and petted his muzzle while the vet administered the shot that would end his life. He hadn't even known he was sobbing until Beatrice and Murf pulled him away from the dead animal and forced him to get checked out by the paramedics. They wanted to give Vronsky a shot for the pain from his most likely broken ribs, but he wouldn't let them. Vronsky welcomed the pain as a punishment, because he was filled with the bitter taste of regret. Honestly, he had expected to win the whole damn thing, and his plan was to give Anna the silver cup that came with his victory. Murf had found him right before the race and told him Anna thought it was too dangerous, but if anything that only made him want to do it more. He was driven by the need to keep Anna looking at him with the same inestimable esteem she had of late. Not only was he in love with her, but he was also in love with the way her respect and admiration made him feel. She made him believe he could do anything, and since he had never been lacking in the confidence department, she now made him feel invincible. When he heard the sharp crack of the other horse's hoof hitting the hurdle, he reacted immediately, pulling Frou Frou's reins to the left. Vronsky asked himself over and over why he hadn't just let Frou Frou's experience guide the way instead of his own fear. If he had, would Frou Frou still be alive today?

His first thoughts when he hit the ground were of Anna. Whether she was watching, which he knew she was, and whether she would still love him now after witnessing the folly of his stubbornness. Only later, after the X-rays showed no internal bleeding, and his ribs were taped up by the ER doctor, did Murf and Beatrice tell him what had happened with Anna. How everyone there had seen her run out onto the field in a blind panic, desperate to know if he was okay. When he heard it, he smiled for the first time since, but Beatrice went on to tell him that Alexander and Eleanor had shown up minutes before the race and witnessed the whole spectacular fiasco. "The proverbial cat," Beatrice said, "just managed to claw its way out of Anna's bag. I've never seen the unflappable Greenwich OG so, well . . . flapped."

Vronsky texted her through the WWF app over and over that night, but she never texted him back.

XVIII

Vronsky loved high tea, though he'd never admit it to any of his male counterparts. He loved the beauty of the details, the three-tiered silver trays, the beautifully sculpted petits fours on the top tier, the delicate crustless sandwiches in the middle, and the crumbly warmth of the scones that sat on the bottom. He adored the tiny ramekins of clotted cream and flavored jams, but most of all he loved the tangy sweet and sour of the lemon curd, his favorite. He had shared high tea with his mother countless times all over the world, but their favorite teas were still after a weekend matinee of a Broadway show.

This teatime with Geneviève ranked as his least favorite right away. As soon as he sat down across from his mother, she scowled. "You look horrible, Alexia," she said. "You need a haircut and some sun, your coloring is abysmal."

"Lovely to see you, too, Mother," he replied, looking around the room to see if he recognized anyone in the crowd who could act as a buffer for him. His attention flew back to his mother when she slapped the palm of her hand down hard enough to make the Limoges china jump and rattle.

"I'll slap that sarcasm right out of your mouth if you're not careful," she hissed. "Today is not the day to test my patience, I'm not feeling jovial."

"Well that makes two of us," he said. "Get on with it."

Though Geneviève's ankle was healed, she had purchased an antique gold-topped walking stick that had once belonged to a Russian emperor at Sotheby's and hadn't tired of its beauty yet. She now wielded it to slap the legs of her son's chair. The noise made every patron at the surrounding tables turn and gape, including Vronsky, who sat up straight in his chair, sucking in a deep breath that did no favors for his sore ribs. "Mother, you're causing a scene," he whispered. "Please."

"Alexia," his mother said, her voice loud for emphasis. "You're the one who should be ashamed for making scenes, not I." She went on to tell her youngest son that she had been patient long enough with his girl-crazy antics, but she was angry enough to intervene now. Knowing that her niece, Beatrice, would never betray her cousin's confidence and tell her what was going on, Geneviève had demanded that Kiril find out what he could about his brother's recent behavior.

"I am a firm believer that men should sow their wild oats when they are young," she continued. "But making a fool of yourself over a young woman of high breeding who is not yours for the taking is as unacceptable as it is repugnant. Your chasing around Anna K. like a puppy panting after a squeaky toy is all anyone can talk about in Greenwich, and now the rumor mill has set up shop in Manhattan."

"I love her," Vronsky said brazenly, meeting his mother's disapproving eyes with his own. "And it's not my fault."

"And whose fault is it?" she enquired. "Is it Greenwich's favorite son's fault that while he convalesces from a terrible car accident, his once loyal girlfriend is running all over town with you? You could have killed yourself during that race, but instead you killed the horse!"

At the mention of Frou Frou, Alexia lowered his eyes in shame. He knew his mother had heard about the timber race tragedy because she had been traveling with Beatrice's mother, her sister-in-law, at the time. When she hadn't reached out to him, he'd hoped that she was so relieved he came out unscathed that he wouldn't be punished.

"I'm buying Penelope a new horse," his mother informed him. "With your money, of course."

"It was an accident and I've apologized to my aunt many times," he said, unable to meet his mother's eyes when the subject wasn't on his beloved Anna. "I feel terrible about Frou Frou."

"And you should," she snipped. "But you're not here to discuss that. You're here to tell me you're done chasing Anna and are moving on. Why not go up and visit Kiril at school? I'm sure a college girl could bring back some color into your cheeks."

Vronsky shook his head slowly, appalled at his mother's suggestion. The thought of any girl that wasn't Anna was ridiculous to him and had been since the moment he had seen her at the train station. He picked up a cucumber-and-cream-cheese finger sandwich and folded the entire thing into his mouth. "Forget it, Mother. I have zero interest in anyone else."

His mother sighed and sat back in her chair, staring at her youngest son. He looked terribly sad and far more pathetic than she had expected, which pained her. She was all too familiar with the heartache of love affairs gone wrong. She had cheated and been cheated on too many times to count.

"Having met the girl, I understand the appeal," she said softly. Geneviève had no problems staying angry at her oldest son, but there was something about her youngest child, who so clearly took after her with his good looks and mischievous spirit, that made it impossible for her to give him the tough love he needed. She had been sent a video of the crazed Anna K. running out onto the field after Vronsky's fall from the horse, and even though she couldn't see the young girl's face, Anna's anguish was apparent in her stricken posture and gait.

Geneviève had always known Alexia would grow up to be a heartbreaker, but she never expected he'd be such an accomplished lothario by the tender age of sixteen. Anna K. was quite a trophy for his wall, and while she respected what it probably took for him to get her, it was her job as his mother to make sure he understood that her notch should be carved on a bedpost, not in the chamber of his heart.

Hearing her son use the word "love" for another woman was not to her liking. She wanted to be the sole owner of his deepest affections for his entire life, and she had no plans to let go of him so easily. Geneviève knew she should send him away to school and that geographical distance was what was required in this case, but looking across the table at him, she knew he wouldn't go. His older brother Kiril only lasted two days without money, but she knew Alexia was made of stronger mettle than his brother and was crafty enough to get by for much longer. She needed to handle this situation very delicately, using all the wisdom and savvy she had accrued in her own life. One wrong move on her part could drive a wedge between her and her favorite son, which was not her intention. "Alexia, darling, the whole ugly business has become too public. Stop seeing her for a while, and if you still feel the same way about her in a year, I'll be the first one to offer you both my blessing."

"I haven't seen her in nine days, Mother," he said, as if nine days was nine years.

"That's a great start! Only three hundred and fifty-six left to go . . ."

"It's killing me!" Vronsky continued, ignoring his mother. "And it's not by my choice. She promised Alexander she'd take some time to decide what she wants."

"You're certainly the better man, my darling," his mother conceded. "But she's a young woman and Alexander W. could secure her entire future. He'd be a wonderful first husband." Geneviève was tired of the glumness, and too much talk always made her tea go cold. It was time for her to bring a little levity to the discussion.

"And I could give her nothing?" he asked. The thought of his mother siding with Alexander made him want to sweep his arm across the table and send the silver trays and fine china crashing to the floor, giving the patrons a juicy morsel to pocket and feast on with their gossip-loving friends later.

"You're a child, Alexia," his mother said. "Why would you want the headache of a girlfriend now? You have the whole world at your disposal and there are plenty more girls out there who'll make you say, 'Anna who?'"

"Mother, don't!" he interrupted. "She's the one I want. There is no other girl for me."

"Fine, but if she doesn't choose you, my dear, don't come crying to me. I'm offering you the chance right now to go to any school anywhere in the world. The offer expires as soon as we're done here."

"Thank you, but no thank you," he said, drinking the last of his oolong rosehip tea.

"Very well . . ." she said.

Vronsky waited for his mother to finish her tea and was relieved there was no further discussion of his love life. Instead Vronsky's mother recounted all the new couture pieces she had just purchased in Europe while Alexia listened dutifully. Only later, when they were outside waiting for Leonard to pull the car around, did Geneviève tell her son about

Claudine, the daughter of her Parisian friend, who, she informed her son, he'd be escorting to Coachella. "I've already told Beatrice about her and I know there's room on the plane."

"I don't know if I'm going anymore, and even if I do, I'm not a babysitter," Vronsky said, his anger returning now that his mother's meddling had resumed.

"You are going, and you're going to make sure Claudine has a wonderful time," his mother said. "You need some sun, and the distraction will do you good. Trust me, I know all too well the agony of awaiting your fate from a lover. It's its own special circle of hell."

#

Kimmie stood outside in the dark smoking a cigarette across the street from Dustin's mom's apartment, while she waited for Steven and Anna to leave. She had heard from Lolly that Steven and Anna went and sat shivah with Dustin and his family every day after school. Kimmie had wanted to be there, too, but she wanted to see Dustin alone more. So, she waited. She placed the small terra cotta–potted cactus on the ground next to her feet and stared down at the round prickly plant she had picked out. She had planned to buy flowers, but as she stood in the florist's, none of the bright fragrant flowers seemed like the right gift to bring for the occasion. A cactus was probably too far in the other direction, but something about it spoke to her, and these days she was navigating her life by her gut instincts.

Finally, Kimmie saw Steven and Anna emerge, and she stepped into the shadows, not wanting to be seen. She was wearing her Natalia jacket, black jeans and boots, and a black beanie over her new short haircut. She had spent five hours at her mother's hair stylist after school, and her hair was back to her normal blond shade. She'd insisted on retaining a touch of color and so had two strips of hair dyed pink on either side of her part. After her color was finished, she told Angela that she wanted to get a haircut as well. Something short, rebellious, and easy to care for. She showed the stylist a picture of Molly Ringwald in *Pretty in Pink*, but Angela had insisted on texting her mom before undertaking something so drastic. Kimmie's mom texted back a hard pass on the Ringwald cut and sent over a few approved pictures to choose from. Kimmie pointed to a cute blonde with a shaggy above-the-shoulder cut.

"Who is that?" Kimmie asked. "She looks familiar, but I don't know her name."

"That's America's sweetheart," Angela said. "Meg Ryan. *When Harry Met Sally?* God, I feel old right now."

Kimmie didn't like the sound of America's sweetheart, but she did like how happy this Sally person looked. "Happy" was Kimmie's new goal, because she had begun to realize that while Natalia pulled off the whole fuck-the-world attitude with edge and aplomb, on Kimmie it just looked as if she was making an I-stepped-in-dogshit face 24/7.

When Kimmie got the text from Lolly that Nicholas had died, the first thing she did was call Natalia, but the phone number was suddenly and suspiciously out of service. She then checked Natalia's Instagram and Snapchat accounts, but they were gone as well. Clearly the wine coolers at her going-away dinner were an ominous sign of the trouble to come. She wondered if Natalia had tried heroin with Nicholas, worrying that she might have OD'd, too, but she felt like she would have heard about it by now. Plus, Natalia had told Kimmie that heroin was the one drug she feared the most. Her mother had told her if she ever caught her daughter sticking a needle in her arm, she'd shave her head as punishment. Since Natalia's favorite pastime was coloring her locks, that was reason enough to take her mother's threats seriously.

Kimmie stubbed her cigarette out on the sidewalk, opened a pack of gum, and chewed several pieces at once. She waited on the corner for the walk signal and then she crossed the street, taking her time. *What am I going to say to Dustin's mom? What am I going to say when I see his dad? "Hello, sir, you don't know this, but we were in the same apartment the last time you saw your oldest son alive. I heard you yell at him. I heard you reveal something that your other son asked you not to tell. I heard you say you were* done with your son, and even if you hadn't really meant it, you said the words and will never have the chance to take them back." *What am I going to say to Dustin?* She knew she had to tell Dustin she was there in Arizona, hanging out with Natalia and his brother, but she really didn't want to. *This never would've happened if Vronsky hadn't screwed me over. My god, why are you even thinking of that little punk right now?*

Kimmie was really working hard on owning up to her own shit, but it was so easy to fall back into her childish habit of blaming everyone else for her problems. Why was it so hard to be the person she wanted to be? She'd felt so much better after she told Vronsky off that day. Her therapist had been proud of her for saying what she needed to say without too much drama, and she honestly hadn't thought of Vronsky at all since then, which was a relief because that proved she had never really been in love with him like she had thought. True love lasted way longer than just two months, right?

She took a deep breath.

Dustin was alone in the living room when the buzzer sounded. He glanced at the kitchen clock and saw it was after eight, which meant shivah was officially over. But as he walked over to answer the intercom a calm came over him. He knew who was at the door.

When Kimmie announced herself, Dustin smiled as he pressed the button. He was pleased that she had stayed true to her word about coming to visit at some point during the week. He had only said four words to Kimmie after the funeral, "Thank you for coming." It was what he said to everyone that day. He had been so drained by the whole ordeal he wasn't able to say anything more, even to her.

He remembered Kimmie's purple hair from the funeral, but when he opened the door and she pulled off her hat, she revealed her normal blond color, only her hair was much shorter. He must have been staring, because she immediately announced she had just gotten it dyed that day and then decided on an impromptu new haircut.

"You look like Meg Ryan in my favorite movie of hers," Dustin said. "She was . . ."

"America's sweetheart?" Kimmie said with a smile, not the one she had been practicing in the elevator, but a real one. She was happy to see Dustin and thankful it wasn't as awkward as she had feared. "I have to admit I don't know who she is. My mom sent her picture to my hair stylist."

"You've never seen *When Harry Met Sally?*" Dustin asked. "My mom dragged me and Nicholas once for . . ." He trailed off, his face crinkled in a mix of surprise and sadness at his casual mention of his brother's name. It had been the first time since Nicholas died that he had spoken about him and not remembered he was gone. He took a deep breath and continued. "She made us see it with her on Mother's Day once. Nicholas and I watched it every time it came on TV after that, but we would never admit we liked it, saying we were only watching it out of respect for the woman who raised us."

"Let's watch it," Kimmie jumped in. "I mean, if you're not busy or anything."

"*When Harry Met Sally?*" Dustin asked. "Don't you have school tomorrow?"

"I do, but I've finished my homework already," Kimmie said. "Public school is way easier. My mom's out with her boyfriend, and Lolly's home online shopping for Coachella, so she'll cover for me. But if you don't want to, we don't have to."

"No, let's do it," Dustin said. "I'm sure my mom owns it on Apple TV. It's one of her favorite movies. She's watched it like a hundred times."

Kimmie told Dustin how her mom watched *Sixteen Candles* while on Ambien and her imitation of her mom made Dustin laugh for the first time since he had found out he no longer had a big brother. He felt guilty for a split second, enjoying himself and having a good time when Nicholas was dead, never able to laugh again, but then he remembered his brother's advice from his letter: life was about love, and if a hard-ass, rap-lovin' guy like his brother could get all mushy about love, then he should definitely give it another chance himself.

And the only girl who made such a thing possible was standing before him. When she looked at him there was something in her eyes he couldn't quite read. She paused for a second then took a deep breath. "I need to tell you something."

"What is it?" he said, staring at Kimmie, her face a montage of guilt or shame or he didn't know what. "It's okay, you can tell me anything."

He could see her gathering the courage. She hesitated then spoke: "When I was in Arizona . . ."

That was all she had to say before he knew exactly what it was. He had been grappling with the idea of bringing it up to her himself, but had decided against it, at least for now. "I already know what you're going to say."

"You do?" she asked, both hopeful and frightened.

Dustin reached into his back pocket and pulled out the letter Nicholas had written him and unfolded it. "There was one more P.S. on the letter that I didn't read at the funeral," he said and recited his brother's final words aloud: "'P.S. I met your girl Kimmie out here. What a fuckin' small world, eh? She didn't know I was your brother and I didn't tell her. I don't know why, but I didn't. She's a real sweetheart, a little lost, but hell, aren't we all? Natalia said that she talked about a boy, the one that got away . . . and of course I thought it was the pretty-boy who stole her from you, but it wasn't him. It was you. She said you were the smartest boy she ever met, and when Natalia asked her why she didn't get with you she said it was because she wasn't ready yet. Dude! You should go for it. Listen to me, I know what I'm talking about, because I'm your brother, which means some of your smarts must've rubbed off on me, too . . .'" He paused and stared at her, both their eyes glistening with tears. "But you didn't know it was him, did you?"

Kimmie nodded. "I did, but only at the end. Do you hate me? Please don't hate me . . ."

"Why would I hate you?"

"Because maybe I could have done something, told someone, gotten him help. I could have stayed, but I left. But I never saw him using, Dustin, I swear he was trying to be good. He loved Natalia. They were my friends. I feel so stupid. Please don't hate me."

Without even thinking, Dustin took her hands in his own and looked deeply into her eyes. "Kimmie, I tried to hate you once. It didn't work."

She let go of his hands and grabbed him by the face, smashing her lips into his mouth and slipping her tongue between his lips. Her eyes were closed; his eyes were wide open. He wanted to remember this moment forever, but as they kissed, he let his eyelids shut, realizing that this memory wasn't about the image of her. It was about the sensation of her touch, her taste, her smell. In this moment, he was blind.

Later, sitting on his mother's couch in the living room, Kimmie and Dustin watched *When Harry Met Sally*. He remembered how he and his dad had sat on the couch together and cried over Nicholas months ago, but where they had been sitting on opposite ends of the seven-foot couch, Dustin and Kimmie now sat in the center, her head resting on his shoulder. She was enthralled by the film. When the movie was over, Kimmie turned to him and said, "I loved it. It's a wonderful story."

"Yeah?" Dustin asked. "What did you like the most about it?"

"I like that they were friends first. And then they weren't friends. And then he loved her. And then she loved him. And then he lost her, and then he realized his mistake and ran through the streets to tell her he'd made a mistake. And that it ended on New Year's Eve because that's when we met for the first time. You know, I'm Harry though."

"What do you mean?"

"I'm the one who didn't know what I had when it was right in front of me. I'm the one who made a mistake and let a good thing slip through my fingers."

Dustin stared at Kimmie in the dimly lit living room. His mother had never replaced the broken lamp, even after all these months.

"I didn't know," Kimmie said quietly. "I didn't know myself. I didn't know what I wanted. I didn't know anything back then."

Dustin nodded slowly. "Okay, so, I'm Meg Ryan and you're Billy Crystal? What exactly are we talking about?"

Kimmie smiled. "I'm saying I want you to ask me to go to prom with you again. Now that I'm a full-on feminist, I'd ask you myself. But it's not my prom."

"Kimmie," Dustin said, hoping that there was a heaven and his brother was up above watching his little brother's own personal rom-com movie moment, *When Kimmie Met Dustin*. "Will you go to prom with me?"

"Fuck yeah I will," she said and snuggled back into him, knitting her fingers into his and clasping them tight.

She left a short while later and they made plans to go see a movie the following day. She had refused to let him walk her outside, insisting that she was a different person than she'd been before. "I'm not saying I know who I am yet," she told him. "But I'm trying to figure it out." After he let her out and watched her through the window getting into a cab, Dustin leaned his head against the door and, looking up at the ceiling, he spoke out loud to his brother. "I owe you one, dude. Big time."

XX

It was the day before they were supposed to meet at the Greenwich airport to board Beatrice's father's recently purchased Gulfstream G500 for Coachella. The Spring Beak trip was meant as a mini reunion for the A-list dinner guests from Beatrice's costume party. They were going to see LiviX2 perform, and they had artist VIP passes which meant they could be upfront at every performance and could travel on the secret paths in the backstage areas. Everyone was going except for Rooster, who was on a football recruiting trip.

Anna had already texted Beatrice her decision not to go; however, she didn't put up much of a fight when her brother argued that a trip West was exactly what they needed.

"We need to make ourselves scarce," Steven told his sister. "Who knows what shit's going down with Mom and Dad this weekend?" After the long ice-out, Steven woke up for school to find his mother sitting on his bed. She told her son she had ended her affair with the Dude with the Dragon Tattoo and that she would confess her transgression to his father when he returned from Germany in two days. When Steven questioned why his mother would tell her husband about the affair if it was over, he was surprised to hear the reasoning behind her decision.

She explained that she had long known about her husband's infidelities and chosen to look the other way. She kept telling herself it was something all powerful men did and that she would accept it as long as it never affected their family name. But the double standard of unfaithful men who expected their wives to be loyal had slowly started to fester within her. Time and time again she thought of confronting him but never found the strength or the courage. She went on to tell her son that she had only been unfaithful to Steven's father with this one person, and the humiliation of being caught by her own son shamed her to no end. She was confessing to her husband as a way to start the conversation. If he wanted the freedom to keep lovers outside their marriage, then he had to grant her the same rights, or it was time to part ways.

Steven felt empathy for his mother, and though he would normally be loath to discuss his own sex life with the woman who gave birth to him, he decided perhaps his recent experience with Lolly might be helpful. "If it wasn't for Anna convincing Lolly to forgive me, and Lolly finding it in her heart to do so, I could have grown up to be like Dad. Things between me and Loll are the best they've ever been. We're really happy now."

"I'm happy for you, Steven," she replied. "See? Even a young girl like Lolly respects herself enough to not put up with bad behavior. I have to put my foot down with a husband who says he loves me."

Steven reassured his mother that it was obvious how much his father loved her, and he was sure everything would work out. It was easy for him to say, but not as easy for him to believe. Steven wished his mother would just confront her husband about his betrayals, without telling him of her own. Steven's father's pride was fierce, and his Korean heritage was deeply ingrained. In Korean culture, men were held in much higher regard than women and the standards of behavior were quite different. Steven suggested they should go away for the long weekend, especially as he and Anna would be in California.

The second and more important reason Anna eventually agreed to go to Coachella was that she'd finally made up her mind what to do about Alexander and Vronsky. Alexander was now off bed rest and would be leaving for Cambridge that weekend, hoping to salvage at least a few credits for the semester. He had already enrolled in summer classes, and a private physical therapist had been hired to help him until he made a full recovery. Anna had seen Alexander only three times in the past weeks since he'd asked her to take some time to think about their relationship, and the visits had been torture for her. It didn't help that Eleanor ambushed her each time she was leaving, demanding to know whether Anna had made up her mind yet.

Eleanor was under strict orders from her older brother to be nice to Anna, so she faked it as much as she could, but her contempt oozed out with every syllable she uttered. One time Eleanor couldn't hold back after they had said their good-byes. "He's T-G-F-Y," Eleanor whispered.

Anna knew she should keep walking to her car, but she clenched her fists and turned around to confront her headband-wearing nemesis. "What was that, Eleanor?"

"Too. Good. For. You," Eleanor repeated. "I've always known it. The fact that he's willing to give you a second chance makes him a saint."

Anna didn't bother to respond, which she knew would leave Eleanor twisting in the wind, worried that Anna would tell Alexander on her. But when she got into her car, her hands betrayed her as she white knuckled the steering wheel. She pulled her car over to the side of the road as soon as she was out of sight and wept. Over the last two weeks, Anna had replayed the last three years with Alexander in her mind. And though he had never been the most exciting boyfriend, he had put her on a pedestal and treated her like a queen, so her complaint list wasn't as long as she would have liked.

Oddly, it was Eleanor's very words that helped Anna make up her mind the next morning when she woke up. Anna didn't agree that Alexander was too good for her, as he had flaws like everyone else. She did agree that Alexander would be anointed a saint for taking her back, and the idea of being the girlfriend of a saint made her want to fill her pockets with rocks and walk into a river like Virginia Woolf. It was trying enough to be the girlfriend of the favorite son of Greenwich, so why would she want to be the girlfriend of the Saint of Greenwich?

After her last midterm, Anna drove over to tell Alexander her decision. He took the news calmly and admitted he hadn't been holding out much hope for a reconciliation. She told him she hoped one day he'd forgive her for her behavior, but she also wanted to thank him for pushing her to take the necessary time to really think about what she wanted for her life. "I'm going to see what it's like to be Anna K. for a while with no added labels," she said. "I don't want my name to be associated with a boy. I'm going to spend some time alone."

When she spoke these words, she meant them. But she also knew that she was ready to see Vronsky again. She had missed him terribly. If they decided to start dating, then that would be fine, too, but she wasn't going to be "Vronsky's girlfriend." If she had learned anything from sitting in a closet listening to Kimmie go off on him for how he'd treated her, it was that Vronsky was not ready to be her or anyone else's boyfriend yet.

The separation from Vronsky had been good for her. It cleared her mind and body from the overwhelming feelings she had been suffering during their secret affair. She had spent the time catching up on her studies, catching up on sleep, and hanging out with Dustin, who always made her feel like being the person she wanted to be. Of course, there were a million times she wanted to text Vronsky, or call him, or even drive to the city in the middle of the night to watch him sleep, but she didn't do it. Each day that passed got a little easier, the physical withdrawal symptoms lessening, though it was impossible for her to stop thinking of him. Because her feelings for him stayed true, she felt certain she was truly in love for the first time in her life, and she wanted to see what happened once they were able to spend some unadulterated time together.

She decided not to reach out to Vronsky and let him know she'd broken up with Alexander but would instead give herself another day or two of boy-free drama. She'd share her news on the plane to Coachella. A musical festival on the other side of the country seemed like the perfect place to start off her new life as a single girl who could dance with or kiss any boy she chose, though there was only one boy with whom she'd wanted to do either of those things. Anna asked Steven if he had convinced Dustin to come along as well, but her brother said he felt it was too soon for him to leave his mom. "Not to worry, Dustin won't be alone. Kimmie showed up on the seventh day of shivah after we left, and the two of them have been spending some time together."

Anna felt an incredible rush of warmth at this news. Perhaps something good would rise out of the ashes of Nicholas's death after all. The coincidence of Kimmie spending time with Nicholas and his girlfriend in the weeks before his untimely death, as well as the letter that Nicholas had written to Dustin, had inspired Anna and played an influential part in her decision-making process. She believed love was a power greater than all else, and everyone who was under its spell had no choice but to be beholden to its capricious and magical whimsy.

Anna had a selfish interest, too, in rooting for Kimmie and Dustin. If she ever decided to start to date Vronsky, it would be far less awkward now that Kimmie and Dustin were together. As she finished packing her suitcase for Coachella, Anna felt a spark of hope within her that perhaps everything was going to work out for everyone after all.

XXI

Vronsky asked Beatrice to let Anna know he was going to Coachella but he'd fly back for her at a moment's notice. Beatrice rolled her eyes and told her cousin this was the last time she would get involved with them. In her entire life, she had never grown weary of "the drama," but this was getting a little ridiculous. Their sordid affair and subsequent separation wasn't just bumming him out, it was bumming Beatrice out, too, which frankly was just unacceptable.

Beatrice arrived at the plane early, wanting to make sure it was properly stocked with the food and beverages she had special-ordered for her friends. She loved California and wanted everyone to get in the right mood for their four-day holiday in Indio hobnobbing with the Hollywood elite. Beatrice was bored of the East Coast's usual suspects and was itching to pry salacious la-la land gossip from the pretty people of the West Coast.

When Vronsky and Claudine arrived, Beatrice was in a fine mood and happy to see her mopey-faced cousin looking better than the last time she saw him. But she was far more excited to meet his traveling companion. When Vronsky introduced his cousin to Claudine, she realized she had met her once before when their families traveled from Vienna to Paris on the VS Orient Express when they were little kids. Claudine was two years younger than her and had been going through an un-fun awkward phase that only made Beatrice's blossoming beauty more apparent, which in turn made Beatrice like Claudine immediately. Now years later, Claudine walked onto the plane and was totally unrecognizable. All remnants of her awkward gangliness were gone, replaced by curves that made the teenager look even older than Beatrice. Claudine displayed her ample assets in a way that only a Parisian woman could, with a voluptuousness as elegant as it was enticing.

Vronsky had no interest in the bait his mother had graciously laid at his feet. But even he had not been completely immune to Claudine's ample attributes. The French girl was more than happy to be dispatched to America in Geneviève's husband's plane to distract Geneviève's love-stricken son from the girl who had abandoned him in the wasteland of her indecision. Claudine was certain she'd be successful, for no boy had ever been able to resist her charms. But Claudine had another agenda for her trip as well. Her sights were set on an even more delectable trophy than the boy known as Count Vronsky.

Adaka, DandyZ, and Clement arrived next, which meant they were waiting for only Murf, Steven, and Lolly to complete their party. Beatrice received a text from Steven that they were five minutes away and that Anna had decided to come after all. Bea wasn't unhappy over Anna's change of heart, not like she would have been fifteen minutes ago. Now she was pleased. Beatrice had sensed Claudine's interest in her from the moment Claudine hugged her and whispered in her ear that she had been counting down the days until she saw her again. "I've never forgotten you letting me practice the proper way to kiss on your wrist," Claudine said, not caring that Beatrice didn't remember.

Now Steven and Lolly walked up the stairs of the private plane with Anna trailing behind them. Beatrice blocked Vronsky's view of the door while Claudine taught him how the Parisians made their martinis. As soon as Anna entered, smiling with anticipation of seeing Vronsky, Beatrice moved out of the way just in time for her to witness him eating the cherry that Claudine was dangling above his mouth. Bea loved her front-row seat to the lightning storm of jealousy that flashed in Anna's eyes, believing for a second that Anna would turn and run. Instead Anna called out to Claudine, "Think you can make me one of those, too?"

At the sound of Anna's voice, Vronsky promptly choked on his cherry. Anna watched as Claudine lifted Vronsky out of his seat, clutching him from behind and performing the Heimlich maneuver until the cherry shot out of Vronsky's mouth and landed at Anna's feet. Claudine rubbed Vronsky's back and said, "There you go, strapping boy. The big bad cherry will not hurt you any longer," to which Anna stifled a laugh, her moment of jealousy eclipsed by gratitude that this voluptuous French girl had saved her love from a most embarrassing fate.

"You're here," Vronsky managed to gasp in a raspy voice.

"So, who's your new friend?" Anna replied.

"I'm Claudine. You must be Anna," Claudine said, shaking her hand. "This poor boy cannot stop talking about you."

"Pleased to meet you, Claudine."

Right behind them, Murf showed up carrying a very large bong that he used as a microphone in his own rendition of Katy Perry's "California Guirls," which he sang as "California Kush" to the delight of the whole plane.

Vronsky pulled Anna outside and told her how happy he was to see her.

Anna stared at him until he finished. "Is she with you?"

"Anna, she's no one. She's the daughter of one of my mother's friends from Paris. My mom insisted I bring her."

"So your mother hates me now?" Anna asked in all seriousness. She could barely control the disappointment in how their reunion was going so far. "Such a shame because I felt like she, of all people, wouldn't hold my mistakes against me."

Vronsky wasn't pleased that Anna referenced his mother's past, as it seemed beneath her to do such a thing, but he told himself she had every right to be upset at his mother's intent to sabotage them. He remembered what Anna had said the last time they had seen each other, the day Kimmie had shown up and thrown gasoline on the fire of Anna's greatest insecurity. Anna had said she wanted to believe him when he told her that she was different than all the other girls from his past, and he had sworn on his knees that she was his one and only.

"Please," Vronsky said. "It's been torture not seeing you. Can't we just focus on the now? You're here now. We're together now. I don't want to waste a second. I love you, Anna."

This was the first time he had ever told her this directly, and he would have preferred to tell her at a time when he wasn't under duress, but it was too late for that. He needed her to understand what she meant to him, so he told her the truth. "I super love you, Anna; I super fucking love you in a big fucking way."

Anna smiled. "Well that's good, Alexia," she said. "Because if I catch you checking out Claudine's rack again, I'll kill you myself and bury you in a shallow, desert grave."

He laughed, surprised at Anna's sudden change of attitude, also noting she didn't say the L-word back to him. He knew he didn't deserve it given the situation, but he wanted to hear it nonetheless.

"So you've forgiven me?" he asked.

"There's nothing to forgive. You said so yourself," Anna replied and then breezed past him into the idling plane. She popped her head out the door and held out her hand for him. "We need to get you to California; you're in desperate need of a tan."

At the front of the plane, Beatrice kept an eye on her cousin and shook her head as he and Anna snuggled next to one another in the hand-stitched custom Italian leather seat.

XXII

The plane ride was torture for Anna and Alexia. They held hands and whispered to each other in their seats at the front of the plane, ignoring the large group in the back who played a version of Marry, Fuck, Kill as a drinking game, using all the celebrities that were reported to be on their way to Coachella. Unable to stop himself, Vronsky began to kiss Anna, and soon they were locked in a hot and heavy embrace that rocked their seats in a way that became too ridiculous for the others to ignore.

"For chrissakes!" Beatrice called out. "Get a room, you two!"

Anna didn't need to be told twice. She stood up first, holding her hand out to Alexia who grabbed it for dear life, and together they walked down the center aisle toward the back of the plane where there was a large bedroom with a California-king bed. Anna didn't care what this looked like (though she avoided looking at her brother) and smiled when everyone slow clapped their approval. She was a single girl for the first time in her life.

In the beautifully decorated bedroom, Anna locked the door and ordered Alexia to get undressed. After he had, she slowly slipped out of her own clothes and stood just out of his reach. When he touched himself, she commanded him to stop, telling him the only person who could touch him was her. When she crawled up onto the bed, she teased him until he squirmed and begged for more. She felt powerful and free. Gone were her fears that their passion had been extinguished by their recent separation. If anything, she was even more enraptured by the beautiful boy who lay naked below her.

She forced herself to go slow, wanting to make it last for as long as possible, offering up the measured ache of their pleasure to the gods who'd fated them to meet, to kiss, to fuck in secret, and who had seen fit to rip them apart, so they could right their wanton ways and come together properly as two people who could belong to one another without anything standing in their way.

When he was inside her, she refused to let him move and instead buried her face in his neck, whispering she wanted to lead this dance. She started moving her hips above him, and she felt him gasp beneath her. "Alexia, my Alexia," she whispered as she grinded against him. She was already at the peak of her excitement and wanted them to ride down the waterfall together. "Now, now, now," she cried out.

"Oh god, I love you Anna, only you!" he cried out as they came together. He imagined the plane falling out of the sky, ready to accept death in this moment of bliss, better to die entwined with the girl he loved than die alone in the distant future.

They lay in each other's arms for the next hour, basking in the ecstasy of their new life together. Anna told him she wasn't going to be his girlfriend, because she needed to be her own woman for a while. She stated that she had no interest in anyone but him, and if he had outside interests in anyone else, well, too bad for him. He laughed and readily agreed to her terms. They were together now and that was the only thing that mattered to him. He didn't need to label her. She wasn't his to own. And he would gladly work each day to earn her affection if that was what it took. They made love once again and fell asleep, lulled by the roar of the engines, not waking until the plane landed at Palm Springs International Airport in the California desert.

Anna and Vronsky dressed quickly and decided they would walk out the door and pretend like nothing had happened. As Anna stepped into the main cabin she saw everyone strapped into their seats staring at their phones in silence. Even though she was embarrassed to face her older brother after what had just transpired, when she caught his eyes she was surprised to see his face was a mask of pure rage.

"Steven?" she asked, feeling frightened. "What's wrong?"

Steven unbuckled his seat belt and was in the aisle in seconds. He pushed his sister out of the way and grabbed Vronsky's shirt, his face red in fury. "You fucking asshole!" he screamed.

Anna tried to grab her brother's arm before he punched Vronsky, but it was too late. Steven's fist slammed into Vronsky's face and sent him reeling backward across the doorway and onto the bedroom floor.

"Stop it!" Anna screamed, but her voice was lost in the chaos. Murf pulled Steven off Vronsky before he landed a second punch, struggling to keep Anna's brother from pummeling Vronsky into a pulp.

Everyone grew silent as the plane rolled to a stop.

"What's going on?" Anna demanded. She was now standing next to Lolly's seat in the aisle, and Lolly held up her phone to Anna, who squinted at it. It was a video, but the lighting was dim so it took Anna a while to understand what she was seeing. "Oh Anna," she heard Vronsky's voice moan out of the phone's speakers, and her eyes flew wide in disbelief. The video zoomed in on her own face now and everything became horrifically clear.

The video showed Vronsky and her having sex in her bedroom. Vronsky's head was cut off in the frame, but it was his naked backside that was thrusting between her open legs with a raw lust that made her cringe. The video had arrived in a mass email to undisclosed recipients originating from a sender: CountV1219@gmail.com. Anna dropped the phone to the floor.

She didn't know where to look, or what to do, so she turned to see Vronsky still sprawled on the floor. He was watching the same video on Murf's phone. She looked away, not wanting to see his face ever again. Who else but him could have videotaped their most intimate moments?

Anna slumped down in the empty seat next to Lolly and looked over at Beatrice and Claudine, who were seated next to each other at the front of the plane. Claudine had the good sense to look away, but Beatrice met Anna's gaze and mouthed the words, "I have no idea . . ." which was true, Beatrice didn't have a clue who would release the revenge porn video for all to see. She had already texted several friends back in Greenwich and found out it had been sent to the entire school. It wasn't obvious from the angle that the guy in the video was Vronsky, though everyone on the plane knew. But it was, without a doubt, the face of Anna K., eyes half-closed in lust, on full display.

Beatrice had the power to fix many a social faux pas, but something like this was beyond her control. Even if Beatrice wanted to, and she didn't know if that was the case yet, there was no saving Anna K.

Anna started laughing, which was hardly the reaction anyone on the plane expected. It started as a giggle, a schoolgirl who had just received a dirty note from a friend in class, but then it grew louder into a crazed laughing fit. She looked like a deranged maniac, sitting next to a terrified Lolly, who was staring at Steven, begging him with her eyes to do something. Steven spat at Vronsky, who was still on the floor with his head in his hands, and then walked up the aisle. "Lolly!" he barked. "Get Anna's bag, we're getting the fuck off this plane." Anna stood up when Steven grabbed her arm and followed him as he headed out the open door.

Still giggling like a psycho, Anna grabbed a bottle of Tito's vodka from an ice bucket at the custom bar as she passed it. "I think I need this more than you, Bea!" she called back, erupting once again in laughter. "Peace out! Anna has left the plane . . ."

XXIII

Steven was relieved he'd let Lolly convince him weeks ago to accept the invitation of one of her mother's friends who owned a place at the Lexington Club, instead of staying at the six-bedroom house Beatrice had rented for the week, which was also in the gated country club community. Their place, a two-bedroom bungalow, technically a pool house behind the main house, was down the street from where Beatrice and the rest of the gang were staying. His anger hadn't subsided and Steven wanted to keep Anna as far away from Vronsky as he could.

Anna tried her best to get drunk in the Uber on the way, but the driver threatened to dump them on the side of the road if she didn't put the booze away. Steven pried the vodka bottle out of his sister's hand and gave it to Lolly for safekeeping. Lolly put the bottle in her purse, happy to have something to do because she was silently freaking out. She just couldn't believe she was front and center during a real live sex tape scandal! Anna could become the next Paris H. or Kim K.! (And what was really crazy was that Kim K. herself was rumored to be staying a few houses over from them; Kanye was performing his Sunday Service on Easter.) Lolly stared out the window at the barren desert landscape. She couldn't believe how dry her skin felt already even though they had only been in the desert for twenty minutes. She was super stoked she'd remembered to pack her extra moisturizing Creme de Corps lotions.

Lolly had so many questions to ask Anna, but she kept her mouth shut and decided to give her some space. She had never seen Steven hit anyone before and wondered if the pool house would have an ice machine since his hand was probably swollen. Lolly couldn't fathom why Vronsky would have released a sex tape of him and Anna. Anyone could see he was the smittenest little kitten ever for her. Why would he blow everything up by sending out a sex tape? She had tried to tell Steven this right after the plane landed and everyone's phone started going nuts with all the texts about it. She had over one hundred missed messages that came in, a new record, though it had freaked her out initially because she assumed someone had died. Honestly it seemed teenagers cared far more about a sex tape than a death. But Steven was already seeing red by then.

Poor Anna, Lolly thought. Anna was positively glowing with satisfaction when she opened the door from the back bedroom only to find everyone on the plane unable to meet her eyes. Well, if there was any consolation, which there probably wasn't, Anna looked stunning on the video and she had obviously gotten milk for cookies. Lolly wondered what she looked like when she and Steven were having sex. Maybe they should film themselves so she could find out. Though, they'd have to delete it right afterward.

Who could have done this? Lolly worried briefly that Kimmie could be involved somehow, since Kimmie definitely had a bone to pick with Vronsky, especially when it came to Anna. The thought made her sweaty with panic, but when she watched the video a second time she could tell that they were in Anna's bedroom at the house in Greenwich, not her CPW bedroom (where Anna had an antique mahogany sleigh bed that was over a hundred years old). Her bed in Greenwich was a matte-finished wrought-iron canopy. As far as Lolly knew, there was no time after Kimmie had returned from Arizona when she could have traveled to Greenwich, filmed them having sex, and come back without her or her mom knowing.

Anna changed into a killer Valentino camo bikini as soon as they arrived at their bungalow. She then filled a glass with ice and took back her bottle of vodka and set herself up poolside with headphones. Lolly was impressed Anna wasn't hysterically bawling. If something like this happened to her, she'd for sure be crying her eyes out.

"What are we gonna do?" Lolly whispered to Steven. "Should we go back home?"

"You don't have to whisper, Lolls," Steven said. "She can't hear us over the Adele she's blasting. I haven't heard from my parents, which means it hasn't hit their radar yet, but it's only a matter of time. My dad is gonna shit a cinder block when he finds out. He'll be more upset over this than my mom cheating. This is his Anna, Daddy's perfect little girl."

"Surely there's some damage control we can do," Lolly said.

"The internet is forever, Lolly," Steven reminded her. "Every teenager in Manhattan and Connecticut has seen it by now. You're still checking TMZ, right?"

Lolly nodded. "All they're covering is Coachella arrivals, and I was thinking about it. They can't post the video because Anna's underage. It's technically child pornography."

Steven was thrilled at this news. He immediately got on his phone and replied-all to the mysterious email, alerting everyone who watched the video that posting it was a federal offense due to Anna and Vronsky's age. He didn't know if this would do anything, but he had to try something.

"Can you go over to Beatrice's for a temperature check?" Steven asked. "I'm gonna try to talk to Anna and see whether she wants to stay or go home. I doubt we can get a flight out tonight, short of renting a private plane. I can't make such a huge charge on my AmEx without Dad's approval, and no way I'm gonna be the messenger who gets killed by delivering the news that his favorite child is the new star of a sex tape."

Lolly said she'd go as soon as she changed clothes. She had packed a big suitcase full of cute new Coachella outfits, and if they were leaving tomorrow she at least wanted to get in a few looks before they left. She wondered if Steven would get mad at her if she posted a Coachella selfie right now. She decided to take a few pics in her room but would hold off posting them until the smoke had cleared.

Twenty minutes later Lolly entered the arid backyard of the mansion Beatrice had rented, after no one answered the front doorbell. She found Beatrice and Claudine skinny-dipping in the enormous lap pool. Beatrice gave her a friendly wave, as if it was any other day, cheerfully informing Lolly they were killing time until the Ecstasy they took kicked in. "Join us!" Beatrice called out. "The water is supes warm. It's like a big saltwater bathtub."

Neither naked girl brought up the whole Anna and Vronsky situation, which forced Lolly to awkwardly ask Bea where she might find her cousin.

"Use your nose, Lolly," Beatrice singsonged from the deep end. "Follow the trail of smoke. V and Murf are around here somewhere, trying take the sting out of his throbbing face. Your hunky bf sure can throw a punch, though I'm surprised Steven didn't just karate chop him."

Lolly wrinkled her nose at Bea's vaguely racist comment but let it go. Maybe Bea was pissed about Anna's sex tape, because if ever there was a high school girl who was ripe to get famous off one, it was Beatrice. "Steven shouldn't have hit him," Lolly replied quietly. "I know he didn't send the email. I mean, he couldn't have, right?"

"Don't know, don't care Lollygirl, sex tapes are so ten years ago," Beatrice said with an edge of stolen thunder in her voice. "Can't you see I'm busy with my new BBFF Claudine? The first B is for Buxom, the second B is for Beautiful and the first F is for what we're about to do to each other after the X kicks in."

Lolly nodded and went into the house. *Could Bea have sent the sex tape? She did brag about having her own IT guy on retainer. Maybe she timed its release for when they were flying to make sure no one suspected it was her. But why would she do that to her cousin? It just didn't make sense.* Vronsky seemed like the one person on the planet that Beatrice genuinely cared about, and he'd never forgive her if he lost Anna over it.

Lolly wandered through the enormous house, checking all the rooms, and finally found Vronsky and Murf sitting on a small upstairs balcony. As Beatrice had predicted, the two boys were sharing a fat blunt, and Vronsky held a box of frozen mixed vegetables against his face.

"You should open the box, silly," Lolly said, taking it from Vronsky. She opened it and removed the plastic pouch of veggies, then handed it back. His right eye had already started to blacken, but it didn't look like his nose was broken, which would have been a shame because he had a perfect nose. If these weren't such extenuating circumstances, Lolly would have asked him if it was his real one or whether some doctor had sculpted it for him.

"You didn't send the email, did you? Sorry, I have to ask." Lolly took the blunt that Murf held out for her and took a big hit as she waited for his answer. Vronsky shook his head no, and she believed him even though she couldn't see his eyes because of the frozen vegetables.

"He definitely didn't send it, Lolly," Murf said. "But what about Kimmie? Vronsky said your sister showed up at his house unannounced and stalker-like when she first got back in town."

Lolly did not react, because she didn't want either of them to know this was new information to her, though she was hurt Kimmie hadn't bothered to tell her about it. "The thought crossed my mind," Lolly admitted, already feeling the effects of the pot. "But it couldn't have been her. She's never been to Anna's house in Greenwich. That tape was made in Greenwich, right?"

Vronsky removed the bag of frozen vegetables from his face and nodded. "Yeah, that was Anna's bedroom. I swear, Lolly, I didn't make that tape. I would never do that to Anna, or anyone!" Vronsky stared at Lolly to see if she believed him and decided she did. He knew he shouldn't ask, but he had to know. "How is she?"

"Not great, obvi. She was by the pool, drinking vodka straight from the bottle when I left, which is very un-Anna-like. Steven said he'd try to talk with her while I'm away. He's ripshit. But I guess you know that already."

"Don't you think it'll blow over in a week or two?" Murf asked. "You rich kids always have some high-key drama goin' on, right? Maybe another sex tape will surface and then everyone will forget about Anna's. Hell, I got a few videos on my phone that might do the trick."

Lolly shook her head. "That's wishful thinking, Murf. This is huge. Anna's no regular girl. She's like royalty in New York and it's a long fall from the top. That email was sent an hour after we took off, and as we flew across the country it had traveled to every private school kid in the country."

"Yo, y'all think it was the Greenwich OG? I mean he got burnt bad. Though revenge-porning a girl would be some bitch-ass shit on his part. Or how 'bout that Eleanor chick?"

"No way Alexander did this," Lolly said. "He's too proper. If people found out, he'd be ruined, too. I mean not ruined like Anna, because it's always worse for girls. He'd never risk his future law career. And Eleanor? Not a chance, she's too much of a goody-goody."

"Ooooh, gurl," Murf said. "You're all *SVU*-ing this shit! You're like a sexy boho detective, I love it." He started to chuckle and lay back, looking up at the cloudless sky.

"Don't pay any attention to Murf, he's baked," Vronsky said. "If I find out Alexander was behind this I'll go up to Boston and kill him myself."

"Alibi!" Murf screamed out at the top of his lungs for the whole neighborhood to hear. "I'm down to be your black Kato Kaelin, man!"

Despite the serious nature of their discussion, all three of them started howling. Lolly had to sit down, she was laughing so hard. She knew it was the pot that was making this terrible situation funny, but it felt good to get the tension out. It had been one thing after another for so long. "What's this stuff called?" Lolly asked Murf. "It's so strong."

"California Dreamin', though we oughta rename it California Nightmare," Murf said. "Hey, hold up." He turned to Vronsky. "This is the first time I've ever been happier to be in my shoes than yours, mostly because you got them all-white Bertolucci kicks I'm super jealous of, but also royally fuuuuucked . . . and not in the good way, my friend, not in the good way."

Vronsky put down the frozen veggies and flipped his Thom Browne sunglasses down, lying back as he stuck up his middle finger and flipped off the whole entire world.

XXIV

Anna woke up the next morning with a screaming headache. She dragged herself to a strange bathroom she didn't recognize and made herself puke, which wasn't difficult. Not much came up, just some yellowish bile, which smelled rancid. All she wanted to do was crawl back into bed and sleep. She wondered if her brother had any sleeping pills or Xanax.

Lolly and Steven were snuggling in the smaller bedroom, and Anna felt a pang of guilt for having taken the big king bed for herself, though she didn't remember how she ended up in bed at all. Seeing her brother peacefully spooning his girlfriend made her think of the nap she and Vronsky took on Beatrice's plane only yesterday, and the thought made her want to vomit again.

She knew Steven kept his drugs in the bottom of a beautiful orange leather jewelry box she had given him two Christmases ago. It was a special place to keep his cuff links and watches when he traveled. She'd had his initials engraved into the fine leather and there was a picture on the inside lid of the two of them as children eating Mister Softee on a park bench. Under a fake leather bottom, built to hide your most valuable things, she found an assortment of pills, an eight ball of coke, and a slip of paper that had two rows of emoji stickers. When she picked up the stickers to examine them more closely, she recalled that Steven had told her he and Lolly were going to drop acid together at Coachella.

Steven had done LSD a few times at tennis camp with a friend from LA and loved it, but he said the trip lasted so long, it was impractical to indulge in it too often. Acid and shrooms were an event drug, he had said. Anna had been surprised that Lolly was willing to try a psychedelic, but as Lolly would follow her brother to the ends of the earth and back again, it made sense that she'd take a twelve-hour hallucinogenic trip with him, too.

Twelve hours sounded like forever to Anna, and when Steven asked if she wanted to join them she'd politely declined. But right now, on the first day of the rest of her shattered post-sex-tape life, it sounded like a perfect escape. She pulled off a sticker, grimacing at the stupid yellow winking smiley face, and placed it on her tongue. She was expecting it to have some sort of taste, but there was no flavor at all. She kept the sticker on her tongue until it started to dissolve and then woke her brother up to tell him what she had done.

Steven took her news calmly and motioned for Anna to bring him the leather box. He said that she needed a trip guide so he was gonna drop one now, too. Lolly woke up and when Steven told her what they were doing she yawned and then stuck out her pretty pink tongue. No way was she going to be left behind.

"What do we do now?" Lolly asked.

"We do what we came here for," Steven replied, sitting up in bed. "We rock Coachella."

This was Steven, Lolly, and Anna's first time at Coachella, though like every teenager in America they had watched videos and seen pictures of the festival for years. It was hotter, dustier, and more crowded than they thought it would be, but they weren't the most reliable narrators as all three of them were tripping hard by the time they reached the VIP security check.

Walking through the main VIP area, they decided to check out the smaller stages and maybe ride the Ferris wheel before it got too crowded. As soon as they passed the white fence of the VIP lawn, Anna clutched at her brother's arm and told him she didn't like how crowded it was. Steven told her it wasn't far to the VIP Rose Garden area and she would have access to shade again. He kept a firm grip on both Anna and Lolly as the wide-pupiled trio slowly made their way through the excited throng of concertgoers, many of whom were dressed in outrageous outfits and probably rolling or tripping as hard or harder than they were. There were sixty-six different musical acts performing on day one and LiviX2 was scheduled to perform at sunset on the Mojave stage. Steven's number one priority was to see Anderson .Paak & The Free Nationals while Lolly and Anna were desperate to see Billie Eilish.

Steven stopped at a vendor and bought three waters, advising Anna and Lolly to keep hydrated. Lolly announced she needed to go to the restroom and Steven said they should wait until they got to the VIP area, but Lolly said she couldn't. Steven pointed the girls toward the port-a-potty line and said he'd stay close by. As they stood in line, Lolly and Anna didn't talk and held hands so they wouldn't get separated accidentally. There were people of all ages at Coachella, some dressed in the same California desert-chic style, a sea of cutoff jean shorts and tank tops, cowboy boots, sun hats and bandanas, while others went all out with their getups, the most extreme being ass-less chaps with biker boots, but the platinum-bobbed girl in front of them had on skin-tight pink leopard-print bell bottoms and a matching halter top. Lolly told her she liked her outfit, and the girl proudly announced her mom had made it for her special to wear to Coachella. "It's my third time," the girl said. "It gets better and better, but the bathroom lines get longer and longer." When Anna asked her name, the girl said Eleanor, and Lolly told her she liked her name even though they knew a girl back East named Eleanor who was way different. The girl laughed and put on a pair of pink heart-shaped sunglasses.

As soon as she put on the sunglasses, Anna felt a wave of panic consume her like an unwanted ghost who had just possessed her body. The sunglasses appeared distorted and huge, and the hearts were stretched out and appeared to be beating like real human organs. "Lolly, I can't be here," Anna whispered. "I'm going to find Steven. I feel weird." Lolly nodded and asked the LA Eleanor if she'd hang with her because she had dropped acid for the first time and was a little scared. The girl smiled and said she was shrooming herself but was more than capable of trip-sitting her while they waited.

Anna wandered around looking for Steven but couldn't locate him, even though he was wearing a bright red HEY BRIDGET baseball cap. The problem was that all the colors were bleeding together, so staring into the crowd to find Steven was like rescuing the exact color crayon from a ninety-six-color boxed set before it melted into a waxy multicolored blob because you had put it in the dryer accidentally while you were tripping. The sun was too bright, and she was feeling overheated. Some guy in a clown wig came up to her and asked her name. "Why do you want to know?" Anna asked, suddenly afraid. "Do you know me?" Her voice was rising in terror, and the clown held up his big white-gloved hands and slowly backed away, telling her he had mistakenly thought she was someone else.

"Who did you think I was?" she cried out. "Who? Tell me!"

The clown yelled out, "Juliet. I thought you were my Juliet."

This made Anna overwhelmingly sad, a Romeo in a clown wig had lost his Juliet. *How will he ever find her here?* The ground seemed to be shifting and slanting under her feet. *Oh my god!* she thought. *It's an earthquake!* She spotted a white tent in the distance and, remembering what Steven had said about the VIP tent, ran toward it, dropping her water bottle in the process.

When she got to the security gate she placed her yellow wristband on the sensor and it glowed green. She found herself walking through a beautiful rose garden and almost sat on a bench but as the roses swayed in the desert breeze she felt as if the flowers started whispering to her, so she kept going, wanting to avoid any hallucinogenic conversations. The VIP area was less crowded, and everyone was better looking, less sweaty, and not dressed as clowns. She found a small area that had a couch, where a couple was holding hands and vaping, and squeezed in, mumbling an apology. She felt queasy, and the ground felt like it was moving. *It's not an earthquake. You're just tripping. You're fine.*

There was a small area to the side where people were standing by a fence listening to the group performing at the closest stage. Anna became transfixed by the dancing crowd, watching the trails of colors waving off everyone's clothes. Then she saw him. Alexia was dancing, surrounded by three girls, each in a bright pink wig. The girls were laughing and holding hands, a ring-around-the-rosie with Vronsky as their maypole.

He's already forgotten about me. He's moved on and replaced me with three Asian girls with cotton candy for hair. Anna hated the girls and their stupid pink party wigs. She hated their faces and their long tan legs. She hated the cropped pink denim jacket and the short turquoise-and-red cowboy boots that the prettiest of the three was wearing. She wanted to beat up the blond dancing boy. She wanted to rip every curl from his stupid head, but she couldn't move. She felt like she was part of the couch, like she was sitting on a melted clock from a Dali painting. *Time is melting. I'm melting Anna, tick turning into tock, and soon I'll be gone.* She held up her hand, and her fingers looked longer than they should have been. *Alexia is the pied piper playing his flute and luring all the pretty dancing girls back to his bed, where he will fill them up and film them up, fill and film, just like he did to me. . . .*

Anna looked over again and saw the three pink-haired girls had morphed into one, and she was no longer positive the blond boy was Vronsky after all. Wanting a closer look, Anna got up but immediately lost her balance and fell to the ground. She bit her lip, and when she touched her face, there was blood all over her fingers. *My life is spilling out of me.* Terrified, Anna scrambled up and looked for the exit. A security guard saw her bleeding and came over to ask her if she was okay. "No, I'm not," she cried.

Anna spent the rest of the day in one of the medical tents, where she confessed to the nurse she had taken LSD. They gave her water, an ice pack, and a cot. She spent the next five hours curled in a little ball, squeezing her eyes shut, seeing swirls of colors that moved too fast and were too bright, but when she opened her eyes she saw a Japanese girl next to her throwing up into a plastic bedpan.

"What's your name?" Anna asked the girl after she stopped hurling. "I'm Anna."

"I'm Juliet," the girl said, sniffling. She had popped a blood vessel from puking and now had one bloodred eye. Anna thought about telling the girl that her rainbow-wigged Romeo was searching for her, but she didn't. *Why should I help them find each other?* Romeo and Juliet had ended badly. *Why do people call it a love story when they both end up dead? It doesn't make sense. Why does nothing make sense?*

XXV

By now it was dark and Murf had spent the last three hours searching for Anna, but with over one hundred thousand people and spotty cell phone reception, it was an impossible task. Steven, who was tripping hard, had run into him, explaining he'd lost his sister and couldn't find her. Murf told Daler and Rowney he'd meet up with them later and texted Vronsky the situation. Vronsky, who had decided to skip the day's performances, was back at the house getting drunk by the pool, so when he showed up at the fairgrounds, he was wasted. Murf had to threaten him with a second black eye before he agreed to go, explaining he didn't have the time to babysit his drunk ass. Vronsky nodded and started the long and lonely walk back to the fairground exits, but only after begging his friend to please text him once he found Anna.

By the time Murf did find Anna in the medical tent, she was shivering in the night air even though she had a blanket around her shoulders. The nurse didn't want to release Anna to Murf, explaining she needed to call Anna's parents. Murf said Anna's parents were dead, and even though Anna was almost back to normal, when she heard Murf's fib she started to cry. The nurse told them she wasn't paid enough to deal with this kind of bullshit and asked them to leave.

Coachella after dark looked totally different, and if Anna weren't so miserable, she would have found it gloriously and magically beautiful. The large-scale art installations lit up the night sky but pockets of darkness made it hard to see. Murf put a dust mask over her face as the wind had picked up, and they weaved their way through the crowd back toward the larger VIP area where Steven said he was going to be. Suddenly Anna stopped walking, refusing to continue on.

"Let's go, we're almost there," Murf said.

Anna pointed at a nearby screen that was glowing red with flames. "Listen! She's talking about me."

Murf stared at the massive screen with Anna, unfamiliar with the seventeen-year-old wunderkind on the stage singing, *"Don't say I didn't warn ya. All the good girls go to hell . . ."*

"Anna, you're fucked up. It's just a song. You're not going to hell."

Anna started crying and sat down on the grass and put her face in her hands, which was when Murf had no choice but scoop Anna up in his arms and carry her like a child.

Murf took Anna back to the bungalow and waited with her until Steven and Lolly returned after the Childish Gambino headliner. Lolly, who was still tripping, came dancing in and declared that Coachella was a religion and she was its newest disciple. Never in her life had she ever had such a magical and wild time.

Murf told them Anna was packing to leave, which made Lolly burst into tears at the thought of not staying to see Ariana Grande's headliner show on Sunday night. Steven told Lolly he needed to do what was best for his sister and although Lolly rationally understood his words, she irrationally couldn't help pouting and stomping about. Overhearing the commotion, Anna came running out of her room and said she couldn't handle any more misery and agreed to stay for the rest of the weekend. Unable to control her emotions, Lolly ran over to Anna and hugged her so hard and for so long Murf had to pry Lolly off of her. Lolly, crying once again, swore her tears were tears of gratitude for all the many blessings she was currently experiencing. She then did a cartwheel in the living room and ran to her room to change into yet another outfit.

"So I'm assuming what I just witnessed was what a good acid trip looks like?" Anna asked with a rueful smile. Steven explained that psychedelic drugs feed off the internal psychic energy of your current emotional state and Anna's unfortunate nightmare trip was more than likely unavoidable given everything that was going on. He told his sister if she still wanted to leave Coachella, he would absolutely go with her and that she shouldn't worry about Lolly.

Anna shook her head and said there was no point in leaving because honestly, there was probably nowhere to hide anymore. She hugged her brother and told him she was going to bed and would see him in the morning.

Murf followed Anna into her room and tried one more time to talk about Vronsky, but as soon as he brought up his name Anna just covered her ears and said, "Lalalalalalalala!" until he stopped. Before he left, Murf gave Anna his word that he knew unequivocally that Alexia had had nothing to do with the sex tape. Anna didn't comment and just grabbed his face in her hands and said, "You saved me, Murf. I was lost and you saved me." As Murf walked back to Beatrice's he knew two things: one, he was not going to try LSD tomorrow as he'd planned because acid seemed stupid AF, and two, that he wasn't going to see Anna tomorrow. In the morning, when he woke up between Daler and Rowney, the first thing he thought was, *She's gone.*

Later at Coachella, Steven confirmed Murf's suspicion and told him he woke up to a note from Anna, informing him she needed to get the fuck out of Dodge and was headed to the beach. Unable to sleep, she decided there was no point in leaving the music in the middle of the desert only to face the music in New York, albeit a very different kind. Knowing her home life would never be the same once she confessed her appearance in a sex tape to her parents, she decided she might as well take the rest of the weekend for herself. She told her brother not to worry; she wouldn't be alone.

Her dad's younger sister, Jules, lived in Los Angeles and worked in "the business" and on a whim Anna called her and asked if she could come there. Anna didn't know her aunt Jules very well, because she was estranged from her mother, Anna's grandmother, and when forced to pick sides, Anna's dad had sided with his mom. As far as Anna knew, her dad only talked to his sister a few times a year, and Anna had only met her when she was a toddler. Anna and Steven received birthday gifts from their aunt, usually some fancy Hollywood swag or a limited-edition pair of sunglasses, but there was no other substantial contact between them.

Jules didn't seem fazed to receive Anna's call at 4 A.M. and texted Anna a pin with her address in Malibu. When Anna arrived, she was amazed to see her aunt had a giant brown Newfoundland that, when it stood on its hind legs at the wooden fence surrounding the house, was as tall as Anna.

"How did I not know you had Newfies, too?" Anna wondered out loud. "Why wouldn't Dad tell me?"

Anna's aunt said it was Anna's father who had gifted her her first Newfoundland twelve years ago. This one was her second. She told Anna her brother had sent her the picture of Anna's dog placing at Westminster. "You looked so happy in those pictures!"

Aunt Jules told her that her husband was still sleeping, so she put Anna in the guest room, a converted garage with a heavy sliding wooden door. When Anna crawled into the loft bed, she smiled because she could hear the ocean down the street.

Anna spent the entire next day under an umbrella on Broad Beach, sitting next to her aunt, who was reading a book and hadn't asked her one question about why she was there, except to inquire if her father knew where she was. Anna explained her parents thought she was at Coachella, and they weren't expecting her home until Monday night. "Okay, I'm not going to pry," Aunt Jules told her. "When you're ready to talk, we'll talk."

Anna was so grateful for her aunt's laid-back attitude that she welled up, but before one tear fell, Kimba, her aunt's brown Newf, sat up and licked her face. Anna had never swum with a Newfie before, but she did that day. She texted Steven and told him she was in Malibu and that she'd meet him and Lolly at LAX on Monday, so they could fly home together. She apologized for stealing off like a thief in the night, but what she wanted, no, what she *needed*, was some time alone. Steven was happy to hear from her and apologized for not being the best acid trip guide, but promised to help her navigate their parents' anger, since he had plenty of experience in that department.

Anna spent the following day at the beach, from the moment she woke up until after dark. Dogs weren't allowed on the beach, and the rangers came twice a day to ticket the rule breakers, but once they left, Kimba was welcome to come down. Anna texted Aunt Jules when the coast was clear, and she and Kimba appeared ten minutes later. There was something incredible about watching a giant dog navigate the mighty Pacific Ocean, and Anna felt like she could sit there and do this forever. After dark, Anna and her aunt walked down the beach, and Anna told her the whole story. It felt good to talk about it with an adult who wasn't a parent, and since Aunt Jules wrote for TV and movies, Anna figured she wasn't the type to judge her.

After Anna finished, her aunt asked whether she wanted advice or whether she had just needed to get this off her chest. Anna had never been asked that question, but when she thought about it, she said it had felt good to talk about everything openly and honestly and perhaps she still needed some more time alone with her thoughts. Her aunt agreed that sounded sensible and explained she and her husband used to live in West LA but eventually moved to Malibu because she felt the ocean helped her think things through, which for a writer was important.

That night Jules's husband, Wilson, grilled four filet mignons and eight ears of fresh corn, and they ate together outside on the deck, with Kimba getting her own steak at the end of the meal that she ate in one hilarious bite. Anna loved hearing gossipy Hollywood stories that had nothing to do with her. She didn't think of her own problems once that night, and when she went to bed, Kimba joined her. Anna's dogs were never allowed to sleep on the bed, but Aunt Jules said they lived their lives by beach house rules, which meant sand was gonna get everywhere anyway so to hell with rules.

The next morning Aunt Jules drove Anna to the airport, but they didn't talk much. Anna stared out at the Pacific Ocean to her right and fantasized about never going back East and just living at the beach forever. When they pulled up to the terminal, Anna felt her anxiety rise like the tide and said, "Okay, I'm scared. I think I need advice now."

"Trust your gut, Anna," her aunt said. "I know that sounds lame, but from what I've heard you made every right decision you could over the last few months. You fell in love, you fucked up a little, but it's all gonna work out. Just keep your head down, and eventually you'll make it through the shit pipe to freedom."

"Okay . . ." Anna replied tentatively. "What's that?"

"Have you seriously never seen the movie *The Shawshank Redemption*? Tim Robbins plays a man wrongly accused of his wife's murder and after years and years and years of scraping at his cell wall with a tiny geology pick finally breaks out of prison and then must crawl, painstakingly crawl, through a long sewage pipe full of shit. And once he's out you've never seen a happier guy. It's one of the most satisfying endings in the history of cinema. That's what you're flying home to: your own personal shit pipe. So accept it and just move forward, inch by inch, and you'll get through it. The whole sex tape thing? That's just the bad luck on your part growing up in the age of smartphones and zero privacy. My money says Vronsky didn't do it. That video was meant to fuck you over. It's revenge porn."

Revenge porn, Anna thought, were two of the ugliest words in the English language.

Anna and her aunt hugged for a long time at the curb with Kimba sticking her head out the back window, panting.

"You're going to be okay," Jules said one more time. "I promise. Being a teenager sucks, but it gets easier the older you get. Actually, that's a lie. It gets easier when you don't give a fuck what anyone else thinks. Oh, be sure to tell your dad I say hello, okay?"

"Aunt Jules, can I ask you a favor?" Anna asked. "Can you call him and tell him what happened? I don't know if I can do it. Please?"

"I guess that's what estranged aunts are for," she said. "'Hey, big bro, I know we haven't seen each other in five years, but nothing brings a family together like a sex tape!' Kidding! Just shoot me the video and I'll text it to him . . . Kidding! I'll call him. Now go, don't miss your flight."

When Anna walked through the automatic doors into LAX, she felt as prepared as she possibly could be to crawl through the sewage pipe to salvation.

XXVI

Since it was nearly the end of the year, and given the extenuating circumstances, Greenwich Academy agreed to let Anna work with a tutor and finish the semester at home. After a thorough investigation by school officials, the origin of the video could not be determined and was left to the FBI to handle, as it was a federal crime to distribute a video of minors having sex. At every private school in the tri-state area, every student who had initially received the email (and there were many) had to have their phone checked for the video. All found copies of Anna K.'s sex tape were deleted. (Of course, there were still plenty of copies floating around if you knew who to ask.)

As promised, Anna's aunt Jules had called her father while Anna was flying home. Jules told her older brother what had happened, leaving out the bad acid trip, and finally ending with the X-rated sex tape of his daughter that had now been seen by pretty much every teenager on the East Coast. Edward listened to his sister relay his daughter's story as he stared at the Atlantic Ocean from the porch of the Portland, Maine, house he and his wife had rented for the weekend.

"She called you?" Edward asked Jules, who he hadn't spoken to since Christmas, and then only briefly. "Why wouldn't she come to me?"

"You're missing the point, Eddie. Get over your stupid pride! If you were Anna and just found out someone released a tape of you having sex, would you tell you? Be happy Anna knew she needed help and called an adult."

"Oh, is that what you are now?" Edward said, pissed that none of their supposed friends, who had doubtless heard the news by now, had bothered to reach out.

"I saw the tape. It's bad. You know, if she wants to come to LA and finish high school she's always welcome."

"I'd send her to Mars before I sent her to the land of fruits and nuts."

"God, you're still an asshole. It's a miracle you managed to raise a good daughter. Look, she asked me to call. I did. But now I gotta go see my fridge about a sandwich. Later, Eddie."

It didn't take long for Edward to locate the video of his daughter entangled with some boy in the throes of ectasy. He hit pause on a frame of the girl's face. It was unmistakably Anna. The grainy close-up sickened him, but that feeling was soon washed away by the sea change of his fury.

If this were Steven, he wouldn't be surprised. But Anna? She was only seventeen. Given his recent weekend with his wife, who'd confessed to her betrayal, Edward was already in a foul mood. Back home in his study, Anna's father stared at the Jay Strongwater picture frame, a jeweled heart in red and purple, which he kept on his desk. Two years ago, Anna had given it to him for Father's Day. It contained a picture of the four of them sitting on the porch of their house in Maui, a rare photo where the entire family looked happy to be together. He stared down at the picture, at this seemingly perfect family. Good-looking, wealthy, a family that seemed to have everything going for it. He hurled the frame across the room, and watched it smash into an antique Korean vase that had been in his family for two hundred years, the very one he had planned to give to Anna one day.

When Anna and Steven arrived home from the airport, Edward sent Anna to her room without looking at her and requested his son's presence in his study. Anna ran off to her room in tears, and Steven followed his father. Edward took out his anger on his son, even though he knew it was unfair. Steven shouldered his father's blame with a stoicism he'd learned from the old man. He'd endure his father's wrath if it meant protecting Anna. Steven waited, knowing to never say a word until he was asked a direct question.

"Should I send her away to boarding school?" his father asked.

"I don't know," Steven said. "Maybe you should ask Anna what she wants."

"She's a girl," his father said. "She doesn't know what's best. She can't possibly understand the scope of this . . ."

"It wasn't her fault, Dad. It just happened," Steven said, knowing his father was too angry to listen to reason.

"Things don't just happen. Things happen because of other things. I failed her as a father and you failed her as a brother. Why weren't you looking after her, or were you too busy partying with your friends and spending my money? You think I don't know what's going on?"

Steven swallowed hard and took note of his father not including his mother in the blame game even though he was certain she was probably topping the list.

"Maybe boarding school isn't such a bad idea. Anna could attend Deerfield with me next year."

"Provided they would even accept her after what happened."

"Dad, this isn't the nineteenth century. I know you keep saying she's ruined, but she's not. She's the victim here. Someone did this to her, and sure, maybe her reputation is no longer spotless, but there are so many kids in this city who have done so many worse things than—"

"I don't care about anyone else's kids!" Edward yelled, slamming his fist on the desk. "I only care about mine."

A knock at the door and Anna poked her head inside, her eyes cast to the floor and her voice trembling. "Can I talk with you, please? Can we talk?"

"I can't look at you right now, let alone talk. . . ." Edward answered, averting his gaze away from his daughter, who slunk back into the hallway. Steven's chest ached for his sister.

Later she was told by her brother that their father had decided she was to remain in the city, grounded indefinitely. Her dogs were sent for and she would miss her horses, but she was happy to be living in the same house with Steven again. And at least her dogs treated her exactly the same, even though she wasn't allowed to walk them. The day after they got back, their mother called Steven and Anna into her bedroom and told them she and her father had decided to take some time apart. For now she'd be living in Greenwich while he stayed in the city with them. When Anna inquired if this was because of her, her mother said that hers wasn't the only life imploding. All she would say was Maine had not gone well. Their trial separation was decided before they learned of their daughter's downfall. "Obviously," she pointed out, "your bullshit isn't helping."

"Are you getting divorced?" Steven asked.

"I don't know," was her response.

Dustin was now paid double to tutor both Steven and Anna with their schoolwork, but Lolly was no longer allowed to come over and sit with them. She didn't take it personally, as she was busy after school every day with rehearsals. Each private school in the city had been asked to select one musical number from their school play to be performed at a large end-of-year concert at Lincoln Center. The proceeds from ticket sales would go to charity. Lolly was the student chosen to represent Spence, as she had played Eliza in her school's all-female production of *Hamilton*. She would soon be making her Lincoln Center debut in front of a thousand people who'd paid five hundred dollars a ticket to fund arts education for the city's underprivileged youth.

The month passed faster than Anna thought it would. She didn't know the extent of the fallout from her sex tape, because she hadn't seen anyone from the outside world to discuss it. She spent her days reading books, playing lots of sad songs on the violin, and learning how to paint dogs and horses by watching YouTube videos. She was happy to see Dustin and had noticed the change in him immediately. There was a lightness about him, the glow of newfound love, which she recognized as the same look she'd had when she looked in a mirror during her affair with Vronsky. Her time of happiness was all too brief, but at least she knew such a grand feeling was possible. Dustin and Kimmie were a couple now, and though Dustin was too polite to talk about it in front of her, Anna was happy for him and made a point of telling him as much. She took comfort in knowing that at least some people, Dustin and Kimmie, and her brother and Lolly, could have a chance at finding happiness together, even if it hadn't worked out for her.

XXVII

The night of Lolly's concert performance at Lincoln Center, Anna got dressed and was standing in the foyer when her dad and Steven came out of their bedrooms dressed for the show. "I'm going, too," Anna said. "Or am I still a prisoner in my own home?"

Before he could answer, their mother entered, her high heels clicking softly on the marble floor. Anna and Steven's parents had not told anyone of their marital problems and were still keeping up appearances at social events, with most people assuming their sparse attendance was due to the trouble with Anna.

The four of them stood awkwardly for a moment, before Anna's father opened the door and the four of them took a car south in silence.

Anna had no idea what her first public appearance in New York since the sex tape would be like. Surely all the fuss would have died down by now. Steven had told her that every school in Manhattan had worked together to delete as many of the videos as possible, thanks to their father calling in a few favors in Washington and offering up donations like Halloween candy to trick-or-treaters. Vronsky's mother's fixer had done what he could as well, but the culprit was still at large, and everyone speculated about the person who'd taken down the great Anna K. Many assumed it was the Greenwich OG, as he had the greatest motive for revenge in the situation. Anna had heard from Steven about the many rumors, but she didn't believe it was Alexander's doing. Sure, he was a likely suspect, but it didn't seem like his style, and so she accepted the mystery of her downfall as just that, a mystery. Because what did it matter anyway?

When Anna's family arrived at Lincoln Center, a hush fell over the lively crowd. Polite hellos were offered to the parents, but as Anna stood there, she couldn't help noticing no one would look at her. She and Steven sat up front with the other students in attendance, and Anna was glad, thinking her own peers would be easier on her than their disappointed parents who didn't want to be reminded that if a girl like Anna could get caught in a sex tape scandal, then God knows what could befall their own progeny.

But it wasn't easier, not by a long shot.

Every single girl turned away from Anna, but that was nothing compared to the looks she received from the boys as she passed by: snickers, leering glances, and crude gestures, once they knew Steven couldn't see them. What hurt Anna the most was the whispering that began the moment she walked by. Anna held her head high and bit her tongue to keep the tears at bay, but when she saw Vronsky sitting with Beatrice and Claudine she faltered. Vronsky stood up immediately to greet her, genuinely thrilled to see her. He was about to reach out, but Anna took a step back, looked down at her Louboutin Mary Janes, and shook her head.

"Please, Alexia," Anna said quietly. "Don't."

Vronsky was stunned, but respected Anna's wishes and sat back down, never taking his eyes off her when she sat down next to her brother two rows ahead of them.

"You could have said hello," he whispered angrily to Beatrice. "It would be the nice thing to do. It could have helped her. Everyone is being such assholes."

"Dear cousin, that girl's beyond help," Beatrice snapped back. "And you of all people should know I'm not nice. Besides, I have more important things to do with my mouth." She smiled at Claudine and blew her a kiss, licking her lips.

Anna sat frozen next to her brother, trying to process what had just happened. Not a single person had greeted her besides Vronsky. It was like she was a ghost at her own funeral, invisible to everyone and yet the subject of their gossip.

"Do you want to leave?" Steven asked. "It's okay if you do."

"No," Anna said. "This is the shit pipe that I have to crawl through, and I have to start sometime."

"What does that mean?" Steven asked.

"It's *The Shawshank Redemption*," Dustin said, appearing beside them. "Steven, I really need to shore up your film studies education. It's pathetic."

Anna smiled at Dustin, who was crouching next to her seat in the aisle. She stood up to hug him, and when she pulled back, she saw Kimmie standing behind him. It was the first time Anna and Kimmie had come face-to-face since the night at the club so many months ago. Anna was scared, unsure if her fragile ego could take another hit, but her fear faded immediately when Kimmie stepped forward and embraced Anna warmly.

"Always the most beautiful girl in the room," Kimmie said. "No wonder everyone hates you."

Anna could have laughed or cried, but laughter won out, because she could tell Kimmie was joking even if it was true. "Kimmie, I really want to apologize for . . ."

Kimmie interrupted Anna. "Please don't. I knew the risks. I didn't have to be there. If it rains, you get wet."

Dustin explained, "It's a quote from *Heat*. We watched it this weekend."

The lights flickered on and off, indicating the show was about to start. Kimmie and Dustin rushed off to their seats, excited for Lolly's performance. When the lights went down, Anna felt better, relieved for a short reprieve from everyone staring at her with disdain. She was trying to steer clear of negative thoughts these days, but she couldn't help her growing anger at the unfairness of everything that was happening. Yes, she was in a sex tape. It happened, so what? Everyone knew it was Vronsky with her, but that didn't seem to matter. How was it that he could still walk around while no one blinked an eye?

Lolly's song was the closing number of the first act before the intermission. She came out onstage, wearing a gorgeous lavender Monique Lhuillier dress she'd gotten from Rent the Runway, which Steven later purchased for her, because she had never looked more beautiful to him. She stepped forward to the microphone, introducing herself and the school she was representing. She then looked down, about to begin her song, but instead leaned forward into the mic and said, "I'd like to dedicate my song tonight to my boyfriend's sister, and my very good friend,

Anna K. I picked this song for you." The crowd murmured in the dark, but Lolly didn't care. She'd spoken from her heart and wanted to do this for Anna, because, in her eyes, no one needed this song more.

Lolly began to sing "It's Quiet Uptown," the song from *Hamilton*, which told the story of Eliza and her husband dealing with the heartbreaking aftermath of the tragic death of their son in a pointless duel. It spoke of two people learning to forgive each other for the mistakes they'd made. It was also a song of redemption and forgiveness, about how Eliza learned to let go of the past and forgive her husband for his affair with another woman. The bereaved husband and wife bonded over the death of their son and learned to love each other again, despite all the odds stacked against them.

We push away what we can never understand
We push away the unimaginable.

Steven had never loved Lolly more than when she dedicated her song to his sister. Anna had never been so touched by another girl, bravely speaking up on her behalf to a crowd of disapproving hypocrites. Kimmie had never been prouder of her beautiful sister, who she once thought was superficial and shallow, but who surprised her by being anything but. And Dustin had never been so happy to sit in the dark theater, holding the hand of the girl he loved. And Vronsky? Vronsky stared at the back of Anna's head in the dark and wondered if she was thinking of him the way he was thinking of her. Even though he hadn't seen Anna in a month, she was still the first thing he thought of when he awoke each morning and the last thing he thought of before falling asleep.

Lolly received a standing ovation, and when the lights came up, Anna and Steven noticed that both their parents were wiping away tears. Lolly came and found Steven and Anna during intermission and was thrilled that they'd been so moved by her performance. Anna gave Lolly a fierce hug and thanked her for her incredible display of kindness. "Lolly, I hope I don't bring down your reputation."

"Oh, Anna, stop it!" Lolly replied. "I used to only care about what everyone thought of me, but not anymore. Now I only care about what the people I love think of me, and everyone else can rot in hell! If it wasn't for you pushing me to find it in my heart to forgive Steven, I wouldn't be here right now. I'm a better person for it, and I will never forget what you did for me. For us. I'll be forever grateful to you for showing me the way."

The two girls hugged again, and Steven, overcome with emotion, wrapped his arms around his two favorite girls. Anna was crying now, but her tears were joyous. For the first time in a very long time she felt grateful for the people around her. She had gone through the unimaginable and was still crawling through the shit, but she now had hope that one day, eventually, she'd crawl out the other side and be free again. She excused herself to go to the ladies' room and sat for a while in the stall drying her eyes. As she stood up to leave the stall, she stopped at the sound of some girls talking at the mirrors.

"Can you believe she showed her face here? If I were her, I'd have left town. She deserves everything she got . . ."

"All dressed up like a lady, but still a two-timing whore, just like her mother. Did you hear? They're actually separated and the mom's living in Greenwich alone."

"Did you see? Poor Alexander's here with Eleanor. He must hate himself for all the years he wasted on that half-breed piece of trash."

Anna waited until the bathroom emptied out before she left. She felt awful but was too stunned to cry. She exited the stall, washed her hands, and looked at herself in the mirror for a long time. She didn't like what she saw, and she knew what she had to do. She walked out of the bathroom straight into Alexander, who was leaning up against the wall waiting for her.

"Hey" was all she managed to get out in her surprise. She noticed his eyes looked glassy and wondered if he was feeling all right.

"Are you okay?" he asked before she could ask him.

Anna was about to say she was fine, but that would have been a lie. "Not really," she admitted.

"Yeah, I can imagine," he replied. "Actually, I can't."

Anna waited for him to say more, but he didn't. She wasn't sure what he wanted from her and she didn't know if she wanted to know. "Is there something you wanted to ask me?"

"Did you ever love me?" He hated himself for being pathetic, but it was something he desperately wanted to know. Even though he wasn't in that much pain anymore, he was still taking Percocet. And though his doctor said it was time he weaned himself off them, he hadn't been able to. He still felt pain every day, but perhaps it wasn't in his leg, perhaps it was his pride. He couldn't stop feeling like a wounded animal over Anna leaving him for another. Some OG he turned out to be. Over and over he replayed their relationship in his head, always regretful over things he should have done differently.

"You're better off without me," she replied. There was so much she wanted to say to him. Why did it take all of this happening for them to talk to each other openly? For a moment she wished she could go back in time, start again, request a do over, go back to her old life when everything made sense. Was that the better version of herself? Was that a girl who could look at herself in the mirror without feeling ashamed? "I'm sorry, Alexander. For hurting you. I made so many mistakes." And with that she turned and walked away, crossed the expansive foyer of Alice Tully Hall, and left out the front entrance into the dark and rainy night.

XXVIII

When Alexander W. took his seat in the back of the theater next to Eleanor, he felt terrible. He had seen Anna walk in with her family, and a tsunami of sorrow washed over him. He was angry and hurt when she ended things with him before he left for Cambridge but felt only pity when he found out about the video. She had made some mistakes, yes, but certainly did not deserve such a terrible fate. He wanted to say something, but when he had his chance he realized he didn't know what to say. Instead, he found himself taking a good look at her for what seemed like the first time ever. He had known she was beautiful and accomplished, but maybe he'd never taken the time to really know her. He'd loved her from the first moment he saw her, but what did that even mean? Eleanor was fidgeting in her seat. "I didn't see her return. Did you? Maybe she left. I cannot believe she has the gall to show her face in public."

"Eleanor, please shut up," Alexander said. "Let it go."

"Why are you still defending her?" Eleanor hissed. "She made a fool of you and our family. I'm happy she's disgraced. She deserved it, and I have no regrets. *Vengeance is mine; I will repay, saith the Lord.*"

It took longer than it should have for his half-sister's words to sink in. Eleanor quoting obscure Bible references was nothing new, but what was she saying exactly? And then, he knew. Even though the second half of the show had started, he got up and walked out of the theater. As he stood alone in the lobby, he tried to gather his thoughts, but was at a loss for what to do. He heard a door close and looked up to see Vronsky enter from outside. He had been out looking for Anna, because he'd noticed she hadn't returned after intermission. Vronsky saw Alexander standing alone and their face-to-face meeting was unavoidable.

"Alexander," he said, nodding curtly.

"Vronsky," Alexander said.

Vronsky was at the theater door, about to walk in, when he heard Alexander speak. "Wait." He turned and walked back to the man that was at one time his greatest rival.

"Eleanor released the video," Alexander said bluntly, his voice strangled with the atrocity of his sister's misdeed. "I thought it was you, but I was wrong."

Vronsky stared at Alexander, speechless. He had assumed it was Alexander, to get back at Anna for dumping him.

"I saw Anna leave. She didn't look well."

"Maybe she went home," Vronsky said.

"If you love her, you should find her. She needs you," Alexander said, even though the truth pained him. Alexander watched as Vronsky ran out the front doors into the dark Manhattan gloom. Alexander decided he no longer wanted to stay, either. He certainly couldn't go back and take a seat next to Eleanor after what she had done. Alexander knew something that Eleanor didn't know yet. His father was planning to divorce her mother. The news would devastate Eleanor, as it meant they would no longer share a home, and part of him wanted to go in and deliver the news, to hurt her the way she had unjustly hurt Anna, a girl he still loved. But Alexander made the moral choice not to act out of anger and, with the help of his cane, slowly hobbled across the lobby and exited the building. It was raining now, and he didn't have an umbrella. But he didn't care in the slightest.

Out in the New York streets, Anna was soaked to the bone, but after leaving Lincoln Center, she didn't want to go home, and so she walked. Just like in the song that Lolly had sung so beautifully only fifteen minutes ago to a packed house, Anna stalked the same avenues as Alexander Hamilton once did over two centuries ago, grieving for her love, a golden object turned to dust in her hands as though she were a King Midas in reverse.

For the first twenty blocks she zigzagged with the lights, but as she walked through the eerily empty theater district, she realized there was only one place for her to go.

By the time she entered Grand Central, she was a half-crazed, bedraggled mess. She wiped her wet hair from her face and continued with purpose, passing everyone who couldn't help but stop and stare at the beautiful girl, wearing a maroon silk dress that dragged a trail of inky water behind her like the residue of some phantom, or the trace of a wraith.

She took the escalator down to Track 27. This was where she'd met him for the first time. The platform was empty, and she walked to the far end where Johnson, the homeless man, lay on Valentine's Day, grieving over his lost dogs.

At least I had one good Valentine's Day, she thought bitterly. *How did I get here? What should I do? What's to become of me?* Her thoughts swirled. She couldn't stop hearing the girls' voices from the bathroom. *They call me a whore. They think I deserve everything I get. They hate me. I've disgraced my family. I've disgraced myself. No one will ever love me again. I'm damaged goods, the inherent vice of high society.*

Anna didn't know how long she had been sitting there in the silence, but she was cold and wet and had never been more miserable in her entire life. When she heard his voice, she thought, *I'm going mad. Now I'm a delusional girl who hears voices.*

"Anna?"

Anna turned and saw Vronsky standing before her. He, too, was wet, but he had on a rain jacket, which he took off immediately and dropped to the ground. He took off his sports coat and hurried to the pitiful girl on the bench before him, draping it over her shoulders.

"What are you doing here?" Anna asked.

"I came to find you," he said, unable to tell her anything but what was true.

"Well, here I am," she said. "Now please go away."

"It wasn't me, Anna. I didn't make that video, and I didn't release it. It was Eleanor."

Anna looked up at him. "What? How do you know?"

"Alexander," Vronsky replied. "He told me. He just found out."

"That conniving bitch!" Anna whispered. "I should have known!"

"I'm so sorry, Anna," Vronsky said. "I've been desperate to see you. I've called every day and left letters with your doorman. Did your parents tell you?"

Anna shook her head. "I've been under house arrest. No one tells me anything. It doesn't matter anyway, Alexia. Haven't you heard? As my father says, I'm ruined in this town."

"I don't care about any of that," Vronsky said. "I love you, Anna!"

"My dad wants to send me away to give me a fresh start," Anna said, her voice shaking from the cold. "But I told him I wouldn't. Do you want to know why?"

"Yes, tell me . . ."

"Because just like you need to be where I am, I need to be where you are," Anna said, finally answering the plea in Vronsky's pale blue eyes. "I love you, too. Even though it'd be easier to hate you. But my father said though the easier path is always more tempting, the harder path is better in the end. Ironic that his words are bringing me to the last decision in the world he'd want me to make."

Vronsky couldn't contain the hope that was building within him. Anna had never uttered those words to him, not once had she said she loved him back. Hearing her speak them was like hearing all the angels in heaven put on a concert just for him. He crossed over to her and tried to sit beside her but she jumped up, recoiling from his touch.

"Get away from me!" she cried out in anguish. "It can never work! It's too late for us. Everything is shit!"

"But it doesn't have to be," he said. "Anna, who cares what people think? I don't! Fuck everyone but us. We love each other."

"No, my father would never allow it. And I won't go back to sneaking around and lying again. I can't. That's how this all began, with lies and betrayal. We were doomed from the very beginning!"

"You're wrong!" Vronsky said. "We didn't betray anything. We were loyal, Anna, loyal to our love for each other. And we're not doomed, dammit! We don't have to be doomed if we don't want to be. We're not living in the nineteenth century. Fuck all these stupid society rules of conduct. We have choices, we have free will, we can do whatever we fucking want."

Again, he approached her. All he wanted was to hold this rain-soaked girl in his arms. She let him hold her, but only for a second before she started hitting him in his chest with her fists, crying hysterically, "No, no, no! It's too late, Alexia!"

Suddenly, Vronsky felt himself ripped away from Anna. He hadn't even heard anyone approach, but a pair of hands were pulling him away from his one true love. "Leave her alone!" a man roared. "She's a good one! She's a good one!" Anna recognized him immediately. Johnson, the homeless man whose lost dog they returned, was soaking wet, too, his filthy face streaked with sludge.

"No! Wait, you don't understand!" Anna screamed.

Vronsky wriggled in the fearsome grip of Johnson's strength, having no choice but to elbow the older man in the stomach so he could be free. Balboa, the dog they had rescued and who had been watching at a distance, now ran into the fray, snarling and barking. The dog leapt at Vronsky, the man who'd struck his master. Vronsky screamed in pain as the dog's teeth tore into his leg, and he whirled around, kicking the dog, who yelped, backed off, then attacked again, this time leaping onto the boy's back as he crouched down, clutching at his bloodied pant leg. Vronsky spun about, moving across the platform, trying to keep the angry beast from ripping into his neck. Anna grabbed the dog's back leg, yanking with all her might, and Balboa flew off Vronsky, skittering across the floor and dropping down onto the train tracks and out of sight.

Anna screamed and ran to the edge of the platform, and Vronsky watched in horror as she jumped down after the dog.

"Anna! Get back here!" Vronsky cried out, running over as she tried to approach the snarling dog, who stopped baring its teeth, sensing that Anna was a friend.

Vronsky felt a wind from the tunnel and looked to his left at the faraway headlights of an oncoming train. In a flash, he jumped down onto the tracks and grabbed Anna around the waist, but she struggled against him, screaming hysterically. "He fell because of me! How many animals have to die for us? A dog, a deer, a horse! Not another one!"

"The train's coming!" Vronsky shouted. "I'll get him, I promise." He dragged Anna to the side where Johnson was waiting. The homeless man reached down, pulling Anna to safety. Vronsky saw his jacket, which was once on Anna's shoulders, now crumpled on the tracks. He threw it over the dog's face and in one quick motion, lunged at Balboa, scooping his wriggling canine body into the jacket and passing him up to his owner.

The train was close, and the unseen conductor laid on the horn, filling the platform with a deafening noise. Vronsky scrambled to the edge, but just before taking Johnson's outstretched hand, he spotted the shiny silver heart charm he had given Anna for Valentine's Day with the words YOU and ME engraved on either side. His heart filled with joy, as he realized Anna had been holding onto his heart all along, the whole month when he was wondering if she had given up on him. She had carried the silver charm with her always. Anna loved him. She always had. He had to get it for her.

He doubled back, reaching down and picking up the first gift he had ever given her, then ran back to the ledge, where Johnson was still reaching down as the train shot out of the tunnel. Vronsky grabbed Johnson's hand, but as Johnson pulled up to lift him out of harm's way, Vronsky's hand slipped from the man's slobbery, rain-slick grasp.

"Anna!" was the last word from Vronsky's lips, as he fell backward in front of the train.

XXIX

Dustin had stopped by the apartment to see Anna the day before she was leaving to go abroad for Vronsky's funeral with Steven, Lolly, and her father. He hadn't seen her since Vronsky's tragic death a week ago at Grand Central, though he had been checking in with Steven daily to see how she was holding up. Dustin had wanted to offer his condolences in person, especially as Anna had been so kind to him after his brother's death a few months previous. He found her in her room packing a large suitcase. When he entered, she gave him a rueful smile, and when he hugged her she started to cry.

"It's good to see you, Dustin," Anna said.

"Anna, I have to say it in person, and I'm sure you don't want to talk about it, but I need you to know how very sorry I am for your loss," Dustin said. "I know how much you loved him."

"Thanks. I did, I do. I love him so much," Anna said. "But please, I can't talk about it. I just can't. Let's talk about something else. When is prom?"

Dustin shook his head. "We may not go. It just seems like such a silly thing in light of everything else."

Anna interrupted him with a ferocity that took him aback. "No!" she cried. "If you and Kimmie don't go, then you're just perpetuating the cycle of misery. Please, be happy and dance together. Love needs a victory."

Dustin didn't know what to say. Anna's words were so incredibly sad. Instead he nodded, took a deep breath and said, "We'll go. You're right. Love does need a win."

"Good." Anna sat down on the bed, suddenly tired from her outburst.

"Please send me a picture. I'm sure Kimmie will be the prettiest girl there."

Dustin nodded in agreement, while he remembered how foolish he had been with his silly youthful goal to walk into prom with a girl from the Hot List, as if something so frivolous would have meant anything in the grand scheme of his life. He'd been a boy then, with stupid notions about life and love, and though only five months had passed since, his entire outlook on the world was radically different. He was a new man, who understood what was truly important. It wasn't about winning some girl's affections, it was about finding someone who gets you and who you get right back. It wasn't about lamenting your losses, it was about celebrating the lives of those you lost by living your own life well.

"So you're leaving tomorrow?" Dustin asked, motioning to Anna's suitcase.

"Yes, we're going to Italy for the memorial service," Anna said softly. "His mother wasn't going to let me come, but she changed her mind after she found a lot of sketches of me and a few poems he had written in Alexia's room. She decided Alexia would want me to be there, so she stopped by and invited me herself. We had a good cry together when she gave me copies of his poems." Anna trailed off and looked down at her hands, hands that would never touch her beloved's golden curls again. "Though I won't say good-bye, because I can't. I'll love him forever." Anna was crying again, but she knew Dustin wouldn't mind, as she had sat by his side while he wept many times over the loss of Nicholas.

Dustin stared at Anna, his heart twisting in his chest for her. He couldn't even begin to imagine what she'd witnessed, though Steven told him Anna kept repeating she wouldn't have wanted to be anywhere else.

"At least I got to tell him I loved him before . . . before . . . I just wish I had told him sooner. I wish I had told him every day."

"The important thing," Dustin offered, "was that he knew."

"It was my fault, Dustin," Anna whispered. "I haven't said this to anyone, but I'm going to tell you. It was me who insisted on saving that damn dog. He did it for me. If we had left him behind, then Alexia would still be alive."

"You can't think that way," Dustin said, sitting down next to her. "It was a terrible accident. That Johnson guy had him, but he couldn't pull him up in time. It's not your fault. How could you have known? You were down there yourself trying to save the dog. It's not like you asked him to do it while you stood by and watched."

"But he died saving my life."

"And I would gladly die to save Kimmie's. That's love, Anna. It gives us purpose and strength. Vronsky had no other choice but to save you. He couldn't have lived with himself if anything happened to you."

"But now I'm the one who's alone. How am I supposed to go on without him?"

Dustin put his arm around Anna's shoulders and gave her a squeeze. "We just do. It could have been you who died by that train, but Vronsky gave his life to make sure it didn't happen. He did it because he loved you, which, as my brother told me, is the only reason to do anything. You need to honor his love and live the life you were meant to live."

Anna bit her lip, trying in vain to stop her tears. She wanted to change the subject. "I heard you deferred MIT so you could be with Kimmie for another year," Anna said.

"Yes, that and I'm also staying in the city to look after my mom. She helped me find a job working at a youth center that specializes in drug addiction."

Anna looked out her window. "I'm really going to miss the city, and all you guys, Steven and Lolly . . ."

Dustin furrowed his brow. "I thought Steven and Lolly were going with you."

"They are, but I meant after. Did Steven not tell you? I'm not coming back with them after the trip. My father thinks it's better if I finish school abroad. You know, a fresh start. He's going to work out of his office in Seoul and I'll be attending a private girls' school there."

Dustin was a little shocked. "I don't understand, when did this get decided? What about your mom and Steven?"

"This morning. My mom's going to stay here. They haven't said they're getting divorced, but it's not looking good. And Steven's going to Deerfield.

But since New York's much closer than where I'll be, I am counting on you to look after my brother for me, okay?"

"Are you sure about all this?" Dustin asked, staring into Anna's face, suddenly feeling uneasy. His hands were now clammy.

"My father thinks it's what's best."

"But what do you want, Anna?"

She looked at him for a long time. "I guess right now, I don't want anything." She paused and then continued, "Actually that's not true. I do want one thing. For you and Kimmie to have fun at prom."

Dustin and Kimmie left for Dustin's senior prom when it was still light out, because after taking pictures at Kimmie's mother's apartment, they had to go to his mom's place, where his mom, dad, and a noticeably pregnant Marcy were waiting to snap some photos of the happy couple, as well. Normally, Dustin would not have agreed to the extra hassle, but his mom was finally out of bed and had asked to share in the occasion, so he couldn't refuse. He was surprised when she informed him that his father and Marcy would be coming over, too, but it made sense. The loss of their son had allowed them to set some of their past differences aside, at least for a little while. Life brought tragedy with the same hand that it brought joy, and Dustin and his beautiful girlfriend going to prom was one joyous moment they would treasure. His parents were rallying around him and Kimmie, and it was springtime in the city, a season of rebirth and renewal.

As Dustin and Kimmie danced to Tina Turner's "Better Be Good to Me" in the ballroom of the St. Regis hotel, Kimmie listened to the words with a smile because she knew it wasn't something she needed to worry about when it came to Dustin. She just hoped all the other girls dancing around them took Tina's words to heart when it came to the boy they were dancing with.

"What are you thinking about, Dustin?" Kimmie asked the boy of her dreams, the boy who she now knew was her first and only true love, as he twirled her on the dance floor. Kimmie had let go of her anger and her black nail polish and combat boots and was back in the color she looked best in—pink. It was okay to be girlie, as long as it was her choice. Lately she had been teaching Dustin to ice-skate, which was going slowly because of his weak ankles, but she didn't mind. They had plenty of time now that Dustin wouldn't be leaving for college for another year.

He looked down at the beautiful girl in his arms and told her the truth, his truth. "I'm thinking about . . . you and me."

Epilogue

It took a while for Jon Snow and Gemma to settle down on the plane. They had flown private a few times before to Maine, Hawaii, and once from Newfoundland, Canada, which was where they were born. Anna had it in her head after Doozy, her first Newfoundland, died that she couldn't possibly get another Newfie after she'd already had the perfect one, but a few sleepless nights after Doozy's death, she was sitting in the dark of the living room in the CPW apartment when her father came home late from work. He didn't even see her curled up on the couch, but she watched him come into the dark living room and make himself a drink. She was afraid she would scare him, so she stayed very still. But she had been crying and sniffled, and her dad heard.

"Anna?" he asked. "Is that you?"

She nodded in the dark, even though he couldn't see her. Her father came over and sat next to her. She put her head in his lap like she was still a little girl and cried, telling her dad that it didn't make sense. Doozy had just celebrated her ninth birthday. (Anna always had a birthday party for Doozy every year, complete with a buttercream frosted cake.) When she came home from the dog park two months later, she'd had a slight limp and then seven days later she was gone, just like that. Her father reminded Anna she was only thirteen years old, so she'd have many more dogs in her lifetime, and that death was as much a part of life as learning to love again was. Love cannot last forever or it wouldn't be special.

"That's the dumbest thing I've ever heard, Daddy," she had said. "No offense."

She told her dad then that she had decided Doozy would be her last Newfoundland and she was already trying to decide what breed her next dog would be.

"Or because you loved Doozy so much," he said, "you get another one, or even two. Don't think about it like you're replacing Dooz, think about it like you are honoring all that was good about her. Loving her, slobber and all, will only make you love your next Newfie even more."

Anna fell asleep, and her dad carried her to her room, even though she was much too big to be carried off to bed like a baby. The next morning, she felt like she had dreamed the whole thing, but when she looked over onto her bedside table, her dad had placed a piece of paper mentioning a breeder who lived in Newfoundland that was expecting a litter of championship bloodline pups any day now. "We'll fly there in a few months and you can pick out two. Maybe a brother and sister like you and Steven," said her father's handwritten scrawl at the top of the page.

Jon Snow was lying across her feet and Gemma was lying down in the aisle on her left, literally barricading Anna into her seat by three-hundred-plus pounds of dog. She had made the right decision in getting them, or rather, her father had helped her make the right decision.

Anna looked over at her dad who was reading the *Financial Times* across the aisle from her. Sensing his daughter's gaze, Edward turned, reached out, and squeezed her hand, but didn't say anything. After Vronsky died, there were security and cops everywhere. A police officer asked Anna who she wanted him to call, and even though her father had barely been able to look her in the face since the sex tape scandal and had only spoken a handful of sentences to her, she said, "Please call my daddy. He'll come for me."

And he did. Since that tragic night at Grand Central, Anna's father had been doing what he could to mend the relationship with his daughter. He had come to realize he had treated her terribly after the tape scandal and he was ashamed that it took witnessing another parent's loss of a child to make him see the misguided error of his ways. Every evening after the accident he'd come in her room and apologize to her. Anna said she forgave him. That he shouldn't even apologize, none of this was his fault. He was a good father. There was something in his daughter's voice that frightened him when she said this. A week later, the day before they were leaving for Vronsky's funeral, she awoke to find her father sitting on her bed. He told her after their trip to Italy he had decided they were going to stay abroad. He really felt that what they both needed was a fresh start, and the change of scenery would be good for both of them. She listened while he told her about a famous girls' school in South Korea where she could finish high school. "You're only seventeen, baby girl," he whispered. "You have your whole life ahead of you and I know it's too soon to say this, but you will love again."

She didn't verbally agree to her father's new plans but had nodded, which satisfied him. She didn't say yes, because she didn't want one of her last words to her father to be a lie. Since the moment she lost Alexia on Track 27 in Grand Central, Anna had known what she was going to do. There was no way to go on living without him, even though she knew she'd go from Anna K., rich society sex-tape girl, to a modern-day Juliet, who died for her Romeo.

She went through the motions of packing for the trip, all the while knowing that she'd never board the plane. She had hidden her intentions well, though she was nervous that Dustin may have sensed something was amiss when he had stopped by earlier to wish her farewell. When her mom came in to say good night, she hugged her and told her she loved her. Anna said it quietly back, though she couldn't remember the last time they had said it to one another.

At midnight she got up, waking her dogs and shushing them, got dressed, and slipped out of the apartment, leaving letters for her father and Steven under her pillow. She was going to walk to Grand Central, but she was tired, and it seemed so far away, so she hailed a cab, got in and said, "Please take me to Grand Central." The cab driver asked her where she was going so late at night, and she whispered back, "I'm meeting the boy I love there. His name is Alexia."

When she got to Track 27, she wanted to cry. The platform was now the home of her greatest happiness and her greatest sorrow. It seemed right that they would both die in the same place, and she hoped if there was an afterlife, she would be better able to find him if they died in the same location. But her tears didn't come, because she was surprised to see someone sitting on the bench at the end of the platform. This was not part of her plan, having to deal with some stranger on her last night on earth. Anna was too frightened to throw herself in front of a train, which seemed a bit too messy and extreme for her taste. She had googled the right dosage of sleeping pills she would need to get the job done and had gone about finding them around the house. Her mother was a troubled sleeper, so there were all sorts of medications floating about. Her plan was to take them and fall asleep on the bench, like she was waiting for her beloved's train to come in.

Anna thought about leaving and going back upstairs to wait until the person on the bench left, but before she could, a female voice called out to her. "Yo, you over there. You got a light?" Anna did have a lighter in her purse, because she had also brought a candle, which she had planned to light in Alexia's honor. She wanted to do a quick memorial service of her own, since she would miss his, and had brought the poems he wrote for her so she could read one aloud.

Anna walked over and handed the girl on the bench her pink lighter. The girl had dark hair, which Anna thought was black like her own. But as she got closer she realized it was in fact a dark emerald green. She had many piercings going up both ears and a ring of roses tattooed around her ankle. She was dressed in all black and wore a black motorcycle jacket that looked familiar, though she couldn't quite place it.

"Thanks for the light. Want one?" the girl asked, holding out a cigarette.

Anna had only smoked a handful of cigarettes in her life, though she and Alexia had shared a few post-coitally once, which made her smile, because she felt at the time like they were kids pretending they were far older, smoking in bed after sex.

"Sure, thanks," Anna said, taking the outstretched Marlboro Light and firing it up with her pink lighter.

Anna sat down next to the girl, and the two of them smoked for a bit. "I know why you're here," the girl said.

This totally freaked out Anna, and she wondered if she had somehow already taken the pills and was now hallucinating. Or maybe she was already dead, a ghost stuck in purgatory like that famous movie about the kid seeing dead people, and this girl was her guide.

"You read that fucked-up story in the paper, right?" she said, exhaling smoke through her nose like Khaleesi's dragon Drogon. "And I thought I had it bad. That poor girl had to see her boyfriend get hit by a train! Whammo!" She clapped her hands for emphasis, which shocked Anna for its vulgarity, given the subject matter. "I mean, that's gotta suck some big ol' balls. And I should know because I lost the guy I loved, too. Two months ago in Arizona. It wasn't as romantic, because he wasn't saving my life and dying in the process, but I was with him when it happened."

"What happened?" Anna asked. "How did he die?"

"Overdose. Smack. H-bomb. Horse. Heroin. He's just another statistic of the opioid crisis in America, I guess. But he's buried up here and I just needed to be near him, you know?"

Anna knew the girl was talking tough, but she could hear the sadness in her voice.

I need to be where you are.

Alexia's words haunted her. He had said it so many times to her, and she didn't always understand it, at first, thinking it was a line on his part. But after he died, she understood it perfectly. She had to be pulled kicking and screaming by her father when he tried to make her leave the platform the night he died. She didn't want to leave him. She needed to be where he was. She refused to leave until after they wheeled him away in the black zippered body bag, but that was after hours of photographs and police interviews. Her father let her stay because he had no choice. She had said then that if he didn't let her stay, she'd kill herself. Her words had frightened her father so much he left her with a cop and ran to an upstairs bathroom, throwing up at the very thought.

"Anyway, so I'm here in the city, my first time ever in the famous Big Apple. I'm hanging out in Union Square Park, and a newspaper blows onto my feet. I mean, who the fuck reads newspapers anymore? But when I try to kick it away, I see the headline of 'Tragic Teen Love Story, the Train of Doom,' or some shit like that, and I pick it up because, hell, I'm eighteen and I have a tragic love story, too. So, I read this fucking nutso story, and I'm obsessed. And where I've been all, 'Poor me, my boyfriend died from an accidental overdose like a dumbfuck,' I really felt for this girl whose boo got run over by a train. By the way, even though I'm calling my dead bf a dumbfuck, I'm saying it with love. I fuckin' loved that guy. Figures that the one guy who's sweet to me, who actually really loved me, kicks the bucket right after he proposes."

"He proposed to you?" Anna asked.

"Yeah, the dummy. I told him we were too young to get married, and we had to wait a few years, but I said yes. It was pretty romantic."

"And you loved him," Anna volunteered.

"And I loved him," the girl agreed. "But he loved me more, which I know is bitchy of me to say, but it's true. My mom always says it's more important for the guy to love the girl more, because if it's the other way around, then it always ends badly for the girl."

"What do you mean?" Anna asked, genuinely interested now.

"Look, we girls get the raw end of the stick on pretty much everything. Men make more money than us. Men are stronger than us, physically; you know, with muscles and shit. They always dump women when they get older, while they get more distinguished and celebrated when they age, which is total bullshit, you know? Like men have always had all the rights and the power forever, where we girls have had to fucking take the scraps. But my mom, and she's smart about men, dumb as rocks about money and parenting, but she knows dudes . . . well, she said the only arena where we women have a leg up on men is in love. 'Cause the only thing that can bring down a big strong man from his high-horse ego is when he loves a woman, like truly loves-her-loves-her. It's the only time we girls get to win big. So that's why it's better if the guy loves the girl more, because if she loves him more, it never works out good for her. I know I sound crazy, my mom explains it better."

"No, I get it," Anna said softly. "Women have suffered throughout history forever at the hands of men. Why should we suffer in the romance, too? I mean, if we don't have to."

"Exactly! You said it, sister." She stared at Anna, a flicker of recognition passing over her face, but Anna didn't flinch. Her picture hadn't been in the papers, because she was a minor and her father had made sure it didn't happen. "So what's your dealio? Why are you here on track twenty-seven in the middle of the night?"

"Same as you," Anna said. "I heard about the story and found it sad. I wanted to come here and . . . I don't know . . . see where it happened. Try to understand it."

"It's simple. This boy loved his girl so much he saved her life, literally pulled her ass out of the tracks, then he saved a homeless dude's dog, but then didn't make it out in time. He's a goddamn romantic hero."

"Yeah, but what about the girl?" Anna asked. "How is she going to live on when a boy loved her that much? He's dead, and her life is ruined forever."

"Yeah, that's one way to look at it," the girl said. "Look, no doubt she's gonna be fucked up forever about it. But think about it. She now gets to live her whole life knowing some boy loved her so much that he died for her! I mean, if that's not power, then I don't know what is. She can be like a superhero with magical love powers or something, you know? Once the smoke clears, and she stops feeling like shit about it, she's gonna feel good forever. 'Cause she will always know she's worthy of some big-ass type of super love. Girl, sorry, I don't know what's gotten into me lately. Normally I'm a total pessimist about love and shit. But this story, I dunno . . . it just makes me hopeful. About love, you know?"

"Yeah, I do know what you mean," Anna said, standing up and stubbing out her cigarette. "I have to get home. But it was great talking to you. And I'm sorry for your loss. I know your boyfriend really loved you, too."

"Oh yeah?" the girl asked. "You don't even know him, so how the hell do you know that?"

Anna shrugged and then smiled. "I just know. One of my superpowers, I guess."

"Cool," she said. "Hey, then you should have this. I was gonna keep it because I found it, but a love superhero should have it instead. It can be your logo like Superman's 'S.'"

The girl flicked something at Anna, something shiny and silver. Anna thought it was a coin, rotating in the air, and she watched as it arced through the air before she reached out and grabbed it.

"It's a little smushed. I think it got run over by a train, but it's cooler that it's not perfect because love ain't ever perfect," she said. "You can still read it though."

Anna looked down in wonder at the object she was now holding in the palm of her hand. It was bent and scuffed, but it was still somewhat heart-shaped.

It was the silver charm Alexia had given her for Valentine's Day, the one he had been holding when he died. She stared at the word ME printed on one side, and then flipped it over to the other side and smiled at the word YOU.

"Thank you," Anna said. "I promise to keep it forever." Anna waved to the girl as she walked toward the stairs, on her way back home to bed, with his heart in her pocket. She needed to get home, tear up some letters, and go to sleep, because tomorrow she was flying off to start her new life, stronger now, because a boy she loved with all her heart had loved her more. And she deserved it.

Author's Note
When Jenny Met Anna

I first read Leo Tolstoy's *Anna Karenina* when I was fifteen. I had recently gotten spectacularly busted sneaking out of the house and "borrowing" the family car to go cruising around our tiny town of Paris, Tennessee, population 11,000 and Home of the World's Biggest Fish Fry. I was grounded for three months with no TV, no boom box, and, to top it all off, my dad called the owner of the local McDonald's and got me a job working the drive-thru.

My only source of pleasure while grounded was reading. My older sister Helen had just finished taking Russian Lit at Brown and sent me her copy of *Anna Karenina* with a note: "Everyone makes mistakes. Anna Karenina had it *way* worse."

An 864-page book set in Russia was a little daunting, but with nothing else to do I figured I'd give it a shot. To say I loved *Anna Karenina* was an understatement. I devoured it, adoring the massive cast of characters and all the family dramas. As a teenage girl, my favorite story line, of course, was the doomed love affair between Anna and Count Vronsky, and I cried when she threw herself in front of the train because I knew Vronsky's love for her was true, even if she couldn't see it. Upon finishing *Anna Karenina*, I crowned it my new favorite book.

I read *Anna Karenina* for the second time fifteen years later when I was living in Cambridge, Massachusetts, married to my first husband, a doctor. With my husband working all the time, me desperately missing my friends and NYC, where I'd spent my entire twenties, I was in dire need of escapism. During my second reading, I was once again mesmerized. This time, however, I was not only taken with Anna and Vronsky's romance, but with the Kitty and Levin love story and Dolly and Stiva's marriage, as well.

Five years later, I was divorced and living in Los Angeles, working as a TV writer. Single again, I spent the Christmas holiday in Manhattan with my very strict Korean mother, who was still not happy with me over divorcing my perfect-in-her-eyes-only doctor husband. My mom had also read *Anna Karenina* twice (once in Korean and once in English), and she and I went to see the Keira Knightley film adaptation at the Ziegfeld Theater. Afterward, we walked back to the St. Regis hotel, where we had a heart-to-heart about the movie and the book. My mother and I rarely see eye to eye on anything (nor do we ever have heart-to-hearts), but this was one of the rare occasions where we found a tiny patch of common ground.

My mother had been born, raised, and married before she moved to the United States from Korea at the age of twenty-eight with my father. She rarely talked about her past, but that night she shared with me how Korean women were still not afforded the same status in society that men were given. I asked if this made her angry, and she said no, because she had been raised to believe that women were valued for their roles as wives and mothers, which was why she couldn't reconcile with my choice to leave my marriage over something as seemingly unimportant in her eyes as my career. I was disturbed to hear that there clearly hadn't been much progress for women in Korea in the 150 years since *Anna Karenina* was published. I, in turn, shared with her that I would be forever grateful to be born and raised in the United States, where as a woman I was afforded the right to live my life however I chose. To me, this meant that if I wanted to leave my marriage and pursue my own career ambitions, then it was my prerogative to leave.

That night, I woke up at three in the morning and headed down to the lobby with my laptop. Sitting in the quiet, next to a gorgeously decorated hotel Christmas tree, I had one of those amazing light bulb moments: what would *Anna Karenina* look like as a young adult novel? Excited by the idea, I emailed Sally, my book agent, and then went back upstairs to bed. My last thought before falling asleep was that in my teen version, Anna would be half-Korean, in honor of my mother's heritage and my brother's half-Korean children. I woke up to an email from Sally saying, "Love the idea! Write it now!"

I made a few attempts, but I always hit a wall and eventually got busy with whatever TV show I was working on at the time. Then, a couple of years later, I met my soon-to-be second husband, John, on a book tour in Naperville in February 2014. (Our meet-cute, like Anna and Vronsky's, also occurred during a snowy winter). When we met, I lived in LA and he lived in Brooklyn. I thought it was a fling, but he claims he knew immediately we were fated for much more. (How very Vronsky of him!) We embarked on a cross-country, long-distance love affair, and even though I said I'd never marry again (being a "wife" didn't seem like my kinda thing), we eloped in Vegas the next year and have been extremely happy ever since.

At Christmas, as my husband and I drove from LA to Nashville with our giant 120-pound Newfoundland puppy, we discussed book ideas we hoped to write the coming year. This was when I told John about my idea for *Anna K.* My husband said, "You should write it now. You're ready." When I asked him what he meant by "ready," he replied, "The best time to write a great love story is when you're living one." I laughed, reminding him that Anna and Vronsky's love story didn't end so well, though as I said it, I was already wondering if there could be a different fate for my Anna K. I started rereading *Anna Karenina* for the third time that night on my Kindle in a hotel outside of Oklahoma City.

Turns out my husband was right. The best time to write a love story *is* when you're in love.

Acknowledgments

There are so many people who deserve a shout-out for their contribution to my first young adult novel, *Anna K*. The list is long, and I will not be going in order of importance; rather I will be mentioning based on height . . . KIDDING. I joke because I have an intense fear of leaving someone out accidentally. If by chance that happens, you should call me and parlay it into me feeling guilty forever and plying you with gifts and desserts. (I don't mess around when it comes to dessert.)

Okay, now you understand why my book is so long, right? I'm a bit of a blabbermouth and have always been this way. The book is dedicated to my husband, John G. Kloepfer, and deservedly so because I cannot even begin to tell you how much praise and love needs to be heaped upon him for everything he has done for the book and for me as a human. He's truly the best husband, and the best early reader I have ever met. He was the first person to read every single page of this book . . . and his edits and smarts have elevated it tremendously. My second reader was the amazing Jenna Hensel, whose unrelenting cheerleading and upbeat attitude was super helpful to me and I'm forever grateful for all your love and support with all my writing. The only thing sunnier than the actual sun out here in L.A. is you. Eleanor Bray, you're next . . . because wow, you really were so fabulous throughout this whole process. Thanks for all your research and your willingness to deep dive into every topic of interest I tossed your way, whether it was Coachella or the right club the characters would go to in Manhattan. Countless texts were exchanged between us when it came to the most au courante teen lingo and you handled all my neurotic questioning with grace and aplomb.

Early readers are always such a necessary part of the writing process and with so many pages it was a big ask. I appreciate everyone's time and effort on my behalf. Thank you Hannah Kloepfer, my amazing little sister-in-law; thanks to my bestie, Stephanie Staal; thank you Erika Kelley, for reading on a plane; thank you Diana Snyder, for all things Greenwich; and to Dustin Morris, you're so special you get a major character named in your honor.

And I'm nothing without my friends: much love to Laura Clement, Tasha Blaine, Jenner Sullivan, Christine Zander, David Holden, and Nadine Morrow—you all accepted my neurotic phone calls graciously and your continual unwavering support and tough-love you-can-do-it attitudes were appreciated. Big warm hugs and thanks to my family: Haekyong Lee, John Lee, Susan Stonehouse Lee, Benjamin, Addison, and Olivia. My lovely in-laws: Deborah and George Kloepfer, Sarah and Bob McLynn, Brayton and Livingston. I should also mention my late father and older sister, my father for grounding me for sneaking out and Helen for sending me my first copy of *Anna Karenina* to help me pass the time. And if we're going there, hell, thank you Leo Tolstoy, because you're the true OG of the literary world.

Sally Wofford-Girand, my literary agent and my friend. You were instrumental from the very beginning, predating everyone else since I first came up with the idea of a teen version of *Anna Karenina* in 2012 after seeing the movie in New York. Thank you for your brilliant mind of knowing this was a great idea and your emails through the years reminding me to get cracking on writing the book. You have been such a rock during this whole process, and I am so grateful for not only your publishing business savvy, but also all your insightfulness when it comes to story and characters. I'm so lucky to have you as an agent and I'm thrilled we're on this ride together. And a big shout-out to Taylor Curtin at Union Literary . . . I have appreciated all our many phone chats during this process and thanks for being so generous with your enthusiasm and support.

I have many people to thank at Flatiron Books, but I must start with the two women who really made this all possible in the first place: my amazing editors Sarah Barley and Caroline Bleeke. (It's rare to get one fabulous editor; to have gotten two has been a real joy in this whole process.) I immediately felt you both understood my vision immediately, how I wanted it to be soapy and fun and girlie and exciting, while also imparting a strong female message without sacrificing any of the swoony romance and love. Your brilliant and astute edits and continual support for *Anna K* has been exceptional, and frankly it's been so much fun to work with you both. I'm really lucky to have two such smart, cool women to share my hopes and dreams for Anna and the whole cast of characters in this book. Special thanks to my publishers, Bob Miller and Amy Einhorn; Keith Hayes and Anna Gorovoy for the amazing cover and design; Lena Shekhter and Lauren Hougen for production; and Cat Kenney and Marlena Bittner, Katherine Turro, and Nancy Trypuc for the incredible publicity and marketing campaigns. And thanks to our cover model, Moon Choi. I adore the kismet of your birthday being the same day as the pub date!

For getting *Anna K* out to the world at large I'd like to thank my foreign agents and those who are publishing the foreign editions: Anthea Townsend, Michael Bedo, Harriet Venn, Claudia Young, Paul Sebes and Lester Hekking, Txell Torrent, Monica Martin, Ines Planells, Nynke de Groot, and Luna Wong.

And I wouldn't be a good Hollywood writer and executive producer if I didn't thank all those involved in helping *Anna K* go beyond the pages and onto the screen. My amazing executive producer team, who have been beyond supportive and amazing: Scooter Braun, James Shin, Drew Comins, and Scott Manson; special thanks to Jake Eagle and Chloe Borenstein-Lawee. Entertainment One, my studio: Jacqueline Sacerio, Pete Micelli, Pancho Mansfield, Mark Gordon, Kristen Barnett, Amanda Gerisch, Greg Clayman, Gary Gradinger, Sam Grodsky, and Michael Kagan. My Paradigm team: Zac Simmons, Doug Fronk, Kim Yau, Martin To, Sam Fischer, Tyler Mathews, Aja Marshall, and

Courtney Jackson. My entertainment lawyer team: Jonathan Gardner and Molly Fenton, Roxana Soroudi and Maddie Silver.

As I started with my darling husband, I will end this long list by saying that a writer has no better companion then a dog, and my dog, Gemma Bunny Kloepfer, is the best. You and Doozy were the inspiration for Anna owning Newfoundlands, because you make my life so rich and grand.

Anna K
by Jenny Lee

PLEASE NOTE: In order to provide reading groups with the most informed and thought-provoking questions possible, it is necessary to reveal important aspects of the plot of this novel—as well as the ending. If you have not finished reading Anna K, we respectfully suggest that you may want to wait before reviewing this guide.

1. Discuss the novel's first line: "Every happy teenage girl is the same, while every unhappy teenage girl is miserable in her own special way." What do you think the author means? Do you agree?

2. Although the novel is called *Anna K*, each chapter alternates between the perspectives of six different characters and features an even larger cast of friends and family. Did you have a favorite character in the novel?

3. *Anna K* is a modern reimagining of Leo Tolstoy's *Anna Karenina*. If you were already familiar with *Anna Karenina*, did *Anna K* make you think about it in a different way? Why do you think there are so many adaptations of classics, from Shakespeare's plays to Jane Austen's novels? Do you think it's ever possible to write a truly new and original story, or is every story a kind of retelling?

4. There are three main teen love stories in these pages: Anna and Vronsky, Lolly and Steven, and Kimmie and Dustin. How are each of these relationships similar and different? What obstacles do each couple have to overcome?

5. In addition to romantic relationships, there are sibling relationships and platonic friendships at the heart of *Anna K*. Compare and contrast these different kinds

of bonds, using examples from the novel. In your experience, can the relationships between siblings and friends be just as powerful and important as romantic relationships?

6. Wealth and status play a major role in the characters' lives. How are their identities shaped by their parents' money and the expectations that come along with it? How do you think their privilege influences the choices they make?

7. Discuss the role race plays in the novel. Although most of their friends are white, Anna and Steven are Korean American, and Dustin and Murph are black. Are the characters of color shaped by their racial identities? If so, how? Do they face any particular challenges, in terms of societal and familial expectations?

8. Were you surprised to learn that it was Eleanor who released the sex tape? Did you have a different theory of who did it?

9. When Anna overhears two girls disparaging her in the Lincoln Center bathroom, she is devastated: *"They call me a whore. They think I deserve everything I get."* Why do you think she feels that way? Discuss the double standard for girls and boys, as reflected by the fallout of the sex tape for Vronsky and Anna. Do you think that double standard is prevalent across our society?

10. After the scandal, Anna's father tells her he is taking her to South Korea, so she can finish high school in Seoul. Do you think a change of scenery is a good idea for Anna? Does it give her a chance to start over, or does it feel like she is running away?

11. How do the six main characters change over the course of the novel, and what triggers their most significant changes? How much do you think you changed during high school?

Read on for a sneak peek of
Anna K Away, the sequel to
Anna K

Anna wanted to scream. This feeling was not new; she had been feeling unhinged for the last ten days, when she had boarded her father's private plane in Teterboro for her summer abroad. She hadn't been sleeping well and really just wished she could be with her dogs, Gemma and Jon Snow, back at their English country house in the Cotswolds, waiting to be transported to Seoul. Their itinerary had them hopping from one country to the next, so traveling with two giant-breed show dogs was a logistical nightmare. It was decided the dogs would stay in England for the first month.

Once Anna and her father left the UK and headed to Rome, her sleepless nights began. Anna had a tendency to replay the last few months in her head, as if by going over it again and again she'd be able to understand how things got so fucked up so quickly. It was like a complicated word problem she just couldn't solve.

Problem #1: If a sixteen-year-old girl with a perfect reputation were on a train traveling at fifty miles an hour and met the love of her life in February, how long would it take for them to fall in love, despite the college boyfriend everyone assumed she would marry even though she didn't even have her driver's license yet? Answer: about three milliseconds.

Problem #2: How long can a sixteen-year-old girl keep her secret love affair secret? Answer: not long enough.

Problem #3: How long can the couple finally be happy once she breaks up with her boyfriend? Answer: five hours, or the time it took to fly from New York to Indio, California, for Coachella, whereupon a sex tape scandal ensued and her life as she knew it imploded.

And the most important question of all: how long can a sixteen-year-old girl grieve for her love after he is tragically killed trying to save her life? Solving this was what kept Anna up late into the nights leading to Vronsky's memorial service in Italy.

The answer currently was she had no fucking idea.

It had been two days since the service, and Anna didn't feel a dot of closure and was pretty sure she never would. It was Anna's second funeral in less than six months. Dustin L., her brother's homework tutor and new best friend, had lost his older brother, Nicholas, to a drug overdose in late March. That was the first one. And now Vronsky's was the second. She really hoped that the celebrities-dying-in-threes things didn't apply to her, because she didn't think she could deal with another tragic death.

She knew funerals were all about saying good-bye. She watched as Alexia's mother sobbed behind a black-lace veil during the brief ceremony. She stared as Alexia's older brother Kiril picked up a handful of dirt and dropped it into the grave after they lowered the coffin. Where Alexia was fair, blonde and blue eyed, his older brother was tan, dark-haired and had the Bowie one-blue-eye-one-green-eye thing, which Anna found unnerving when he looked directly at her. Everyone present was then allowed to take a small gardening spade to drop in some dirt and to say their farewell. When it was Anna's turn, she grabbed a handful of dirt with her left hand and tossed it in, along with two white oleanders she had brought. Standing there, she had tried to open her heart and release all her feelings for him, as if that were even possible. She felt empty when she returned to the hotel afterward, wrung out like a dish towel, sad and spent.

But then it all came flooding back, and she was barely able to keep her head above the rising tide of pain and regret—all because of a box filled with love letters from a beautiful boy who had just been buried in Sicilian soil.

When Anna's mother had handed her the box, shortly before Anna and her father had left for the airport, it was wrapped in plain brown paper.

"What's this?" Anna asked quietly.

"It's not a gift, but it's something you should have. You'll understand why when you open it. And don't tell your father."

"When should I open it?" Anna asked.

Greer sighed, her expression softening for a moment. "Wait until after his memorial."

"His name is Alexia Vronsky," Anna said with more spark than she'd mustered in quite some time. "Was. His name was Alexia." Her eye felt twitchy, more from the lack of sleep than anything else.

"Yes, that was his name. May he rest in peace, and once he is, I hope you can find the strength to put all of this behind you. You have your whole life ahead of you, Anna. You need to be wiser with the choices you make. It's the summer and a good time to find a way to rein in your life."

Rein in my life? Like it's an unruly horse who broke free and ran away? You think it's so easy to just gather up the pieces of my exploded heart and put them back together again? So I can be, what? An ice queen like you? This is what Anna wanted to say, but instead she said nothing. She knew her mother wouldn't understand, and these days, she didn't even know herself. Lately she wondered if her life devolved so rapidly because she'd always had everything pulled in too tightly. And even if she wanted to, which she didn't, she doubted she could ever go back to living her life in the same way she had before she fell in love with Vronsky. It had changed her, and she didn't want to change back. Anna took the box with a nod, slipping it into her nylon Prada duffel.

After the memorial service, Anna told her father she needed sleep, which was the truth. But though her body was exhausted, her head couldn't shut itself down. She decided it was finally time to open the box. Lifting the lid, she pulled out tissue paper and found a stack of letters tied with black Net-A-Porter ribbon. There were probably more than a dozen envelopes of all shapes and sizes. When she untied the bow, her hands were shaking. She picked up the first envelope on top and turned it over in her hands. Seeing his handwriting made her chest ache. Each letter had a date on the back of the envelope, every day he had dropped them off for her after they had been forbidden from seeing each other; the last one was dated the day he died.

With a parched mouth and trembling hands, Anna opened the first letter.

April 2019

Dearest Anna,

I'm going out of my mind not being able to see you or talk to you, so I'm kicking it old school and writing to you with pen and paper. I doubt your parents will pass these on to you, but I have every intention of bribing your doormen with doughnuts and Yankees tickets. The hope is they will take pity on me and agree to slip this to you while you're walking the pups.

I keep thinking back to our time on the plane and how those will be my last happiest hours until I see you again. My feelings for you are unchanged, and when the smoke clears you will see me standing, steadfast and waiting. I'm sure your father probably hates me, but I will do whatever it takes to gain his trust. I can be quite charming when necessary, as you well know. (Is it too soon for a little levity?)

Hmmm. My letter sounds whiny and sad . . . am I whiny and sad? You have to tell me if I am; I'm a big boy, I can take it.

I love you so much.

Forever and always yours,
Alexia V.

About the Author

Jenny Lee is a television writer and producer who has worked on BET's *Boomerang*, IFC's *Brockmire*, Freeform's *Young & Hungry*, and the Disney Channel's number-one-rated kids' show *Shake It Up*. Jenny is the author of four humor essay collections and two middle-grade novels. *Anna K* is her debut YA novel. She lives in Los Angeles with her husband and 135-pound Newfoundland, Gemma (and, yes, it's a toss-up on who's walking who every day).

Instagram: @jennyleewrites
www.jennyleewrites.com